D0455632

KEVIN O'BRIEN

THE BAD SISTER

PINNACLE BOOKS
Kensington Publishing Corp.
www.kensingtonbooks.com

PINNACLE BOOKS are published by

Kensington Publishing Corp.
119 West 40th Street
New York, NY 10018

All Kensington titles, imprints, and distributed lines are available at special quantity discounts for bulk purchases for sales promotions, premiums, fund-raising, educational, or institutional use.

Special book excerpts or customized printings can also be created to fit specific needs. For details, write or phone the office of the Kensington sales manager: Kensington Publishing Corp., 119 West 40th Street, New York, NY 10018, attn: Sales Department; phone 1-800-221-2647.

First Pinnacle printing: August 2020

10 9 8 7 6 5 4 3 2 1

ISBN-13: 978-0-7860-4508-2
ISBN-10: 0-7860-4508-6

Printed in the United States of America

Electronic edition: August 2020

ISBN-13: 978-0-7860-4511-2 (e-book)
ISBN-10: 0-7860-4511-6 (e-book)

This book is for Dante & Pattie Bellini

ACKNOWLEDGMENTS

As usual, topping my Thank-You list is my dear friend and editor, John Scognamiglio, who is always there to inspire and guide me. Thanks also to the brilliantly talented team at Kensington Publishing, who always have my back and continue to wow me with their dazzling work.

Thank you to the wonderful gang at Jane Rotrosen Agency—especially Meg Ruley and Christina Hogrebe.

Another thank-you goes to my Writers Group friends, David Massengill, Garth Stein, and Colin McArthur, for helping get this book off the ground.

Thanks to all my Seattle 7 Writers friends, especially Dave Boling, Erica Bauermeister, Carol Cassella, Laurie Frankel, Suzanne Selfors, Jennie Shortridge, and Garth Stein.

I'd also like to thank the following friends and groups who have been incredibly supportive: Dan Annear and Chuck Rank, Dante and Pattie (again!), Pam Binder, A Book for All Seasons, The Book Stall, Marlys Bourm, Amanda Brooks, Terry and Judine Brooks, Lynn Brunelle, George Camper and Shane White, Barbara and John Cegielski, Barbara and Jim Church, Anna Cottle and Mary Alice Kier, Paul Dwoskin, Elliott Bay Book Company, John Flick and Dan Reich, Bridget Foley and Stephen Susco, Margaret Freeman, Matt

Gain, The Girls Gone Wild Reading Books, Cate
Goethals and Tom Goodwin, Bob and Dana Gold, Cathy
Johnson, Elizabeth Kinsella, David Korabik, Stafford
Lombard, Susan London, Paul Mariz, John, Tammy and
Lucas Millsap, Roberta Miner, Dan Monda, Debbie
Monda, Jim Munchel, Meghan O'Neill, the wonderful
folks at ReaderLink Distribution Services, my ever-
faithful friends from Sacred Heart School (you rule),
Eva Marie Saint, John Saul and Mike Sack, the cool
gang at Shelf Awareness, John Simmons and Hulet,
Roseann Stella, Dan Stutesman, George and Sheila
Stydahar, Marc Von Borstel, and Ruth Young.

Finally, thanks to my sibs and their families. Adele,
Mary Lou, Cathy, Bill, and Joan . . . you guys are the
greatest.

CHAPTER ONE

Saturday, October 6, 2018
Rhododendron, Oregon

Nate Bergquist wondered if he'd survive this weekend with his brother.

They were on their way to the family cabin near Mt. Hood National Forest, about an hour southeast of Portland. It was a tradition, going there for their birthdays. The brothers were born four years and one day apart: October seventh and eighth. They'd missed coming here last year. Nate's older brother, Gil, had insisted on this trip. He said he didn't want to see the tradition die. But Nate couldn't help thinking his brother had another reason for this hasty getaway.

Gil drove fast—with his window halfway open. The wind tousled his near-shoulder-length, golden blond hair. Not many people at thirty-six could pull off the long-haired preppy look, but Gil made it work for him.

Riding shotgun, Nate felt his stomach tighten as they took another curve in the highway. He listened to the tires squeal and braced his hand against the dashboard. Route 26 narrowed down to two lanes as it wound through the woods, and at times, it seemed choked with RVs. But that didn't slow down his brother any. He kept passing the trailers and motor homes, one after another. The needle on the speedometer of Gil's Audi coupe hovered near eighty.

"Hey, Steve McQueen, what's the goddamn hurry?" Nate almost had to shout to be heard over the wind whipping through the car. "The cabin isn't going anywhere. Would you mind slowing down?"

Leaning to his left, Nate spied his girlfriend, Rene, in the rearview mirror. She and Gil's new girlfriend, Cheryl, sat crammed together in the backseat. The wind had done a number on their hair. Rene rolled her eyes and mouthed *thank you* to him.

"Pussy," Gil muttered, shifting gears.

Nate half turned in the passenger seat to address the women: "Are you sure the wind isn't too much for you back there?"

"Right now, it's the least of my worries," Rene replied, shouting over the sound of the wind. She was pretty with green eyes, freckles, and long, wavy tawny brown hair. A yoga instructor, she had the taut, trim body that came with the job. She was Nate's age: thirty-two. She leaned forward and put a hand on his shoulder. "Please, tell me again, there will be alcohol when we reach our destination—*if* we reach our destination."

"Every time he gets behind the wheel, Gil puts pedal to the metal," Cheryl announced. She smoothed back her blond hair. "I've gotten used to it. Actually, he's a very good driver."

"*I'm an excellent driver,*" Gil said, imitating Dustin Hoffman's character in *Rain Man*, a movie the two brothers had seen multiple times while growing up. The two of them often launched into their own language of movie quotes that no one else understood. "*Kmart sucks,*" Gil grumbled. "*We have pepperoni pizza for dinner Monday nights . . .*"

Cheryl laughed. Rene rolled her eyes again.

"For a thousand dollars, what was Dustin Hoffman's name in that movie?" Gil said.

"Raymond Babbitt," Nate answered without hesitation. He turned forward again and noticed the speedometer had gone down to sixty-five. "And Tom Cruise was Charlie, the much cooler, better-looking younger brother."

"That's only true in the movies, bub," Gil said.

Nate was grateful his brother had eased up on the accelerator. For a while, he'd thought Gil might have someone on his tail—not just because of his crazy driving, but also from the way he kept checking his rearview mirror. Gil was a private detective, and weird little episodes of intrigue were a hazard of his profession. If someone was indeed following them, it would be like Gil not to say anything that would *worry the women folk*.

Nate checked the side mirror. No one was behind them.

Now that they weren't driving so fast, he could actually enjoy the scenery along the way: the familiar creeks and small waterfalls, the evergreens bordering the highway, and all the other trees ablaze with autumn colors.

Nate knew Gil had slowed down mostly for Rene's sake. His brother and Rene were like cordial adversaries. They managed to tolerate each other. As Rene put it: "I like Gil, but he's an asshole a lot of the time. And I don't like the way he treats you—especially in front of me."

She'd made that painfully clear when Nate had introduced her to Gil—over dinner at McMenamins two years ago. After ninety minutes of listening to their brotherly banter, Rene had cleared her throat. "Excuse me, Gil," she'd said calmly over her crème brûlée. "But I don't appreciate you calling Nate 'pussy,' 'douchebag,' 'doofus,' or 'wuss.' I know you're trying to be funny, but I don't find it amusing at all."

"Well, okay . . ." Gil had said, looking stumped. He'd turned to Nate. "So—how about those Trail Blazers, bro?"

At first, Nate had been embarrassed. He'd wanted his brother to like Rene, and here she was slamming Gil's standard shtick—and a tradition of verbal abuse that had thrived for at least a quarter of a century. It was really none of her business. Yet, Gil respected her. Nate noticed he tapered off on the name-calling after that—at least, in front of Rene. Gil still liked to goad her on occasion, but never pushed it too far. He was pretty much behaving himself for this trip—so far.

"What was I talking about before you interrupted and jumped on my ass about my driving?" Gil asked, his eyes on the road.

"You were telling me that I should switch jobs, and I wasn't listening," Nate answered.

"Just let me say this," Gil went on. "Frank—at the agency, you know my friend Frank—he wrenched his back. So he went to Kaiser and they had him see this physical therapist there. The woman spent forty-five minutes showing him some stretching exercises. Then she printed up some exercise instructions for him and sent him on his way. They charged Frank three hundred and ninety bucks. I'll bet that's a hell of a lot more than you get per hour at the veterans hospital. According to Frank, this girl was like—phoning it in. She didn't exactly break into a sweat."

Nate squirmed in the passenger seat. "I'm sure Kaiser gets most of that three hundred and ninety bucks," he said. "And maybe the therapist seemed apathetic because she doesn't like her job. I happen to love where I work. I love the guys. I like helping these veterans put themselves back together again."

Nate hoped Rene would keep her mouth shut. Earlier this week, he'd complained to her that one of his new patients had spit on him. In truth, the job wasn't always the lovefest he made it out to be. Occasionally he got patients who were genuine jerks. That was true in any job. But most of the guys who came to him were still traumatized and in pain. And his job was to inflict even more pain on them and teach them to tolerate it. Whether it was on an exercise mat, on a pair of parallel bars, or in the shallow end of a pool, he had to push these broken men to their limit. Many of them were amputees. Nate had to help them adjust to using prosthetics, and he might as well have been torturing them. But by the time they'd completed their therapy, most of his patients were grateful. Nate became like a war buddy with some of these guys. He'd wiped away their tears, lifted and carried them, and cheered them on. Once they were whole or pretty much independent, Nate always got a lump in his throat saying goodbye to them. They made him feel essential and seemed to look up to him. It was a feeling he never got from his older brother.

"All I'm saying is that you work like a dog, and they pay you shit," Gil said. He checked the rearview mirror again. "It took seven years to earn your degree, and for what, Nate? How much do you rake in a year? Fifty? Fifty-five grand?"

Nate turned toward his window. "Around there," he mumbled.

He was pretty sure his brother didn't make much more as a private detective.

Nate used to look up to Gil, who had been kind of wild when they were growing up. He attracted people with his charm, his good looks, and his athletic prowess. He was a tough act to follow. Much of Nate's identity was wrapped up in being Gil Bergquist's kid brother— and that had made him proud until late high school. Then he'd started to resent it.

Time had shifted things around a bit. Nate was in great physical shape from working out with his patients every day. He was tall, with blue eyes, wavy black hair, and a goatee. As for Gil, though still handsome, he'd gotten paunchy. He'd had two failed marriages and rarely saw his only child, a nine-year-old daughter who lived with the first ex-wife in Ashland. His private investigation business was unsteady. He was probably in debt up to his elbows and certainly couldn't afford the Audi. If someone was actually following them on the highway, it was probably a repo man.

Gil was always pushing the envelope, living beyond his means.

Two nights ago, when he'd called Nate about this trip, Gil had mentioned that he was about to "score a shitload of money."

"And how exactly is that going to happen, Sherlock?" Nate had asked.

"I'm not at liberty to say, but it involves some information I've dug up for a client—valuable information, it turns out."

"This doesn't sound very aboveboard," Nate had said warily. "In fact, it sounds way under the board. What's going on?"

"The less you know about it, the better. But if everything goes according to plan, I'll be sitting pretty next week."

"Jesus, Gil, I can't believe this. What are you doing, pulling a bank heist or something?"

"That's it, I'm *Thomas Crown*." He'd chuckled. "Relax. It's nothing that serious. Forget I even said anything."

To Nate, it sounded like extortion—what with that talk about the *valuable information* Gil had dug up for a client. Gil had gotten into trouble before with other shady get-rich schemes. He'd been lucky not to have his detective's license revoked or been arrested or worse.

And yet, here was Gil, Mr. Shady Deal, doling out career advice to him.

"If I were you, I'd tell the VA hospital to *take this job and shove it*," Gil said as he took a curve in the highway. "Then I'd find some cushy work at one of these health care providers. Or you could start your own business— like I did, work out of your house for a while, no overhead. Anything but that miserable hospital job . . ."

"I'll take that under advisement," Nate replied.

He didn't say anything else to his brother. He turned and asked Cheryl about her job behind the Enterprise Rent-A-Car counter at PDX. That kept her talking for the next thirty minutes. They turned off the highway onto a rural road, and then to a gravel trail that snaked through the woods.

Nate listened to the pebbles ricocheting against the underside of the car. He noticed the turnoff to their closest neighbor's cabin, which meant they had a half mile to go. It was getting dark, but Nate still spotted certain landmarks along the way—including an old metal Smokey Bear sign he'd nailed to a tree twenty years ago, and Gil's initials carved in another tree closer to the cabin. Then there was their mother's birdhouse on a pole that never stood straight: the Leaning Tower of Pisa Birdhouse, the family used to call it. The birdhouse was pretty dilapidated now.

The vacation home—a three-bedroom log cabin with big windows and a porch in front—looked slightly neglected as well—at least, from the outside.

Parking by the porch, Gil popped the trunk. They unloaded their overnight bags, some groceries they'd bought for the weekend, and a cooler full of perishables. While the women turned on the lights and opened some windows to air out the place, Nate went to the side of the cabin and got the water pump going. He noticed Gil at the end of the driveway, glancing up the gravel trail.

Nate caught up with his brother as he started back toward the cabin. "What's going on?" Nate asked. "Are you expecting someone?"

Gil squinted at him. "What do you mean?"

"On the way here, the way you drove and the way you kept checking the rearview mirror, I thought someone might be following us or something."

Gil chuckled and shook his head. "We're fine. God, what an imagination. Y'know, you always used to get spooked out whenever we stayed here for the weekend with Mom and Pop. Nothing ever changes . . ."

Once they stepped back inside the house, Gil switched on the porch light.

Nate wondered why he'd turned on the outside light if they weren't expecting anyone.

The plumbing in the cabin was ancient, but reliable. Nate could hear the pipes moaning. Gil was upstairs in the shower. Rene and Cheryl were in the kitchen, knocking off a bottle of red wine. The cabin had sufficiently aired out and was now getting chilly. Nate made the rounds from room to room, closing the windows again.

He noticed that Gil had turned on all the outside lights—including the ones in back and two floodlights that were fixed on trees by the driveway. So everything was illuminated around the cabin. Beyond that, it was just a wall of trees—and darkness. The moon wasn't out tonight.

From his parents' CD collection, Nate had James Taylor's *Greatest Hits* playing on the old boom box in the living room. "Fire and Rain" was just the tune for his nostalgic mood.

His brother used the family cabin a lot more than he did. Nate hadn't been here since they'd lost their dad.

Their mom had been the first to go—three years back. She'd died from pancreatic cancer at age fifty-nine. His dad remained alone in the Lake Oswego house Gil and Nate had grown up in. He started drinking heavily. Nate tried to intervene and even moved in with him for a while. But nothing he did seemed to help, so eventually Nate gave up and moved back into his own apartment in Portland. One Friday night eighteen months ago, their dad got drunk, slipped, and hit his head on the corner of the breakfast table. He lost consciousness and never woke up. When Nate hadn't been able to get him on the phone the following Sunday, he swung by the house and found his father on the kitchen floor. He'd bled to death from the gash in his head.

Nate was devastated and blamed himself for giving up on his father months before. In his job, he never quit on his patients. But his dad was so selfish in his grief. As Gil had pointed out to him, "The old man didn't make any effort to be strong for us after we lost our mother. He just wanted to numb himself with booze and shut everyone else out." At the time, Gil was dealing with divorce number two—and he was kind of bitter about everything.

While Nate made the funeral arrangements, Gil had an estate broker go through their parents' house. This guy cleared out the place before Nate had a chance to go through his parents' things.

Gil didn't seem to understand why he was so incensed. His brother assured him that they'd split down the middle whatever the estate broker raked in from the sale of their parents' earthly possessions. That didn't include their mother's jewelry. Gil's second wife had made off with most of the valuable pieces the year before. In the end, Nate got a check from his brother for $2,300, which was probably less than what the dining room set was worth. Never mind all the other furniture in the house, the electronics, the silver, china, and various antiques. Nate wasn't sure if it was the estate broker ripping them off or if Gil was holding out on him.

Nate paid a lot more attention to the details when they sold their parents' house. But by then, things between Gil and him were slightly strained. It wasn't so much that he minded getting cheated out of the money—though he didn't like being treated like a chump. He figured Gil was desperate for funds. He was always in some kind of financial trouble. No, what really bothered Nate was that he hadn't been able to hold on to some of the things that reminded him of his mom and dad and his childhood.

Since their dad's death, the two of them had gotten together only a few times—for lunch or dinner. But for Nate, it was always sort of a chore. They both knew their relationship wasn't the same. And they both knew it wouldn't do any good to discuss it.

But just a couple of days ago, Gil had the bright idea about this trip—with Rene and Cheryl in tow. He was adamant about it. As an extra lure, Gil said he had several items from their parents' home, items the estate broker hadn't wanted. Nate didn't understand why his brother hadn't told him about these rescued family "treasures" until now. In fact, the sudden urgency for this "birthday getaway" seemed oddly suspicious. Nate couldn't help wondering if, for one reason or another, Gil needed to get out of town for a while. Perhaps things were so dicey he even needed to make sure his girlfriend and his brother weren't left behind.

At least he'd been telling the truth about the family treasures on display in the cabin—like the big oil painting of a Swiss chalet, which now hung over the sofa. The picture had been painted by their mother's best friend. Nate had never liked it much, but he was happy it hadn't ended up with strangers. The semi-kitschy painting had been in his parents' living room for as long as he could remember.

Gil had shoved most of the things he didn't know

what to do with into the small bedroom off the kitchen. The junk was still there in boxes. Nate figured he'd sort through all of it after dinner. He saw that Gil had placed some familiar knickknacks and framed family photos on the mantel of the river rock fireplace in the living room. Nate had always thought the room resembled a lodge with its hardwood floors, knotty-pine walls, and the high-vaulted ceiling. In one corner, there was a winding staircase to the other bedrooms and bathroom. Another corner had an alcove with a desk. When he was a kid, Nate used to spend his evenings in the tilt-back swivel chair, drawing. Sometimes, he'd imagine a bear emerging from the dark woods and crashing through the big window in front of the desk. As he grew a bit older, Nate's imaginary killer bear was replaced by a man in a hockey mask, carrying a machete.

Gil was right about his overactive imagination—back when they were kids, at least.

Nate heard the pipes squeak and realized his brother was finished showering upstairs. Gil had mentioned starting a fire in the hearth after dinner. Nate stepped outside and gathered up some logs from the stack on one side of the cabin. During a second trip for another load, he thought he heard something moving nearby in the woods. It sounded like footsteps, twigs snapping.

He stopped and listened for a moment. He didn't see anything, just the tree branches swaying in the night wind. Nate gathered up the logs, brought them inside, and unloaded them in the brass bin by the fireplace. He went back to the door, and closed and double-locked it.

"Nate? Could you come in here and help us with this damn stove?" Rene called.

None of the appliances in the kitchen matched—
and each one was older and quirkier than the next. The
"biscuit"-colored fridge made all sorts of ghostly
noises. The dishwasher was a dull stainless steel, and
left all the glasses looking cloudy. And the ancient gas
range/oven was chipped white enamel—with a tempera-
mental pilot light.

Nate caught a whiff of shrimp when he stepped into
the kitchen. A big bowl of them sat on the counter. Tonight's dinner menu was garlic butter shrimp, steamed
vegetables, and pasta.

"We've used up a box of matches trying to get this
stupid oven lit," Rene announced. Moving over to the
counter, she poured some more wine into her glass.
"And speaking of getting lit, I'm having another glass of
this cabernet. Cheryl, can I top you off?"

"You don't have to twist my arm." Nibbling on a
cracker, Gil's girlfriend stepped away from the stove and
held out her wineglass for Rene.

Nate chuckled. "I have a feeling you two will be
hammered by dinnertime."

"You almost say that like it's a bad thing," Rene
quipped.

Nate kissed her shoulder as he stepped around her
to the counter. He started to open the junk drawer where
they kept the extra matches. That was when he saw
something outside the kitchen window.

He froze as two people staggered from the shadowy
woods.

"Oh my God," Rene said behind him. She must have
seen them, too.

It took Nate a moment to figure out it was a man and

a woman, both wearing dark jackets. They didn't look like hikers or campers. At least, they weren't wearing backpacks.

In all the times he'd stayed at the cabin, Nate had never encountered a stranger anywhere near the house. It didn't make sense that this couple had just come out of nowhere. The man was balding and about thirty. As he approached the cabin, he seemed to notice Nate in the window, staring back at him. The guy waved, and then started limping.

The woman's short-cropped dark hair was messy, and she had dirt on her face. She looked exhausted. "Help us!" she cried. "For God's sake . . ."

Suddenly Nate heard the back door being unlocked. He turned away from the window in time to see Cheryl opening the door for the two strangers. "Are you hurt?" she called.

"We couldn't get any goddamn cell phone service!" the man yelled. "Our car broke down—"

"We started walking and got lost," the woman spoke over him.

The guy almost knocked Cheryl down as he staggered into the kitchen. He pushed the door open wider, and it banged against the wall. His companion followed him in.

"We thought we were going to die out in those fucking woods," he gasped. "We've been walking around for at least three hours . . ."

"Are either of you hurt?" Nate asked. They'd never answered Cheryl's question.

"My ankle—I twisted my goddamn ankle," the man said, plopping down in a chair at the breakfast table. He accidentally knocked over Cheryl's wineglass. It hit the floor and shattered. Red wine spilled across the worn linoleum tiles. "Oh fuck," he groaned, sounding angry. "I'm sorry, okay?"

The woman half-collapsed in the other chair.

"I'll clean it up," Cheryl said. "Where do you guys keep the mop and the broom?"

Nate pointed toward the broom closet. "There, thanks, Cheryl." He turned to the man again. "Where's your car?"

"I don't know," the man grumbled. He looked down at his foot and winced. "Hurts like a son of a bitch."

"He's a physical therapist," Rene said. "You should have him look at it. He knows what he's doing." She filled two glasses with water, and then stepped around the mess on the floor and set them down in front of the couple.

The woman greedily drank her water. But her friend, still gasping, scowled at his glass. "Shit, don't you have anything stronger?"

Nate hesitated. Something was wrong. It wasn't just the unsettling way these two strangers had barged into the house and wreaked havoc. Nate could have sworn that when he'd first spotted him emerging from the thicket, the man hadn't been limping at all. And the dirt smudge on the woman's cheek looked phony— almost clichéd. Nate wasn't sure about the cell phone reception in the middle of the woods, but he'd always been able to get phone service in the cabin—and certainly on the highway.

"Something stronger?" Nate repeated. He couldn't believe the balls on this guy, turning down a glass of water and practically demanding that they raid the liquor cabinet for him.

"I'll get you some brandy," Gil said.

Nate swiveled around to see his brother in the doorway to the kitchen. He was dressed in jeans and a V-neck sweater. His hair looked damp, and he was barefoot.

"We keep the hard stuff in the living room," Gil explained to the man. "Nate, check out his ankle for him, okay?" He turned and headed toward the living room.

Nate wondered why his brother didn't seem the least bit wary of these two. Plus, he wasn't exactly dying to look at this guy's ankle.

Rene was using paper towels to soak up the spilled wine while Cheryl, with the broom, swept the glass into a dustpan.

Nate turned to the man again. "Let's have a look. Which ankle is it?"

The guy immediately pulled his foot away. "Don't bother yourself. I just need to stay off it for a little bit . . ."

Nate noticed, for someone who had been traipsing through the woods for three hours, his shoes didn't look very dirty.

Past James Taylor's singing and the sound of Cheryl sweeping up the glass, Nate thought he heard Gil whispering on the phone in the next room.

"So—you don't have any idea where you left your car?" Nate asked—to distract the man.

"Alongside one of the roads off the highway," the woman answered for him.

"And you didn't walk back to the highway for help?" Rene asked, dropping a wad of soggy paper towels into the sink. She turned to them. "Why in the world did you go into the woods? You'd have had a lot more luck getting help by flagging down a car on the highway . . ."

"Yeah, well, we were at least a couple of miles from the goddamn highway," the man said impatiently—as if Rene were an idiot. "Okay? Jesus."

"Hey, pal," Nate said. "I know you've been through a lot. But that's no way to talk to us. We're just trying to help you."

The guy gave him a defiant stare. Then his gaze shifted, and he straightened up in the chair.

Nate turned to see Gil in the kitchen doorway again.

"We're all out of brandy," Gil said. "What were you guys doing in the woods anyway? It's private property."

The man frowned at him. "Oh shit," he muttered. He slid his hand inside his jacket and glanced at his companion.

The woman suddenly shot out of her chair and grabbed Cheryl, who screamed. The broom and dustpan dropped to the kitchen floor with a clatter. Shards of glass scattered across the tiles. It happened so fast, Nate barely saw the woman take the pistol from inside her jacket. She jabbed the gun barrel against the side of Cheryl's head.

The balding man jumped to his feet, knocking over the chair. He pulled out a gun, too—and pointed it at Gil. "Get your fucking hands up," he growled.

Glaring at him, Gil was obedient.

Nate automatically raised his hands as well, holding them halfway up.

"I know Mr. Hot Shot Detective has a license to carry firearms," the man said. "So keep those hands up, Gil, and turn around, nice and slow . . ."

Nate couldn't believe this was happening. He stole a glance at Rene, over by the sink. She didn't move a muscle. Tears welled in her eyes, and she looked terrified.

The guy's female companion still had the gun to Cheryl's head. Cheryl was trembling. The expression on the woman's face was cold and passionless. Nate had a feeling that, without even flinching, she'd put a bullet through Cheryl's head.

Nate once again looked at his brother, who still had his hands raised. Following the stranger's orders, Gil had gradually turned around until his back was to them. The handle of a gun stuck out of the waistband of his jeans.

"Let the others go," Gil said, his back to them. "They don't know anything. You can send them on their way without their phones or the car. It'll be at least an hour before they reach the highway. That'll give you plenty of time to get away . . ."

"I don't think Nate wants to leave his big brother behind," the man said.

Stunned, Nate stared at him. The guy knew him, too.

The man nodded at Nate. "Take the gun from your brother. Slowly."

With a shaky hand, Nate reached for Gil's gun. Holding it by the grip, he pulled the revolver out from where it was tucked in the waistband of Gil's jeans.

"Now, drop it on the floor—in front of my feet," the man whispered. "No fucking funny business."

Biting his lip, Nate bent over slightly and then let the gun slip out of his hand.

The man kicked it to a far corner of the kitchen.

As Nate straightened up, he saw the guy raise his gun over his head, but it was too late to react.

The man slammed the grip of the gun against Nate's face. He fell to his knees onto the kitchen floor. After the shock came the blinding, searing pain. Past a high-pitched ringing in his ears, he heard Rene scream.

"Son of a bitch," Gil yelled. "Leave him alone . . ."

The second blow was to the back of Nate's head.

He collapsed facedown on the kitchen floor—amid the shards of wet glass.

Nate woke up on the floor of the small, darkened bedroom. Some light seeped in from the kitchen through the doorway. He was lying on his side. He wasn't sure how long he'd been unconscious. His head throbbed, and it felt like one side of his face was smashed in. Blood dripped from the gash alongside his temple to the floor. Just opening his eyes hurt.

Still, he tried to move. But then he realized his hands were tied behind him—and his feet were bound together at the ankles with duct tape. Straining, he lifted his head and saw Cheryl lying on the bed, gagged and hog-tied. Her eyes met his, and she whimpered weakly. In a panic, Nate glanced around for Rene, but she wasn't in the bedroom with them. What had they done to her?

He could hear the two intruders talking in the living room. Their words weren't clear, but it sounded like they were firing questions at Gil.

"Go fuck yourselves," Gil said loudly.

That much Nate heard. He also heard someone strike a blow—and Gil gasping in pain. It sounded like they were asking about someone named Rachel Bonner.

Nate heard her mentioned twice. He wondered if this Rachel Bonner person had something to do with the *valuable information* Gil had alluded to the other day on the phone. Was all of this connected to his brother's involvement in some shady deal to make a quick "shit-load of money"?

Though it made his awful headache even worse, Nate writhed around on the floor, struggling to loosen the rope around his wrists. All the while, the muted conversation continued in the living room. He flinched every time he heard another punch thrown. He wondered why his brother was holding out. Or maybe Gil was stalling for time. If he had indeed phoned someone earlier, maybe they were on their way.

Nate thought he heard Rene's muffled crying in the kitchen. He imagined her tied up in there—maybe on the floor or in a chair. Rene always came across as strong and composed—especially to the students in her yoga classes. But she actually scared easily and often had nightmares. Nate hated to think of her alone in the next room, frightened and helpless, all her nightmares coming true.

He could smell the shrimp they had planned to cook for dinner. It was spoiled now. But beneath the stink Nate picked up another odor: gas.

Nate realized they must have left the unlit oven on. How long had the gas been leaking from the oven?

"Okay, hot shot, have it your way!" Nate heard the guy say loudly. "Maybe you'll start talking if I bring one of those bitches in here and start working her over."

Her eyes full of panic, Cheryl started squirming on the bed. Nate kicked and thrashed on the floor, but the rope around his wrists hadn't slackened at all. He heard footsteps in the kitchen and Rene's stifled sobs.

Nate bellowed out: "Leave her alone!"

The footsteps stopped, and there was an awful silence. Nate held his breath.

After a moment, the floorboards creaked again and the footsteps got louder—closer. A shadow swept over the bedroom. Nate lifted his head and saw the man, in silhouette, standing in the doorway, holding a knife.

"You just gave me an idea," the guy said, stepping into the room. He stood over Nate for a moment. Then with a grunt, he hauled back and kicked him in the stomach.

Stunned, Nate clenched into a ball, bringing his knees up to his chest. The blow knocked the breath out of him. An excruciating pain spread through his gut. He felt it in his shoulders, too. He'd almost torn his arms out of their sockets when he'd recoiled. His head spinning, he desperately gasped for air. He was barely aware of the man hovering over him, cutting the duct tape around his ankles. If he'd been thinking clearly, Nate might have kicked the guy in the face. Instead, he let the man pull him to his feet. Nate was still bent over from the pain in his gut.

"You could use some fresh air," the guy said mockingly. "Come on with me."

The man had the revolver in his hand now. He led Nate into the kitchen, where Rene was tied to one of the dinette chairs. A dishrag was stuffed in her mouth to keep her from screaming. Nate stopped. He tried to say something to her, but he could barely get a breath. The man pushed him toward the back door. Nate stumbled and almost tripped.

"Stinks in here," the guy said, opening the back door. He shoved Nate outside and shut the door behind him.

The cold night air actually revived Nate a bit.

"What has Gil told you about Rachel Bonner?" the man asked.

Nate shook his head. "I—I don't know who that is."

"Fuck," the guy muttered. He grabbed Nate's arm and pulled him around the side of the house—to the front of the cabin. "You better pray your asshole brother tells us what he knows."

He led Nate up the front porch steps to one of the big living room windows.

Nate shivered. He could see his breath. He gazed inside toward the desk, where, as a kid, he used to draw. He was horrified to see what they'd done to his brother.

Stripped down to his underwear, Gil was tied to the desk chair. He looked like a defeated boxer slouched in the corner of the ring. His handsome face was a swollen, bloody pulp. Cuts covered his body. On his right arm and shoulder were square patches where it looked as if they'd carefully cut off some layers of skin.

The woman was sitting on the edge of the desk, her back to them.

Tightening his grip on Nate's arm, the man knocked on the window.

The woman quickly turned, the gun readied in her hand.

"Open the window," the man called. "I want Gil to hear his brother beg for his life."

The woman nodded—almost as if she approved of the idea. She moved to the window and opened it a crack.

The man jabbed the muzzle of the revolver against Nate's temple and then took a step away.

Trembling violently, Nate realized the guy didn't want to get splattered with blood. Nate remembered that image from the Vietnam War—of the prisoner being shot in the head. He was certain he was going to die. "Goddamn it, Gil!" he cried out. "Tell them what they want to know!"

"I'm really tired of this," the woman announced. Returning to the desk, she started hunting through her purse. "We're giving you ten seconds. If you don't start answering our questions, my friend is going to shoot him. Do you understand, Gil? You have ten seconds to start talking or you'll see your brother's brains all over that window."

One of Gil's eyes was swollen shut, but he seemed to focus on Nate with his one good eye. He winced and slowly shook his head.

The woman pulled a pack of cigarettes and a lighter out of her bag. "Ten . . . nine . . . eight . . ."

"Your brother's a real asshole," the guy muttered, the gun just inches from Nate's skull. "It's too bad for you . . ."

"Gil, for God's sake!" Nate yelled. "Cooperate with them!"

Her butt against the edge of the desk, the woman kept counting as she tried to light her cigarette. But the lighter didn't seem to be working. Nate could almost hear the failed clicks.

Then he remembered the gas.

"Four . . . three . . ."

"No, wait!" Nate screamed.

She clicked the lighter one more time.

It sparked a flame that erupted into a deafening blast. The windows shattered as flames and fiery debris spewed out of the cabin. Everything shook. The blaze shot up higher than the treetops. Logs, cinders, splintered wood, and glass flew through the air.

The explosion knocked Nate off his feet; it all happened in a flash, so fast he barely had time to realize that everyone inside the cabin was now dead.

Then, all at once, something hard and heavy fell on top of him.

Buried under the scorched, smoky wreckage, Nate knew that he was as good as dead, too.

CHAPTER TWO

Two years later: Thursday, September 3, 4:04 P.M.
Lake Forest, Illinois

Hannah O'Rourke had made it her mission to learn everything she could about Rachel Bonner.

Seated in the upper deck of the North Suburban Chicago commuter train, the willowy, dark-haired eighteen-year-old studied her phone screen—and Rachel's photo. Hannah hadn't met Rachel yet, and she felt a bit like an online stalker. But she had a good excuse. Rachel Bonner was going to be her college roommate.

Hannah was on her way to start freshman year at Our Lady of the Cove University in the small town of Delmar, two stops from now. Thanks to Google and Instagram, Hannah had already learned that Rachel Bonner was twenty, extremely pretty, and extremely rich. She was the only child of Richard and Candace Bonner of the Chicago Stock Exchange, Lake Shore Drive, and North Shore Country Club. Rachel was all over the Internet, mostly because of her parents' wealth, but also due to her involvement in a lot of high-society charity work. A junior at Our Lady of the Cove, she would be living with Hannah in one of the dorm "bungalows." Rachel would be acting as their "big sister" and adviser. Hannah had been worried that her big-sister-roommate might turn out to be a first-class snob, a goody-two-shoes Patty Simcox (*Oh, we're going to be such good friends!*), or maybe just a major drip.

Taking off at eight-forty this morning, Hannah had flown from Seattle to Chicago, accompanied by her half-sister, Eden, who, much to Hannah's chagrin, would also start her freshman year at the university.

For the trip, and to make a good impression on the kids at Our Lady of the Cove, Hannah looked pretty smashing in khaki slacks, a new blue sleeveless top, and blue flats. Meanwhile, Eden wore a black tee under a pair of hideous, unflattering yellow overall shorts, with red sneakers—just what every fashion-forward lesbian was wearing in Wyoming eleven years ago. Hannah had been totally embarrassed sitting next to her on the plane. And there was just enough family resemblance between them for people to figure out they were related.

Together, they'd taken the CTA from O'Hare to Union Station and then caught the Metra commuter train from there. It had been a long, grueling day so far. Eden had picked these seats on the upper deck because she'd thought it would be cool to sit above everyone else in the train car. But it wasn't so cool lugging four big pieces of luggage up the winding, narrow metal staircase. No sooner had they gotten settled in their upper-level seats and secured the suitcases on the luggage rack than Eden promptly got to her feet again. She announced that she wanted to "explore" and then disappeared, leaving Hannah alone to look after all the bags.

That had been forty-five minutes ago. So typical.

Eden had driven Hannah's parents crazy by disappearing for hours at a time—or even for a day or two—without telling anyone. She was always off on some stupid, Kerouac-like mini-adventure, hitchhiking or taking the ferry someplace, and switching off her phone so no one could reach her. During spring vacation last year, Hannah's parents had called the police when Eden disappeared. It had been three whole days before she finally called them from Oregon, where she'd been picking apples on some farm.

So Hannah told herself not to be too alarmed that her half-sister had wandered off. Still, it was unnerving. Every time Hannah heard the doors between cars whoosh open, she'd anxiously glance down in that direction, hoping to see Eden returning.

It was weird, because months back, when she'd learned that Eden would be going off to college with her, Hannah had been horrified. After the last two awful years at home, she'd desperately wanted to leave Seattle and start fresh someplace where no one knew her. Then, it turned out, the person who had caused her so much grief, humiliation, and shame was accompanying her to Our Lady of the Cove. So much for a fresh start. Hannah had hoped something would happen—like maybe her half-sister would pull another one of her disappearing acts and this time, not come back. Hannah didn't want Eden dead or anything. She just wanted Eden out of her life. Why couldn't her half-sister just run away and join a cult or something?

Now, Hannah was worried one of those wishes had come back to bite her in the ass.

She hated the uncertainty. Had Eden gotten off at an earlier stop to look around, and then missed getting back on the train? Maybe right now, she was on the train platform five stops back.

Hannah sent her a text:

Where R U? R stops coming up.

Just moments later, her phone buzzed.

But it wasn't Eden.

Riley was texting her. His photo came up, the one of him in shorts and a T-shirt, standing on the deck of a boat. He was so handsome with his wavy blond hair, a tan, and that lean, athletic build. He was a sophomore at Northwestern. Several train stops back, in Evanston, Hannah had found herself smiling at the thought of that stop becoming a frequent destination.

Though she'd dreaded attending Our Lady of the Cove with her half-sister, Hannah did have a few things she looked forward to—and at the top of the list was Riley McCarren.

She hadn't actually met him yet, but they'd been texting, video-chatting, and talking on the phone for weeks now. Hannah couldn't help feeling that he was *the one*.

She touched the phone's text icon:

What's up? R U in Chicago yet?

Hannah worked her thumbs over the phone screen:

On the train. Delmar in 2 more stops! U were right. It's not that far from Evanston.

Told U.

My stupid half-sister has totally disappeared. I keep thinking
she might've gotten off at the wrong stop sometime back. I
have 4 big suitcases here and don't want to lug them all by
myself. She's got 2 B somewhere on this train.

Maybe she's locked in one of the bathrooms. LOL.

UR a big help. When R U getting in? Can't wait to C U.

Riley lived in Boston, and with his accent, he
sounded like Mark Wahlberg on the phone. Hannah
couldn't remember if he was flying in tomorrow or Saturday morning. They'd agreed to meet this Saturday
night.

Her mother had pitched a fit about her communicat-
ing and setting up a date with this guy she hadn't even
met yet. For all she knew, her mom said, some pervert
could have been using a photo of a J.Crew model to lure
her into his web.

Her mom was naturally cautious because of the thing
that happened.

The thing that happened—that was what Hannah
called the series of horrendous events that accounted
for the last two miserable years. The thing that happened
had made national news headlines for several days. She
and Eden had become reluctant Internet stars, and they'd
each garnered their share of stalkers. Though most of
the whack-jobs had moved on ages ago (probably to
other teenage girls in the news), a few nutcases were
still out there.

But Riley wasn't one of them. As he explained, his
freshman year roommate had developed an Internet
crush on her for a while—until he'd gotten a girlfriend
and transferred to U of I mid-year. But last spring,
the former roommate had forwarded Riley one of

Hannah's Instagrams about getting into Our Lady of the Cove—just a few Metra stops away from Northwestern. Riley couldn't resist sending her a message and suggesting they get together when she came to the Chicago area. He'd said he thought she was "pretty cute, too."

According to her mother, Hannah was only encouraging stalkers by posting so much stuff on social media. But really, she wasn't about to give up the things she loved—just because of a few obsessive creeps. Besides, she took precautions. Unlike her half-sister, she didn't talk to strangers or wander off alone for hours at a time. She watched out for herself.

Plus, if she hadn't been posting regularly on social media, she never would have connected with Riley.

And Hannah was no fool. After a few texts back and forth, she'd insisted on some FaceTime sessions with Riley. She needed to make sure the gorgeous photo was real. She was delighted to see he was the genuine article. Making things even better was the fact that he was already a college guy. Plus he knew all about her, and he still liked her. After two years of feeling like a freak at her high school, Riley made her feel cool and desirable.

Nevertheless, her mother kept warning Hannah that she was telling this stranger way too much about herself. Maybe that was why, in the back of her mind, Hannah wondered if Riley was too good to be true.

From the three dots in the text box, it looked like Riley was writing something. It was taking him a while.

The train car doors hissed open, and Hannah glanced down, hoping to see her half-sister returning. Instead, some guy in a business suit stepped into the car.

Hannah glanced back at her phone. Riley's text finally came up:

> Bad news. I'm not flying in until later this week. Family emergency. Major hassle, but it can't B helped. Looks like I won't C U until next weekend . . .

Hannah's heart sank. She was crushed. She'd been looking forward to this all summer, and now she had to wait at least another week.

What if, by then, he met some other girl he liked better than her?

Of course, she couldn't let him know how disappointed she was. She swallowed hard, typed in a sad face, and then quickly erased it.

> I'll miss U! Family emergency? Hope it's nothing 2 serious. Is everyone OK?

There was no response, not even a wavy dot, dot, dot. She waited about twenty seconds and then texted:

> U still there?

Then she waited another few moments, until he finally texted back:

> I got a call here I need to take. Text U back soon!

Frowning, Hannah texted back *OK*. Then she clicked off.

"Shit," she muttered, glancing out the train window. They sped past trees and phone poles. Some of the houses near the railroad tracks looked slightly neglected and sad.

The prospect of seeing Riley tomorrow was the one thing that had kept her from being totally homesick today. She wouldn't see her parents or her brothers again for another three months. She'd never been away from them for more than a weekend—until now. She'd been so miserable at home for the last two years, and yet she'd give anything to be back there now. She particularly longed to go back to that time before *the thing that happened*, before Eden had come into their lives, before the murders and the headlines—back when they were so happy and didn't know it.

Where the hell was Eden anyway?

Hannah glanced down toward the train car's doors again. No sign of her.

Maybe if she wasn't sitting here all alone, she wouldn't feel so depressed. She couldn't depend on her half-sister for anything. Ever since Eden had moved in, the two of them had been at odds. Fortunately, Hannah's bedroom was in the basement, which had made it easier to avoid everyone—especially Eden, whose room was on the second floor. Their respect for each other's turf was probably what kept them from killing each other.

Two weeks ago, in an email from the college, they both received the distressing news that they'd be rooming together in one of the dorm bungalows—along with Rachel Bonner.

Hannah tried to assure herself that Rachel would be cool. This was one "big sister" she didn't have to worry about. She had a good reputation and a pedigree background. Unlike Eden, she wouldn't come with a shitload of problems.

"Delmar!" the train conductor announced as he walked through the car. "Next stop, Delmar and Our Lady of the Cove University!"

From the upper level, Hannah glanced down toward the car doors again. Still no Eden.

"Shit," she muttered again.

The train started to slow down.

Hannah got to her feet and started gathering up the bags.

CHAPTER THREE

"The class lists went out last week, Ellie," said Jeanne, the clerk in the bursar's office. She was in her early sixties with close-cropped, beige-colored hair and glasses. She stood behind the counter, where a small, dirty-looking plastic fan was blowing on her. The air-conditioning didn't seem to be doing much good. "I really wish you'd check your email once in a while," Jeanne added. She started typing on the keyboard in front of a computer monitor on the counter.

"Sorry," Ellie sighed. She had a regular Gmail account for family and friends. But she purposely hadn't checked her university email account all summer. "I appreciate this," she said.

"You're just lucky I like you," Jeanne replied—over the sound of the printer running. "How is it out there? Still miserable?"

"Stifling," Ellie replied as she leaned against the counter. She pulled the strap of her bulky, cloth purse off her shoulder and lowered it to the floor. Ellie was thirty-three, but looked younger. The tan helped. She taught four different journalism classes at Our Lady of the Cove—and except for teaching one summer school class, she'd spent most of her summer goofing off: swimming in Lake Michigan and working in her garden in back of her townhouse apartment.

Slim and pretty, she wore her shoulder-length, chestnut brown hair in a ponytail today. Since classes weren't in session, and it was ninety-nine degrees out, she'd dressed casually in a pink-and-white-striped tee, khaki shorts, and sandals. She had her sunglasses pushed up on top of her head—a look she knew some people hated (including her dad and her ex-husband). But she was too hot and tired to care right now.

The printer spit out three sheets of paper, and Jeanne handed them to her.

"Thanks," Ellie said. She glanced at the enrollment list for her Introduction to Journalism class: twenty-two students. *Manageable*. She scanned the names, and showed the listing to Jeanne. "I should know this, but what does this double asterisk by *Jensen, Nicholas* mean?"

Jeanne squinted at the page. "He's not a registered full-time student," she explained. "He's adult continuing education."

This was a red flag for Ellie. "Did he sign up for any other classes in the college or just my freshman journalism class?"

The printer had churned out four more pages, and Jeanne handed those to her. "Jensen, Nicholas?" she said, pausing at the keyboard.

Ellie nodded.

Jeanne typed on the keyboard and checked the monitor. "Nope, just Intro to Journalism."

"Do you have an address for him?" Ellie asked.

Jeanne consulted the monitor again. "Eight-twelve Sunset Ridge Road, number seventeen. Highland Park."

That was about fifteen minutes away. Ellie figured maybe it was just a temporary address for this Nicholas Jensen person—if that was even his real name. Then again, if someone was out to get her, would he really go to all the trouble of moving into an apartment in Highland Park and enrolling in one of her classes? It would be a hell of a lot easier just to hang around the liberal arts building, Lombard Hall, one morning. If he asked enough students, he'd eventually find out where she taught her class. Then he could just walk into her classroom and start shooting.

Ellie told herself that she was being paranoid.

But sometimes, it was hard not to be. That was why she'd deliberately avoided checking her college email account all summer. Too many people had access to that email address, and too many cranks were out there.

Ellie decided Nicholas Jensen was probably just some old guy who wanted to write his memoirs. She'd had an adult continuing education student like that last year—a baggy-eyed, gray-haired, middle-aged man who thought he knew more than she did—and he didn't hesitate to tell her so in front of the class. He was a major pain in the ass, but more or less harmless.

Ellie glanced farther down the list of students in her freshman class. "Eden O'Rourke . . . Hannah O'Rourke?" she read aloud. She looked up at Jeanne. "Are they the same Eden and Hannah O'Rourke from Seattle, the half-sisters?"

She shrugged. "Beats me. Am I supposed to know them?"

"They were all over the news about two years ago,"

Ellie explained. "It was a big story—murders, infidelities, real juicy stuff. Their father is Dylan O'Rourke. Does that ring a bell?"

Jeanne shook her head. "O'Rourke," she repeated as she typed on the keyboard again.

"Dylan O'Rourke—married, father of three, extremely handsome," Ellie explained. "If you saw his picture, you'd remember him. Quite the looker—or at least, he was. He was also a serial cheater. Two years ago, this sixteen-year-old girl, Eden, dropped in on him and his unsuspecting family. She was the result of a brief, extramarital fling Dylan had with her trampy mother. The woman dumped the baby with a friend of hers named Cassandra, who, more or less, raised Eden on her own. Then, just in time for Eden's sweet sixteen, this Cassandra woman said she was moving away and gave Eden back to her birth mother, who months later, died in an apparent suicide. Are you following me so far?"

"I think so," Jeanne said with uncertainty.

"Anyway, Dylan didn't even know he had a daughter. It was a big surprise for everyone. With Cassandra gone and the mother dead, the girl had no place to go. So after making her take a paternity test, Dylan and his wife— who was either a saint or a total doormat—took the girl in. This Eden is only a few months older than their daughter Hannah. Apparently, she turned everyone's lives upside down—and not in a zany, cute *Parent Trap* way either. The whole situation was more like *Psycho* than any Disney movie."

Jeanne's eyes widened. "What happened? You mentioned a murder . . ."

"Turned out Eden's mother hadn't committed suicide after all. She'd been killed by Cassandra. The two were more like lethal frenemies than friends. Cassandra was obsessed with Dylan. She killed a couple of other women, who had both slept with him. Then she tried to kill Dylan's wife and one of Hannah's younger brothers, too. I forget the wife's first name. This crazy woman shot Dylan while he was driving his car, and he crashed into a tree. The accident definitely changed his looks. Depending on who you talk to, it's up for grabs just how much he deserved getting his handsome face messed up. I feel a lot sorrier for the wife and his kids. Apparently, the wife had a sister who committed suicide years and years before—and the sister might have slept with the husband, too. At least, it was intimated in some of the reports. The whole thing was very sordid and scandalous. It was national news for several days."

Jeanne glanced at the monitor. "The wife's name is Sheila. It's here as the emergency contact for both girls: Dylan and Sheila O'Rourke. And it's a Seattle address. Looks like you're right. Both girls are incoming freshmen."

"Why do you suppose they're coming all the way here to attend this little school? I mean, I know we've got a good reputation, but come on . . ."

"Maybe they just wanted to go to college where no one has heard of them," Jeanne said with an arched eyebrow. "And no one will gossip about them."

Ellie nodded sheepishly and sighed. "Okay, point taken."

Still, as a former news reporter for the *Chicago Tribune*, she was naturally curious about the half-sisters. Ellie hadn't even met the girls yet, and already, she wondered if they'd allow her to interview them. Maybe she could write a follow-up article about the half-sisters two years after being thrust into the national spotlight. Then again, perhaps Jeanne was right. They probably wanted to be left alone.

Ellie slipped the class lists into her purse. Heading out of the bursar's office, she thanked Jeanne for her help.

"Check your email for God's sake!" Jeanne called after her.

Ellie realized the building's air-conditioning must have been working after all—at least somewhat—because she got a blast of hot air as she stepped out into the blazing sun. Fortunately, the trees alongside the walkways between buildings offered some shade, especially here, in the campus's older section. It was quite pretty—with a sweeping view of Lake Michigan. The tall church tower loomed above the other rooftops on the campus. Though their architectural styles varied, all of the buildings somehow seemed to blend together harmoniously. The old brownstone housing the bursar's office had a certain charm, and so did the women's four-story white stucco dormitory next door—despite some signs of decay. A creek snaked through the old section of the campus, and around every corner, there was a quaint footbridge or a garden patch with a shrine or a statue of some saint.

As lovely as it was, this picturesque old section of the campus took on a sinister air at night. Woods bordered the area on two sides, and there were just too many shadowy nooks, too many places for someone to hide. Those pious saintly statues became slightly menacing once the sun went down. This part of the campus reminded Ellie of a cemetery—beautiful during the day and downright creepy at night. Or maybe she just felt

that way because she knew about Our Lady of the
Cove's history—and what had happened there in 1970.

It was hard to imagine it now—with the sun shining
through the trees and the birds chirping. Since school
wasn't yet in session, the place was practically deserted.
Everything seemed so peaceful.

Check your email for God's sake!

It was the last thing Ellie wanted to do. During the
summer, when she'd purposely avoided her college
email account, she'd actually had some days when she
hadn't been afraid. She'd slept easier at night. She'd
even taken the steak knife out from between her mattress and box spring and put it back in the kitchen
drawer, where it belonged.

She was going back to work in a few days. A lot of
people—including everyone associated with Our Lady
of the Cove—used her college email address to reach
her. She couldn't put off checking it any longer. She had
her laptop in her bag.

She headed across the brick-tiled quad toward the
student union—a big, ugly steel and glass monstrosity
in the newer section of the campus. The attached coffee
shop, Campus Grounds, was air-conditioned.

Ellie stepped inside and shuddered gratefully from
the delicious chill. She was practically the only person
in there. She didn't have to wait in a line to place her
order. She took her iced latte to a window table. The
barista had Sting on the sound system.

With a napkin, Ellie dabbed the perspiration from her
forehead. Then she pulled the laptop notebook out of
her bag. Switching it on, she logged into her email account through the college, and found 772 unread emails.

"Oh spare me," she murmured.

Sipping the iced latte to fortify herself, Ellie started weeding out all the junk mail and spam. She managed to whittle down the unread messages to sixty-three, most of them from the college's administration office and senders whose names she didn't recognize.

With reluctance, Ellie clicked on the first unfamiliar email name. The date was May 29, and there was no subject name.

I hope you get AIDS and die, you skanky bitch. Your whole family should get AIDS and die. Do you even have a family? I'll bet your a lesbian, you dried-up—

Ellie didn't read any more.

"Sweet," she whispered, clenching the wadded-up napkin in her fist. She was sorely tempted to reply and tell them she wasn't a lesbian, and that it's "you're a lesbian," not "your." But the unwritten rule in cases like this was not to engage. Besides, the asshole didn't even leave a name. So she deleted the message.

With a sigh, she moved on to the next email, also dated May 29. The sender was ninar402@chevyd.com, and the subject line was "Your Arson Story":

Dear Ms. Goodwin,

I have written a very, very compelling screenplay version of your newspaper coverage of all those arsons in Chicago from two years ago. I know there's currently some film deal about that going on, but I also know that some of these film deals can go bad really quickly. I'm really hoping for you to read my screenplay (attached-152 pgs) and let me know what you think. I know, after you read it, you'll want to talk to the people making your movie about using my brilliant screenplay. Let me

know as soon as you get this, because I think the timing of
this is very, very important. I do not have an agent, but I don't
think I really need one, because I'm very, very confident you
will find my screenplay excellent . . .

It went on for three more paragraphs, but Ellie skipped
down to the sign off: *Sincerely, Nina Rumble.*

"I'm very, very sorry, Nina," she said under her breath.
When she had some downtime, she'd email Nina an
excuse as to why she couldn't drop everything and read
her brilliant screenplay. She tagged the email "Keep as
New" and then noticed that Nina R had sent three more
emails over the summer. Ellie clicked on the most recent
one—from two weeks ago. The subject line was "My
Screenplay":

Dear Ms. Goodwin,

I think you are extremely rude and very, very inconsiderate.
I sent you my screenplay over two months ago, and have
never heard back from you. I spent a lot of time writing my
screenplay based on your story. How long would it take for you
to read it? Just a few hours at the very, very most. You should
be flattered that I was even interested in your newspaper
articles. Now I don't even think you're even that good a writer . . .

"Oh terrific," Ellie murmured. "Now someone else
hates my guts."

There was no use writing back to Nina and apologizing, because then, she'd end up having to read the stupid
screenplay, which was bound to be very, very bad. With
a pang of guilt, Ellie deleted Nina Rumble's emails.

Then she opened the next one, sent on June first from

ggma@gbrewer.com with the subject line "Thinking of the Children." There was no salutation:

> Because of YOU, my brother, Ted Brewer, is in prison, and his wife is left without a husband at home, and his three children are left without a daddy. They had to move from their nice house to a small apartment in a terrible neighborhood on the south side. You should know that all three of Ted's kids are now having problems in school and "acting out." The oldest, Ted, Jr., has been in fights and arrested twice. My sister-in-law is now suffering from depression, and she drinks as a way to self-medicate. You've ruined my brother's family and so many other families. You did this. You took Ted away from his family, and put him in prison. You are godless . . .

It went on for another five paragraphs and was signed *Gloria Georgina Brewer*. Ellie wanted so much to write back—just one sentence: *Ted put Ted where he is*. But what good would that do? Gloria had had her say. There was no use in trying to argue with her. She wanted someone to blame, but not her brother. It was easier to blame the former newspaper reporter.

However many angry or threatening emails waited for her now, the numbers had been a lot worse two years ago, when the messages had come through her news-paper email address—dozens by the day. Ellie had written a six-part exposé for the *Chicago Tribune* about an organization called American Family Preservationists. Eight of its most ardent members—including Ted Brewer—carried out a string of arsons in the city. They set fire to a Jewish cultural center, a mosque, a branch of Planned Parenthood, a GBLT youth center, and even a yoga studio. Three people perished and another seven ended up hospitalized from those fires. Thanks to Ellie's exposé, Ted and his cohorts were arrested, convicted, and imprisoned. Ellie won a few local awards for her reporting, and the series was syndicated nationally. For a while, there was even some movie interest. Ellie got an agent—and a film option netting her one hundred and eighty thousand dollars. But the movie people couldn't come up with a decent screenplay. There wasn't much glamour, sexiness, or cloak-and-dagger stuff in Ellie's painstaking investigative work. She'd conducted scores of interviews and had dozens of doors slammed in her face. She'd also done a ton of research online, in the library, and at the Cook County Hall of Records. But that kind of thing didn't really transfer well into film. Yet, according to Ellie's film agent, there was still a lot of buzz about the project, and once it was off and running, she would receive half a million dollars on the first day of the movie's principal photography.

So—nineteen months ago, when the newspaper downsized and Ellie was encouraged to take a buyout, she didn't feel too bad about it. Unfortunately, once that happened, film interest in her story dried up and her option wasn't renewed.

Ellie glanced at Gloria's email again. She wanted to write back and point out that the people killed or permanently scarred by Ted Brewer's handiwork had families, too. But she knew it was pointless.

She imagined—while she'd been unemployed last year, watching her film deal and her marriage unravel—that maybe all of it had been the answer to some fervent prayers from the Brewers and families like them. If they had known what a horrible time that was for her, they'd have said she had it coming.

In the wake of it all, Our Lady of the Cove seemed like a good place to recuperate—and hide.

But someone—probably her film agent—had updated her Wikipedia page, which mentioned that she now taught journalism at the university. So Ellie was still getting hate emails through her college email address. Even with all the misspellings and bad grammar, some of those notes were damn disturbing. As a precaution, she kept three fire extinguishers in her small townhouse. And she felt wary about non-students—like Nicholas Jensen—taking her freshman journalism class. The Brewers and their kind had a lot of friends. Two of the men convicted of arson were now out of jail. Ellie knew all their names and faces. Nicholas Jensen wasn't among those arrested and convicted, but it could be a fake name.

She'd have to wait until the first day of her journalism class on Wednesday to see if Jensen looked at all familiar.

Ellie slurped the last cold drops of her watery latte, and then she pulled the class list out of her purse. She glanced at the names again—and then stopped once more at *O'Rourke, Eden* and *O'Rourke, Hannah*.

She returned to her laptop screen, closed the email page, and tried a Google search for the half-sisters. The results came up, a long list of news articles from two years ago, when the story in Seattle first broke.

Under the Google headings, Ellie clicked on *New* to see if there were any follow-up stories on the two girls. There were no articles. But Hannah O'Rourke was active on Snapchat and Instagram with all sorts of posts over the summer. The most recent was from yesterday: a selfie, taken at a high angle with her looking up at the camera so that the shot also included a half-packed suitcase on her bed.

> Heading to Chicago tomorrow to start college. 99 degrees there! Packing my swimsuit!

For someone whose family was part of such a scandalous news story, Hannah didn't seem publicity shy. Then again, she was a teenage girl, and some of them lived and breathed social media. If they didn't photograph it and post it online, then it never really happened.

Despite what Jeanne at the bursar's office had said about the girls wanting to be left alone, Ellie once again considered the possibility of talking to the half-sisters. The notion of writing a follow-up story—or even another series—intrigued her.

She couldn't help it. Once a reporter, always a reporter. Because of her last big scoop two years ago, she was still getting horrible, hateful emails.

Yet, all she could think about right now were the two half-sisters and the potential story there.

CHAPTER FOUR

Thursday, 4:16 P.M.

Hannah hadn't really noticed the businessman sitting nearby on the train car's upper deck until he asked if she needed help with her suitcases. He was thirty-something, and nerdy-cute with receding light brown hair. He must have taken off his suit jacket and loosened his tie before coming to her aid. Hannah figured he probably heard her cursing under her breath as she struggled with the four big bags on the luggage rack—among them, a heavy as hell and embarrassingly ugly canvas suitcase with Eden's moronic Magic Marker doodling all over it.

He grabbed that one and a second bag, then led the way down the narrow winding stairwell to the train's main deck. He took one of the suitcases from her while she was still in the stairwell, creating a pile of bags at the foot of the steps.

"This is really very nice of you," Hannah said. "My sister is supposed to be here helping out, but she wandered off. I think she must have gotten off at the wrong stop."

"Did you try calling her?" the man asked.

She sighed. "Twice. She must have turned off her

phone. This is pretty typical of her. I'm sure she'll ma-
terialize eventually."

Nodding, the stranger gave her an awkward smile.

Hannah wondered if her Good Samaritan recognized
her from the news stories. Though it had been a long
time since all the headlines, people still occasionally
stopped her on the street or in a store. She got everything from "Hey, you look familiar" to "Oh my God,
you're the one from that screwed-up family!" Some guy
had actually said that to her. "Were you there when that
whack-job tried to shoot your father?" he'd asked.

In fact, the night that happened, Hannah wasn't
even home. She was having the time of her life at a
slumber party—at the house of Taylor D'Arcy, who
basically ruled their junior class. After years of feeling
like the Invisible Girl at school, Hannah was—at last—
in the in-crowd.

Then bam, *the thing that happened* made headlines
all over. She convinced herself that the horrible dark
cloud hovering over her family had a silver lining. She
assumed her new A-list friends would be there for her.
Plus, practically all of the girls had noticed her father
at different school functions because he was so good-
looking. It was a little creepy when they referred to her
dad as a hunk or a hottie, but Hannah kind of liked it,
too. They acted as if her dad were a movie star or royalty
or something. Suddenly, he was in the hospital, possibly
crippled for life. Though her family was in a shambles,
at least her friends would rally around her and she could
take comfort in that.

But she was wrong. The news coverage didn't pull
any punches.

All at once, she, her friends, and the entire world

knew about her father's extramarital affairs. Yes, *affairs*, plural. There had been other women besides Eden's mother, a lot of others. He went from being her cool dad to being this total sleaze-bucket, a national joke. Hannah felt like everyone was laughing at her, too. She knew she wasn't supposed to care what other people thought of her, but it still mattered.

Hannah had had a crush on this jock, Ian Westerlund. He was tall and ruggedly good-looking with dark blond curly hair. His family had moved to Seattle from Australia a few years before. Hannah became frazzled and breathless if Ian even so much as looked at her. A while back she'd mentioned to Taylor D'Arcy that she thought Ian was cute.

On her first day back at school after the thing that happened, just before third period English Lit class, Ian approached her desk. He made eye contact and said, "Hey . . ."

"Hey," Hannah managed to reply.

Here it is, she thought. In his sexy Australian accent, Ian was about to tell her that he saw her on the Internet— and how sorry he was about what had happened to her family. Hannah's heart pounded furiously.

"Hey," he said again. "Listen—"

"Hannah's got the hots for you, Ian," Taylor interrupted— for the whole class to hear. She sat behind Hannah. "But I don't know if you should go out with her, because her dad has really screwed around a lot. For all you know, he could have screwed your mom. You and Hannah could be brother and sister . . ."

It was a stupid, mean, tactless thing to say, but since Taylor D'Arcy had said it, everyone laughed. Even Ian chuckled awkwardly.

But all Hannah could do was look down at the floor and try to keep from cringing.

Before the end of the school day, everyone was quoting Taylor.

In the corridor, after sixth period, some stupid-ass senior Hannah barely knew came up to her. "Hey, aren't you Hannah O'Rourke?" he said. "I hear your father can't keep his dick in his pants. So—do you party around a lot, too?"

Hannah hoped it would all go away and everyone would forget soon. But it was in the news for days. Plus, after a brief absence, her bastard half-sister, Eden, was back at school—a walking, talking, breathing reminder that Hannah's father was a womanizing scumbag.

Even though she was older, Eden had started out at the high school a year behind Hannah—in her brother Steve's grade. It didn't seem to bother Steve much. But then Eden was quickly moved up to Hannah's grade, and Hannah was utterly humiliated.

Eden had cleaned herself up a bit and lost the Goth look she'd featured when she'd originally shown up at their house. She could actually be pretty with a little effort. But she still had the dark eyebrows and platinum hair (à la Emilia Clarke in *Game of Thrones*). She also had horrible taste in clothes, and looked just plain trashy half the time. It might have helped if she'd worn a bra more often. She had big boobs, too, so it was hard not to notice.

Even if she weren't the "braless wonder," Eden still would have stuck out. In class, she questioned and debated their teachers at every turn. She seemed openly hostile to the people Hannah thought mattered. Even though they'd been pretty awful to her, Hannah still cared what they thought. She remembered Ian Westerlund saying something really funny in their world history class, and once the laughter had died down, Eden could be heard muttering to no one in particular: "What a fucking idiot."

Eden seemed determined to befriend the class losers and misfits. While that might have seemed noble or kind, it was also pretty stupid. Sure, kids sometimes were pegged as losers for no discernible reason. But most of the time, they didn't fit in because they were just damned impossible to get along with. And yet Eden sought them out.

"She's kind of *contrary*, isn't she?" Hannah's mother had once said, describing Eden. "She seems bent on being different from everyone else."

For some reason, Hannah hadn't expected Eden to pull her vanishing act on their very first day away from home together. Hannah kept telling herself, *I'm not responsible for her*. Hell, her half-sister was lucky she didn't just leave her stupid bags here on the train.

Hannah worked up another smile for her Good Samaritan businessman. "Is Delmar your stop, too?" she asked.

"No, but you looked kind of overwhelmed, so I thought I'd help." He nodded at the suitcases crammed in the aisle. "I can hand these down to you once you're on the train platform. Are you at the college?"

She sighed. "I'm starting my freshman year. And not a very good start, I guess . . ."

He smiled again. There was nothing flirtatious about it. In fact, it was almost fatherly, like he felt sorry for her.

As much as her half-sister could be a pain in the ass, Hannah hated the notion of getting off the train without her—alone in this strange town. She told herself she wasn't going to cry—not in front of this nice man. Never mind how Riley had just burst her bubble with the news that he wasn't seeing her this weekend. And forget that she was so homesick her stomach ached.

She glanced down at all the bags again and wondered how she was going to manage lugging them around all by herself.

The rest of their stuff had been shipped off to Our Lady of the Cove last week.

Except for a virtual tour online, neither Hannah nor Eden had visited the college. Of course, she'd read up on the place. It was a small Catholic university with about four thousand students. It had been a women's college, but now about twenty percent of the students were male. The school had a good reputation, but neither Hannah nor Eden would have chosen it for themselves.

For a while, it had seemed they might need to put their college plans on hold. Their father's hospital and physical therapy bills had put a huge burden on the family finances. The insurance covered only so much. Eden was due to inherit a large sum from the woman who had raised her, but she wouldn't see a dime of it until she turned twenty.

At just about the time Hannah should have been applying herself academically and planning for college, total apathy had set in. She'd hated her family and hated the kids at school. She'd spent most of her time watching TV and on social media. She might not have had many friends at school, but thanks to all those headlines, she had more social media followers than all her classmates put together. Studying was the last thing on her mind. So her grades were hardly scholarship-worthy. By the time Hannah realized she'd blown her chances of getting away from her miserable existence and into a decent college, it was too late.

But then, out of the blue, both she and Eden received scholarship offers from a Chicago-based financial firm, the Slate-Gannon Group. Both the girls' tuition and their room and board were covered. Apparently, the firm had a connection to the university, and every year, they selected a few financially challenged students for their scholarship program. Though the O'Rourkes weren't exactly destitute, no one questioned the offer.

The one condition was that the half-sisters were going off to college together. Hannah knew Eden wasn't exactly thrilled at the prospect either.

Maybe that explained why Eden had disappeared. Maybe she'd decided to run away, and hopped off the train at the first stop back in Chicago.

Hannah felt so utterly pathetic and alone. Tears filled her eyes.

The man was still smiling at her. It felt like they'd been standing there forever at the bottom of the steps to the train's upper deck, waiting for her stop. She cleared her throat. "I—I really appreciate this . . ."

"First time away from home?" he asked.

She just nodded. She was afraid if she tried to talk, she'd start crying.

"My daughter's going off to college next year," the man said.

Just then, the car doors whooshed open, and Eden almost barreled into the guy. He must have thought she was slightly demented—what with her spacey, baffled expression and those hideous yellow overall shorts.

"Where the hell have you been?" Hannah barked. She wiped away her tears. "I thought you were dead or something. This is so goddamn typical!"

"God, bite my head off," Eden replied. "I'm sorry. I fell asleep in another car."

With her foot, Hannah shoved aside Eden's canvas suitcase to make room in the aisle. "Well, thanks a lot. Could you possibly be more inconsiderate? You left me with all the bags—"

"Bitch, bitch, bitch," Eden muttered. "I'm here now, aren't I?"

Hannah rolled her eyes. "Yeah, praise Jesus."

The train screeched to a halt, and Hannah grabbed a handle by the doorway to keep from falling over. She gave her Good Samaritan a strained smile. "Thank you very much," she said. "You've been really nice . . ."

"Good luck," he said. He handed her the third bag and quickly backed away.

With a loud hiss, the train doors opened. Eden stepped outside with her bags, and Hannah followed her. Weighed down with the suitcases, she staggered off the train onto the station platform—smack into a wall of wilting heat and humidity. Hannah managed to hobble a few more paces before pausing to plop the heavy, bulky suitcases on the walkway. "Wait up!" she called to Eden.

Her half-sister was shuffling along the platform with her two bags—toward Delmar's quaint, Tudor-style station house. She stopped and then turned to scowl back at her.

Hannah grabbed her bags again and caught up with

her half-sister. Already, she was perspiring. She set down the suitcases once more.

"Y'know, the way you were acting," Eden said, talking loudly over the sound of the train as it pulled out of the station, "that guy helping with the suitcases probably thought you were a total raving psycho. Just saying . . ."

"Well, maybe if you hadn't wandered off and waited until the very last fucking minute to show up again, I wouldn't have been acting so nuts." Hannah stopped yelling as soon as she realized she didn't hear the train anymore. But the sound had been replaced by an almost continuous shrill buzzing. "What the hell is that?" she asked, fanning herself. "Do you hear it? It sounds like— like jungle noises in the Amazon."

Eden rolled her eyes. "It's not the Amazon. It's Lake Michigan, and I'm pretty sure they're cicadas."

But Hannah wasn't listening. With the train gone, she had her first look at downtown Delmar. Among the storefronts, the one that stood out was the Sunnyside Up Café, which looked like a cheap greasy spoon. Its name was on an old, battered 7UP sign on a pole at the edge of the parking lot out front. Corn dogs were probably their specialty. Next door was a locksmith, and beside that, Verna's Hair Salon. It looked like just the place to go for a poodle cut and a blue rinse. Who, under the age of eighty, was named Verna?

For the past hour, Hannah had been looking out the train window as they stopped in each north suburban town: Wilmette, Winnetka, Hubbard Woods, Glencoe, and so on. The towns seemed affluent and charming— full of quaint shops and classy-looking restaurants.

Even the cars parked by the stations appeared expensive. But this Delmar place was a dump.

Hannah's phone buzzed. She dug it from her purse, and on the screen, she saw Riley's handsome photo again. She opened up his text:

> Had to take a call from my mother. Sorry today got screwed up. If all goes well, let's count on seeing each other a week from Saturday. OK? It'll B a crazy week ahead 4 me, but I'll try to be in touch. Talk to you soon. OK?

Squinting at her phone screen, Hannah shook her head. It seemed like a total brush-off. *If all goes well,* they'd get together? He'd *try* to be in touch? Nothing definite, no promises, no commitments. He didn't even say what this big *family emergency* was. Maybe he'd met someone else already.

I don't understand, she started to type. But then, she erased it and just typed *K*.

She sent the text and then clicked off the line. She worked her thumbs over the phone again. "I wonder if they even have Uber in this shithole," she said, her voice strained and shaky. "Do you suppose the college is far from here?"

"About a mile, I think," Eden answered. She dug her sunglasses out of a front pocket of her overall shorts and put them on. "Who was that on the phone?"

"Nobody," she murmured. In a weak moment, Hannah had told Eden about Riley, and couldn't help bragging that she had a date with him that weekend. She wasn't exactly dying to tell her that the big date was off. She didn't want to give Eden anything to gloat about.

She ordered the Uber. "I'm roasting, aren't you?" she

asked her half-sister. "If our dorm *bungalow*—or whatever they call it—isn't air-conditioned, I swear, I'll slit my throat . . ."

"Bitch and moan, bitch and moan," Eden muttered.

Hannah didn't look up from her phone. She swiped back to Riley's photo and studied it. She had a feeling he was lying to her, and maybe he'd been lying all along.

Right now, she was pretty certain she would never meet him at all.

If her stupid half-sister weren't here, she would've burst into tears. She was so disappointed and miserable, she wanted to die.

From behind the wheel of an old minivan parked across the street from the train station, he watched them, the phone still in his hand.

He'd been waiting and sweating inside the hot vehicle for over an hour now. Hannah hadn't been on the last two trains.

Actually, he'd been impatiently waiting for her for at least eight months. That was how long he'd been following every move Hannah O'Rourke made. She was all over the Internet—from the old news stories about what had happened to her family two years ago, to her own frequent posts on social media. He'd become utterly fascinated with her.

After all their texts, the phone conversations, and the FaceTimes he'd carefully arranged, he felt he knew her better than anyone else.

And now, at last, she was coming to him.

But he wasn't ready to meet her just yet. So he remained slumped in the driver's seat with the car window rolled up—even in this oppressive heat. He just wanted to look at her.

Even at this distance, he could see Hannah was as pretty as her photographs. The sister, Eden, was attractive, too—in a common, earthy way. She lacked Hannah's elegance and style.

He watched Hannah and her sister on the train platform with their large suitcases. It looked like they were arguing. From all the texts and conversations, he knew she didn't get along at all with her half-sister.

If Eden O'Rourke suddenly disappeared, Hannah might even be grateful, most grateful.

He was all set up for it. He just had to wait for the right moment.

Hannah was looking at her phone right now. He would wait and watch them until their ride came.

He set Riley McCarren's phone on the passenger seat.

Right now, Riley was soaking in the old claw-foot tub in the second-floor bathroom of the house.

Because of the heat, five bags of ice had been dumped into the tub with him—to keep his body from rotting and stinking to high heaven.

At the 7-Eleven, the clerk who had rung up all the ice asked if he was having a party.

"Sort of," he'd told the guy with a cryptic smile.

It was more like a funeral than a party.

Riley would stay on ice for a while. It was supposed to rain later tonight. After that, the ground would be a lot softer, and it would be easier to dig a grave in the woods. The spot had already been picked out. The grave didn't even have to be that deep, not if he chopped him up. The tub was the perfect place for it.

Just three hours ago, Riley had been tied to a chair

with a belt around his neck, crying and pleading for his life.

He was such a handsome, clean-cut guy, it was hard not to like him. He kept saying that he wasn't going to talk to anyone. *I know I said that she was pretty and that I liked her, but that doesn't mean I'd give you away. You—you can't do this. I mean, you might need me again for another FaceTime session. What if she wants to video-chat again? C'mon, please, cut me a break, man. I've done everything you've asked. I don't even need the money. You can have it back. I've cooperated. I don't get why you're doing this. You don't have to . . .*

He wouldn't shut up. He kept begging and weeping and talking—right up until the old snakeskin belt around his neck choked the life out of him.

Riley's phone buzzed again.

He grabbed it off the passenger seat. He knew it was Hannah. She was the only one who called this number. It was a text.

Hope everything turns out OK with UR family. Also really hope 2 C U next week. Take care.

He looked out the window at her—on the train platform. Smiling, he texted back:

I'll C U. U can count on it.

CHAPTER FIVE

Thursday, 4:52 P.M.

From the backseat of the air-conditioned Uber car, Hannah had gotten a good look at the town of Delmar and Our Lady of the Cove's campus. The sleepy little town wasn't as awful as her first impression of it. Delmar had a supermarket, a movie theater, and some decent-looking restaurants, but it wasn't Seattle. The campus was actually kind of pretty with its trees and gardens, and a view of the lake.

She and Eden asked the Uber driver to wait while they reported to the administration building, Emery Hall, where they were given freshman orientation packets and keys to their quarters: bungalow twenty, St. Agnes Village. Hannah suspected the squat, elderly woman at the reception desk in Emery Hall's lobby was a nun. She wore a white blouse, a brown skirt, and what looked like orthopedic shoes. A crucifix dangled from a chain around her turkey neck. She cheerlessly informed them that the dorm cafeterias weren't open yet, but the student union served food until nine, and the Grub Hub market attached to the student union carried some prepared meals to go. It was open until midnight.

Back in the Uber vehicle, they continued down the

campus's main drag. Hannah noticed a turnoff ahead marked by a tall marble post at the edge of a garden. The words ST. AGNES VILLAGE were carved into the post, which looked like a tombstone. On top of the marker was a four-foot statue of a haloed girl, holding a lamb and a palm leaf. She was looking up at the heavens with a forlorn, pious expression on her face.

Eden was checking her phone. "Says here that Saint Agnes was a virgin martyr, thirteen years old," she announced. "She refused to give up her chastity, and so the Romans executed her by stabbing her in the throat."

"Swell," Hannah sighed. "I'm just going to love it here, I can tell already."

"Didn't you say something back at the train station about wanting to slit your throat?" Eden asked. "Well, you and Saint Agnes are like peas in a pod. And you're both vir—"

"Oh, shut up," Hannah muttered.

The Uber driver turned down the winding road, where a series of old, two-story, white stucco cottages were lined up close together on both sides of the street. Above every front door was a wooden crucifix—along with the bungalow number.

Hannah hadn't noticed many other students milling around the campus. But then, freshman orientation didn't officially begin until tomorrow afternoon, and most of the regional and local freshmen probably wouldn't be arriving until then. She doubted the tiny school attracted many students from either coast.

"It's bungalow twenty," Hannah reminded the driver. She noticed the ground-floor windows on the sides of the cottages all had bars on them. The lawns in front were tiny and well-maintained. Hannah saw the even-numbered cabins on her right. They were approaching bungalow sixteen. "We're coming up to it," she said.

But just after number sixteen, there was a slightly overgrown garden with a couple of Japanese maples, a bird bath, and another saintly statue. Hannah noticed the next bungalow down was number twenty. "Um, here we are," she said. "This is us."

"What happened to eighteen?" Eden asked.

Hannah was wondering the same thing.

As the driver pulled up in front of the bungalow, Hannah saw the front door was open already—and so were the front windows. "That's weird," she murmured.

"No shit," Eden whispered.

The driver popped the trunk. But Hannah didn't want to get out of the car until she knew what was going on inside the bungalow. Eden didn't move either.

A young man stepped out of the cottage. He wore a blue-and-white-striped T-shirt and khaki cargo shorts. Hannah guessed he was no taller than her, but he had a lean, athletic build and a healthy tan. His dark brown hair was combed to the side and fell over his forehead. As he approached the car, he broke into a smile—and all at once, Hannah forgot about Riley. This guy was so damn cute. "Eden? Hannah?" he called.

She could hear him on the other side of the Uber car's closed window.

He opened the car door, and the hot air rolled in. "I'm Rachel's friend, Alden, at your service. I'll get your bags. Go on in. You're just in time for the smudging ceremony . . ."

"Hi, I'm Hannah," she said, stepping out of the car.

"I know," he replied. As he headed toward the trunk, he smiled briefly at Eden. "And you're Eden, hi." He started to hoist the suitcases out of the trunk. "Rachel and I stalked you guys online. You're both even prettier in person. Or is it creepy of me to point that out?"

"Borderline creepy," Eden said.

Hannah laughed. "It's not creepy at all!"

"Are these my little sisters?" someone called.

Hannah turned toward the bungalow and saw Rachel Bonner in the doorway. She held a smoking sage stick over a bowl. "Welcome to bungalow twenty, girls!"

For a second, Hannah thought, *Oh my God, she's bat-shit crazy.*

She was wearing an outfit right out of the 1960s— Capri pants with a splashy, flowered pattern and an orange sleeveless top. Her brunette hair, which had been shoulder-length and wavy in most of her online photos, had been sheared off. It was cut in a pixie style with short bangs. Rachel ducked back inside with her sage stick and bowl.

Hannah and Eden each grabbed a suitcase and followed Alden as he carried the two other bags through the doorway. They stepped into a living room, impeccably furnished in mid-century modern style—like something out of a West Elm catalog. There was a huge framed poster from the Audrey Hepburn movie *Sabrina* practically taking up a whole wall. Frank Sinatra was singing "Let's Get Away from It All" on the music system.

The bungalow was like something out of the 1950s. But it was the *glamorous* 1950s. A big-screen TV in the corner of the room seemed out of place.

The burning sage, along with the heat, made the place seem stuffy. A window fan stirred the smoke around a little, but didn't cool down the room much.

Chanting quietly, Rachel flitted around and used a feather to distribute the smoke from the sage stick. "Excuse me, roomies, but I can't stop and break the spell," she announced. "I'm almost done. Throw your stuff in your room, and get your butts right back here."

Her friend, Alden, led the way. "Your bedroom's over here," he said, heading for a door across from a kitchenette, where there was a sink, a microwave, a toaster oven, and a mini-fridge.

Hannah paused and set down the suitcase by a portable bar. It separated the living room from the tiny kitchen area, which had a back door. On top of the bar were four crystal flutes and a silver bucket with champagne chilling. The bar and the matching stools were mid-century modern designs, too. Hannah turned to Alden. "When they said online that our dorm rooms were furnished, I really didn't expect it to be this nice."

Chuckling, he plopped down the bags. "The furniture they give you is crap. All this stuff is Rachel's. She even had someone repaint the place. She's going through a retro phase right now—in case you didn't catch on. Last year, it was bohemian shabby chic shit. I kind of miss the bean bag chairs. By the way, I hope you like Sinatra."

"And Ella Fitzgerald and Nat King Cole and Tony Bennett and Julie London," Rachel said—still fluttering around the living room with her feather and sage stick. "If not, don't bother unpacking!"

Alden opened the bedroom door. "Give it a few months," he whispered. "And she'll be into new wave or rap or some such shit."

Hannah and Eden followed him into the shadowy, hot, claustrophobic bedroom. There was barely space for the three of them and the suitcases. Last week, from

Seattle, they'd shipped two big boxes of bedding, posters, books, and things they couldn't live without. Both parcels were now on the stripped twin beds, which seemed crammed into the tiny room—along with two desks that had built-in bookcases and a dresser that, obviously, they were supposed to share. All the furnishings were old, ugly, and slightly battered—not in the same league as the sleek, beautiful pieces in the living room. The one window was open and had bars on the outside. The view was of the garden next door. Hannah wondered how she and Eden would manage to cohabit in this tiny space without killing each other. Already, she found it hard to breathe. The room was like an oven and still smoky from the burnt sage.

Alden set the suitcases on the bed. There wasn't any space for them on the floor. "The boxes arrived yesterday," he said. "I dumped them in here. Hope that's okay."

"Do you live here, too?" Eden asked.

"No, I'm at O'Leary Hall, the boys' dorm," he explained. He stepped over Hannah's suitcase and pushed open the window more. "The smoke should dissipate soon. Not that I totally buy into this *smudging* shit, but if any spot in this dump needed it, this bedroom's the place. The previous occupant, Rachel's roommate last year, turned out to be a total pain in the ass, lots of personal problems. No one could stand her."

"Why?" Hannah asked.

"Let's not be unkind, Alden," Rachel said, stopping by the doorway again. "Let's just say it wasn't a good fit!" She headed into the living room with her sage stick again.

He rolled his eyes. "For one, she was a lazy slob, a

total pig," he whispered. "Rachel got sick of cleaning up after her all the time. Didn't even flush the toilet. She was one of those 'if it's yellow, it's mellow' people. Anyway, Rachel's right. I shouldn't be mean. Let's just say we were in here a while trying to smoke out her essence."

"Well, then I guess we should thank you," Hannah said.

"It wasn't just the ex-roommate we were trying to smudge out." He nodded toward the window—and the flower patch beyond the bars. "You're next door to some heavy, bad vibes. There used to be a bungalow where that funky-looking garden is now. It was bungalow eighteen, but they tore it down and retired the number. No one wanted to live there. Hell, they couldn't *pay* anyone to live there . . ."

Hannah's eyes widened. "Why? What happened?"

"Somehow, I figured you might have known about it," Alden said. "Back in 1970, they had a serial killer on the loose. He murdered a bunch of girls here on campus."

Hannah was dumbfounded.

"No shit?" Eden murmured.

"I shit you not," Alden said. He glanced toward the window again. "The guy broke into bungalow eighteen, and he tied up the three girls who lived there. I really don't know how he managed to do it. Maybe he made them tie up each other. Anyway, he had them all in the upstairs bedroom. He dragged one into the bathroom and killed her. Then while he took the second girl out and murdered her, the third girl managed to untie herself and escape. They called the guy the Immaculate Conception Killer. The girls he murdered that night were like his fifth and sixth victims. The police caught him a couple of days later . . ."

"Afterward, no one wanted anything to do with the place," Rachel said, stopping in the doorway again. She stubbed out the smoldering sage stick in a bowl. "So they tore it down and put in the flower garden and the statue of Saint Ursula. She's another virgin martyr. I think they shot her with an arrow or beheaded her or something. You can't throw a rock on campus without hitting a statue of a virgin martyr."

Frowning, she shook her head at her friend. "Alden, you stinker, I can't believe you told them about the murders next door. You could have at least waited until they'd settled in a little. Now they're going to have nightmares tonight, and it'll be entirely your fault. Anyway, it was fifty years ago, and I've smudged the hell out of this place. So let's not be morbid." She turned and started toward the kitchenette. "A champagne toast is in order! Alden, get your cute butt in here and open the bottle for us!"

He followed her out to the living room.

In a stupor, Hannah just stood there. She'd read up on the university. How come she didn't know about these murders from fifty years ago? She looked out the window—at the overgrown garden next door.

"Which bed do you want?" Eden asked. "Window or wall side?"

"Wall, I guess," Hannah said, thinking it might be less drafty in the winter—and a bit farther away from the *heavy, bad vibes* of bungalow eighteen. She dropped her purse on the wall-side bed and then stepped into the living room, where Tony Bennett and Lady Gaga were singing a duet on Rachel's music system.

Alden uncorked the champagne. Eden stepped out of the bedroom in time to join them by the bar for a toast. Rachel handed her a full glass.

"Here's to a marvelous year ahead," Rachel said, raising her flute. "And here's to my 'little sisters' who have traveled so far to be here. May this be the beginning of a beautiful, magical lifelong sisterhood!"

"Hear! Hear!" Hannah said. She got a special little thrill clinking glasses with Alden. She couldn't tell yet if he and Rachel were romantically involved. But she hoped they weren't. With only twenty percent of the school's student population being male, her chances of meeting another guy as cute as him were very slim.

Eden downed her champagne in a couple of gulps. "Thanks a lot," she said, setting her empty glass down on the bar. "Listen, I'm going to check out the campus. See you guys later."

Rachel looked flummoxed. "Have fun!" she called as Eden headed out the door. She waited until the door closed and then sipped her champagne and gave Hannah a baffled smile. "Was it something I said?"

"Or was it me and my big mouth?" Alden asked.

Hannah rolled her eyes. "No, that's just her."

"The independent type," Rachel offered.

"No, just rude," Hannah admitted. "I'm never sure with her. She's my half-sister. We've been living under the same roof for two years, and I still don't get her. Anyway, I'm sorry."

"Oh please," Rachel said with a dismissive wave of her hand. She grabbed the champagne bottle and topped off their flutes, then headed toward the sofa. "C'mon, take a load off and tell us all about this *half-sister* thing. Or shouldn't I ask?"

"I've already fessed-up and told Hannah and Eden that we've googled them," Alden said, sitting in an easy chair.

"Why, yes, you do have a big mouth," Rachel sighed.

"It's okay." Hannah smiled. She sat down on the sofa, making sure not to crowd Rachel. "I checked you out online, too. Your hair was longer in all your photos."

Rachel pointed to her pixie cut. "This is Jean Seberg damage—from last week. I saw a double feature of her movies *Breathless* and *Bonjour Tristesse*. Next thing you know, I was going for the scissors. My stylist cleaned it up the following day."

"Well, I love it," Hannah said. She meant it, too. In just a matter of minutes, she'd done a complete about-face on her first perception of Rachel. Her "big sister" wasn't crazy at all. She was unique, stylish, sophisticated, and fun. Already, Hannah wondered if Rachel might sometime let her borrow that cute top or the Capri pants. She and Rachel looked about the same size.

After only one glass of champagne, Hannah had become quite relaxed and didn't mind telling them all about the *half-sister thing*—and how her family was affected by Eden moving in with them. She even explained how *the thing that happened* had wrecked her friendships at school. After her second glass of champagne, Hannah realized she'd been monopolizing the conversation. "Aren't you sorry you asked about my sister?" she finally asked. "Listen to me. I didn't mean to talk your ear off."

"Are you kidding?" Rachel said. "I read about what happened—with the murders and all. So I was curious. But hearing you tell it, well, suddenly, it's not just some news story. It's real. It happened to you and your family."

She glanced at her wristwatch. "God, I didn't realize how late it is." She turned to Alden. "If you still want to go to Lake Bluff, we should get cracking."

Hannah had a bunch of questions she wanted to ask them—mainly if they were dating each other. But suddenly, the two of them got to their feet. Alden collected the empty flute glasses and set them by the kitchen sink. Rachel switched off the music and then took her cell phone out of her purse. "We should let you unpack and get settled," she said, staring at her phone as she texted someone. "Feel free to turn on the TV or the sound system. Help yourself to whatever's in the fridge. You're probably dying for a shower. The bathroom's upstairs . . ."

"And remember while you're in there, if it's yellow, it's not mellow!" Alden added as he and Rachel headed toward the door.

"Gross," Rachel said. She glanced over her shoulder at Hannah. "If you go out, don't forget to lock up. See you later!" Then she stepped outside and shut the door behind her.

Hannah went to the front window. Rachel and Alden walked to the curb, and a black Lincoln Town Car pulled up. Alden opened the back door for Rachel, and they climbed inside. Obviously, it wasn't an Uber. The vehicle must have been waiting for them down the block. They'd left in such a hurry that Hannah couldn't help thinking she'd talked too much. Or maybe they were just late for something.

She watched the Lincoln Town Car head down the street. The living room suddenly seemed hot and stuffy again. And in an instant, she felt hopelessly lonely. Her eyes watered up. Was this how homesickness was going to hit her—in these awful, unpredictable tsunami-like waves?

She wanted to phone home. But she knew she'd start crying as soon as she heard her mother's voice—her mother, toward whom she'd been so critical and snippy these last few years. Everything her mother did had struck Hannah as stupid and embarrassing. Now, she missed her so much that her stomach ached. Or maybe it was the champagne making her over-emotional. She couldn't call home now anyway. They'd want to talk to Eden.

Wasn't that just like her to disappear? Typical.

Hannah went back into the narrow bedroom, opened her suitcase, and unpacked a few items. It was still smoky in there. She moved over to the window.

She gazed out at the slightly unkempt garden next door and shuddered. She couldn't help thinking about what had happened in the bungalow that had been there fifty years ago.

CHAPTER SIX

Thursday, 8:16 P.M.

By the time Eden reached the parking lot of the Sunnyside Up Café, she was exhausted.

She'd explored the campus. Most of the buildings were closed up—except for a couple of dorms and the student union, which didn't look too interesting. She wanted to check out the recreation center, which included an indoor pool, but a sign on the locked door (she'd tested it) said the rec center didn't open until tomorrow.

Eden also checked out the surrounding neighborhood. A street of old mansions along the lake bluff had been converted to housing for upperclassmen, up to twenty students per house. At least that was the story Eden got from a gabby middle-aged woman walking her Irish setter. Closer to town, large, graceful private homes occupied the lakefront property. Alongside the driveway to one of them, Eden discovered a trail down to the beach. Both the pathway and the beach were probably private, but that didn't stop her.

Taking off her shoes, she must have walked at least a mile along the shoreline, sometimes in the hot sand, sometimes with her bare feet in the cool water. Though it was late, the beach was still dotted with swimmers, mostly kids screaming and laughing. If not for them, Eden would have stripped down and swam in her panties and T-shirt.

She hadn't slept much last night, and it started to catch up with her. Still, she kept walking. That was Eden's trademark. "You're always pushing things to their limit," her stepmother, Sheila, had told her. This criticism usually came up when Eden was driving. She never stopped for gas until the needle was on empty. And she rarely moved into the right lane to exit until the very last minute. It was a game she played, staying in the fast lane for as long as she could. It made life more interesting.

So Eden kept walking—even though she was tired and hungry and had to pee. She told herself that it wasn't really an emergency yet.

But by the time she'd found another trail up from the beach and back to town, it had become a definite emergency.

The Sunnyside Up Café was half-full with customers, and nearly all of them looked up and gaped at her as she staggered in. She spotted a sign for the restrooms and made a beeline toward them.

It wasn't until she came out of the bathroom and sat down at the counter that Eden got a good look at the place. It was definitely a dive. The ramped-up air-conditioning couldn't diminish the strong smell of fried onion rings and bacon. The walls were decorated with framed, sun-faded vintage ads for Coke, Canada Dry, Jell-O, Hunt's ketchup, and the like. The battered pressed-wood and avocado Formica tables looked like hand-me-downs from a Denny's that had closed. The cushioned seats in the booths were covered in orange

Naugahyde that was cracked and taped in places. At least the red tape *almost* matched. "Working My Way Back to You" by Frankie Valli and the Four Seasons was playing over the sound system.

What a surprise, an oldie, Eden thought. The place was from another decade. But she liked it. And the menu had several vegetarian items that looked decent. She could imagine parking herself here at a table for hours in the evening, drinking gallons of coffee while toiling over her homework or maybe chatting with some of the locals. The town probably had some interesting characters.

The waitress was a skinny, tall, sixtyish woman with short gray hair and a dimpled smile. The nametag on her mustard-colored uniform read ROSEANN. "What'll you have, hon?" she asked.

Eden ordered lemonade, a veggie burger, and fries. She guzzled down the entire lemonade a minute after it was set in front of her, and the waitress gave her a refill.

While she waited for her food, Eden dug the freshman orientation packet out of her purse and looked it over. There really wasn't much for her to do tomorrow. She had to report back to Emery Hall to get her photo taken for her student ID and her cafeteria card. There were tours of the campus and sign-up tables for various clubs and activities—none of which interested her even remotely. She'd already registered for all of her classes. It didn't seem worth it, coming in four days early just to have her stupid picture taken. But at least she could sleep in tomorrow. Maybe she'd take the train to Chicago. She could have her picture taken another day. It couldn't be the only day they were making ID cards.

While Eden ate her burger, the waitress asked if she was a student at the college. Eden told her yes, she was a freshman—from Seattle. "I just arrived today," she said. She glanced around. "You must get a lot of students in here, being open twenty-four hours."

"Yep, keeps us in business," Roseann replied. She was behind the counter, making a fresh pot of coffee.

"Have you worked here long?"

"Only since 1992. I've lived in Delmar practically my whole life, born and raised here."

Eden felt a bit sorry for her, but didn't let on. "Did you go to the college?"

"Nope, no college degree. Guess you could say I graduated from the school of hard knocks." She started wiping down the counter.

Eden wiped her mouth with her napkin. "Were you living here when those murders happened on the campus?"

"I certainly was." Roseann nodded. "Boy, do I remember that. Y'know, I don't get many kids asking about the strangler, not anymore. The college has kept that chapter of their history under wraps. Where did you hear about the murders?"

"My new roommate's boyfriend told me," she explained. "What was it like back then—I mean, suddenly having all these murders happening right here in your neighborhood?"

The waitress set down her dishcloth. "I was seventeen at the time, in high school. I know it's hard to imagine me at seventeen, but believe me, I was once. Me and my friends, we were terrified. Our parents were terrified. This used to be one of those towns where no one locked their doors at night. But all that changed. None of us went out after dark. We were all so scared. And when we did go out—during the day—we took all sorts of precautions. I carried my grandfather's old straight razor in my purse. And my best friend kept one of her mother's knitting needles in her bag. I remember walking by the park with her after school. No one dared walk alone, not with that maniac loose. I remember not being able to figure out what was so different, and then it dawned on me. It was the silence. There wasn't any laughing and singing, because the kids weren't there. The swing set, jungle gym, and the slide—they were all empty. It was eerie."

She leaned in close to Eden. "But you know, it didn't happen all of a sudden. It sounds weird, but I was sort of braced for something awful. Before the first girl was strangled, some strange, disturbing things were going on at the college . . ."

Eden stopped eating and pushed her plate away. "Like what kind of things?"

"Like a freshman girl in one of the cottages in Saint Agnes Village," Roseann whispered. "The school was all-girls back in 1970. The girl had managed to keep it secret that she was pregnant. The story goes even she didn't know. She just thought she was sick and getting fat—right up until she went into labor. Can you believe it? She had the baby right there in one of the cottages. She didn't want anyone to know about it, so she choked the baby to death with the umbilical cord."

"Oh my God," Eden murmured, wincing.

Roseann nodded glumly. "It was a boy, the poor little

thing. The mother, the girl—I guess she was out of her mind—she tossed it in a laundry basket with all her blood-stained sheets and things. Then she tried to set it on fire. I guess she wanted to destroy all the evidence, but she didn't do a very good job. The fire alarm went off . . ."

Eden kept shaking her head.

"The school did its best to cover up the whole incident. I hear the archdiocese even got the local newspapers to play it down. But everyone knew."

"What happened to the girl?" Eden whispered.

"They locked her up in Elgin, the state asylum for the insane."

"Is she still there? Do you know?"

"That's not very likely, since they tore down the hospital in 1993," Roseann answered. "Maybe they transferred her to another place. Or maybe she's out. Chances are pretty good she's still alive. She was only a couple of years older than me, and I ain't dead yet." She glanced over toward some customers at a table on the other side of the restaurant. "Excuse me, hon . . ." She came out from behind the counter and hurried to the table.

Slightly dazed, Eden couldn't help wondering about this baby-murder from fifty years ago. In which bungalow did the girl give birth and kill her baby? How could she have not known she was pregnant? She imagined the girl now, seventy years old and still locked up in an insane asylum.

She heard a rumble outside—like a big truck passing by, or maybe it was thunder. When she turned to glance out the window, Eden noticed a man sitting alone in the booth closest to her. He had a half-eaten sandwich on the plate in front of him. He was about thirty and sinewy-looking with a deep tan, receding brown hair, and a thin mustache. Eden couldn't decide if he was borderline handsome or kind of slimy. He winked at her, then reached around and showed her a crinkly paper bag that obviously held one of those twenty-four-ounce cans of beer. She wasn't sure if he was offering her a sip or just letting her in on his little secret.

Slimy, she decided, turning forward again.

As the waitress swung by the man's table carrying a tray of dirty dishes, Eden noticed him hide his contraband beer.

Roseann ducked into the kitchen and then emerged again empty-handed. "Did you save room for dessert?" she asked, taking away Eden's plate.

"Just coffee," she said. "Earlier, you mentioned some *things* that happened before the first girl was strangled. Was there something else?"

Roseann set a cup in front of her and poured the coffee. "A few days after the girl killed her baby, another girl at the college disappeared. People weren't sure if she'd been abducted or if she'd run away or what. But a couple of days later, her sister got a letter from her saying she was okay. And people stopped worrying for a while—until they found the strangler's first victim in a ravine by the college library."

"Was it the missing girl?" Eden asked.

Roseann shook her head. "A different girl entirely. The missing girl was actually being held prisoner by the strangler. He and his mother lived in an old farmhouse outside Waukegan. The girl was locked up in a little shack in their backyard." Roseann's voice dropped to a whisper again. "I guess he was torturing her and doing all sorts of nasty things to her. She was the last one he killed. He strangled four or five girls, the last two together on the same night."

Eden nodded. "Yeah, I heard about that. It happened in a bungalow that they later tore down. I moved in right next door today. You said the killer lived with his mother? How did he keep everything he was doing a secret from her?"

"He didn't," Roseann answered under her breath. "The old bitch was behind a lot of it, pushing him to kill those girls. At the trial, she said it was her son's 'sacred mission' to kill the 'holy sluts.' Talk about crazy. I guess she and her lunatic son were pushed over the edge when that girl had the baby and killed it."

"Was there a trial?"

Roseann nodded. "After he killed the last two girls, he left a witness. The police caught up with him pretty quickly. At the trial, he and Mama were found guilty as sin, of course. She was an accessory. She died in prison less than a year after they locked her up, cancer or something. Sonny Boy got the electric chair a few months after she went. That's what she kept calling him during the trial: *Sonny Boy*."

Eden grimaced.

"Say, you're pretty good with all these questions," Roseann said. "Are you studying to be a reporter or something?"

Working up a smile, Eden nodded. "As a matter of fact, I've signed up for a couple of journalism classes."

"That's nice. Excuse me again," the waitress said hurriedly. "Duty calls . . ."

Eden noticed two middle-aged couples had just come in and taken a table by the door. Roseann fetched their waters and menus.

"Hey, girlie," someone whispered.

Eden turned toward the slimy man in the booth and found him smiling at her.

"It was six," he said.

Her eyes narrowed at him. "What?"

"He killed six women," the man said, "not 'four or five.' There were the two girls he strangled, and a teacher he killed. Then he did the two in one night, and finally the girl he had locked up in the shack. That's a total of six."

"Well, thanks for clearing that up," Eden muttered, starting to turn away.

"Are you signed up for Ellie Goodwin's journalism class?"

Eden scowled at him again. "I don't see how that's any of your business."

"A lot of good people went to jail because of her. She's a fucking busybody and a liar, writing all those stories full of fake news. Stupid, conniving woman, she'll get hers someday . . ."

He slurred his words a little, and Eden figured he was drunk. She turned forward again and sipped her coffee.

"Rachel Bonner, she's your housemate, isn't she? The rich bitch. She's bad news, too."

Eden glared at him. "Are you following me or something?"

He grinned. "You said you lived next door to where both those girls got it back in 1970. So I figured you're in bungalow twenty. That's where Princess Rachel lives in the lap of luxury in her spacious second-floor bedroom meant for two girls. And I'll bet she's got you and some other poor girl crammed into that little closet of a bedroom off the kitchen."

"I don't see how that's any of your business either," Eden said. It was damn creepy that he knew so much about the setup of their bungalow.

"Well, take it from me," he said. "You just give it a week with that Bonner bitch as your roommate and that Goodwin skank as your teacher, and you'll know you should have listened to your old friend Lance. They're both bad news. You want another tip?"

"Not particularly."

"If you're heading back to your bungalow after this, you can save yourself about six blocks by taking the shortcut through the woods. Just hang a right when you step out the door here."

With a sigh, Eden faced forward again.

"Are you listening?" he said, raising his voice a little. "Hang a right, go to the dry cleaners on the corner, take another right, and you'll see the woods across the street—and a little trail. It takes you directly to Saint Agnes Village. You'll save yourself at least fifteen minutes. Are you listening to me?"

"Stop annoying the other customers," Roseann grumbled as she approached his booth. She slapped a check on the table in front of him. "She's too young for you anyway, lover boy."

"Looks like it's about to rain out there," he said. "I'm just telling her about the shortcut back to her bungalow."

And I was just about to tell you to fuck off, Eden thought. But she didn't even look his way. He gave her the creeps. Glancing in the opposite direction, she could see his reflection in the restaurant's darkened plate glass window.

He got to his feet. "Take it easy, honey," he murmured.

Eden kept her head turned away. In the reflecting window, she watched him swagger toward the exit, the beer tucked under his arm. He stepped outside.

Roseann refilled her coffee cup.

"Who was that?" Eden asked. "Do you know him?"

"That's just Lance," she sighed. "He's on the custodial staff at the college. He does some landscaping, too. He's also a terrible tipper. He had a snoot-full tonight. I think he has a problem. He's always sneaking beer in here, like he's fooling everybody. I'd have to be blind not to catch on. Anyway, I'm sorry if he was bothering you. He's harmless enough."

Ten minutes later, when Eden stepped out of the Sunnyside Up Café, she realized the rumbling sound she'd heard earlier hadn't been a truck passing by. It had been thunder. She felt the wind kicking up. Some trash and leaves scattered past her as she headed down the block. She saw a flash of lightning over the lake. For a second the whole sky was illuminated.

It hadn't started to rain yet, but it looked like it might pour at any minute. She remembered Lance's "tip" about the shortcut back to St. Agnes Village. Was he on the level?

Eden turned, and at the end of the block, she saw the dry cleaners he'd mentioned. When she reached the corner, she looked to her right at the darkened woods. Tree branches swayed and rustled with the wind. It seemed like the whole forest was alive and moving.

She couldn't help thinking he was in those woods,

waiting for her. But he'd left the restaurant at least twenty minutes ago. Besides, hadn't the waitress said he was harmless?

From across the street, she could make out a break in the trees. Eden figured it was the foot trail he'd told her about.

Eden told herself that she'd save walking at least six blocks.

CHAPTER SEVEN

Thursday, 11:52 P.M.

Hannah sat up in bed. Through the window, a streetlamp outside provided just enough light to see everything in the small bedroom—including the empty bed across from her.

Eden had been gone six hours. And it was raining out, not the dull, monotonous Seattle type of rain Hannah was used to. This was a downpour with thunder and lightning. She'd purchased a fan earlier in the evening, and it had cooled the bedroom down. She'd also left the window open. The ugly beige curtains billowed with the breeze from the storm. Hannah thought about getting up and checking the windowsill to see if any rain was coming through the screen. But then she figured, if Eden's bed got wet, she deserved it.

This was so typical of her half-sister. She literally didn't have sense enough to come in out of the rain.

After Rachel and Alden had left earlier tonight, Hannah had unpacked, showered, and gotten a feel for the bungalow that would be her home for the next nine months. While upstairs, she couldn't resist checking out Rachel's bedroom—despite the closed door. It was gorgeous and roomy with a queen-size bed; more sleek, mid-century modern design furniture; an amazing, huge framed print of the Eiffel Tower; and a plush shag rug. Rachel even had a vase with freshly cut flowers on her desk—along with a silver-framed black-and-white photo of a sexy, handsome young man. It looked like an old high school graduation portrait. Hannah put it together from a collage of photos on Rachel's bulletin board that the stud in the silver frame must have been Rachel's father. It was weird to see him age—getting balder and paunchier—in so many pictures. Hannah also noticed there was only one photo of Rachel's mother—in a shot with Mr. Bonner.

The bedroom was about thirty degrees cooler than the rest of the bungalow, thanks to the air conditioner humming in the window.

Hannah had hoped that Rachel and Alden would come back in time for the three of them to have dinner together, but no such luck. By eight o'clock she was starting to feel totally abandoned—and hungry. She texted Eden:

Where R U? Alone here at Bung 20. Want 2 go eat?

No reply, of course. She shouldn't have been surprised. Eden had probably switched off her phone again.

Hannah called home and talked to everyone. Earlier, she'd been afraid that, upon hearing her parents' voices, she'd burst into tears. But it was her mother who lost it and started crying. "We miss you so much, honey!" she said, her voice all broken and weepy. Apparently Hannah's twelve-year-old brother, Gabe, kept going into her empty bedroom and coming out with this melancholy look on his face that absolutely broke her mom's heart. Her mother made it sound more like Hannah was dead than just away at school.

Everyone expected to talk to Eden, too, of course. Hannah told them that she'd gone off by herself two hours before and was incommunicado.

"Why am I not surprised?" her mother sighed. "Well, when she *re-appears*, have her call us. Okay?"

After hanging up with her folks, Hannah stuck a Post-it note on the bedroom door:

E –

Gone to the student union for dinner. Call home when you get this.
8:15

The student union was in a big, modern glass-and-steel building that included a coffee shop, Campus Grounds, and a 7-Eleven type of market, the Grub Hub. Hannah had a feeling both spots would be her salvation in the months ahead. The union was like one huge bar—with two pool tables, dart boards, pinball and video game machines, and a couple of strategically located TVs. It was also air-conditioned, thank God. On the wall behind the counter-bar was a chalkboard menu of Italian sodas, juice drinks, and coffee specialties. Exposed pipes, beams, and ducts ran along the ceiling, and concrete support posts were staggered every twenty feet or so. There were about twenty-five people—mostly girls— eating and drinking at the tables. It didn't seem like much of a crowd for such a large space. Hannah guessed most of them were freshmen, like her. She'd hoped against hope that Rachel and Alden might be among the diners, but she didn't see them anywhere. Some students sat in couples or groups, making Hannah wonder how these people knew each other when they'd all just arrived today. Were they all from the same high school?

Or maybe they just had roommates who hadn't deserted them.

Several students ate alone, staring at their smartphones so that they wouldn't look utterly pathetic. Hannah figured that was what she'd have to do.

She sat down at a table close to the entrance so that, if Eden showed up, she'd find her easily. The laminated handwritten menu had eight food selections. Hannah decided on the Cobb salad, and then glanced around for a waitperson. Or did they even have servers? Maybe she was supposed to go up to the counter and order her stupid dinner.

She hated this.

She should have sat near someone else that was alone—and then she could have asked what the hell she was supposed to do to get some dinner in this dump. She might have struck up a friendship, too, if only a temporary one.

She noticed a couple of girls, a chubby blonde and a pretty brunette, about three tables over. They both wore Our Lady of the Cove T-shirts, which Hannah thought was kind of pathetic for any freshman to do on her first day here. But they looked friendly enough, and they smiled in her direction. So Hannah smiled back. Then the brunette got to her feet, waved, and signaled like she wanted her to come over and join them.

Hannah was so grateful. Even if they were total dipshits, at least they were nice enough to invite her over. She waved back and started to stand—just as another girl walked past her. The other girl wore an Our Lady of the Cove T-shirt, too.

Standing there for a moment, Hannah watched the new arrival join her friends at the other table. The blonde whispered something to her two friends, and they all laughed.

Hannah shrank back into her chair. Had they noticed her making an ass out of herself? Was that why they were giggling? She gazed down at the tabletop and started to count to herself. In thirty seconds, she'd get up, walk out, and find something to eat at the Grub Hub. She didn't care if it was a stale hot dog that had been on one of those rotisserie things since Tuesday—just as long as she didn't have to sit here alone.

After twenty-three seconds, she became aware of someone standing beside her table. Hannah figured it was the waitperson, and she hesitated before looking up.

"Please tell me that you haven't ordered yet, because the food here really sucks."

Rachel was smiling down at her.

Hannah sprung to her feet. She almost wanted to hug her.

Ten minutes later, they were headed to town, walking through a residential section with beautiful, big old homes. The tree-lined street ran alongside a bluff overlooking the beach. The sky was darkening and ominous over Lake Michigan. It looked like a storm was rolling in. Hannah could feel the wind picking up and the temperature dropping.

Rachel explained that she'd seen her note to Eden on the bedroom door. She apologized for running off earlier. Alden had needed to pick up a pair of prescription eyeglasses at Target in Lake Bluff. "It didn't dawn on us until we got there," Rachel said. "We should have invited you along. You probably need stuff for your room or groceries. Anyway, we can still pick up anything you need while we're here in town tonight."

Hannah asked where Alden was. With Riley out of the picture—if not completely, then at least until a week from Saturday—she couldn't help wondering about Alden.

Rachel shrugged. "Beats me. I dropped him off at his dorm about fifteen minutes ago."

As they approached the town, Hannah spotted her first firefly. She wanted to chase it, cup it in her hands, and watch it light up. Rachel was amused. "God, you're like a little kid! It's just a lightning bug."

"Well, they don't have them in Seattle," she replied, out of breath. She gave up on the chase. There was something so magical about the glowing insect—and this moment with her cool, sophisticated "big sister." Just minutes ago, she'd been so alone and depressed. But Rachel had come to her rescue, and they were on their way to have dinner together. A part of her was actually glad Eden had disappeared. It would have been a real drag to have her half-sister along.

In a cozy Italian restaurant called Bellini's, they ate the most delicious pizza Hannah had ever tasted. She'd never seen pizza cut in squares before, but apparently, that was how they did it in Chicago.

They were just finishing up dinner when Hannah worked Alden into the conversation again. She finally had the nerve to ask: "So—are you guys like—dating or anything?"

"Me and Alden?" Rachel laughed. "God, no. He's practically like my brother. We grew up together. His mother was a maid in our house, an Irish girl, and single. She died from a brain tumor about ten years ago. But Alden stayed on—with the house staff looking after him, well, the house staff and me. And now he's looking after me. At least, that's what my father thinks about the setup. Alden started here last year. My parents are paying for it." She picked up a square of pizza, but then seemed to change her mind about eating it and put it back. "Anyway, no, Alden and I aren't dating. Why do you ask? If you're interested in him, you're shit out of luck. Alden will deny it until he's purple in the face, but I'm ninety-nine percent sure he's gay as a Christmas goose. Or he's at least a Kinsey five."

"Oh, I wasn't interested," Hannah lied. She tried to hide her disappointment and fiddled with a breadstick. She should have known. He seemed too good to be true.

Rachel sipped her Diet Coke. "I didn't want to ask you this in front of Alden earlier. But how is it with your dad? I mean, I've read such terrible things about him screwing around all the time, but he really can't be that awful."

Making a face, Hannah squirmed in her chair. "I used to think I was so lucky. Most of my friends, their parents are divorced, or if their parents are still together, they can't stand each other. But my mom and dad seemed happy, always hugging and kissing, very lovey-dovey, almost nauseatingly so. As far as fathers go, my dad seemed pretty cool. I mean, all my girlfriends thought so. Then the shit hit the fan, and I found out he was this sleazy serial cheater. And so did everyone else, because the whole thing became a media sensation. Anyway, while all that was happening, he was laid up in the hospital with major injuries—"

Rachel nodded. "Yeah, I read that he was shot and crashed his car."

"As angry as I was, I kind of felt sorry for him, too," Hannah admitted. "But I couldn't really forgive him, y'know? I don't think I ever will. He hasn't been the same since all this happened. He doesn't even look the same—thanks to the accident." She shrugged and worked up a smile. "Anyway, aren't you sorry you asked?"

"Not at all," Rachel murmured. She actually seemed fascinated. "I read something about your dad and your aunt having an affair. Is that true? Him and your mom's sister?"

Hannah snapped the breadstick in half. "Yep, it's true."

"What was she like? Or don't you want to talk about it?"

"Oh, I don't mind talking about it with you," Hannah said. "Actually, I never knew her. She died before I was even born. It was a suicide. She took a swan dive off the roof of a high-rise apartment building."

"Yeah, I read about that, too. But did your mom or dad ever say anything about her?"

"Up until two years ago, my younger brothers and I had no idea she even existed." Hannah sighed. "My parents kept it a secret that she had a kid sister. But last year, I got my mom to open up about her. Her name was Molly, and I guess she was a major flake—really irresponsible, sort of a wild child. But she was pretty. My mom was so mad at her about the affair that she destroyed every photo of Molly she had. Then a couple of years ago, she had a change of heart and contacted some of Molly's high school and college friends for any pictures they'd saved. She managed to track down a few. I've seen them. Molly really was a knockout. Anyway, I don't know much else about her. It's not like my mom and dad talk about her. And for obvious reasons, bringing her up in a conversation with them tends to be a real buzz-kill."

"That's so sad," Rachel whispered. She must have meant it, too, because she actually had tears in her eyes. "I feel so sorry for her . . ."

"I feel a lot sorrier for my mother," Hannah said. "Anyway, enough about my parents. That's one big soap opera. What about your folks?"

Rachel wiped her eyes with her napkin. "What about them?"

"I don't know," Hannah said. She'd thought she should change the subject so the conversation wasn't only about her. "Are you all close?"

Rachel shrugged. "Yes and no. It's your standard poor little rich girl story. When I was growing up, my dad was away a lot on business. My mother was an heiress. Dad took over her father's company and made it into this huge corporation. I was raised mostly by a series of nannies and household staff members. If it weren't for Alden, I'd have been awfully lonely. I don't have any brothers or sisters or cousins. But I always had great birthday parties, packed with my father's business associates' kids and a ton of presents. I made quite a haul every Christmas, too. It's still that way. Anything I want, I just ask for, and I usually get it. My dad sort of dotes on me now. I think it's to make up for all the time he wasn't around when I was a kid. He's really over-protective. That's why I'm going to school here. It's only forty-five minutes away." She made a face. "My mom and I don't exactly get along. She's the Botox queen of the Gold Coast. It's gotten so her expression never changes. I honestly can't tell anymore if she's mad at me or happy. I'm terrified I'll grow up to be just like her, because she was an only child, too. And I'm an heiress, like her. She went to school here, too."

"Was she here when those murders happened?" Hannah asked.

"No, that was like fifty years ago. She came here years after that. She's fifty-seven." Rachel glanced at her wristwatch. "God, it's twenty to ten. I didn't realize it was so late. The Jewel's closing soon. We better get going. I'm buying you guys a fan for your bedroom. It was like a sauna when I was smudging in there this afternoon." She waved at the waiter. "Dante! Check, please—and could you box this up?" She pointed to what was left of their pizza.

Hannah reached into her purse, but Rachel insisted on paying for dinner, since she'd invited her. Hannah thought it was a pretty sweet deal having a rich roommate.

Minutes later, they stepped out of Bellini's—right into the beginnings of a thunderstorm. The rain was just starting to come down—sporadic, heavy drops.

The two of them hurried across the street to take cover under some shop awnings. Hannah spotted the sign for the Jewel-Osco supermarket down at the end of the next block. Delmar's main drag was only three blocks long and didn't even have a stop light. She figured it was about a mile back to St. Agnes Village—and they were going in the opposite direction.

"Maybe we should head back now before it really starts to pour," Hannah suggested, glancing over her shoulder. "I don't really need to go to the store. I can survive without a fan for one night."

"Nonsense, I'll just call Perry," Rachel said, talking loudly to compete with the patter of rain on the awning overhead. She fished her cell phone out of her purse. "He can drive us. No sense getting caught in a monsoon."

"Who's Perry?" Hannah asked. There was a crack of thunder, and she flinched.

"He's our ride." Rachel kept walking, but slowed down as she worked her thumbs over her phone screen. "Did you see Alden and me when we took off earlier? Perry was driving the Town Car. My father hired him. Like I told you, my dad's overprotective. When I first started school here, he actually had three guys working in shifts on *bodyguard* duty. I think my parents were worried I'd get kidnapped or something. Twenty-four-seven, one of them was always in a car parked by the entrance to Saint Agnes Village—like it was a stakeout or something. Totally ridiculous. After a couple of months, I persuaded my father to narrow the team down to one guy. Anyway, that's Perry. He's sort of like my bodyguard and babysitter. But mostly, he's my chauffeur."

"Like your own personal Uber," Hannah said. "Is he still staked out by the front gate to the village?"

"No, thank God," Rachel said, putting her phone away. "He lives here in town, and he's on call. Talk about a cush-cush job. I don't think he's much of a bodyguard. If somebody actually wanted to kidnap me, I'd be in real trouble. Still, it's nice to have him around in situations like this. He'll meet us outside the Jewel."

Rachel was right. After they picked up a few items—

including the last box fan in stock—Rachel and Hannah stepped out of the supermarket to find the Lincoln Town Car waiting for them. A stocky, thirty-something man with a crew cut and a five o'clock shadow stood by the car. He had an umbrella ready, and opened the back door for them. Hannah barely got wet, even with all the rain.

"Perry, this is Hannah, my roommate and 'little sister,'" Rachel said, once he pulled out of the parking lot. "You're going to see a lot of her in the coming year."

"Hi," Hannah said.

The rain beat on the car roof, and the windshield wipers squeaked a bit. Hannah saw the driver glance at her in the rearview mirror. He nodded.

"Perry's a man of few words, aren't you, Perry?" Rachel said. "What were you in the middle of when I texted? Don't tell me you had a hot date. I'll hate myself for interrupting."

"Nothing that important," he answered seriously. "I'm here to serve."

Hannah had a feeling he didn't like being teased. She noticed him eyeing her in the rearview mirror again.

After he pulled over in front of the bungalow, he jumped out and opened their door. Then he held the umbrella over both of them—while he walked in the downpour—right up to the cottage's front door.

It was completely dark inside, and Hannah realized Eden still hadn't come back.

She noticed Perry unlocked the door with his own key. "I should do a house check," he announced. He nodded at the front of the bungalow. Beside the big picture window was a smaller one they'd left open. "I don't like that open window."

"C'mon, give me a break," Rachel said, stepping

inside and switching on the light. "The window's got a screen on it, and all the other windows have bars on them . . ."

"Just doing my job," he said. Collapsing his umbrella, he started in after them and then slipped off his shoes. Hannah was startled to see him head right into Eden's and her bedroom.

Rachel rolled her eyes. "Tightly wound," she whispered. "But he means well." She set down the fan, plopped on the sofa, and switched on the end-table lamp. Then she glanced around. "Where's Eden anyway?"

"Beats me," Hannah sighed. She set her grocery bag beside the fan on the floor. "This is classic Eden behavior, disappearing for hours at a time and being incommunicado."

Perry came through the living room again. He stopped by the window and got ready to close it.

"Oh please, spare us!" Rachel cried. "We'll suffocate."

"Some rain's getting in," he said.

"I don't care. I can live with a wet floor. I promise, we'll close and lock the stupid window before we go to bed."

He gave a curt nod and then headed up the stairs.

"There better be nothing missing from my underwear drawer when I check later tonight!" she called.

"That's inappropriate," he replied from upstairs.

She grinned at Hannah. "God, I love teasing him. Anyway—that's really weird about your sister. She's been gone, like, five hours. You're not worried?"

"A little bit, I guess," Hannah admitted.

"Maybe you should call her."

"She always turns off her phone. I think she does it just to be perverse."

Still, Hannah dug her phone out of her purse so she could once again text her wandering half-sister.

That had been nearly two hours ago, and there was still no response.

When Perry had left, he'd reminded Rachel to bolt the front door. But they couldn't, not while Eden was still out there somewhere.

Rachel had headed up to bed about an hour ago. Hannah had dug out the bedding from one of the boxes and made up both Eden's and her beds. She'd thought of that line from her dad's favorite baseball movie, *Field of Dreams,* something about, *If you build it, he will come.* In the case of Eden's bed, Hannah had thought, *If you make it, she will come back.*

Now the bed was probably damp with rain in the spot under the open window. The curtains kept fluttering. Beyond the jail-like bars, Hannah saw another flash of lightning. The overgrown garden next door was briefly illuminated. She noticed the lonely, solemn statue of St. Ursula, unmoving against all the swaying foliage and flowers. The two Japanese maple trees on either side of the martyred saint looked like they might snap in the rain and wind.

Hannah glanced at the digital clock on the desk behind her: 12:26 A.M. She wanted to switch on the lamp and read a little. But she hated the idea that anyone walking by could see her in here—on the ground floor. Of course, who in their right mind would be out walking in this rain? Who, besides crazy people and her half-sister? That was just the problem. She didn't want any psycho out there peeping in at her. They could walk right up to the barred window if they wanted. And she couldn't close the curtains without stifling the cool breeze.

She really wished she were in her own bed at home, where it felt safe, where worrying about Eden was her parents' job. Hannah couldn't help thinking that the move to college—along with this sudden sense of responsibility for her half-sister—was turning her into her mother. Really, why should she give a shit if Eden wanted to stay out all night carousing? *Carousing?* God, she was even thinking in terms her mother used.

Beyond the sound of the whirling fan and the pelting rain, Hannah thought she heard a strange click—inside the house. She threw back her sheets and jumped out of bed. In her blue gingham summer pajamas, she crept out of the bedroom. She checked the kitchen—and the back door. Nothing. She listened for a moment.

A lock rattled. Someone was trying to get in the front door.

Please be Eden, please be Eden, she thought.

Hannah stepped out toward the kitchenette and paused by the bar. She noticed the empty champagne bottle on the counter. If she had to, she could clobber an intruder over the head with it. Biting her lip, she watched the front door open.

Soaking wet, Eden stepped inside and closed the door behind her. Her blond hair was in damp tangles.

With an exasperated sigh, Hannah stomped back into the bedroom, dug a towel out of one of the boxes, and returned to the living room with it. "Here," she hissed, practically shoving the towel in Eden's hands. She brushed past her, double-locked the door, and secured the bolt. Then she swiveled around. "Where the hell have you been all night?" she whispered. "And could you at least take off your stupid shoes? You're getting the floor wet."

"God, get off my ass," Eden muttered, patting herself down with the towel. Her T-shirt and ugly yellow overall shorts were drenched and clinging to her. "What are you having a cow for anyway? It's not that late. It's only like ten-thirty Seattle time."

Hannah shushed her. "Rachel may be sleeping."

"Sounds like she's got an air conditioner up there," Eden said, lowering her voice. "I doubt she can hear us. I don't think we're interrupting the princess's beauty sleep . . ."

She headed into the bedroom, and Hannah followed her. "Here's a crazy idea," Hannah said. "Why don't you turn on your stupid phone once in a while? Did you even bother reading my texts? You're supposed to call home."

"I texted them about an hour ago, and they all texted back," Eden replied. She started to peel off her wet clothes. "God, nag, nag, nag . . ."

Hannah plopped down on her bed. "Where were you all this time?"

"I told you—I wanted to check out the campus. I ended up having dinner at the Sunnyside Up Café. I met this creepy guy there. Or maybe he just seemed creepy because he was drunk. He's a janitor with the college. He sure knew enough about this place."

"What do you mean?" Hannah asked, concerned.

"He knew the setup, that we're sleeping in this closet, and that Rachel has deluxe accommodations upstairs. Maybe she's had him clean in here or something. I don't know, beats me. Anyway, he also told me about a shortcut through the woods."

Except for her panties, Eden stood there naked and ran the towel over herself some more. She didn't seem to care that the window curtains weren't drawn. "It started raining when I left the diner," she said. "I almost took the shortcut, but then I decided, screw it. There was something I didn't trust about that janitor guy. So I went back to the café. I had some coffee and started talking to a few of the locals. One of them gave me a ride to the gate down the street. God, I really need a shower . . ."

She wrapped the towel around her and headed out of the bedroom.

Hannah remained on the bed and listened to Eden climbing the stairs. She was wondering about the creepy janitor when she noticed Eden had left her wet clothes on the floor in the middle of the bedroom. What a slob. And it hadn't even registered with her that her bed had been made. Did she think it had just magically happened?

Oh God, she thought, *I really am turning into Mom.*

This living arrangement wasn't going to work out. For the sake of everyone's sanity, Eden had to go. Maybe there was a vacancy in another bungalow—or in a girls' dorm. Eden would probably be happier there. And she'd be someone else's headache.

Hannah would talk about it with Eden in the morning. Right now, she was too upset to broach the subject. The two of them would just end up getting into a huge argument.

Hannah climbed under the bed sheet and turned her face to the wall. If she could fall asleep before Eden returned, she wouldn't have to talk to her at all.

But Hannah was still wide awake when Eden wandered back into the room with a towel around her.

Hannah wondered what kind of mess she'd left in the bathroom.

"You didn't have to make the bed for me, y'know," Eden said. "I could have done it myself."

Hannah didn't reply. She wondered if this was her half-sister's version of a *thank-you*. She glanced over her shoulder. Eden now had on an oversized V-neck T-shirt. She crawled into bed. She'd left the towel on the floor.

Hannah sighed and stirred under the thin bed sheet. More than anything, she just wanted to fall asleep, but she knew it was impossible. She held her tongue for another few minutes, but finally caved. "Y'know," she said quietly. "I think we're going to end up killing each other if one of us doesn't find another place to live. You obviously aren't crazy about Rachel. Well, I happen to like her—a lot. I want to stay. I've unpacked most of my stuff already. It can't really matter to you where you live. Maybe at this orientation thing tomorrow, you can ask about relocating."

There was no response. Then Eden let out a moan and a single snore.

Hannah couldn't believe it. Was she actually asleep already? Her head had hit the pillow less than three minutes ago. Amazing. And in a strange, new bed, too.

Hannah sat up and gazed at her half-sister, dead to the world.

There was another crack of thunder, more distant and muffled this time.

Hannah glanced toward the window to see the lightning flash—which illuminated the garden next door for a second. She saw a man standing by the over-grown plot.

Her heart stopped. She wanted to scream, but couldn't. She could hardly breathe.

It had happened so fast. She'd glimpsed him only in silhouette. But she could tell it was a man lurking out there in the rain—right by the spot where those girls were murdered.

With a shaky hand, she reached over and shook Eden. "Wake up!" she whispered. "There's someone outside."

Eden barely stirred. "What?" she murmured, her eyes still closed.

There was another flash of lightning. Hannah expected to see the man on the other side of the window, peering in at her through the bars.

But she saw no one—just the garden, so much like a little cemetery.

Eden let out another solitary snore and rolled over in bed.

Hannah grasped the bed sheet to her chest. She was afraid to move. She could feel her heart racing wildly. She hadn't imagined the man. She knew he'd been out there in the downpour. But she couldn't say for certain that he was peeping in at them. For all she knew, he could have just been walking by. Maybe he had a girlfriend in one of the bungalows, and he was meeting up with her in secret.

Hannah told herself that if she was going to sleep in a bedroom on the ground floor, she'd better get used to seeing people walk by at all hours. She settled back in bed and closed her eyes. She was being paranoid. There were bars on her window. The front door was locked and bolted, and Rachel had a bodyguard on call who was just five minutes away.

As much as she tried to calm down, Hannah knew it would be hours before she fell asleep tonight.

She opened her eyes and gazed at the window again.

She couldn't help wondering if they put the bars up after the girls next door were murdered.

CHAPTER EIGHT

Friday, September 4, 2:35 A.M.

He wasn't very impressed with the results.

The Sony compact RX100 had been featured in an online article about the best cameras for taking photographs underwater without a flash. He needed the camera for shooting at night. He thought it ironic that, with all the rain, he may as well have been underwater while using it earlier tonight.

The video looked murky once he watched it full-screen on his computer monitor. Of course, he'd videotaped the two half-sisters in their bedroom with the lights off. The bars on the window kept getting in the way. Still, he was able to zoom in on them: Hannah, in her flimsy pajama set, and Eden, naked except for her panties as she patted off the rain with a towel. She was completely nude as she changed into a V-neck T-shirt before slipping into bed. He captured some good full-frontal shots from that. Why couldn't it have been Hannah?

He had better-quality video images of them in the well-lit living room, when Eden had come home from her night of prowling. He backed up the digital recording to watch it again. His eyes lingered on Hannah's long, bare legs, and her breasts jiggling beneath the delicate pajama top. Watching the girls snap and snarl at each other amused him. But mostly, he was aroused.

One of the first things he'd done when he'd gotten back here to his home base was peel off all his rain-drenched clothes. Watching the video of the girls in various stages of undress had made him extremely horny. There was something so intimate about being naked, too. He couldn't help playing with himself.

He sat at a long desk in the second-floor bedroom of a mostly empty, deserted-looking farmhouse. The place was a leaky, decaying dump. But the utilities were paid up, and that allowed him to keep all the outside cameras running. They were planted around the house—out in front, in the backyard, and one inside the tool shed. On the desktop he'd set up the computer, the monitors, and all his surveillance equipment.

The rain had died down. A cool breeze drifted through the bedroom's open window. It felt delicious and slightly erotic against his bare, damp skin.

He didn't want to think about what he still had to do tonight. The awful smell from down the hall had been a reminder—until he closed the bathroom door. Most of the ice in the tub had melted, and Riley's body was starting to decay. Opening the bathroom window and spraying some air freshener in there had helped. But then it smelled like something rotting in a watermelon patch. So he'd lit a few candles while he'd set out the saw, knives, and plastic bags on the bathroom floor. He figured, with all the blood splattering, he'd be naked when he cut up the body; then he could just shower afterward. The burial spot he'd selected was a higher elevation in the woods, so it wouldn't be too muddy. He figured on finishing up by dawn.

But he didn't want to think about that now.

In the distance, he could hear a muffled barking. But he really had to concentrate and listen for it.

He looked at the monitor, the one picking up an image from the camera mounted near the ceiling of the little tool shed out back. Inside the cramped space, there would be enough room for a small table, a chair, and a cot. Right now, the shed was empty—except for the stray mutt he'd picked up the day before yesterday. It was a medium-size brown dog, part-retriever and part-something-else. The mutt hadn't been wearing a collar. With a few Milk-Bone treats, it had been easy to lure him inside the car.

Also up near the ceiling in the shed were a microphone and a speaker. He'd tested the mic, and even standing on the chair, he couldn't reach any of the equipment bracketed up there. The walls were soundproof. At least, he hoped so. It had taken the better part of a weekend to install all the damn panels.

On the desk in front of him, he pressed the sound button to the receiver box. With the volume turned up only to three, the restless mutt made a hell of a racket as it barked, paced around, and intermittently jumped up against the bolted door.

Switching off the receiver, all he heard was a faint echo of the barking. No one else would hear. The closest neighbor was nearly a mile away.

This test with the dog was a success. Now he knew. No one would hear any screaming.

Naked, he got to his feet and walked over to the window. He looked down at the shed at the edge of the patchy, neglected backyard. It stood near a tall, old maple tree with a tire swing hanging from one of the branches. The tire swayed in the wind.

No one would be looking for a missing girl in there.

In the morning, after he buried Riley, he would come back here and feed the dog. Then he would let it go.

But the girl taking its place wouldn't be as lucky.

Once Sonny Boy murdered all the other holy sluts on his list, he would kill her, too.

CHAPTER NINE

Wednesday, September 9, 2:47 P.M.

The sun streamed through the big windows of the old classroom. It shone directly on the thirty-something man sitting at one end of the long table in the back row.

From her desk in front of the class, Ellie could now see that his chiseled, handsome face wasn't quite as flawless as she'd first thought. A scar covered the left side of his forehead. It looked as if he might have been burned at one time.

All she could think about were the arsonists she'd helped put in prison. A couple of them—along with another suspect who had gotten off—had been burned in the fires they'd set. No surprise there, as those morons weren't exactly adept. Ellie wondered if he'd been one of them.

It had been almost a week since she'd looked at the class list and noticed that *Jensen, Nicholas* was the only adult continuing education student taking her Introduction to Journalism course. Ellie had done a search for his name in the computer files of her arson series, and hadn't come up with a match amid the couple of hundred names in her notes. A Google search hadn't led to anything substantial either.

She'd told herself it would be easier to determine just who Nicholas Jensen was once he showed up in her class and she saw his face.

All week long, she'd been distracted by the hate-emails she'd managed to avoid during the summer. Some were pretty scary—enough so that she took the steak knife out of the kitchen drawer and hid it between her mattress and box spring again. She made hard copies of the most overtly threatening emails and filed them—in case she needed them as evidence for the police. Then she blocked the addresses of the senders and deleted the emails. Still, she couldn't help feeling vulnerable.

A few of the haters had managed to track her down through LinkedIn, which made her extra wary of a stranger who had contacted her through the website on Monday. He'd claimed to be Alistair Thorne of *Chicago Huff Post*. He'd wanted to meet with her regarding writing a series of follow-up articles on the convicted arsonists and their connections to American Family Preservationists, which still had several active chapters throughout the country. After making a few inquiries, Ellie had discovered there was no one named Alistair Thorne working for *Chicago Huff Post*—not even as a freelancer.

Now that she'd seen Nicholas Jensen sitting in the back corner of the hot, stuffy classroom, she couldn't help wondering if perhaps one of the haters had indeed found her. Still, except for the scar, he looked innocuous enough. His dark blond hair was cut short—with enough product in it that the sexy bed-head look must have been intentional. None of the American Family Preservationist creeps she'd encountered in the past seemed like the type to use hair products. They were more the type that beat up guys who used hair products. But perhaps this guy was going out of his way to look collegiate. He wore a white polo shirt, and she noticed another scar—a long, pinkish patch on his muscular arm. There was no wedding ring on his finger.

Nicholas Jensen didn't look at her much. Instead, he seemed fixated on Hannah O'Rourke, sitting one table up and a row across from him. Of course, she was arguably the prettiest girl in the class. So there was really nothing too suspicious about him staring at her.

For this first class session, Ellie had been going around the room, picking students at random and asking them to explain why they'd decided to take a journalism course. Did they want to become reporters?

For the last few minutes, Robert Danagold, one of five men in the class (including Nicholas Jensen), had had the floor. At first, Ellie had been impressed with his answer to her question. He said he'd read about Daniel Pearl, the *Wall Street Journal* South Asia bureau chief who had been beheaded by terrorists in Pakistan. He'd pointed out that there weren't many other professions "worth dying for." He went on about the importance of the pursuit of truth, and he made some good points. But after a while, he started to sound like an op-ed piece he must have written for his college application. Ellie's mind—and her eyes—had started to wander.

She was still sizing up Nicholas Jensen when she realized Robert Danagold had finally stopped talking. Everyone was staring at her now, waiting—including her mystery man in the back row.

"Thank you, Robert," she said, recovering quickly.

Then she nodded at Jensen. "Nicholas Jensen, how about you?"

With a slightly apprehensive look on his face, he straightened up in the chair.

"I'll ask you the same question." Ellie gave him a cool smile. "In this age, when newspapers are downsizing and journalists are being maligned and threatened, why are you interested in a journalism class?"

"I hope to sharpen my writing skills. I figured taking a journalism class might help."

"Do you want to become a reporter?"

"Not particularly. I just hope to become a better writer."

She nodded but couldn't help probing a little deeper. "I noticed on the class chart, you're a continuing education student. Do you want to improve your writing skills for your job? What kind of work do you do?"

He cleared his throat. "I'm self-employed. My interest in journalism doesn't really have much to do with my job. As I said, I just want to become a better writer."

Eden O'Rourke's hand went up briefly. She didn't wait for Ellie to acknowledge her before she spoke. "On the subject of jobs," she said, lowering her hand and flicking back her platinum-colored hair. "You used to be a newspaper reporter, and now you're a teacher. Why did you stop being a reporter?"

Ellie managed to smile at her. "My newspaper, the *Tribune*, had to do some downsizing. They offered me a severance package, and I snatched it up." She took a deep breath. "So how about you, Eden? Why are you interested in—"

"Do you miss being a reporter?" Eden interrupted, staring intently at her.

Nodding, Ellie kept the smile plastered on her face. "Sometimes. But teaching is also very fulfilling. So I started to ask, what made you—"

"As a reporter, when you get ready to interview somebody for a story, you go in with an agenda, don't you? I mean, you've already made up your mind about the person you're interviewing and how you're going to write your story. Isn't that true?"

"Not necessarily," Ellie answered. "Still, I'm glad you brought that up—"

"But you do research on your interview subjects ahead of time. You can't help forming an opinion before you meet them. So that makes you prejudiced, doesn't it? It means the story is slanted to your bias from the start. So you aren't really going after the truth, but more like *your version* of the truth."

Ellie finally let her cordial smile vanish. "Good journalists will research interview subjects, yes. But good journalists will also allow their interview subjects to answer the questions, and that's how they get to the truth. They listen, Ms. O'Rourke. They don't constantly interrupt."

Eden O'Rourke shifted in her chair and then opened her mouth to talk again.

"But a good journalist is also curious and relentless," Ellie added—loudly, to cut her off. "And you seem to have those qualities—in spades." She glanced at the clock. "The class assignment for Friday is to bring in a newspaper or online article you think is exceptionally well written and be prepared to discuss it. Extra points if you pick an article on a subject that ordinarily wouldn't interest you. So if you don't like sports, bring in something noteworthy from the sports page; or if you're not into politics, bring in a political story. You get the drift. All right? See you on Friday . . ."

People started to get out of their seats. Ellie thanked God Eden O'Rourke didn't blurt out another irritating question. Eden grabbed her backpack and got to her feet. She didn't look at all annoyed or peeved. It was as if she'd said what she'd wanted and now was moving on.

But her half-sister, Hannah, looked exasperated. Rolling her eyes at Eden, she stood up and picked up her tote bag.

Ellie caught a glimpse of Nicholas Jensen as he headed toward the classroom door. He carried a small backpack by the strap. He took one look back over his shoulder—not at her, but at Hannah O'Rourke.

That was Ellie's last class of the day. As she cleared her desk and loaded up her big purse, she still wasn't sure what to think about Nicholas Jensen. The college offered English composition and creative writing classes. If he really wanted to improve his writing skills, he could have signed up for one of those courses. She also wondered what field he was "self-employed" in. At the same time, if he was here on a mission for the American Family Preservationists, he'd clearly let himself get distracted today by Hannah O'Rourke and her youthful beauty.

Or had he come here *for* Hannah?

Stepping out of Lombard Hall into the hot afternoon sun, Ellie spotted Hannah sitting on a stone bench by the dahlia garden near the entrance. Hannah quickly got to her feet and approached her. "Ms. Goodwin?"

Ellie stopped and smiled at her. "You may call me Ellie. After the first class session, I usually drop the formalities."

"I'm Hannah O'Rourke."

Ellie nodded. "I know. I recognized your name—and your sister's—in the class list."

"*Half*-sister," Hannah said. "And I want to apologize for her. She can be awfully obnoxious sometimes."

"That's okay. I know what your family went through. I'm sure Eden must have encountered some bad reporters back then."

Hannah sighed. "Still, that's no reason to go after you. Eden has this irritating habit of questioning authority wherever she goes. She drove all of our high school teachers crazy."

"Well, don't worry about it," Ellie said. "No offense taken. I'm just sorry I didn't get a chance to ask her why she was taking the course. I didn't ask you either. I'd have thought you'd be pretty fed up with reporters, too."

"Most of them were nicer to me than they were to Eden." Hannah nervously fidgeted with her hair. "The whole experience made me realize that reporters still have a lot of power and influence. Anyway, it got me thinking. What I'd really like to do is interview celebrities and write about them, cover film premieres, award shows, rock concerts."

"Oh, so that's why you're interested in journalism." Ellie had been hoping Hannah's ambitions would be a bit loftier. But she nodded and kept smiling. "Well, that—that's valid. Plus as an entertainment reporter, you'd know from your own experiences what it's like to always have a microphone shoved in your face wherever you go—having everything you say get written down. You'll have a lot of empathy for your celebrity subjects."

"Exactly," Hannah said. She leaned in close and spoke in a whisper. "So—do you mind me asking? What's Jennifer Lawrence like?"

Ellie gave her a puzzled smile. "Jennifer Lawrence, the actress?"

Hannah nodded. "Isn't she playing you in the film version of your story?"

Ellie laughed. "Oh that! Someone posted about it on Instagram, didn't they?"

Hannah nodded again—eagerly.

"That was over a year ago. It's true, Jennifer Lawrence's people were interested in the film project for a while. But after about two weeks, the whole thing went kaput."

"So—you don't know Jennifer Lawrence?"

Ellie shook her head. "Sorry. I never got to meet her or talk to her or anything like that."

Hannah looked crestfallen. She said nothing.

Ellie couldn't help wondering if her flimsy connection to Jennifer Lawrence was the driving force behind Hannah enrolling in her journalism course. Maybe Hannah had imagined her teacher and the film star as best friends—with Jennifer popping in on her class from time to time just to study her in action.

"The film deal kind of stalled out on me last year," Ellie admitted. "So—it's doubtful that any movie stars will be portraying me any time soon. I hope that didn't have too much to do with your decision to take my journalism class."

"Oh, not really," Hannah replied. She was a terrible liar. She still looked disappointed.

"I have to admit," Ellie said, "when I saw Eden's and your names on the class list, I wondered what brought the two of you all the way out from the West Coast to this little school."

"The two of us got full scholarships. The deal was too good to pass up. A corporation out of Chicago paid for everything, the Slate-Gannon Group."

"You mean, Rachel Bonner got you and Eden scholarships?" Ellie asked.

Hannah squinted at her. "Why would Rachel have anything to do with Eden's or my scholarship? It's this company . . ."

Ellie nodded emphatically. "Yes, the Slate-Gannon Group. It's owned by Rachel's father, Richard Bonner. They're big contributors to the school. Rachel helped arrange for a couple of the scholarships last year. If I remember correctly, one of the recipients ended up becoming her roommate, and the other was a friend Rachel grew up with."

"Eden and I are rooming with Rachel now," Hannah murmured, looking completely baffled. "I don't understand. Rachel's the one who set all this up? Why?"

Ellie shrugged. "I—I have no idea. You and Eden were pretty famous a couple of years ago. Maybe she followed you on the news or social media and figured . . ." Ellie trailed off and shrugged once again. "I honestly don't know. I'm just guessing."

"Well, this is weird," Hannah said. "Rachel's practically like my new best friend. And she hasn't told me a thing about this. Are you sure she's the one behind the scholarships? Are you sure this Slate-Gannon place is connected to her?"

Wincing, Ellie nodded. "Yes, it's one of Richard Bonner's many businesses. It's not common knowledge, but I know from working at the *Tribune*. Still, it's quite possible Rachel had nothing to do with the scholarship. She might not know about it. I really think I spoke out of turn. I'm sorry, Hannah. I shouldn't have said anything."

Hannah shook her head. "No, it's okay. I'm glad you said something. Still, this is so screwed up. I better talk to Rachel. Would you excuse me?"

"Sure," Ellie said, feeling strange about the whole thing. "See you in class on Friday."

"Bye," Hannah said. She brushed past Ellie and headed toward the quad.

As Ellie watched her walk away, she spotted Nicholas Jensen, standing across the small courtyard—in front of another building. He had his phone in his hand.

But his eyes seemed to be on Hannah.

"Was that the famous Hannah O'Rourke I just saw you talking to?"

Ellie swiveled around to see Diana Mackie, a student she'd befriended last year when the girl was a wretchedly unhappy freshman. Ellie had been new to the college and pretty miserable as well. She hadn't fully recovered from losing her newspaper job, her film deal, and her husband. Suddenly, there had been this scared, homesick, friendless freshman even worse off than her. Diana had been like a needy kid sister she could look after, and soon Ellie had stopped feeling sorry for herself. After a couple of months, Diana had started doing a lot better, but they continued to get together for dinner every couple of weeks or so.

Diana was pretty and slightly plump with freckles and short, wavy red hair. Hugging her books to her chest, she smiled at Ellie from behind a pair of sunglasses.

Ellie was surprised to run into her. "Well, hi, Di. Yes, that—that was Hannah, in the flesh." Ellie had had coffee with Diana on Monday, and had mentioned that the O'Rourke sisters were in her journalism class.

She looked over toward where Nicholas Jensen had been standing a moment ago. But he was gone now.

"Is everything okay?" Diana asked.

Ellie glanced around the courtyard. She didn't see Jensen anywhere. It was as if he'd vanished. "Um, everything's fine," she said, still distracted. Then she focused on Diana and worked up a smile. "How are you? How's your new guy-friend?"

"We talked last night, and we have a date on Saturday—after he finishes up at the rec center."

"Well, that's wonderful," Ellie said.

"I'm taking your advice and not overanalyzing it." Diana gave her a curious, sidelong look. "What were you and Hannah O'Rourke talking about? From where I stood, things looked pretty intense."

"We were just talking about her sister—and her roommate."

"Who's her roommate?"

"Rachel Bonner."

"Hannah's roommate is Rachel Bonner?" Diana uttered an ironic laugh. "Well, that's a position I wouldn't want to fill."

"Why would you say that?"

Diana shrugged. "I just figure it might be bad luck. Rachel's roommate last year was Kayla Kennedy . . ."

"Was that her name?" Ellie asked. "I knew Rachel had a hand in getting her roommate a scholarship."

"Don't you know the rest of the story?"

"I guess not," Ellie admitted.

"Kayla was from outside Sheboygan, not too well off, the only child of a struggling single mom. You get the picture. Anyway, a couple of years ago, Kayla was riding her bicycle—she was a big bicyclist—she was crossing a bridge when she saw a car spin out of control. It crashed through the guardrail and plunged into the water. Kayla came to the rescue just as the car was sinking. She dove into the water and saved the passengers—a young mother and a toddler. She was a hero. It was big news. It was in all the papers."

Ellie wondered how come she didn't know about it. She must have been dealing with the arson investigation at the time. "Did Rachel Bonner know her?" Ellie asked.

"No, but I guess she read about her, and the next thing you know, Kayla Kennedy had a full-paid scholarship to Our Lady of the Cove, and for her freshman year, she was sharing a bungalow with Rachel Bonner."

Ellie realized that it must have happened the same way for Hannah and Eden O'Rourke. Rachel must have read about them, and then set up the scholarships and the same living arrangements she'd had with Kayla Kennedy.

She frowned at Diana. "So why is that bad luck?"

"Well, because Kayla Kennedy's dead. She was killed in a bike accident over the summer."

Dumbfounded, Ellie just stared at her.

Diana winced a bit and then nodded. "That's what I mean when I say, being Rachel Bonner's roommate isn't a position I'd want to fill."

CHAPTER TEN

Wednesday, 3:12 P.M.

Hannah stopped by the small shrine to St. Lucy near the library. Rachel had been right. Practically every time Hannah turned around—especially in the older section of the campus—she found herself looking at a statue of another virgin martyr. After nearly a week at Our Lady of the Cove, Hannah barely noticed them anymore. This shrine by the library was yet another little garden patch with a stone bench. Amid the roses was a weather-worn statue of Lucy, who, like St. Agnes, was executed with a sword-thrust to the throat.

Hannah sat down and texted Rachel:

I'm headed home. Need to C U. It's important.

For the last six days, Rachel had been her best friend, her guide, her touchstone. Hannah couldn't have survived here without her. Rachel was just like the "big sister" she said she was. She'd even helped Hannah get over the whole Riley heartbreak.

Over the weekend, Hannah had sent him three texts. *Just checking in*, she'd told him. She'd expressed concern about his "family emergency." In only one of the texts had she asked if they were still on for Saturday. She'd done her best not to put any pressure on him.

The son of a bitch didn't respond at all.

Rachel said she'd done everything right. Hannah had shown her the photo of Riley on the boat deck. "Yeah, he's a stone fox," Rachel had told her, "but a lot of good that does you if he's totally unavailable. This early in the relationship, he shouldn't be ignoring you like this. I don't care if his entire family is being held hostage by terrorists. The guy could answer a simple text. I say, move on! Why do you want to be with somebody who leaves you feeling this insecure?"

Hanging out with Rachel had been a wonderful distraction. Alden had also helped her get over Riley. Hannah always got a little thrill whenever he dropped by the bungalow. Rachel had said Alden was gay, but as far as Hannah was concerned, the jury was still out. She hadn't had the nerve to ask him point blank. Maybe it was because she didn't want to hear the answer. It was too much fun having a little crush on him—and wondering if it was reciprocal. Sometimes, she caught him gazing at her with a certain look in his beautiful brown eyes, and it took her breath away. Or was she imagining things? Maybe it was just wishful thinking.

The other guy who helped take her mind off Riley was J.T., a lifeguard at the campus rec center's pool. Although the pool was indoors, he still had a gorgeous, dark tan. He was boy-next-door cute with a swimmer's build and flecks of gold in his shaggy brown hair. So far, Hannah had gone swimming in the rec center twice, and both times, she'd caught him looking.

"It's his job to watch you, stupid," Eden had pointed out. "God, vain enough?"

J.T. was a junior, and according to Rachel, he'd slept with a ton of girls on the campus. But Hannah didn't care. It was still nice to have an extremely cute guy noticing her. And it gave her extra incentive to go swimming and get her exercise three times a week.

One man whose attention she didn't appreciate much was Lance, the creepy janitor Eden had told her about their first night on campus, the one from the Sunnyside Up Café. Eden had pointed him out to Hannah during one of their rare outings together on campus. He'd stared at them, nodded, and smirked. For the rest of their walk to the O'Donnell Hall cafeteria for breakfast, she and Eden had argued:

He was looking at you.

No, it was you, Hannah. I'm sure he was checking you out.

No, it's obvious he has a serious crush on you. And I'll be honored to be a bridesmaid at your wedding.

Hannah kept noticing him again and again—all over the campus. He was usually operating a leaf-blower, but other times, he just seemed to be lurking. Hannah had a feeling he was the one prowling outside her bedroom window in the thunderstorm on her first night in bungalow twenty. Rachel maintained he was quite harmless. Lance had an on-again-off-again thing going with a divorcée in Waukegan. That was also where he lived—in a house with his mother. The property was owned by one of Mr. Bonner's corporations. Rachel rented the place to them for some ridiculously cheap price. It was practically like charity. Lance's mother, Alma, was Rachel's cleaning woman and laundress. Once a week, she cleaned the bungalow—everything except for Hannah and Eden's room. Hannah had run into her in the living room last week—a sullen, sixty-something, copper-haired woman who smelled like disinfectant. Around her neck, she wore a chain with a clunky-looking fake-gold crucifix. Her pale pink sweatshirt had a photo of two kittens on it. According to Rachel, Alma came by at least one other time during the week to pick up or drop off Rachel's laundry. She had her own key. It made Hannah nervous to think that Alma's creepy son had such easy access to the key to their bungalow.

She could have used Alma's services in Eden's and her bedroom—or at least, for Eden's half of it. Hannah had settled in, put art posters on the wall, throw-pillows on the bed, and fun knickknacks on the shelf. But Eden's side of the tiny room was a mess, and the wall was still bare. Eden said she didn't see any point in decorating or unpacking since she'd be moving out. Apparently, that was also her rationale for not making her bed and leaving her dirty clothes wherever she goddamn pleased.

Eden was now on a waiting list for a room in O'Donnell Hall or one of the other bungalows in St. Agnes Village. Rachel claimed she wanted Eden to stay: "I'd hate to break up our team—our sisterhood."

Hannah had no idea why Rachel was being so nice to Eden, who had made no effort to be friendly to her. Practically every time Rachel and Hannah had stepped out together, Rachel had invited Eden along. But Eden had continually shot her down, preferring instead to go explore on her own.

Hannah felt so lucky to be Rachel's roommate and friend. She got a rush just hanging out with her. Not only was Rachel fun, stylish, and generous, she was also Chicago royalty. It was like being friends with a celebrity.

Rachel was a bit of a mystery, too. Hannah still didn't feel she knew her very well. Of course, their intense, whirlwind friendship had been going on for only six days.

And now, this bombshell.

Why hadn't Rachel told her she was the one who had gotten them their scholarships? The whole thing had been arranged. Now their friendship, the roommate setup, and all of it seemed so forced and fake. She and Eden were Rachel Bonner's charity cases—like Lance and his mother.

Was Ellie Goodwin right when she'd said Rachel must have read about them in the newspapers or on the Internet? And then what? Had she felt sorry for them and decided to pay their way through school? It made Hannah feel like a freak—a sad, pathetic freak. She wasn't Rachel Bonner's friend. She was her *project*.

Her back to St. Lucy, Hannah got up from the bench and headed for St. Agnes Village. Just as she reached the front door to the bungalow, her cell phone buzzed. It was Rachel texting back:

B home in 15 min. Wuzzup?

Biting her lip, Hannah replied:

Tell U when U get here.

She shoved her phone in her tote, took out her key, and unlocked the door. As she opened it, she spotted Eden coming down the stairs—obviously from the bathroom. Eden stopped on the bottom step and gave her a look. "Oh shit, what did I do now? Are you pissed because

I asked Ellie Goodwin a few hardball questions? She's a big girl. I think she handled it okay."

"I'm not pissed about that, at least, not anymore." Hannah took a deep breath and shut the door behind her. "I was just talking to Ellie. Guess who owns the Slate-Gannon Group."

Eden leaned against the newel post at the bottom step. "I haven't a clue."

"Rachel's father," Hannah said. "She set up the whole thing—our scholarships and this whole living arrangement. Can you believe it?"

Eden seemed to ponder the question. "Huh" was all she said.

"That's it?" Hannah asked. "Aren't you upset?"

Eden shrugged. "Well, now that I know she's paying for everything, I guess I should suck up to her more. Then again, you've been sucking up enough for the two of us." She stepped down and headed through the living room toward their bedroom.

"I haven't been sucking up to her," Hannah argued, trailing after her. "I've genuinely liked her. I thought she was my friend. Don't you feel deceived—and manipulated?"

Eden took off her shirt as she entered their bedroom. She tossed it on her unmade bed. "I really don't see why you're having a cow."

"I don't like being somebody's charity case," Hannah grumbled, dropping her tote on her bed.

"Well, I guess I'm used to it."

Hannah plopped down in her desk chair. She realized that Eden had accepted charity two years ago when Hannah's parents took her into their home.

Eden peeled off her jeans. "Besides, we knew it was

charity when we took the scholarships. We just didn't know that your BFF, the princess, was behind it all." Eden left her rumpled jeans on the floor and stood there in her bra and panties. She put her hands on her hips. "If I were you, I'd get over it pretty fast and just enjoy the free ride. You want to piss her off and have her cancel our scholarships? I don't know about you, but I happen to like it here." She reached over and switched on the fan. "Then again, if you're really so outraged, maybe you should be the one to move out, and I'll stay here."

Hannah sighed. She hated that her half-sister almost made sense. "I didn't tell you the other thing. You know the girl who lived here before us? Well, Rachel got her a scholarship, too."

Eden dug a pair of cut-offs and a T-shirt out of her moving box. "You mean, the girl they couldn't stand? *If it's yellow, it's mellow*?"

Hannah nodded glumly. "She and Alden were Rachel's charity cases last year."

Eden paused for a moment before putting on her clothes. "Well, he's still around," she said—almost to herself. "I wonder what happened to her."

On one of the desktop monitors, he watched Eden O'Rourke step into her cut-offs.

He wished Hannah had been the one to get undressed for him. But she was still sitting at her desk.

On Tuesday morning, while the three girls were at classes, he'd snuck into the bungalow and installed a nanny-cam in the small bedroom. It was a wireless model, less than three inches tall and three inches wide, very hard to detect. He'd taken apart the box fan and hidden it in the corner inside. It peeked through the grillwork in front. The fan blades didn't obscure anything. The picture quality was pretty good, too.

Last night, he'd watched Hannah strip down to her panties. He'd only caught the most fleeting glimpse of her breasts before she turned her back to the hidden camera and donned a robe. But he'd seen enough to replay it again and again while masturbating.

He really wished she would get undressed now. She'd been wearing those clothes all day, running from one class to another. And it was hot out again. Didn't she want to slip into something else, something more casual and lighter?

He should have planted a listening device in there—so he could hear what Hannah and her half-sister were saying. It looked like they might be having another argument.

He wondered if Hannah would miss her when she was gone.

It didn't look like Hannah intended to get undressed any time soon. So he got to his feet and moved over to the window. He looked out at the backyard—at the tool shed.

It was empty right now, but wouldn't be for long.

CHAPTER ELEVEN

Wednesday, 3:20 P.M.

Ellie had compiled three "Arson Story" computer files containing mug shots, police sketches, and captioned photos of various suspects in her investigation. Each file had at least one hundred subjects. She was almost done going through the second file. So far, she hadn't found anyone who even resembled Nicholas Jensen. She'd had one false alarm—a police sketch of a suspected arsonist who looked like a mustached version of Jensen, but his approximate height was listed as five feet, five inches, which made him about eight inches shorter than the man in her journalism class.

She sat at her desk in her closet-size office on the fourth floor of Lombard Hall. But she had a window—with a fire escape and a view of the lake if she pressed her cheek against the glass. There was just enough room for her desk and chair, a file cabinet, a bookcase, a visitor's chair, and an old-fashioned radiator. The wall was covered with awards, citations, and plaques she'd received for her newspaper reporting, most of them specifically for the arson series. At first, Ellie had kept the awards stashed in her closet. She'd never had her own office at the newspaper, just a desk. And she'd never been interested in exhibiting her awards at home. But now, in her little shoebox of an office, she had a place to display her citations—which impressed no one except maybe a few people in Our Lady of the Cove's administration department. It was good for the college to have an award-winning journalist teaching there.

As she stared at the computer screen, Ellie couldn't help wincing. She hadn't looked at these mug shots since she'd written the arson series two years ago. Each image was a reminder of all her hard work, the sleepless nights, and the constant fear. During the investigation, Ellie had known the deeper she dug, the more she put herself in danger. And these were scary-looking guys. The police sketches were the worst—flat, cartoon faces with cold, staring eyes. The mug shots weren't much better. They all looked so sleazy and cruel. She remembered how some of those faces haunted her. She used to imagine waking up and finding one of those men standing in her bedroom.

Now, she could too easily see one of them marching into her classroom with an assault weapon.

Every time she clicked on a new image, it was with apprehension. She really didn't want to remember any of these guys. Some of them were still out there, sending her emails. Every once in a while, Ellie came upon the image of someone with the American Family Preservationists—a lowlife, petty criminal turned warped, self-righteous crusader. She'd helped put some of them in jail—and wondered if they were out now.

As she clicked on the last mug shot of the second file, Ellie wanted to give up—or at least take a break before looking at the final batch. She didn't think she'd find

Nicholas Jensen among these creeps. He'd seemed far more interested in Hannah O'Rourke than he was in her.

Ellie wondered if she should be worried for Hannah rather than for herself.

Instead of opening up the last file of arson suspects, Ellie clicked onto Google and typed in the search box: *Kayla Kennedy death.*

The subject had been gnawing at Ellie since her friend Diana had brought it up. "A bike accident" was how Diana had described the death of Rachel Bonner's roommate. She hadn't said if anyone else had been involved or if there had been witnesses.

The first search result Ellie found was an article from the *Milwaukee Journal Sentinel* dated June 7. Kayla couldn't have been home from school for more than a week before she was killed. The headline read:

SHEBOYGAN GIRL DIES
IN BICYCLE ACCIDENT
***

*Kayla Kennedy Was Known
for Heroic Rescue of
Drowning Mother and Child*

A photo of Kayla accompanied the article. With her short-shorn dark hair, she looked like a tomboy. She had a cute, impish smile.

According to the article, Kayla was riding her bicycle to Pine Hills Country Club, where she worked the morning shift as a waitress. Ellie imagined that it hadn't been light out for long, and the roads must have been nearly deserted. Somehow, Kayla had lost control of her bike, careened into a gully, and been killed. No vehicles were involved. There were no witnesses.

Ellie couldn't find any follow-up articles in the *Journal Sentinel* that gave further details about the accident. There was nothing about an investigation.

She found a brief follow-up piece in the *Sheboygan Press*. It was about Kayla Kennedy's memorial service, and it featured a photo of a young woman walking down the church steps. The caption read:

> Chicago's Rachel Bonner, former roommate to Kayla Kennedy at Our Lady of the Cove, was among those who attended the memorial service on Saturday.

Rachel looked very stylish in her black dress.

CHAPTER TWELVE

Wednesday, 3:29 P.M.

"Oh, that stupid Goodwin woman and her big mouth," Rachel grumbled.

She paced back and forth in the living room in front of Hannah and Eden, who were seated on the sofa. As usual, Hannah couldn't help admiring Rachel's outfit— splashy pink, green and white floral-patterned slacks with a white sleeveless top that barely reached her tan, trim midriff. Rachel looked at them and shook her head. "You guys weren't supposed to know, not just yet. I wanted to be the one to tell you."

"Well, why all the secrecy?" Hannah asked. "Why didn't you just tell us right away?"

Rachel sighed. "I wanted to see how well we got along first."

"Is that because of your last roommate?" Eden asked pointedly. "You gave her a scholarship, too, and you guys ended up hating each other."

"I wouldn't say that," Rachel murmured, looking uncomfortable. Her eyes suddenly avoided them. "Alden spoke out of turn about that. Kayla was just different. Anyway, I'm not about to bad-mouth her, because the poor girl's dead. She got smashed up in a bicycle accident over the summer."

Her mouth open, Hannah said nothing. It took her a moment to realize that she'd been sleeping in this dead girl's room.

Eden folded her arms in front of her. "Well, Alden made it pretty clear you were smudging the place to get rid of her essence. So she must have been a real piece of work."

"I was smudging in there because she *died*. And okay, I'd be a hypocrite if I said we ended the school year the best of chums. But that was Kayla. With you guys, I could tell you were different from her. I liked you both right away."

"Which bed was hers?" Hannah had to ask.

"Neither," Rachel answered, rubbing her forehead. "She had this awful futon in there. It was hers. Kayla took it with her when she moved out. I admit, having her for a housemate was a mistake. I really should have met and screened her beforehand. This woman with Slate-Gannon who helps arrange the scholarships read about Kayla rescuing someone from drowning. It was written up in the local papers. She was a hero, and it sounded like she was in a financial pinch. So we figured she'd be an excellent candidate for a scholarship."

"Is that how you found us, too?" Hannah asked. "Did you read about us—and what happened to our family a couple of years ago?"

"Yes, I read about you guys, but that's not all of it." She stopped pacing and let out an exasperated sigh. "I could wring Ellie Goodwin's neck. What a blabbermouth. I wasn't going to tell you about the scholarships until we discussed another matter." She turned and headed for the stairs. "Wait here. I have to show you something . . ."

Hannah watched her hurry up the stairs.

Eden patted her arm and gave her a lopsided smile. "Gosh, now I'm really sorry I'm moving out," she whispered. "I hope you enjoy having that dead girl's bedroom all to yourself."

"Very funny," Hannah hissed, jerking her arm away and squirming on the sofa.

"Oh, relax," Eden muttered. "It's not like she croaked in there."

It took another minute before Rachel came down with a piece of paper in her hand. It looked like some kind of document. "I was going to wait until we got better acquainted before I sprung this on you guys." She seemed a bit breathless. Hannah couldn't tell if it was from running up and down the stairs—or if she was nervous. "Anyway, I may as well tell you now. I—well, I was adopted."

This was news to Hannah, who had already read several online articles about Rachel. But she wasn't exactly stupefied by the revelation.

Rachel rolled her eyes and then shrugged. "It's no big secret. I grew up knowing. My parents couldn't have children, and they arranged to adopt me when I was an infant. It was a private adoption. Anyway, last year, when I turned nineteen, I finally asked my mother and father about my birth parents. So . . . it turns out, that twenty years ago, there was this pregnant college student at the University of Oregon, and she wanted her baby to have a good home."

She handed the document to Hannah. "Anyway, I think you know these people."

Hannah gazed at the birth certificate for a baby girl. The mother's name on the certificate was *Mary Michelle Driscoll*, Hannah's aunt Molly, the one her mom had kept a secret for so many years.

But it was the father's name that knocked the breath out of her: *Dylan O'Rourke*.

"Oh my God," Eden murmured, reading over her shoulder.

Hannah couldn't wrap her head around it—her father and her mother's sister had had a baby together. She knew they'd had an affair. But she couldn't believe her father had created yet another illegitimate child—and with his sister-in-law, no less. Did he even know? He hadn't had any idea about Eden until she was sixteen and showed up at their door two years ago. Chances were her aunt Molly hadn't said anything to him. Hannah figured her mom probably didn't know either.

Dumbfounded, she gazed up at Rachel. She swallowed hard. "Does my father know about you? Does my mother?"

Rachel shook her head. She plopped down in the chair across from her. "That's why I wanted to help you guys," she said. "That's why I felt it was so important we meet—and like each other. The three of us are sisters."

Hannah was so upset, she felt sick to her stomach.

Eden took the birth certificate out of Hannah's shaky hand and gave it back to Rachel. With a sigh, she leaned back on the couch again. "So . . . how do your parents feel about all this?"

Rachel narrowed her eyes at her. "What do you mean?"

"This whole setup," Eden said with a look around the room. "You giving us scholarships and making us your roommates. How are they taking it?"

Rachel glanced down at the birth certificate in her lap. "To be honest, they're not exactly crazy about it. They pretty much leave me alone to work out the scholarships with the Slate-Gannon people. They just found out about all of this last week. Anyway, it was my decision, and they've accepted it."

"So, are you hoping to meet our father now or what?" Eden asked.

"Not right away," Rachel said. "I figured it was something the three of us could discuss and agree on. For now, I'd like to keep this between just the three of us—well, the three of us and Alden. But he's sworn to secrecy."

Hannah still couldn't fathom it. She looked across the coffee table at this young woman who was her older half-sister. She could see a family resemblance—especially to the photos of her aunt Molly.

She turned to Eden. "You're certainly taking this well. I don't know how you can be so calm right now."

Eden looked at her and sighed. "I already knew about Dylan's other love child." She turned to Rachel. "I just didn't know it was you. Cassandra, the woman who raised me, hired a private investigator to look into our father's various extracurricular activities while he was married to Sheila. This started when I was a kid, and I guess, over the years, this detective kept digging up dirt on Dylan. I think Cassandra got a bunch of paperwork from him. She stored it away someplace. I don't know where. And I never could find out the detective's name. But I knew there was a daughter, a year older than me. My stepmother let that much slip. Every once in a while, she'd remind me of how lucky I was. 'Don't complain,' she used to tell me. 'I'm sure you're a lot better off than his other bastard.'"

Hannah let out a stunned little laugh. Considering that Rachel grew up in a palace on Chicago's Gold Coast, the woman who had raised Eden had been way off in her assessment.

"I never said anything," Eden continued. "But I had a feeling the other child was born to Hannah's aunt Molly. When you talked to your parents about this, Rachel, did they ever mention a private investigator?"

With a baffled look on her face, Rachel shook her head.

"My half-brother—I guess *our* half-brother, Steve, got some weird emails a couple of years ago, just before everything went to shit. The emails were about Aunt Molly. We never found out who sent them. Do you know if your parents could have sent those emails—or some friend of your parents?"

"I doubt it. I mean, why would they?"

"And it wasn't you—or maybe Alden?"

Rachel frowned at her. "I told you. I didn't even find out about my birth parents until after I turned twenty—last December third. And I didn't tell Alden until last month."

"When you were a kid, did you have a stuffed animal named Micky? It was a monkey, Micky the Monkey . . ."

Rachel slowly shook her head.

"Back when my father was recuperating in the hospital, some young woman came by the nurses' station and dropped off a stuffed monkey for him. She didn't leave her name. The monkey used to belong to Hannah's mom, Sheila, but then 'Aunt Molly' took it. And years later, it turned up on my father's nightstand by his hospital bed—in Seattle."

Hannah stared at Eden, eyes narrowed. "How come I didn't know about this?"

"Because Dad told me," Eden said. "I guess he didn't tell you because you would have gotten all upset and made it all about you—like you usually do." She turned to Rachel. "Are you sure you weren't the one who gave him that monkey?"

"I think I'd remember taking a trip to Seattle," Rachel said, a bit huffily. "And I never had a stuffed animal monkey named Micky. I think I'd remember that, too."

"Well, somebody sent those emails, and I think that same somebody—a pretty, young woman, the nurse said—left that stuffed animal for our father in the hospital. If it wasn't you, maybe it was someone you know."

Rachel shrugged, but she looked exasperated, too. "I'm telling you, I don't know a thing about it. This is all new to me."

"I don't understand any of this," Hannah finally piped up. "I mean, what are we supposed to do now? Are we supposed to keep this a secret? What did you want us to do with this information?"

"We're sisters!" Rachel cried. "I wanted to help you out. I wanted us to be close! Is that asking too much? I grew up alone, knowing my real parents didn't want me—"

"So did I," Eden interjected, "minus the silver spoon."

"Then you should understand how happy I was to realize I had two half-sisters. You should understand how much I've wanted to hear about my real parents. Is it so horrible that I wanted to help you guys and get to know you?"

Before Hannah or Eden could answer, Rachel jumped to her feet. "Listen, I'm going to leave you guys alone to talk this over. It'll give us all a chance to calm down. Maybe by the time I get back in a few hours, cooler heads will prevail." She snatched her purse off the table near the stairs. "I must have been crazy to think this would be a happy thing. This isn't how it was supposed to be, not at all."

She headed outside and slammed the door after her.

Hannah sat in silence with Eden beside her.

She watched the birth certificate flutter off the edge of the chair and gently land on the floor.

CHAPTER THIRTEEN

"**A**ctually, she's my half-sister, but she's your half-sister *and* your cousin," Eden drolly pointed out as they gathered up their dirty clothes—Hannah, from the corner of their closet floor, and Eden, from wherever she'd dumped each item as she'd removed it from her body.

"God, is our father a pig or what?" Hannah muttered, stripping her bed. "I think we should call home right now. He should know about this. And so should my mother."

"Why don't we chill out a bit, and process it first?" Eden suggested. She sniffed a pair of socks that she had picked up off the floor and then tossed them in her laundry bag. "I think that's one thing our *big sister* is right about. The three of us need to discuss it first before we let anyone else know. Besides, it's really her scoop, not ours."

"I hate this," Hannah said. "*The Society of the Secret Sisterhood,* that's us. Just when I was starting to feel normal, we're freaks all over again. Do you loathe our father as much as I do right now?" She stuffed her sheets into the laundry bag.

"I grew up knowing all the dirt about him, so none of this is much of a surprise. He's not that bad. He's a nice guy and a pretty good father—just a shitty husband. I think—"

Eden fell silent at the sound of the front door opening.

"Hello?" It sounded like Alden.

"We're back here!" Hannah called. She automatically touched her hair to make sure it wasn't a mess. Then it occurred to her that perhaps Alden had been nice to her all week merely because she was Rachel's half-sister.

She could hear him and Rachel whispering. Then he poked his head in their bedroom doorway. Rachel was behind him with her head on his shoulder. She looked half-asleep.

Eden gave them both a flippant smile. "Hi, Alden. Hi, *sis*!"

Rachel waved at them. "We were in Kenosha!" she announced, slurring her words.

Alden nodded. "Only forty minutes to a tavern that never cards anybody, and we had a designated driver at our beck and call."

"Thank God for Perry," Rachel said. "Did we drink to Perry? I forget."

"We sure did, hon," he said.

Hannah could tell he wasn't drunk. But Rachel could barely stand. She backed away and leaned against the bar.

"She's really sorry you guys weren't happy about the news," Alden murmured. "Not that anybody blames you. But she was feeling pretty raw about it. Laundry night?"

Hannah nodded and then she stuffed a pillowcase in her laundry bag.

"We're going to hydrate and put some solid food in our stomachs," he said. "We've got a chicken basil pizza from Bellini's. Do either of you want a piece before we whisk it away?"

"I'm perfectly willing to share," Rachel muttered, her back to them. "They're my little sisters. What's mine is theirs . . ."

"Pizza?" Alden whispered to the two of them.

Both Hannah and Eden shook their heads. "No thanks," Hannah whispered.

"I think it's best if we take ourselves upstairs, give everyone a little space." Alden led Rachel away. He stopped at the bar to grab the pizza box. "C'mon, Rachel. We'll watch some bad TV up in your room."

Neither Hannah nor Eden said anything. Hannah could hear Rachel quietly whining about something. She sounded like a little girl on the verge of a crying fit.

Alden shushed her. "Don't worry. They're nice girls. They'll come around . . ."

Hannah felt awful. She listened to the footsteps on the stairs. Then after a minute, there was a faint murmuring from the TV in Rachel's room.

She turned to Eden. "Do you feel like a complete shit? Because I sure do."

"You know how I feel?" Eden whispered. "Like you must have felt two years ago when I dropped in on your family and announced that I was your bastard sister. I didn't expect anyone to be happy about it or throw a party for me. She's a major delusionoid if she was expecting us to jump up and cheer. But I do feel sorry for her. I know how lonely it is for her right now—even though she's got Cutie Pie and a pizza keeping her company at the moment. It still sucks to have your family reject you."

"We're not rejecting her," Hannah said. "We're just trying to get used to the idea that she's our sister."

"Believe me. *I* know. It feels like rejection."

Hannah finished loading her laundry bag. She was still in a daze. Rachel had obviously thought her revelation would bring the three of them closer together. Instead, it just made Hannah bond more with Eden, who seemed calm and levelheaded throughout the whole thing. Hannah was so grateful Eden hadn't decided to go off on her own tonight, because she really needed her right now. She suddenly realized how much they had in common—besides their father. They'd spent the last two years living under the same roof. And yes, they'd avoided each other most of that time. But they knew each other, too. She didn't have to explain anything to Eden. She was the one person here at this school who didn't feel like a stranger.

She and Eden hunted around for quarters and then headed out of the bungalow with their bulging laundry bags. Hannah hoped no one else would be using the laundry room. She wanted to hang out there with Eden and talk. The three sets of coin-operated washers and dryers were in a one-room bungalow about half a block down the row of residence bungalows. It also had some plastic chairs and a couple of vending machines full of soda and junk food.

It was a beautiful, clear night—with a whisper of fall in the air. Some of the trees along the winding street had started to shed their leaves. Moths fluttered around the streetlights. In the distance, music blared from one bungalow, and a girl's laughter rang out from another.

Hannah remembered how horrified she'd first been at the prospect of going away to college with Eden. But now, she was glad her half-sister was here beside her. She wanted to tell her so, but figured Eden would just say something sarcastic. So Hannah kept her mouth shut.

"Y'know, Rachel seems to have the best of intentions," Eden remarked, "even though the road to hell is paved with them. I mean, thanks to her, we're here and not day-hopping at some community college in Seattle. I'd like to stay here—and stay on her good side. I don't want her canceling our scholarships. I mean, I haven't even explored downtown Chicago yet."

"Do you think she'd really do that?" Hannah asked. "Cancel our scholarships—just because she's mad at us?"

"You tell me," Eden said. "You know her better than I do. Up until today, the two of you have been the best of chums. But I wonder if she'd still be paying that Kayla girl's way through school if she hadn't died in a bike accident."

They turned down the stone pathway to the laundry bungalow. Through the front window, Hannah noticed something flickering inside the room. At first, she thought it might be a faulty overhead light.

But then Eden opened the door and gasped.

From in the doorway, Hannah saw something wrapped in a towel, inside a plastic laundry basket. It was on fire. She heard a baby shrieking. For a few horrible seconds, she stood there paralyzed. She felt the heat on her face.

Eden dropped her laundry bag and ran to grab the small fire extinguisher bracketed to the wall by the Coke machine.

The room filled with smoke and the smell of burning plastic. The flames went out of control. A flower-patterned sheet on a nearby clothesline caught fire. The alarm went off with a deafening blare. It drowned out the baby's cries.

Hannah rushed to the basket to try to smother the flames. But the searing heat was too much, and she couldn't see past the thickening black smoke.

Eden struggled with the fire extinguisher and finally got it off the wall. But she obviously didn't know how to operate it.

Choking on the fumes, Hannah kept thinking the baby would be dead before either one of them got to it.

Eden finally figured out how to use the extinguisher, which emitted a blast of dense white spray. She aimed it at the fiery sheet and then at the charred bundle inside the laundry basket. A grayish cloud billowed over half the laundry room, dousing the flames. Ember-like bits of burnt cloth flew around the room.

Covering her mouth, Hannah ran toward the burnt, partially melted plastic basket. She held her breath as her hands reached out for the scorched, small object swaddled in the towel. But then she saw that the blistered, blackened thing was just a doll.

Still, she had to touch it—just to make certain. The intense heat must have destroyed the mechanical crying device. The singed doll didn't let out a peep as Hannah nudged it. But the plastic was still hot, and she burned her fingers.

"It's a doll!" she cried, backing away toward the door. "It's just a stupid doll!" She gagged and started to cough.

Eden tossed aside the fire extinguisher. It landed on the floor with a clank. Through the dissipating noxious smoke, her half-sister moved toward her. "Are you okay?" she yelled over the piercing alarm. Then Eden pulled her through the doorway.

Outside, Hannah finally caught her breath—at least for a few moments.

The alarm had brought at least a dozen girls out of their bungalows. They gathered near the pathway outside the laundry room. A few of them were in their robes or sweats. Hannah spotted Rachel and Alden coming up the road.

"Hannah? Eden? Is that you?" Rachel screamed over all of the noise. She started running toward them. Alden chased after her.

Still in shock, Hannah felt Rachel embrace her.

"Are you okay?" Rachel asked. "Are you both okay? What happened?"

"We're all right," Eden answered for the two of them.

Hannah began to cough again. She let Rachel and Alden lead her farther away from the smoky bungalow. She was still shaking. For a couple of minutes, she'd been certain that someone had set a baby on fire.

She noticed the janitor, Lance, had shown up. He ventured inside the laundry bungalow and shut off the alarm.

Hannah's ears still rang from the blaring.

A campus security vehicle pulled up to the curb. A husky, forty-something, uniformed woman climbed out of the car. She was mumbling into a device clipped to her shoulder. But Hannah couldn't hear what she said.

Meanwhile, several more girls had gathered around to see what all the commotion was about. A few of them were taking photos or videos with their smartphones.

Hannah could catch only snippets of what Eden said as she explained to Lance and the woman from campus security what had happened: "Someone set a doll on fire in a laundry basket . . ." That much Hannah heard.

Lance ducked back into the laundry room, and a few moments later, he emerged holding out the baby doll by its singed little arm.

A couple of the onlookers screamed. But a few others laughed.

Lance coughed. "Somebody's idea of a joke," he announced. He cleared his throat again. "The same thing happened here exactly fifty years ago tonight, same damn thing—only with a real baby. Sick, sick joke."

Hannah felt Rachel squeeze her shoulder.

She heard a siren in the distance. She glanced toward the entrance to St. Agnes Village.

She couldn't see the fire truck yet, but its swirling red strobe seemed to light up the horizon.

CHAPTER FOURTEEN

Friday, September 11, 3:33 P.M.

Ellie was in a lousy mood.

It didn't help that the girl in line in front of her at Campus Grounds had waved her boyfriend to come join her. He butted in front of Ellie without so much as a glance at her, and then he ordered some concoction that took the barista forever to fix. Now he had his credit card out to pay for it. His girlfriend had already paid for her coffee and found a table. Ellie was just itching to tell the guy that the "we're together" excuse some couples used so that one of them could butt in line was bullshit—and totally unacceptable when the couple paid separately.

Jerks.

Ellie tried to remember if she'd ever pulled that "we're a couple" entitlement routine on people when she was married to Mark. Probably. But she couldn't imagine she'd been this rude about it.

She wasn't really upset at the couple. They'd merely added to her frustration today.

Her two o'clock Introduction to Journalism class hadn't gone quite the way she'd wanted it to.

She knew in her gut that Nicholas Jensen hadn't enrolled in the class to sharpen his writing skills—as he'd claimed. But she still couldn't figure out what his angle was. She'd examined over three hundred mug shots, photos, and police sketches, and couldn't come up with anyone who had even a passing resemblance to Nicholas Jensen. She'd googled him again and still didn't find anything that might shed some light on who he really was.

She'd gone back to the bursar's office in Emory Hall and made a copy of Nicholas Jensen's registration record. His emergency contact was listed as *Sarah Jensen (sister)* with a local 847 area code. Ellie had called the number five times in the past twenty-four hours, and it had just rung and rung. No answer. No machine had picked up.

He'd sat in the back row again today, wearing a vintage-looking Hawaiian shirt with pineapples on it. On anyone else, she might have thought it looked kitschy-cute, but on him, it looked tacky. He was the second student she called on. Ellie noticed when she'd said his name—first, *Mr. Jensen*, and then, *Nicholas*—he failed to react right away. Either Nicholas Jensen wasn't his real name or his hearing was atrocious.

For the homework assignment, he'd brought in a news article about a proposed levy for the local public schools. She had him read the first three paragraphs and then describe why he'd chosen it as an example of good reporting.

From his seat in the back row, he read the beginning of the piece, and then added, "I thought the writing was clear and concise, and very informative."

"So ordinarily, you wouldn't be interested in local politics?" Ellie asked.

"Not even remotely," he replied. "I figured that was the point to the assignment—to pick a well-written article I wouldn't ordinarily find interesting."

"So local politics isn't your thing. Have you lived here on the North Shore for long?"

He hesitated before answering, "A couple of years."

"And what kind of work do you do?"

"I'm self-employed."

"Doing what?"

He gave a cryptic smile. "Well, it has nothing to do with local schools or local politics. But after reading this article, I felt I knew something about the proposed levy. So I think the woman who wrote this piece did an excellent job of reporting."

He'd cleverly evaded her question. Still, it was obvious he didn't want to talk about his job—if he had one.

Eden O'Rourke was blessedly quiet and non-confrontational during the class. Ellie made it a point not to call on her.

As the hour ended, Jensen got to his feet and made a beeline toward the door. That was just fine with Ellie. She wanted to talk to Hannah—without him hanging around again. She wanted to apologize for letting it slip about Hannah's and Eden's scholarships coming courtesy of Rachel Bonner. Also, she'd heard Hannah and Eden had put out a fire in one of the bungalows in St. Agnes Village, and she was curious about that.

Hannah must have wanted to talk to her, too, because as the others filed out of the classroom, she approached Ellie's desk.

But just then, another student, Alicia, stepped in

front of Hannah and proceeded to explain to Ellie in excruciating detail why she hadn't been able to do the homework assignment.

Behind her, Hannah waited patiently, but then she started drifting toward the door.

"Excuse me, Alicia," Ellie said. She glanced over at Hannah. "Hannah, did you want to see me?"

She seemed to work up a smile. "It's okay. It can wait. Have a nice weekend!" She hurried out of the classroom.

Alicia went on for another five minutes before she finally left.

Then Ellie had gathered her things and come here to Campus Grounds for her afternoon iced latte pick-me-up.

She was really sorry to have missed talking with Hannah. She cared about her. Hannah's ambition to become an entertainment reporter might have seemed a bit shallow. But Ellie could tell she had a good heart. She just needed some more confidence—and someone to guide her. She'd been through some awful things that became very public. For someone unwillingly thrust into the limelight, she seemed refreshingly normal—and vulnerable.

In many ways, Hannah reminded her of Diana, someone in need of a big sister. Ellie wondered if this was going to become a yearly thing for her—picking out a student to befriend and help. But was she really trying to help the kid—or just trying to feel better about herself?

Ellie got her iced latte to go and headed for the exit.

"Ms. Goodwin?"

She stopped and turned to see the guy who had butted in front of her in line, sitting with his girlfriend.

He stood up. "You probably don't remember me, but my name's Jeff Coughlin. I was in your business communications class last year, and—well, you were like one of the best teachers I've ever had. I learned so much from you about writing and how to communicate—in texts, emails, and letters. It's been so helpful to me. Anyway, I just wanted to say thank you."

Stunned, Ellie stared at him. "Well, thank you, Jeff. I—I really like hearing that. Thanks. It was nice to see you again."

He gave a shy little wave. "Have a good weekend, Ms. Goodwin," he said. Then he sat down with his girlfriend again.

Ellie hurried to the door. For some reason, she just wanted to cry. She should have been flattered the young man had paid her a compliment. But she kept thinking about how resentful she'd been at him and his girlfriend just a minute ago. Had they really been that rude? Or did they simply make her angry because they were a happy, young couple—and she was alone?

Ellie hadn't realized just how bitter she still was over the way things had turned out.

She'd been riding high two years ago with her movie deal and all those awards for her arson series. Of course, it was unnerving to receive the hate mail, but that was at the newspaper, and it somehow felt separate from her personal life. Plus, she shared the emails and letters with her coworkers, so she didn't feel so alone or scared.

She had her husband, Mark, at home about sixty percent of the time. He was a sports recruiter for Northwestern University and traveled a lot. But she always felt safe alone in their apartment in Evanston.

She felt secure in their relationship, too. They'd been married for six years. Mark was a former jock, starting to get paunchy and losing his hair. When not on the road, he was happy to stay home with her and do nothing. She never felt like she had to worry about him. He seemed so devoted to her.

The buyout at the newspaper was like a gift. Ellie decided to freelance and focus on starting a family. They'd been putting it off for a while. Ellie felt it was finally time. Mark didn't agree. He wanted to wait. He pointed out that, with his frequent traveling, he'd end up being a part-time dad—and that wouldn't be fair to her or a baby.

Yet he had no plans to quit his job. So how long did he expect her to wait?

For the first time in their marriage, Ellie was genuinely disillusioned with him. And it lasted weeks and weeks—until she quite unintentionally got pregnant.

Mark did a shabby job covering his disappointment. He kept saying things like, "We'll make the best of this" and "This is a new chapter in our lives," which to Ellie sounded like lame bromides for coping with a tragedy. When she finally got fed up with his clichés and they had it out, Mark admitted that he felt betrayed. He kept throwing in her face the one percent odds of her getting pregnant with her IUD. He refused to believe she hadn't tricked him somehow.

Even though he apologized later, everything he'd said was seared in her memory. Between his accusations and her morning sickness, Ellie was miserable.

After a couple of months, Mark seemed to come around. He even went out and bought a little yellow sweater for the baby—yellow, since they didn't know the sex yet. Ellie kept thinking, *His buying the baby sweater is a baby step.*

Then one Wednesday, in the middle of the deli section at Mariano's in Skokie, she started bleeding. She was grateful the employee restroom was clean. One of the cashiers was so sweet, helping her through the whole ordeal until Mark came. He drove her to the hospital at Northwestern.

He didn't say anything, but Ellie knew he was secretly relieved about the miscarriage. At least, that was her impression. Then again, maybe she was just depressed, a little crazy, and looking for someone to be mad at. But Mark didn't suggest they try to have another baby. It didn't even come up as an option.

It was about a month after the miscarriage that he suggested they get "gussied up" and go out to a nice restaurant. She grudgingly gave Mark points for trying to make her happier and put some romance back into the marriage.

He'd gotten them a lovely, candlelit corner-table at Found Kitchen and Social House, an upscale eatery in Evanston with a bohemian-chic decor and a menu that included three different kinds of caviar.

The menu also had a small selection for kids. But it seemed unconscionable for anyone to bring a bratty, screaming preschooler to such an elegant place at nine o'clock on a Thursday night. But, apparently, the single mom seated on the other side of the restaurant thought it was perfectly okay. Mark had his back to the child and the mother—a vain-looking brunette in her late twenties. Ellie watched her, sipping red wine and checking her smartphone while her pajama-clad child ran amok, shrieking, laughing, and almost barrcling into the waiters and waitresses. Ellie was annoyed, but also sort of amused by the whole thing.

Mark was just annoyed. Every time the little girl ran past their table, Mark would drop his fork on his plate and try to look over his shoulder at her. "Are you sure it's just one kid back there?" he asked Ellie, exasperated. "Because it sounds like three kids—all high on Red Bull. I'm sorry, but this whole dinner is ruined. If I hear that brat scream one more time, I'm saying something to the manager. Where the hell is the mother anyway?"

"She's been on her phone for the last twenty minutes." Ellie took another gulp of wine.

She couldn't help thinking that Mark wouldn't have been a very patient father. Of course, it was always different with one's own kid. And he'd made such a big deal out of this dinner tonight, wanting it to be perfect. Small wonder he was furious. He wasn't the only one either; nearly everyone else in the restaurant looked perturbed.

"Do you still want to have a kid?" he asked pointedly as he cut into his pork chop.

Ellie frowned at him. "Yes, just not that model. Besides, I don't think we'd be the type of parents who wouldn't care if everyone hated our child."

The little girl almost collided with a waiter carrying a tray of drinks. He managed to sidestep her without any spillage. But she let out a shriek anyway.

"Jesus Christ!" Mark hissed, finally getting to his feet and swiveling around.

"Honey, don't make a fuss," Ellie whispered. She

glanced over at the mother across the restaurant. She was staring at them.

"Daddy!" the youngster suddenly cried. "Daddy, Daddy, Daddy!"

Mark seemed to freeze. He just stood there with his hand on the back of the chair while the little girl ran toward him, her arms open. She hugged his leg.

Bewildered, Ellie glanced again at the brunette seated on the other side of the room.

Even from that distance, Ellie could see the tiny smirk on her face.

Her name was Ashley, and she was twenty-nine. She lived in a two-bedroom apartment near Lincoln Square with her four-year-old, Chloe.

It turned out Mark didn't mind being a part-time father after all. For years, he'd been visiting Ashley and his daughter. He'd spent the night with them at least four or five times a month—when Ellie had thought he'd been out of town on business. Sometimes he'd stayed with his mistress and his daughter for an entire weekend, like they were a regular family.

Apparently, Ashley had had enough of the skulking around. Mark had mistakenly mentioned to her that he was taking Ellie to Found. So Ashley had shown up with their rambunctious child, knowing Chloe would eventually spot her daddy.

It was a gamble that paid off for Ashley and Chloe—and even for Mark. He moved in with them, hired some ruthless shark of a divorce lawyer, and actually ended up with a big chunk of Ellie's movie money. She'd been stupid enough to put it in their joint account.

By the time the movie deal had fizzled and Ellie took refuge in the teaching job at Our Lady of the Cove, her ex-husband and Ashley were married. And soon after that, Ashley announced on social media that she was pregnant.

So, last year, when Ellie noticed a miserably homesick, friendless, overweight Diana Mackie in her Introduction to Journalism class, she took the freshman under her wing. She helped Diana feel better about herself and ended up feeling better about herself, too.

This year, Diana had come back as a sophomore, ten pounds lighter than her freshman year, with some school friends, and even a potential boyfriend. Meanwhile, Ellie felt stuck in the exact same place she'd been last year at this time. She'd become acquainted with the other teachers, but didn't really feel close to any of them. While semi-content with her "temporary" job, her garden, and her townhouse, Ellie couldn't help wondering if she'd suddenly wake up one morning in the same place and realize she was fifty.

That was why she'd been so interested for a few days in writing a story on Hannah and Eden O'Rourke. Ellie felt very close to the subject matter of wandering husbands fathering children outside the marriage. She'd figured getting published again would help break her out of her rut. But now, she felt like that would be taking advantage of these two girls who had already had their share of media exposure.

Ellie wondered if she should just look into an online dating site instead. She had to do something to shake things up.

She was approaching the recreation center—a big, ugly, Soviet-Bloc style building in the newer section of campus. There was a balcony walkway around the structure and windows in the back that looked in at the swimming pool.

Diana's prospective boyfriend worked there as a lifeguard. Diana had said his name was J.T. Ellie decided to take the long way around and check him out—if he was there.

Steam condensed near the bottoms of the tall, tinted windows. The afternoon sun made it difficult to see inside very clearly. But Ellie spotted a young man strutting back and forth on the deck on the other side of the pool. He was looking at his phone. He wore red trunks and a tank top that showed off his tan, trim body. He had shaggy brown hair, just as Diana had described.

Ellie counted four people swimming laps in the pool. One of them finished up and climbed out of the water onto the deck. She was slim, young, and pretty, and wore a blue one-piece bathing suit. Ellie recognized Hannah, who turned in her direction. Ellie started to wave at her.

But just then, a man swam over to the edge of the pool and hoisted himself up to the deck. He stood beside Hannah and shook the water off his body. Tall, lean, and sinewy, he wore black trunks. He said something to Hannah, and she laughed.

Ellie stood there outside the window, peering in. She wondered what Nicholas Jensen had said that was so funny.

CHAPTER FIFTEEN

Friday, 3:44 P.M.

At poolside, Hannah turned and seemed to spot her.

Ellie felt as if she'd been caught spying. But she waved at her from the other side of the window.

Waving back, Hannah signaled for her to come in.

Ellie hesitated and then headed around to the recreation center's front entrance. She showed her ID to the girl at the front desk, who gave her directions to the pool. Ellie had to pass through the women's locker room to get there.

She felt out of place in her street clothes. Stepping into the pool area, she got a waft of the chlorine smell that lingered in the humid, near-tropic air. There was a slight echo from two swimmers splashing in the pool, when J.T. called out to her: "No street shoes allowed beyond the line!" He vaguely pointed to a dividing line on the deck, where the white tiles met the concrete. Then he looked at his phone again and resumed pacing along the length of the pool.

Obedient, Ellie halted in her tracks, not far from the pool's shallow end. NO DIVING was spelled out on the floor in blue tiles on that end of the pool.

"Hey, Ms. Goodwin!" Hannah's voice echoed, too.

She approached Ellie, with Nicholas Jensen lagging behind. She'd already dried off somewhat and had a towel wrapped around her shoulders like a shawl. But Jensen was still wet and dripping. Ellie couldn't help admiring his well-sculpted body and the matted-down hair on his chest. But then she noticed the faint, patchy scars, from his shoulder all the way down his left arm.

"Hi . . ." She worked up a smile. "I had no idea you two knew each other."

"We didn't," Hannah replied. She smoothed back her wet hair. "We just met like twenty minutes ago and realized we were both in your journalism class."

"Well, it's sure a small campus." She nodded at Jensen. "Hello, Nicholas."

"Call me Nick."

Ellie wasn't sure if her contempt for him was working overtime, but he seemed to puff his chest out a bit. She tried to keep a pleasant look on her face. "Do you swim here regularly?"

"Actually, this is my first time," he replied. "I just got my membership earlier this afternoon, before your class."

"And right away, you run into someone you know. Well, like I said, it's a small campus, isn't it?"

"Sure is," Hannah agreed. "We were talking about you earlier. Nick didn't know about your movie deal."

"That's odd," Ellie said. "It's one of the first things they say about me after the course description." Ellie looked him in the eye. "It's strange you didn't see it."

"Yeah, I don't know how I missed it."

"Did Hannah tell you what the film deal was all about?"

He ran a hand through his wet hair. "Some kind of exposé you wrote, a series of articles, I understand."

"That's right. I helped put several murderers in prison—a bunch of narrow-minded lowlifes making themselves out to be crusaders." Ellie studied him for a reaction and continued trying to goad him. "They started some fires. A few of them were so stupid they ended up burning themselves. They'd be pathetic if they weren't so dangerous. Because of them, innocent people were killed and wounded. But justice was served."

Folding his arms in front of him, Jensen nodded. "Well, score one for the good guys."

"She won a ton of awards for her reporting," Hannah said.

"I'll have to Google it," Jensen said.

Ellie sensed he was lying. She glanced at the scars on his arm again.

He caught her looking and rubbed his arm. "Kind of a mess, isn't it?" He chuckled. "It's a souvenir from my reckless, misspent youth. I was in a motorcycle accident."

Ellie nodded. To her, the scars still looked as if he'd been burned once. While interviewing witnesses, she'd met with enough survivors from the arsonists' fires to recognize burn scars.

"Well, nice running into both of you," he said, a hand still partially covering his arm. "Have a nice weekend. See you in class on Monday." He nodded at Ellie and smiled at Hannah.

"See you, Nick," Hannah said.

Ellie didn't say anything.

He gave a little wave and then turned and headed toward the men's locker room a few feet away.

Hannah seemed a bit mesmerized as she watched him walk away. Then she turned to Ellie. "That was awkward," she whispered. "Do you think his feelings were hurt? I noticed the scars, too, but I didn't want to say anything. Actually, they're kind of sexy, don't you think?"

"Are you interested in him?" Ellie asked with a wary look.

"God, no." Hannah laughed. "Please. He's at least thirty."

"A veritable relic," Ellie said drolly.

"I didn't mean it like that. It's just that I'm more interested in guys closer to my own age. But he's nice— and good-looking, don't you think?"

"I think he's not very trustworthy," Ellie admitted. "And I'd be very careful dealing with him if I were you."

"Well, like I said, he's too old for me." Hannah leaned in close, and her voice dropped to a whisper. "Actually, I'm sort of interested in the lifeguard. His name is J.T. Isn't he cute?"

Ellie glanced at him, still pacing on the other side of the pool. He looked back at them for a moment and then checked his phone again.

"I hear he's been with, like, half the girls on campus, which should be a real turnoff," Hannah said under her breath. "But I still kind of like him. I don't know why . . ."

Ellie figured Freud would have had a field day with that remark, considering the reputation of Hannah's father. She made a mental note to warn her friend Diana about this J.T. character before she got in too deep with him.

"Maybe I just want to get excited about somebody new," Hannah said, working the towel over her damp hair. "During the summer, I had this long-distance, text and FaceTime thing with a guy from Boston named

Riley. He goes to Northwestern. I thought he might be the one, y'know? We had a date to finally meet each other last weekend, and he postponed. He had a 'family emergency.'" Hannah used air quotes and rolled her eyes. "We're supposed to get together tomorrow, but he hasn't followed up on it. I've texted and called, and he hasn't gotten back to me. So I'm like ninety-nine percent sure I've been dumped—or ditched, or whatever."

Ellie shook her head and sighed. "I'm sorry. That's rough. You know, when I was with the *Trib*, a coworker did a feature story about dating in modern times, and some people out there are device-flirters. They'll talk and text and FaceTime with you, but when it comes time to actually meet you, they back away. They have intimacy issues. Anyway, it's his loss."

"Thanks, I think I needed to hear that." Hannah shrugged and slung the towel around her shoulders again. "God, listen to me go on. You're my teacher, not my girlfriend. I'm sorry."

"It's okay. I think I can be your teacher *and* your friend."

"Anyway, I wanted to talk to you after class, but not about that. I felt bad for running off like I did the last time we spoke. The news about Rachel getting Eden and me our scholarships kind of floored me. I had no idea. It was a weird, major surprise—the first in a day full of weird, major surprises."

"Did you discuss it with Rachel?" Ellie asked.

Hannah hesitated. "Yeah, and she was kind of—disappointed I found out. She planned on telling me later. Anyway, I'm glad you said something."

"There were other surprises on Wednesday?"

"God, were there ever." Hannah heaved a sigh. "That

night, Eden and I walked into the laundry room, and there was a fire . . ."

"Yes, I heard about that. I'm glad you weren't hurt."

"Someone set a doll on fire inside a laundry basket. It was a prank, I guess. Exactly fifty years ago on Wednesday, a freshman in one of the bungalows had a baby in secret. Then she killed it and set it on fire. Can you imagine? Eden heard about it before I did. But when we tried to Google it, nothing came up. Eden swears it's true, but I think it's one of those urban legends."

"No, it actually happened," Ellie told her. "The archdiocese managed to keep it under wraps at the time. The story was buried in the back pages of the *Tribune* and the *Sun-Times*. But you wouldn't have found anything on Google if you went looking under Our Lady of the Cove. Back in 1970, when it happened, this was Blessed Heart of Mary College. They changed the name shortly after that. There was so much bad publicity for the school back then, mostly due to a series of murders that same year."

"So that's why we couldn't find anything about the murders online," Hannah said. "Eden and I tried to look them up, too. We were looking under Our Lady of the Cove."

"You know, I totally forgot it's the fifty-year anniversary of all that," Ellie murmured.

The serial killings weren't discussed much at the school. When she'd first started teaching at Our Lady of the Cove last year, Ellie had been warned by someone who worked for Father O'Hurley, the vice president of the university, not to talk about the murders. None of the teachers were to mention the subject—especially with students. The powers that be at Our Lady of the Cove wanted to pretend the murders had never happened.

And now, someone was reminding everybody about the infanticide that was said to have sparked the "Immaculate Conception" murders.

"I know it sounds paranoid," Hannah said. "But I can't help thinking that whoever started the fire on Wednesday night must have seen Eden and me coming. It couldn't have been going for more than a minute at the most. They must have set it and then climbed out of a back window. The laundry bungalow is the only one that doesn't have bars on the windows."

"You didn't see anybody?"

Hannah shook her head. "The woman from campus security kept asking us that. But Eden and I didn't notice anything until we were right in front of the place. We were distracted. We were still kind of in shock over—well, something else that went down that day."

"*Something else?*" Ellie asked. "Another surprise?"

Hannah opened her mouth, but then hesitated. She glanced over toward J.T. again.

Ellie followed her gaze—across the pool. The handsome, young lifeguard had stopped pacing. He was facing them. The way he held his phone, it looked like he was taking their picture, but Ellie wasn't sure. He stashed his phone into the pocket of his baggy red trunks. Then he climbed up a short ladder to his lifeguard tower and sat down.

Ellie turned once again to Hannah, who seemed deep in thought. "What is it?" Ellie asked.

She sighed. "You have to promise not to tell anyone. I'm still not sure how I feel about it. The reason Rachel arranged the scholarship for us is because—well, we're related to her. Rachel was adopted."

Ellie nodded. She remembered someone at the newspaper mentioning it once. She didn't think it was a big secret or anything.

"She finally found out last year about her real parents. Her real mother was my mom's dead sister, my aunt Molly. She had the baby when she was in college and gave it up. And the father was—*is* my dad. I knew he'd had an affair with my aunt—way back before I was born. But I don't think he or my mother know Aunt Molly had a baby. She must have kept it a secret. Still, my dad's name is on the birth certificate. Rachel showed it to Eden and me. Anyway, all of us are half-sisters."

"God, what a shock," Ellie whispered. "You poor thing. So—your parents don't know anything about this? How's Eden handling the news?"

"It wasn't such a shock to her," Hannah replied, frowning. She readjusted the towel around herself. "The woman who raised Eden hired a private detective to dig up everything he could about my dad. That was ages ago, I guess. Anyway, the detective must have found out about the baby. Eden said she's known for a while. She just didn't know it was Rachel. I'm not sure how I feel." She glanced down toward the floor, and her eyes filled with tears. "When I think about how I used to adore my father . . ."

Ellie took Hannah's hand in hers. She felt so bad for her, and didn't know what to say.

"You have to promise not to tell anybody," Hannah whispered.

Nodding, Ellie squeezed her hand. And at that moment, it hit her. She'd just been handed a major news story. Two years ago, the O'Rourke family had been the focus of a national media frenzy—Dylan O'Rourke, in particular. And, locally, anything concerning the Bonners was news. The meeting of the three half-sisters was a big human interest story, the kind of scoop any reporter would kill for.

But Ellie knew she couldn't live with herself if she betrayed Hannah's trust.

"I won't breathe a word about it to anyone," she promised.

Hannah wiped her eyes and gave her a grateful smile. "Thanks. I'd hug you, but I'm still kind of damp." She looked over toward the clock on the wall. "I think I'll do one more set of laps before I cut out of here. I'm going to some sorority recruitment thing at five-thirty. I'm not sure if I really want to join, but it's a free dinner. Anyway, thanks for listening. I felt funny after I waved at you to come in here, since you're my teacher and all. But now, I'm glad I did."

"I'm glad you did, too," Ellie said.

Then, out of the corner of her eye, she noticed someone in the doorway of the men's locker room. He quickly ducked back around the corner. But Ellie caught a glimpse of his shirt—that tacky Hawaiian thing with the pineapples on it. Was he listening in on their conversation?

"What is it?" Hannah asked.

"Nothing," Ellie said. "I think I'll stick around and watch for a few minutes, if that's okay with you." She didn't want to leave Hannah alone here if Jensen was still lurking about.

"Cool," Hannah said. Draping her towel over the

back of a plastic chair, she padded over to the deep end of the pool and dove in.

J.T. seemed to be watching her.

Ellie glanced back at the men's locker room and didn't see anyone.

She couldn't help thinking that perhaps some of the arsonists from two years ago had never been caught. Maybe one of them had ended up here, and he'd started a fire in the laundry room the night before last.

Then Ellie caught a glimpse of Nick Jensen outside— as he passed by the tall windows.

She wondered how much he'd heard of Hannah's and her conversation. Did he know about the three half-sisters? She felt very protective of Hannah right now.

On the other side of a partially fogged window, Jensen paused for a moment and gave her a halfhearted smile. He waved.

Ellie just glared at him. She wanted the son of a bitch to know she was onto him.

He looked away and kept moving.

CHAPTER SIXTEEN

Friday, 4:17 P.M.

Ellie was determined to have it out with Jensen.

She figured he wouldn't return to the pool within the next hour. Even if he did, Hannah was probably safe. Two more young women had shown up to swim. Ellie had caught Hannah's eye between laps; then she'd waved and pointed outside to indicate she was leaving. Hannah had waved back and resumed swimming.

Ellie had left the copy of Nicholas Jensen's registration form in her office in Lombard Hall. His phone number was on it. She planned to call the son of a bitch and find out once and for all what he was up to.

At a determined clip, she headed toward the old campus. On the horizon, over the lake, she could see dark clouds and a storm rolling in.

Ellie slowed down as she approached the university library, the unofficial dividing line between the campus's old and new sections. The impressive, three-story structure had some Frank Lloyd Wright influence with its tall, stained glass windows and the way the building jutted over the creek that snaked through most of the old campus. It was a beautiful structure, the jewel of the campus, built in the 1960s, when Blessed Heart of Mary College had expanded.

Behind Ellie was a one-lane bridge that crossed over the creek to some of the older dorm buildings and St. Agnes Village. The bridge was about four car-lengths long and twenty feet above the stream. Off the overpass, on the library side, was a concrete stairway with a pipe railing. The stairs curved down under the bridge to a walkway that overlooked the creek for about three blocks in the opposite direction of the library. It led to another set of stairs that came up behind the playfield.

Ellie paused halfway between the start of the bridge and the library's front entrance. From there, she had a view of a spot farther down the creek—as it deepened into a wooded ravine.

The body of the first murdered girl had been found there in 1970. She'd been strangled. She'd last been seen leaving this beautiful library late the evening before.

Ellie felt the wind kick up. She watched the leaves scatter through the gully. She remembered last year, in mid-September, on the anniversary of the first murder, someone had left a funeral wreath by that spot in the ravine. It was clearly visible from where Ellie now stood—as well as from the bridge and the stairway. Ellie didn't know if someone was being solemn or morbid or what. But after only a couple of hours, the wreath was whisked away at the behest of Father O'Hurley— or so Ellie had heard.

Whoever had started that fire in the laundry bungalow knew about the Immaculate Conception murders fifty years ago. Ellie wondered if her extreme distrust of Nick Jensen had muddled her thinking. A doll had been torched in a laundry basket—obviously someone's warped commemoration of the anniversary of that gruesome baby-murder. It had nothing to do with her or Hannah O'Rourke.

Though she could tell it would start raining soon, Ellie sat down on a bench in front of the library. She wondered if she was wrong about Nick Jensen. Maybe she'd let that collection of hate email from over the summer make her paranoid. All the guy had done was sign up for her journalism class. Based almost entirely on intuition, Ellie had convinced herself that Nick Jensen was vile and horrible. It was based on prejudice, too. On the surface, he seemed nice, and he was very attractive. So—immediately, he couldn't be trusted. He was capable of awful things. Had Mark really damaged her that badly?

Ellie told herself she wasn't completely nuts. After all, what was Nick doing earlier, skulking around the entrance to the men's locker room? Those were burn scars on his arm, she was almost certain. And why wasn't his emergency contact person picking up the phone?

She dug her smartphone out of her bag and found the number she'd called several times since yesterday. She hoped Nick's sister, Sarah Jensen, could tell her a few things about him. That had been standard operating procedure for Ellie when she'd been a reporter. When investigating someone, she always did her research first—reading up on them and then talking to the subject's friends, family, and even their enemies. The last person she talked to was the person she was investigating.

She tried Sarah Jensen again—if such a person even existed. Frowning, she listened to it ring and ring.

"Hello?" a man said.

Ellie was caught off guard. "Uh, yes, hello," she said. "Is Sarah Jensen there, please?"

"You've got the wrong number," he muttered hurriedly.

"Um, this is supposed to be an emergency contact number for Nicholas Jensen. Do you, by any chance, know him?"

"No. I told you, you've got the wrong number." The man hung up.

Donald Sewell, fifty-nine, of Niles, Illinois, was the man who had hung up on her—at least that was the name that popped up when Ellie googled the phone number Nick had provided for "Sarah Jensen."

She sat at her desk computer in her tiny, fourth-floor office. It had started raining by the time she'd reached Lombard Hall. The sky had turned so dark that she'd switched on the overhead light in her office. The upper floors were now deserted and quiet. Most of the teachers had already rushed home for the weekend. All Ellie heard was rain pattering against the window and an occasional rumble of thunder. Every once in a while the lights flickered.

She tried to look up *Sarah Jensen, Chicago Suburbs*, and *Sarah Jensen, Illinois* on Google and the online white pages. None of the resulting *Sarah Jensens* had phone numbers that even came close to the emergency contact number Nick had put on his registration form. Obviously, he'd made up the phone number.

Had he made up his own name, too? Was his address really on Sunset Ridge Road in Highland Park? Was this his 847-area code number?

Ellie typed the phone number in the Google search box and entered it. She stared at the first result at the top of the screen:

Healing Hands—Therapeutic Massage by Nick
http://www.hhmassageservices.com
Individual Massage and Bodywork;
Injury—Maintenance—Wellness;
In-Calls/Out-Calls—Nick Jensen, LMT (847-555-4195)
812 Sunset Ridge Road #17, Highland Park, IL 60035

Ellie clicked on the link, and Jensen's site came up. A medium-size photo was there, a serious-looking shot of him, standing by a massage table. He wore a tank top and calf-length shorts that showed off his trim, taut body. She recognized him, but his face was mostly in the shadows. And he was posed so that his scarred arm wasn't in the photo.

It was strange, but Ellie felt sort of disappointed she hadn't found his mug shot or his name on some American Family Preservationists roster. He looked like a legitimate masseur. She'd been looking under *Nicholas Jensen*, and Ellie now realized she would have found him a lot sooner had she tried *Nick Jensen*. With the abbreviated first name, he was listed under several sites. She checked his customer reviews on Yelp. The earliest one was from six months ago, back in April:

5 Stars—Great Massage
I called Nick, and he was able to see me the same day. The massage was in-studio: Clean, comfortable setting, terrific music and a heated table. He was a super-nice guy and very professional. We discussed my back issues upfront. He

worked out the kinks. He didn't talk much during except to check in with me now and then. The time went by way too fast! My stress was gone, the aches and knots were gone. I left there in a state of bliss. I'll definitely be back.

– **Ed G.** (90 minutes/$120)

Ellie checked the other reviews. Everybody seemed to love him. One man and two women mentioned he was "very handsome," making her wonder if he was *that* kind of masseur. Then again, maybe out of habit, she was still looking for something disreputable about him.

She started to read the last review, from *Brad C*, another satisfied customer, who appreciated Nick's "magic work" on his shoulder, injured during a football game.

The lights flickered again, followed by a crack of thunder. Ellie stopped and looked up at the overhead light. She already felt a tad nervous being completely alone here on the fourth floor. The last thing she wanted was to have all the lights go out.

She had an umbrella on the hook behind her office door. Ellie figured she'd wait for the storm to die down a little, and then she'd head home.

Meanwhile, she kept digging for more information about Nick Jensen. She checked some of the other sites, hoping to discover where he practiced before April of this year. She couldn't find anything. She still didn't trust him, not after catching him eavesdropping on her conversation with Hannah. And why had he lied about his emergency contact person?

She was reading some more reviews for him on another massage site when she heard a door slam in the hallway. It was so loud, Ellie flinched. She sat there for a moment, listening. She didn't hear any footsteps, just the rain. With trepidation, she finally got to her feet and crept to her office doorway. Poking her head out, she glanced up and down the long, vacant hallway.

"Hello?" she called nervously. "Is anyone there?"

No answer. Her heart was racing.

All the lights flickered again. There was another rumble of thunder, more distant this time.

Ducking back into her office, Ellie glanced toward the rain-beaded window. She didn't care if it was pouring out, she didn't feel safe here. She could finish this up at home. She sat back down for a minute so that she could log off her computer.

Suddenly, the overhead light went off, and the room was dark.

Ellie glanced up and saw someone in the doorway. The hallway light in back of him kept his face in the shadows. He may as well have been wearing a dark mask.

She let out a gasp.

He switched the light back on. "I didn't know anyone was in here," he said.

It was the custodian, Lance. He still had one hand on the light switch. With his other hand, he took out his music earbuds.

Wide-eyed, Ellie stared at him. "God, you scared me," she said, catching her breath. "What—what are you doing here?"

He frowned. "My job, that's what I'm doing here. I thought this office was empty."

Ellie managed a smile. "Well, it will be in a minute. Carry on."

She didn't know Lance very well, but she had the

distinct feeling he didn't like her or anyone else for that matter. Getting to her feet, Ellie quickly gathered her things, including her umbrella. Her back was to him for a moment.

"Well, have a nice weekend," she said to be polite. But when she turned around, he wasn't in the doorway anymore.

Ellie moved to the doorway and glanced out at the corridor. He wasn't in the hallway, but she noticed a light coming from an office two doors down. A shadow moved across the floor in front of the open doorway.

She switched off the light to her office. Ellie's hands were shaking as she closed her door and locked it. Then she hurried for the stairwell and started down the steps. The lights flickered again as she passed the door to the second floor. She practically bolted down the last flight.

Ellie didn't start to feel safe until she reached the first-floor corridor, where some students were lingering after the last class of the day.

Stepping outside, she finally got her breath. She stood there for a moment, feeling the rain on her face. Then she opened her umbrella and headed toward the teachers' parking lot.

She glanced over her shoulder at Lombard Hall. Her eyes moved up to the fourth floor. She noticed all the office windows were dark—all except one.

She saw his silhouette framed in the window. He was perfectly still.

And she knew he was looking down at her.

CHAPTER SEVENTEEN

Friday, 8:55 P.M.

Eden recognized the man who had just sat down at the end of the counter in the Sunnyside Up Café. It was Nicholas Something, the older guy from her journalism class.

Sitting midway between them, a trucker hunched over his fried chicken dinner. Eden couldn't tell if her classmate had seen her yet. Sipping her lemonade, she made no effort to catch his eye.

She'd been alone at the bungalow earlier, just her and the ghosts in the garden next door. Hannah was at some sorority recruitment dinner—Eden's idea of hell. And Princess Rachel was out on the town with her boy-buddy, Alden.

Life in bungalow twenty was still a bit fractured and weird after Rachel's big reveal on Wednesday. But it was all pretty familiar to Eden, who had gone through this two years ago.

She knew what it was like to reach out to people who were family and have them treat you like some stranger with a secret agenda. Of course, in her case with the O'Rourkes, that was exactly what she was: a stranger with a secret agenda. Still, Eden had tried to let Rachel know that she understood how she felt.

"Thank you, that's really nice of you," Rachel had said, giving her a pinched smile. "But I really don't think it's the same situation at all."

Eden figured what the hell. She didn't have to be Rachel's pal and confidant any more than she'd needed to be buddies with Hannah when she'd first moved in with the O'Rourkes. As long as Rachel kept paying for her scholarship, Eden wouldn't complain.

One bizarre result of Wednesday's news was that Hannah had suddenly become closer to her. Last night, Hannah had even said that she didn't want her to move out. "I'd really like it if you stayed," she'd told Eden. "Just, please, see if you can be a little less of a slob."

Eden wasn't sure how long this strange sisterly bonding would last. Hannah was so fascinated with Rachel that it probably wouldn't be long before the two of them were chummy-chummy again—maybe even closer than before, since they were sisters now. Then, Eden figured, soon enough, Hannah would go back to treating her like somebody's pet reptile.

But in the meantime, Hannah was still pretty torn up about Rachel's bombshell announcement. She wanted to tell her parents. But Eden didn't see what good that would do right now—especially since Rachel and her folks wanted to keep it secret for a while.

Eden had spent most of her life knowing about "Dylan's other bastard." She'd managed to keep it to herself for the last two years while living with Hannah's family. They'd already been shaken up enough—especially Hannah's poor mother, Sheila. And Hannah's two younger brothers didn't need to know about another surprise half-sister. As for Dylan, he was now a beaten, broken man. Why tell anyone right now? They were all in Seattle. It wasn't like they were going to meet Rachel any time soon.

The afternoon thunderstorm hadn't lasted long. But Eden had gotten her sneakers muddy taking the shortcut through the woods. Sketchy as Lance seemed, he'd been right about the shortcut. It was the fastest way to town and back, and only mildly creepy at night now that Eden knew the way.

Roseann, Eden's waitress from the other night, was working this evening. She set a plate of oatmeal pancakes and a sticky-looking glass decanter of maple syrup on the counter in front of Eden. Patsy Cline's "Crazy" played over the sound system. The trucker left his money on the counter and headed out the door.

"Breakfast for dinner is always an excellent choice," Nicholas What's-His-Name commented from the other end of the counter.

Eden hesitated before smothering the pancakes in syrup. She glanced at him. "You won't get an argument from me."

"We're in the same journalism class," he said. "I thought you looked familiar."

Nodding, Eden cut into her stack of pancakes.

"My name's Nick."

Eden nodded again. "I know. And you're . . ." she lowered her voice to imitate him, "'self-employed.'"

He laughed. "Do I really sound like that?"

"Very mysterious," she said. She took her first bite, and the pancakes were delicious.

"Do you mind if I sit next to you?"

She shrugged. "Suit yourself."

He brought his sweater, the menu, and his glass of water to the spot beside her and sat down. Roseann was there in front of him on the other side of the counter with her pad ready. "Can I have the breakfast special?" he asked her. "The eggs scrambled, bacon, and wheat toast. Oh, and a Coke, too, please."

"You got it, hon," Roseann said, scribbling on her pad as she moved toward the kitchen.

He draped his sweater on the back of his barstool and turned to Eden. "So—you've noticed me in class . . ."

"You're kind of hard to miss. You're the only one in the room over twenty—except for the teacher." She ate another forkful of pancakes.

"What do you think of Ellie Goodwin?" he asked.

"I like her. She's smart."

"I like her, too," he said. "But I don't think she cares much for me. I'm trying to figure out why."

"Maybe it's because she can't get a handle on you."

"What do you mean?"

"Well, it's just what I said. You're the mystery man. You stick out. And when she asked, you wouldn't tell her anything about what you do for a living except"— Eden lowered her voice again—"'I'm self-employed.' Even I thought that was weird. And I really don't give a shit what you do."

"I'm a massage therapist."

"Legitimate?"

"No, I'm a male prostitute. What do you think?" He chuckled and shook his head. "I've got a state license, a certificate, and the whole deal. Of course, I'm legitimate. That's the first question you ask? And you wonder why I don't want to announce to the class what I do."

Sighing, Eden cut herself another forkful of her pancakes. "Sorry, my bad. So—are you from around here or what?"

"Yep, I've lived in the Chicago area all my life."

"What's a massage therapist doing taking a journalism class?"

"Like I told the teacher, I just want to become a better writer. It has nothing to do with my job." He sipped his water. "How about you? Why are you interested in journalism?"

Eden had a mouthful of food, so she didn't answer for a moment.

"What I mean is," he said, "I remember reading about you and your sister a couple of years ago. I figured, after all of your experiences with reporters, you'd both be pretty fed up with journalists in general. So it was kind of a surprise to see you two in a journalism class."

Eden stopped eating and studied him. She wondered what his angle was. He was right about one thing. She'd been around enough reporters to distinguish the sneaky ones with a secret agenda and the ones out to trash her. She wasn't sure if he was a reporter or not—or what he was exactly—but she was almost certain this Nick guy was a sneaky one.

She wiped her mouth with her napkin. "Most of the journalists I met were pretty cool," she answered guardedly. "I like talking to people and finding out about them, hearing their stories. I also like cutting through the bullshit and getting to the truth. Plus I enjoy writing. I keep a journal. So, what the hell? I thought I'd take a journalism class."

Roseann arrived with his Coke and his breakfast-for-dinner. She set the plate and the tumbler full of soda in front of him. Then she gave him a straw, a bottle of ketchup, and a bowl filled with packets of various jams.

Nick smiled and thanked her.

Eden kept studying him. He seemed to know he was good-looking. And he seemed to know how to pour on the charm, too. His sleeves were rolled up, and she noticed the scars on his arm. "So, what happened there?" she asked.

He let out a surprised little laugh as he spread jam on his toast. "Most people stare, but they're afraid to ask. Back when I was a teenager, I banged myself up in a motorcycle accident."

Eden narrowed her eyes at him. "Is that what really happened? I get this vibe that you're lying to me. If it's none of my business, just tell me and we can drop it."

He laughed again and squirmed a bit on the barstool. "You really do cut through the bullshit, don't you? Actually, the painful truth is, a few years back, I put too much charcoal starter in a hibachi while barbecuing some burgers, and the thing barbecued me instead." He took a bite of his toast. "Pretty stupid of me. So I say I was in a motorcycle accident. It sounds so much cooler."

Eden just nodded. She still didn't completely believe him. She'd only eaten half her stack of pancakes, but she crumpled up her napkin and tossed it on her plate.

"You know, when I read about you," he said, "I could really relate. I understood what it must have been like for you growing up. I was an only child, too—and adopted. I never knew who my real father was."

"I always knew who my father was," Eden corrected him. "And it turned out I wasn't an only child."

"Yeah, but you were *raised* like an only child," he said, nibbling on a piece of bacon. "And—well, this afternoon, while I was swimming laps at the pool, I overheard your sister talking to Ellie Goodwin. Your sister said something about the woman who raised you hiring a private detective to find out more about your biological father."

Silent, Eden stared at him again. Yes, this guy was

definitely working an angle. She drummed her fingers on the countertop. She'd just told Hannah on Wednesday night about the private investigator. She couldn't imagine Hannah blabbing to Ellie Goodwin about it already—and so loudly that other people could hear. "Too bad for them you're not one of those people who wear earplugs when they're swimming," she said finally.

He sipped his Coke and shrugged. "I just happened to hear them talking, that's all. It got me thinking about my father and how I never really knew him. Maybe I should hire a private detective, too. Did this detective come up with any useful information?"

"I haven't a clue," Eden lied. She wasn't going to tell this stranger her family secrets. "You'd have to ask the woman who raised me, and she's dead. And if you want me to recommend the guy, I can't, because I don't know his name. Besides, I'm pretty sure he was in Portland, and that was years ago. What else did you happen to hear while you were swimming your laps?"

Heaving a sigh, he set his fork down. It clanked against his plate. "God, now you're making me feel like a jerk—like I'm this major snoop or something. I was just taking a break in the shallow end, and I heard them talking. There's an echo in the pool area . . ."

Eden tried not to frown at him. She wondered if, during this poolside chat, Hannah had told Ellie Goodwin about Rachel being their half-sister.

"I'm curious about what else you overheard," she said coolly.

"Well, it sounds like Rachel Bonner is your roommate," he said.

Eden nodded. "That's right."

"She gets written up in the papers a lot—and online."

He picked up his fork again. "Had you heard of her before you came here?"

"I'd never heard of her—not until I found out she was going to be my roommate, and that was about a month ago. What else did you hear in the shallow end of that pool?"

"That's it, nothing else. And I swear I wasn't eavesdropping."

Picking up her check, Eden looked at it. Then she put it down and reached for her purse. She gave him a wary smile. "Well, if you're done with all your questions, the witness would like to be excused."

He laughed defensively. "Hey, I'm really sorry." He swiped her check off the counter. "Listen, let me pay for your dinner. You're right. Sometimes, I ask too many questions. It's just that I read about you, and like I say, I kind of related to you. Can't you stick around and talk some more? I swear I won't pry. I think we started off on the wrong foot."

Eden stood up. "No, that's how we've finished." She grabbed her zip-up sweatshirt. "It was interesting talking to you. See you in class. Thanks for dinner."

She turned toward the waitress, and with her thumb, Eden pointed to Nick. "He's buying my dinner. Thanks a lot, Rosie!" Then she headed toward the door.

Stepping outside, Eden felt a chill. She put on the sweatshirt. As she passed by the restaurant, she stole a glance inside at her dinner companion.

Frowning, he stared back at her.

Eden kept walking. She decided not to take the shortcut back to St. Agnes Village, not just yet.

She would hang out around town for a while—just to make sure Nick, the mystery man, didn't follow her.

CHAPTER EIGHTEEN

Friday, 9:20 P.M.

"What the hell were you thinking?" Rachel wailed. She sat up on the living room sofa, almost knocking over the bowl of microwaved popcorn at her side. She wore a T-shirt and sweatpants, and still held the remote control in her hand. On TV, Cary Grant and Eva Marie Saint were frozen in the middle of a lip-lock while the pause symbol flashed in the upper corner of the big screen.

Perched on the edge of the easy chair, Hannah still had on the cute skirt and blouse combo she'd worn to the boring sorority dinner. It had been build-your-own-tacos, followed by a bunch of awful recruitment speeches. All evening long, she'd felt a bit guilty for sharing their big family secret with Ellie Goodwin earlier at the pool. She'd returned home about ten minutes ago to find Rachel back early from her night out with Alden. Hannah had decided to tell her about the poolside chat with Ellie. She hadn't even kicked off her shoes yet.

"Seriously, are you crazy?" Rachel asked. "No one was supposed to know about this! And of all the people you could confide in, you picked that blabbermouth reporter? She's the reason I had to tell you about us before I was ready. God, what in the world were you thinking?"

Hannah shifted around on the chair. "I'm sorry. I just needed to tell somebody. And she's the only person here I feel close to—besides you. She promised she wouldn't tell anyone else—"

"Oh, she promised? Did she pinky-swear? Because if that's the case, I'll feel a lot better." Rachel rolled her eyes. "Christ, Hannah, at the risk of repeating myself, she's a *fucking reporter*! How could you be so stupid—and reckless?"

"Ellie told me she wouldn't breathe a word about it to anyone," Hannah said, suddenly feeling horrible. "I'm certain she won't say anything."

"Shit," Rachel muttered, plopping against the back of the couch. Some of the popcorn spilled out of the bowl. She started picking up the pieces and eating them. "Listen, I'm sorry. I know you like Ellie Goodwin. But this afternoon, you told a reporter a major news story. *Dylan O'Rourke has another bastard child, and it's the heiress to the Bonner fortune!* Do you really expect your *friend*, Ellie, to keep that to herself?"

Hannah hesitated before she nodded. "I—I trust her," she said, now trying to convince herself as well as Rachel. "I really think it's going to be okay."

"I don't mean to jump on your case, Hannah. It's just that I'm not ready for the whole world to find out about this. I let my parents know that I'd told you and Eden about us being sisters, and they were pretty upset. I mean, they'll live. But they don't want it getting out. They're in the news all the time, but they control everything. They have a whole public relations team handling stuff like that. They're extremely guarded about their privacy. If they knew a reporter found out about this thing, they'd absolutely shit."

"I'm sorry," Hannah murmured, getting to her feet. "If it'll make you feel any better, I have Ellie's email address. I'll write and tell her again that our whole conversation at the pool today is off the record."

"I'm not sure how much good that'll do." Rubbing her forehead, Rachel sighed. "Listen, I'm sorry, too. I was already in sort of a crappy mood tonight. Alden and I planned on a movie after dinner. But when we came out of Bellini's, we ran into his roommate and a bunch of his stupid friends. They were all driving to Kenosha to get drunk, and I could tell that Alden really wanted to hang with them. I said it was okay. So off he went for his boys' night out."

"That sucks" was all Hannah could think of to say. She was reminded once again of Riley. She'd hoped against hope that he'd call sometime tonight about their "date" tomorrow. Now, she knew it was never going to happen.

"Anyway, it didn't help my mood any to hear about your talk with Ellie," Rachel muttered. She picked up the remote and switched channels. A wave of canned laughter from some sitcom came over the TV's speakers.

"Aren't you going to watch your movie?" Hannah asked. "I could watch it with you. It's one of my favorites."

"No, it's spoiled now," Rachel answered, staring at the screen.

Hannah said nothing.

She just nodded and retreated to her bedroom.

CHAPTER NINETEEN

Friday, 9:44 P.M.

Eden couldn't shake the feeling that someone was watching her.

After leaving the Sunnyside Up Café, she hadn't been in any hurry to get back to the bungalow—and loathed the notion that Nick What's-His-Name might follow her through the woods on her shortcut home. So she'd killed time window-shopping around downtown Delmar, which had taken all of fifteen minutes. But it had been an uneventful, stress-free fifteen minutes.

Then, wandering into the Jewel-Osco, Eden had glimpsed someone out of the corner of her eye: a tall man in a pale blue Oxford shirt—like the one Nick, the mystery man, had been wearing. She had no desire to talk with the guy again, so she just kept moving and tried to avoid making eye-contact with him.

Eden picked up a spiral notebook, a granola bar, potato chips, and a liter of Diet Coke. At the end of each aisle, she checked the round security mirrors strategically located around the supermarket. In the mirrors' slightly distorted reflection, she kept spotting the blue Oxford shirt guy—no shopping cart, no basket—at the end of the aisle.

Now, at the U-scan checkout, she glanced around for him. But Eden didn't see Nick anywhere. Nor did she see a man in a pale blue Oxford shirt. It was as if the blue-shirt man had been a phantom that existed only in the warped reflection of the security mirrors.

She hurried outside with her grocery bag. As she backtracked toward the café, Eden realized a beat-up, white minivan was cruising down the street behind her. It was hard to miss. The street was practically deserted—except for some people coming out of Bellini's, across the street. Laughing, they headed off in the opposite direction. Eden kept moving along the sidewalk, and she heard their laughter fade in the distance. She glanced over her shoulder.

The minivan still hovered behind her.

Eden picked up her pace a bit.

The blare of a car horn made her stop in her tracks. She turned around in time to see a Volvo pass the minivan and continue up Delmar's main drag.

"Screw this," she muttered, not moving. She defiantly stared at the minivan, which had stopped, too. She couldn't see who was at the wheel. A streetlight reflected on the windshield.

The minivan was still stationary. To Eden, it seemed like a standoff. Was the driver staring back at her? She was tempted to flip the person the bird.

Then, with a screech of its tires, the vehicle peeled away and sped past her, up the street. Within moments, the minivan's taillights and the sound of its revved motor disappeared in the night.

"What the hell was that about?" Eden said under her breath.

A bit shaky, she crossed the street. Passing the

Sunnyside Up Café, she glanced in the window. The place had filled up with more customers. But Nick What's-His-Name wasn't in there—at least, she didn't see him at the counter.

Heading around the corner, Eden wondered what he was after. It seemed like too much of a coincidence that he just happened to be at the diner the same time that she was—after just happening to be at the swimming pool the same time as her sister. He had to be following one—or both—of them. She was pretty sure he'd lied to her about practically everything he'd said—from how he got the scars on his arm to where he was from. Eden had been here at Our Lady of the Cove for only eight days, but already she could pick out the native Chicagoans from the twang in their speech. He didn't have one. She'd read that people in the Pacific Northwest had no discernible accent. From the way he spoke, he fit into that category.

At the dry cleaners on the corner, Eden turned right and paused for a moment to stare at the dark woods across the street. She could see the start of the shortcut trail. She'd be home in five to ten minutes—instead of at least twenty minutes the long way. This way was creepier and muddier—and yes, maybe it felt like something out of *Grimm's Fairy Tales* or *The Blair Witch Project*. But the trail was quite well traveled. The other afternoon, she'd passed three different people taking the shortcut, and one of them was a priest. Eden told herself that she'd be fine.

Crossing the street, she didn't see the minivan in either direction. At the mouth of the trail, she could smell the dead leaves and wet earth. She headed down the crude, winding pathway and the darkness of the woods gradually swallowed her up. It got harder and harder for her to distinguish the path. Slowing down, Eden took her grocery bag in her left hand and then searched through her purse for her phone. All around her, she could hear leaves rustling. With each step, the ground beneath her feet became more slick and muddy.

Eden thought about turning back. But then she glanced over her shoulder and couldn't see the lights from town anymore. All she saw were trees, their branches swaying slightly in the wind.

She finally found her phone and switched on the flashlight. She aimed it at the pathway in front of her. A man's shoe prints were in the mud headed in the same direction as she was. They looked fresh.

"Shit," she whispered.

She told herself to calm down. After all, wasn't she just thinking about how a lot of people used this trail? Just because some man had recently taken this route, it didn't mean the footprints belonged to that Nick guy or some psycho-killer.

Eden kept walking. The temperature seemed to drop, and she figured she'd reached the middle of the woods— the cold heart center. She hoisted up the grocery bag so she was hugging it to her chest. Her bulky purse dangled from the strap around her arm. It bounced against her thigh as she walked. She heard her keys jangling in the bag.

She heard twigs snapping behind her, too.

God, please let it be another student, she thought. Maybe it was one of the girls from St. Agnes Village. Then they could walk together.

Eden turned around and directed the flashlight's beam on the snaky pathway behind her. She imagined a big,

lumbering man with a stocking mask over his face
coming at her. But there was no one. There wasn't a
sound either. Had he stopped moving when she'd
stopped?

"Fucking stop it," she said aloud.

Why was she doing this to herself? This wasn't like her
at all. She didn't scare easily. She enjoyed adventures—
and pushing the envelope. Getting an adrenaline rush
was usually fun for her.

But talking to Nick What's-His-Name had unnerved
her. And now she was a hostage to these dark, sinister
woods. She felt like a frightened little girl.

Breathless, she pressed on. In her shaky hand, the
phone light's beam wavered on the trail ahead. Eden zig-
zagged around tree roots and divots along the way. She
stumbled a few times, but she didn't slow down. Brushing against a low tree branch, she scratched her neck.
Still, she kept moving. She didn't even check to see if
she was bleeding. She heard the keys rattling, twigs
snapping, and her own hard breathing. The grocery bag
felt so heavy and cumbersome. She was tempted to just
dump it.

Then she saw something ahead that made her slow
down.

Over the treetops, Eden noticed the lights from the
campus. The pathway in front of her widened. It looked
like a straight shot to the road behind St. Agnes Village.
She would be there in only a minute or two.

Eden caught her breath and pushed forward. Clammy
and sweaty, she thought about taking a long, hot shower
when she reached the bungalow.

She could see the end of the trail up ahead—and even
some of the road. She also noticed a vehicle parked on

the other side of the street, close to the fence that ran along the back of the bungalows. For a few awful seconds, Eden thought it was the white minivan again.

But it was a gray SUV.

Eden pressed on—until she caught a glimpse of something out of the corner of her eye. It came from around the bushes and blocked out the light at the end of the trail.

Eden gasped and stopped in her tracks. Then she noticed the nun's habit—the tunic and veil. The nun's face was in the shadows. For a moment, it seemed absurd to see a nun in these woods. But Eden had seen them in their old-fashioned garb around the campus. And earlier in the week, she'd noticed a priest using this trail.

She let out a tiny laugh. "My God, Sister, you scared me . . ."

But she fell silent as the sister took another step toward her. The nun towered over her. Eden glanced down and noticed the men's shoes under the hem of the black garment. Looking up again, she saw his five o'clock shadow—and the cold stare from his eyes.

Before she could move, he lunged toward her.

Everything went out of focus. The grocery bag fell out of her hands.

He took her in a headlock.

Gasping for air, Eden helplessly tugged and clawed at his arm. He pulled something out of the sleeve of his tunic. Eden only caught a glimpse of it—a piece of cloth in a plastic bag. He held the bag up close to her face. She heard the plastic rustling as he plucked out the rag.

She realized he was wearing some kind of surgical gloves. He slapped the piece of cloth over her nose and mouth. It was wet and smelled of some chemical.

Eden tried to struggle, but she couldn't move her head. She thought he might break her neck. She felt her whole body shutting down. Her arms fell to her sides.

Eden desperately tried to get a look at his face. But the way he held her head, all she could see were the treetops. They seemed to be swirling.

Then it was just blackness.

CHAPTER TWENTY

Saturday, September 12, 11:52 A.M.

"**G**od, it's noisy there," she said into the phone. "Where are you?"

Sitting on the living room sofa in her summer pajamas, Hannah was alone in the bungalow. She'd just called her seventeen-year-old brother, Steve. With the two-hour time difference in Seattle, she'd expected to catch him at home, having breakfast. But when he'd picked up and said, "Hey, Han," she'd heard a lot of racket and other people in the background—like he was at T-Mobile Park or something.

"I'm at Biscuit Bitch—at Pike Place Market," he explained.

"What are you doing there?"

"Eating breakfast," he answered. "I'm having a Cheesy Pork n' Bitch. That's a biscuit with gravy and cheddar and shredded bacon. It's bitchin'."

"My guess is you go there so you have an excuse to say 'bitch' a lot."

"Actually, it's really good. Plus I have a gymnastics meet at two, and they say you're supposed to eat a lot of carbs before a big sporting event."

"I think you're supposed to do that the night before,

but what do I know? Are you there at the restaurant with anybody?"

"Nope."

She wasn't surprised. Her brother was always kind of a loner. "Who's keeping the home fires burning?" she asked. "Where are the 'rents?"

"Gabe has a football game. So Mom and Dad went there to cheer him on."

She wondered why her parents were playing favorites with her twelve-year-old brother. "Well, who's cheering you on?"

"Nobody. They offered, but I get nervous whenever Mom and Dad are in the audience—especially Dad. Every time I'm ready to get up on the side horse, they act like I'm stepping in front of a firing squad. Anyway, I have a new routine, and I don't want to screw it up."

"I wish I were there," Hannah said. "I'd cheer you on."

"That's really sweet of you to say," Steve murmured. "Are you feeling all right? Is this really Hannah? Who are you? What have you done with my sister?"

"Very funny." She laughed despite herself. The truth was she'd had a major attack of homesickness this morning.

"How's Eden? Still driving you crazy?"

"She's been out all night," Hannah sighed. Getting to her feet, she wandered over to the bedroom door. "I haven't seen her since about five-thirty yesterday afternoon. I called and texted her, and of course, no answer."

"Of course," he said, sounding unconcerned. "I guess she's up to her old tricks."

Leaning against the bedroom doorway frame, Hannah stared at Eden's bed. Her half-sister had actually made the bed yesterday morning. It was strange to see it looking so neat and tidy—unslept in. "I was up until four this morning," Hannah said into the phone. "I practically climbed the walls worrying about her."

"You really shouldn't, Han. Eden can take care of herself. You know how she gets. She's probably off on one of her solo adventures. I'll bet she's been out all night exploring Chicago. She'll drag herself in there later today, crash, and take a three-hour nap."

Even though she was on the phone, Hannah nodded.

After last night's tense discussion with Rachel, Hannah had hoped to talk with Eden about it. If nothing else, she could always count on her to be honest. Would Eden think it was so horrible that she'd confided in Ellie Goodwin about their big family secret? Hannah had decided to wait up for her.

She'd passed the time online, looking up articles on the murders that took place on the campus back in 1970, when it was Blessed Heart of Mary College. According to the Wikipedia write-up, the "Immaculate Conception" murders were preceded by two disturbing events that occurred at the college the previous week. The first of those events was when eighteen-year-old Linda Mackevich secretly gave birth in one of the bungalows and then strangled her baby and set it on fire. Hannah looked up what happened to the girl after that: She was committed to an insane asylum and, over the years, was moved from one institution to another. Then in 2009, Linda Mackevich died of cancer at age fifty-seven while confined at Garfield Park Behavioral Hospital in Chicago.

The second disturbing event was the disappearance of a sophomore, Crystal Juneau, only a few days after the infant's murder. Hannah saw her photo: a pretty girl with long, dark hair parted down the middle. As a kid,

Hannah had been a fan of *That Girl* reruns, and Crystal reminded her of a young Marlo Thomas. There was some confusion as to exactly when the girl had been abducted. Two days after Crystal had gone missing, her fraternal twin, Cynthia, also attending Blessed Heart of Mary, found a note on her bed from her sister assuring her that she'd just needed to get away, and she was all right. But that was the last communication from her.

Crystal, in fact, had been abducted by the Immaculate Conception Killer, Lyle Duncan Wheeler. He'd forced Crystal to write that note. He kept her locked up in a shed in his backyard, where he routinely raped and tortured her. In a matter of days, he'd strangled two students and one teacher—before breaking into bungalow eighteen, where he stabbed and strangled two of the girls who lived there.

Ensconced on her bed at three in the morning, Hannah couldn't help looking up from her laptop at the overgrown garden outside her window, where bungalow eighteen had once stood. Suddenly, the murdered girls next door had names and faces. Nineteen-year-old April Hunnicutt was a chubby-faced blonde with a dimpled smile and short, wavy hair. She looked like she'd had a wicked sense of humor. One of the articles Hannah read mentioned that April was a Beatles fan, and the oldest of five kids. Her housemate downstairs, eighteen-year-old Debbie Metzger, had studied ballet and theater. She'd been stabbed twenty-six times. In the bedroom, next to where police found her body, stood a bookshelf filled with plays by Tennessee Williams, Lillian Hellman, William Inge, and others.

It was strange to think that, while these two girls were being murdered and a third narrowly escaped, another girl had been sleeping soundly here in this room, so close to all that horror and carnage.

Small wonder Hannah had had trouble falling asleep after climbing into bed and switching off her light at four this morning.

She woke up shortly after eleven—only to see Eden's bed still vacant and tidy. For a few minutes she heard Rachel talking to someone on the phone in the living room. Hannah still felt weird about their discussion the night before, so she stayed in bed—until she suddenly heard the front door open and shut. She thought it was Eden, finally returning home. Throwing off her sheets, Hannah jumped out of bed and rushed into the living room. But it was empty. Out the front window, she spotted Rachel climbing into the backseat of the Lincoln Town Car. Her driver, Perry, closed her door for her. A minute later, he was in the driver's seat, and off they went.

After everything she'd read last night, Hannah didn't especially like being alone in the bungalow, even in the daytime. She was lonely, too. Her brother had a morbid fascination with old true crime stories, especially serial killings from yesteryear. If he weren't such a sweet guy, she'd be worried about him. She'd figured Steve would be interested in hearing about the Immaculate Conception murders. Plus, maybe he'd heard from Eden last night or this morning. Finally, even though she'd gotten into trouble last night for opening her big mouth, a part of her wanted to tell Steve about their father's other child. Why should she be practically alone in this?

"Hannah? Are you still there?" Steve asked over the din in the background.

With the phone in front of her, she sat down on her

bed and sighed. "Yeah, I was just spacing for a second. Listen, how are Mom and Dad doing?"

"Okay, I guess."

"I mean, are they, like, getting along okay together or do they seem on the brink of divorce? I keep thinking, now that Eden and I are gone, one of them will end up moving into her *sty* down the hall or into my room in the basement."

"No, they're still sleeping together."

Ever since things had gone to hell two years ago, their dad hadn't been the same. After having been laid up in the hospital for weeks, he'd come home looking older and paunchier. Plus he'd been publicly humiliated. He'd become a national joke. Yet, oddly enough, he got a lot of fan mail from women, but they were obviously the same kind of crazies who wrote to serial killers in prison. It used to be that people thought her mother was lucky to be married to such a handsome, charismatic guy. That just wasn't so anymore. Besides, once the truth had come out about all her dad's womanizing, the same people who had thought her mother was lucky now considered her a total saint or a total chump.

Hannah had thought her going off to school would change things, and maybe her mom would finally dump her dad. But then, she hadn't counted on her dad becoming so pathetic and needy. Maybe her mother liked him that way.

She wondered how her mother would react to the news that he'd fathered yet another illegitimate child way-back-when—and with her own sister, no less.

Suddenly, Hannah didn't want anyone in the family to know, at least not right now. As much as she wanted to unload the news on Steve, she couldn't do that to her brother. It was too much. And, hell, it would throw him off his game today. For now, it would have to stay a secret between her and her two half-sisters—and Ellie Goodwin.

"Hey, I haven't told you yet," Hannah said. "But I'm living next door to this garden that looks kind of like a cemetery. But there used to be another dorm bungalow in that spot. And two girls were stabbed and strangled there fifty years ago."

"You're kidding."

"I'm serious as a heart attack. I can't believe Eden didn't say anything to you about it. You can look it up online—the Immaculate Conception murders in 1970, back when this place was Blessed Heart of Mary College. It's all really creepy and sad—and right up your alley. Check it out. You'll be all over it."

Hannah talked with her brother for another ten minutes. She kept hoping Eden would walk in before she hung up with Steve, but no such luck.

Slouched on her unmade bed with her back against the wall and the phone in her hand, she listlessly stared out the window. She thought of the two girls murdered in the house that used to be there—where the statue of St. Ursula now stood amid the chrysanthemums. She thought of the others whose young lives had been cut short by the Immaculate Conception Killer. She imagined them as grandmothers now—and not the rocking-chair, crocheting variety either. They would have been around seventy years old, still active, vital, and hip.

After murdering those two girls in bungalow eighteen—and inadvertently letting one witness escape—Lyle Duncan Wheeler returned to his home in a rural area outside Waukegan. He went to the shed in his backyard and slit the throat of his prisoner, Crystal Juneau.

Biting her lip, Hannah glanced down at her phone. She googled the name again. She wondered how many days had passed between the baby-murder and Crystal's disappearance. After a few minutes, she found the answer. It had been only three days. Crystal Juneau had vanished on September 12, 1970.

Fifty years ago today.

Hannah lowered the phone and gazed at Eden's unslept-in bed.

She shuddered violently.

CHAPTER TWENTY-ONE

Eden had no idea how much time had passed—hours or days—since she'd been attacked in the woods. Lying in the dark on a cot, she kept seeing that man disguised as a nun, his face a blur. He'd lunge at her again, and Eden would recoil. She'd want to cry out, but couldn't. As if struggling to wake from some nightmare, she'd try to sit up.

But she was strapped to the cot—like some kind of mental patient. Duct tape around her wrists tethered her hands to the sides of the cot. A wadded-up rag was stuffed inside her mouth. It had been in there for so long that it tasted like puke.

Her last memories were of those woods, that minivan following her, and Nick What's-His-Name being so phony-friendly to her in the café. Sometimes those images came back to her all distorted—like a reflection in one of those store security mirrors.

She'd been sleeping on and off ever since the woods. During the off-periods, she hallucinated. One moment, she was tied to a steamer trunk in the cargo area of a ship; and the next, she was in a crypt hidden in the garden next door to her bungalow. At times, she was lucid enough to figure out where she was—either

someone's garage or one of those storage lockers people
rented out for junk they didn't know what to do with.
The place was cold and smelled musty—like wet, dirty
concrete. It wasn't completely dark. A bit of light fil-
tered in through a vent up on the wall—just enough for
her to make out that someone had set up a couple of
folding chairs near her cot.

She wasn't completely alone the whole time. A man
had come to talk with her every so often. Each one of
his visits was preceded by a click and a mechanical
humming noise. Then the big door would open from
the ground up. In one of those instances, the daylight
blinded her, and she couldn't see who was coming in;
but most of the time, it was dark and she still couldn't
make out his face. In what must have been one of her
hallucinations, she was almost certain her visitor was a
priest. He sat in one of the folding chairs and started
reading to her. Eden thought he was giving her the
sacrament of Last Rites. She remembered crying and
trying to tell him that she didn't want to die.

She could barely figure out what was happening to
her—let alone why. She only knew she'd never been
so scared in all her life.

Escape seemed impossible. Even if she hadn't been
strapped to the cot, she doubted she could make it
halfway across the room because she was pumped full
of drugs. Her visitor had given her several shots in the
arm. He must not have been too skilled with a hypodermic, because her arm was sore as hell. On two of those
visits, after giving her a shot, he had asked her a bunch
of questions. It was the only time he took the putrid rag
out of her mouth. Plus he gave her some water, so she
almost welcomed the interrogations. He also switched

on his phone for some light—enough for him to find a vein in her arm for the needle. She liked the light. And he was always very friendly. He talked in a soothing voice and assured her she'd be all right. She never saw his face, but she kept thinking of Nick What's-His-Name from the café. He served up that same fake-friendly attitude with all of his questions. And this one with the needle was asking about the same things—the detective that Cassandra, the woman who raised her, had hired; Rachel Bonner; and her father in Seattle.

Eden always answered honestly. She didn't know the detective's name. As far as she knew, he'd been hired ages ago when she was a little kid. He might have worked for Cassandra again. Cassandra had been obsessed with Dylan and the different women he'd been with; and it only made sense that she'd had him investigated again and again. But Eden wasn't sure. Yes, the detective probably gave Cassandra documents, but Eden had no idea where they'd been stored. They hadn't been among any of Cassandra's things after she died. Eden knew she had an older half-sister somewhere out there. Dylan O'Rourke was the father. But Eden had no other details. She'd never heard of Rachel Bonner or her family—not until she got the news that Rachel would be her housemate at Our Lady of the Cove.

Eden didn't care that she was giving away family secrets. The guy gave her a little more water whenever she answered a question. And each time, he thanked her for being so cooperative.

She tried to figure out when he'd come in here last. She was thirsty again, and hungry, too. She'd also wet her pants sometime recently. It was so humiliating and horrible. But Eden told herself that she couldn't start crying. Her nose would fill up with snot, and with this awful rag in her mouth, how would she breathe?

She heard a click. She twitched at the humming sound of the big door lifting. Squinting toward the opening, she saw it was nighttime. She'd noticed some light coming through the vent just a minute ago, and now realized there must be a security light outside near the vent opening.

She realized something else: There were two men now. Were there always two? Was she just too out of it to notice? Or had the man recently recruited someone else?

One of them shone a flashlight at her, and suddenly, she couldn't make out a thing—just the blinding light getting closer and closer.

"I see you're awake, Eden," her interrogator said in his fake-friendly tone.

The big door started to descend. The gloomy room turned darker and darker.

"I'm giving you something that will help you sleep, Eden. This will all be over soon. We're letting you go." There was a pause. "Give me some light . . ."

She realized he was talking to his friend now. The flashlight beam swept over the man hovering near her—onto the hypodermic in his hands. As he guided the needle into her arm, Eden winced at the pain. With the light on her arm, she could see the other puncture marks and the purple bruising.

"I hope you're not giving her too much of that shit," the other man muttered. "I don't want to feel like I'm screwing a corpse in the back of that SUV. If that's the case, we might as well just finish her off here instead of waiting to do it in Wilmot Woods. The whole point to nailing an eighteen-year-old is that she's got some life in her . . ."

"Shut the hell up," the one with the needle grumbled.

The light blinded her again. "Look at her," the other one said. "She's so out of it, the bitch has no idea what we're talking about . . ."

Horrified, Eden shook her head and tried to cry out. She knew exactly what he was talking about. They were keeping her alive long enough so the new guy could get his rocks off. Then they were going to kill her in those woods. They'd probably bury her there, too.

She struggled to stay awake because she knew she'd never wake up again.

"Go make sure the coast is clear," said the man closest to her. Tossing aside the hypodermic needle, he pulled his phone from his jacket pocket and switched it on. With the screen glowing, he placed the phone on the cot—just above her shoulder. "She'll be out soon. Pull the car right up to the door so no one sees us loading her in there. They've got security cameras all over the place."

"Hey, no shit, I know what I'm doing," the other one said. "You forget, I chose this locker because the camera coverage on it sucks. That's why I parked the SUV where I did."

The man's flashlight went off. Eden heard a click and then that mechanical humming as the big door started to ascend again. She saw the new guy silhouetted against the moonlight as he headed outside. She noticed a row of other storage units across the way—and a barbed-wire fence beyond that.

"Close the door until you get back with the car!" called the man at her side.

"I know, I know," grumbled his friend.

The humming noise started again as the door descended.

Eden felt her body shutting down. Her eyelids fluttered as she desperately clung on to consciousness.

The man backed away from her. He collapsed one folding chair and then let it drop to the floor with a bang that echoed in the near empty storage room. He did the same thing with the other chair. "Y'know, I tried to cut you a break," he said. "I told them that you wouldn't remember anything with all the drugs I've given you. I said we could just get you high and dump you near one of those homeless areas downtown, leave it up to chance. Everyone would think you'd partied too much or something—even you. But it was too risky, they said. So it's the woods for you. Crying shame—sweet, young thing like you . . ."

Bending over her, he started to unfasten the strap across her feet.

Eden tried, but couldn't move her legs.

"Where the hell is he?" the man muttered to himself. He straightened up and glanced toward the door. With a sigh, he took out a switchblade and hovered over Eden again.

For a second, she thought he was going to stab her.

But he just cut the duct tape that kept her hands adhered to the sides of the cot.

Outside, she heard brakes screeching, and then a car door slammed. There was that click again, followed by the motorized humming. The door started to ascend.

Eden glimpsed the SUV parked parallel to the door opening—and the other man as he headed toward them.

He switched on the flashlight, momentarily blinding her once more.

"Jesus, what took you so long?" asked the man at her side. He straightened up and turned around.

His friend moved toward him at a brisk clip. The new guy had something in his other hand. He held up a little canister and sprayed something in the other man's face.

Eden got a whiff of it—some kind of Mace or pepper spray. She squeezed her eyes shut. She heard the other man coughing and gagging. Something landed on the floor with a clank. She wasn't sure if it was the canister or the flashlight. One of the men bumped against her cot, jolting her.

She opened her eyes again. The flashlight was still on, rolling back and forth on the floor. In the fractured light, she saw the new guy slash his friend's throat. The blood splattered across Eden's face.

The man clutched his own throat as blood seeped through his fingers. Choking and gagging, he collapsed on the floor—right beside her and the cot.

The other man swiveled around and made a beeline for the SUV. He opened the side door and grabbed something. With a grunt, he hauled it out of the vehicle. The corpse made a thud as it hit the concrete floor. He dragged the body over toward the other one, leaving behind a crimson trail.

Breathing heavily, he leaned over her.

Stunned, Eden gazed up at him, but his face was just a blur. She couldn't move. She was helpless.

"Those assholes almost spoiled everything," he whispered. He made a fist and drew back his hand. "You weren't supposed to disappear until tonight."

He punched her in the face.

CHAPTER TWENTY-TWO

Sunday, September 13, 2:08 P.M.

"I'm sorry I'm late," Ellie said, catching her breath.

"No worries. I just got here a few minutes ago myself. Plus it gave me a chance to read. I just started this, and I love it." Diana showed her a paperback copy of Daphne du Maurier's *Rebecca*.

It was a beautiful, sunny afternoon, and Diana had scored an outside table at Campus Grounds. With her fair skin, she'd moved her chair into the shade. She already had her latte. "That's a cute top," she said, nodding at the multicolored, striped pullover Ellie wore with her khaki slacks. "Go get your coffee. It'll give me time to finish this chapter."

Ellie laughed. "Yes, ma'am! And thanks. You look cute, too." She headed into the coffee house and got in line. There were only a few people ahead of her.

Diana seemed like she was in a good mood. Ellie's young friend had had a date the night before with J.T., the lifeguard at the recreation center, the one who was supposed to have slept with half the campus. Ellie hadn't said anything about it to Diana yet. She wasn't sure how serious Diana was about the guy. It seemed like an odd match—this cocky, handsome lifeguard and a shy, vulnerable girl with body issues. Plus he seemed like a bit of a dim bulb, and Diana read the classics for fun. But Ellie had decided to keep it all to herself. While Diana was out on her date last night, Ellie had been binge-watching season four of *The Gilmore Girls*. So she didn't feel very qualified to dole out love advice today. She figured she would just listen to what Diana had to say about the date.

Last night's TV marathon had taken Ellie's mind off Nicholas Jensen for a while. Despite an extensive search online, she hadn't been able to find anything about him before that massage review in April of this year. It was as if he didn't exist before that. But other than giving the wrong phone number for his emergency contact and showing up in her journalism class when she'd just been exposed to a whole summer's worth of hate mail— Nicholas Jensen hadn't done a damn thing wrong. He wore hair gel and made his living massaging men and women—and apparently very well, according to the glowing reviews. That hardly fit the profile of the racist, homophobic misogynists who were out to get her. So why was she obsessing over him? He barely seemed to know she was alive. He paid plenty of attention to Hannah, but very little to her.

"What can I get you?" asked the skinny barista with her hair in cornrows.

A life, please, Ellie wanted to say. She ordered her coffee and thought about how she needed to pay more attention to her own love life—or lack thereof—instead of focusing on Hannah's or Diana's. These girls were under twenty—with plenty of time and opportunities ahead. But Ellie was lonely, and she felt her biological clock ticking.

She took her coffee outside and sat down with Diana. They didn't waste any time with idle chitchat. They got right into Diana's date the previous evening with J.T. He'd taken her to dinner at the student union of all places, not exactly haute cuisine. Then again, the important thing was that he treated Diana nicely.

"He was sweet," Diana said. "But I think he seemed nicer, more interesting, and funnier than he really was, because he's so good-looking. Could it be I'm really that shallow? And the whole time I was with him, I felt like *What does he see in me?* I mean, he could go out with practically any girl he wanted. I kept noticing other people looking at us, especially girls, and I'm sure they were thinking, *Why is he on a date with that fatty?*"

"Oh, for God's sake," Ellie said, putting down her coffee cup. "Don't even start with me on your body-weight issues again. Not every woman needs to look like Kate Moss. He obviously finds you attractive, or he wouldn't have asked you out. What did you do after dinner?"

"We walked to town and saw a movie, the new Keira Knightley."

"Did he pay?"

"I offered to pay, since he picked up the bill for dinner. And he let me. He put his arm around me during the movie . . ."

Ellie nodded. She felt very protective of Diana. Ellie still wasn't sure if she should tell Diana about J.T.'s reputation. She remembered how, on Friday afternoon at the pool, he'd secretly taken a photo of Hannah in her swimsuit. It had struck Ellie as odd—in fact, more than odd, downright creepy.

"After the movie, then what?" she asked.

"He asked if I wanted to go to the rec center, which was closed by then. But he said he had keys to get in, and it was kind of cool at night when nobody else was around."

"Here we go," Ellie said cynically. She shifted around in the café chair.

"Anyway, we went there, and I was a little nervous. He wanted to show me the pool—"

Ellie heard her phone ring inside her purse. "Damn it, sorry," she muttered, reaching into her bag, which hung by its strap over the back of her chair. She glanced at the screen: *847-555-7117, Admin—Our Lady of the Cove.*

Ellie wondered what someone in the college's administration office wanted with her on a Sunday afternoon. "I should take this. I'm sorry, Di." With a sigh, she pressed on the phone screen and answered: "Hello?"

"Ellie, this is Father O'Hurley . . ."

"Hello, Father O'Hurley," she said, making a surprise-face at Diana across the café table. It wasn't just someone in the administration office calling; it was the vice president, who pretty much ran the university. The president, Monsignor Clark, was eighty-seven years old and had been nothing more than a figurehead for years. The last time Father O'Hurley had even acknowledged Ellie had been four months ago, toward the end of the school year, when he'd seen her on campus on a Monday afternoon and good-naturedly chided her for not attending Sunday mass. Ellie remembered, despite his smile, he'd had a certain edge that told her he'd been dead serious about the whole thing.

"Um, how are you today, Father?" she asked.

"I'm fine. Did I catch you at home?"

"Actually, I'm having coffee with a friend at Campus Grounds."

"Oh, then you're practically right next door. I'd like to meet with you in my office at Logan Hall this afternoon."

"What time this afternoon?"

"Well, you're about five minutes away. So let's say in fifteen minutes. My office is two-oh-one."

Ellie was momentarily dumbfounded. He expected her to just drop everything, dump her friend, and run to meet him. "Can I ask what this is about, Father?"

"We'll discuss that when you get here, Ellie. See you in fifteen minutes."

He hung up.

Father O'Hurley's secretary was a skinny, wry-faced old woman. She reminded Ellie of Ellen Corby, who played Grandma Walton in *The Waltons* reruns Ellie had watched as a kid—Grandma Walton minus the warmth and sweetness. When Ellie had walked into the anteroom and told her who she was, the secretary scowled at her—almost as if she blamed Ellie for her having to work on a Sunday. "Take a seat. Father O'Hurley will get to you soon enough."

Except for the church, Logan Hall was the oldest building on the campus. It housed the administration offices. A former mansion, it had a seedy grandeur and seemed like the type of place that was haunted. Despite the sunshine outside, the waiting room seemed gloomy. Ellie sat on a sofa, and on the coffee table in front of her were old copies of *Catholic Digest* fanned out.

The secretary's idea of O'Hurley getting to her "soon

enough" was twenty minutes—and counting. Ellie could have driven home and changed clothes had she known she'd have to wait this long. In her casual pullover and slacks, she felt underdressed for meeting with the head of the school. She'd also rushed Diana through the rest of her date story in order to make it here on time.

It sounded like J.T. had lived up to his reputation last night. He'd taken Diana to the pool and suggested they go for a swim. He'd told her that he sometimes swam there at night—naked, since no one else was around and the lights were off. But he'd told her that she could swim in her underwear if she wanted. Fortunately, Diana had been too smart to fall for that. No one had gotten into the water, and their clothes had stayed on. But they'd kissed and necked on the sideline bench by the pool. J.T. had felt her up, too. But when he tried to get his hand under her sweater, Diana had called it a night. At least he'd been a good sport about it. He'd walked her back to the dorm, kissed her good night, and said he wanted to see her again. Diana had said sure, but in truth, she had mixed feelings about it.

Ellie had promised to call her tomorrow so they could talk about it some more. Then she'd hurried to Logan Hall for this mysterious meeting. That was—she glanced at her watch again—twenty-seven minutes ago.

Grandma Walton's intercom buzzed. She picked up her phone and murmured into it. Then she hung up, cleared her throat, and announced: "Father O'Hurley will see you now."

Throwing Ellie another resentful look, she came around her desk and opened the big mahogany door for her.

"Thank you," Ellie said, stepping inside.

The door shut behind her.

O'Hurley's office was huge—especially compared to Ellie's little cubbyhole of a workspace. It had a slightly cluttered, fussy opulence: oversized antique furniture was arranged around the fireplace, a bookcase was filled with beautiful china, vases, and ornate gold and silver plates, and framed oil paintings hung on the walls.

O'Hurley was at his big mahogany desk in front of a picture window. It had a beautiful view of the treetops and Lake Michigan. O'Hurley stood up. "Sorry to keep you waiting, Ellie," he said. He motioned to the two hard-back antique chairs facing his desk. "Have a seat."

He was in his mid-fifties, about six feet tall, and quite commanding in his priest's garb. He had wavy gray-brown hair and might have been handsome if his complexion weren't so pasty. He also had a strange, pinched look on his face. His mouth was smiling, but the eyes were joyless, without any sparkle.

Ellie sat in a chair, which was uncomfortable as hell. On the wall to Ellie's right hung a painting of a pious-looking woman, a halo encircling her head of long, brownish hair. Unlike the pretty, virginal martyrs commemorated in various statues on the school grounds, the saint in this head-and-shoulders portrait looked dour and middle-aged. A small light shone down on the elaborately framed piece.

"That is a painting of Saint Anne that my mother posed for," O'Hurley explained. "I'm glad you noticed. Isn't she beautiful?"

"She's lovely," Ellie lied. She noticed a sparkle come to O'Hurley's eyes when he looked over toward the painting of his sour-faced mother.

But then he turned toward Ellie, and that gleam vanished—along with his smile. "Well, we have a problem," he said, sitting down. He folded his hands on the desktop, which was cluttered with antique knickknacks—including an ornate crucifix in one corner. "It's been brought to my attention that you've become very close to one of your journalism students— I'd say in record time, too, since she's a freshman and the school year has barely begun." He glanced down at some notes he'd jotted on a yellow legal pad. "The girl is Hannah O'Rourke, and she's here—along with her sister—on a scholarship arranged by Mr. and Mrs. Richard Bonner. But then, you already know that, don't you?"

Ellie couldn't help narrowing her eyes at him. "Yes, it came up in a conversation with Hannah after class the other day."

"I understand, in another conversation—this time at the fitness center pool during a swimming date—you managed to extract some far more sensitive information from the girl."

Ellie shifted around in the uncomfortable chair. "I didn't *extract* anything. And I wasn't on a *swimming date* with Hannah. I happened to be passing by the rec center on Friday. I saw her by the pool, and she waved me inside. And by the way, those are the only times I've ever talked with Hannah O'Rourke outside of class."

Ellie wondered where Father O'Hurley had heard all of this. Did he have someone spying on her? She immediately thought of Nicholas Jensen, who had been hovering close by during both of those conversations with Hannah. Or maybe it was J.T. Perhaps that was why he'd taken their picture at the pool on Friday. She also remembered how Lance, the custodian, had been lurking around Lombard Hall on Friday.

"I'm sorry, Father. I don't understand what all this is about."

He frowned at her. "This is about the fact that you're a reporter. And you gained the trust of a naive girl so you could gather confidential information from her for a potentially big news story."

Gaping at him, Ellie shook her head. "Whoever's telling you this has it all twisted around—"

"Please, don't interrupt me," he said. "This is an extremely sensitive and private issue that Mr. and Mrs. Bonner don't wish to see made public. Rachel's parents are among the leading financial contributors to Our Lady of the Cove. We depend on their generosity to help keep this university running. We have an excellent relationship with the Bonners. And I won't see it ruined by some opportunistic reporter who happens to be a part-time teacher here."

"Are you finished now?" Ellie asked with an edge to her voice. "Because I'd like to say something. First, I think I know what *sensitive information* you're referring to . . ." It was obvious he was talking about Rachel's real parentage. "Hannah told me about it in confidence. I didn't coerce it or extract it from her. She volunteered the information. And I promised her that I wouldn't tell anyone or discuss it with anyone. So—I'm not going to discuss it with you, Father. But I'll say this much. I have no intention of writing some big exposé on the subject. I never did. And I really resent your implications."

"And I resented getting a very angry phone call at the rectory last night from Mr. and Mrs. Bonner. They were quite upset, and I don't blame them—especially after everything they've done for this school and the archdiocese."

Ellie didn't shrink under his intimidating gaze. At least now she realized where he'd gotten all this biased information: Hannah had told Rachel, and Rachel had told her parents.

Ellie took a deep breath and then let it out. "Well, you can call back the Bonners and tell them they have nothing to worry about with me. I have no desire to stir up a scandal. I don't intend to embarrass them or their daughter or anyone in the O'Rourke family. I promised Hannah that I wouldn't say anything, and I meant it."

"I hope that's true," he said, still glaring at her as if she'd done something wrong. He'd probably expected her to cower and apologize all over the place. It was obvious he didn't like being talked back to. He cleared his throat. "In the meantime, I'd like you to stop spending so much time with Hannah O'Rourke. This kind of close friendship between a teacher—an older, single woman—and her young, naive student is very disconcerting."

Ellie almost laughed at the innuendo—and this, coming from a man who kept a shrine to his mother in his office. But Ellie shifted in the chair again and squinted at him. "What exactly are you insinuating, Father?"

"I'm not making any insinuations," he said. "I'm telling you to stop seeing this girl outside of class."

"Well, she's my student. I can't very well prevent her from coming to see me on her own."

"I can," he said firmly. "We have at least a dozen applications on file from journalists who would like to teach here, all of them very qualified." The bland, joyless smile returned to his face. "Of course, we'd hate to lose you. I really don't want it to come to that. You understand, don't you?"

"I'm afraid I do," Ellie replied. "I'll tell you what, Father. Outside of class, I'll do my best to avoid Hannah O'Rourke. Will that make you and the Bonners happy?"

He seemed to consider it for a moment, and then he slowly nodded his head.

"Is there anything else, Father?" she asked, getting to her feet.

O'Hurley stood up, too. "Thank you for coming in on such short notice."

Ellie headed for the door and opened it.

"Oh, and Ellie," he called. "It would be nice to see you at mass on Sundays. It sets such a good example for your students."

She stared at him. "Good afternoon, Father," she said.

Then she got the hell out of there.

CHAPTER TWENTY-THREE

I wanted 2 C Chicago n took d train there. Already made some
new friends. Staying w/them. Don't worry bout me. Having
fun. Screw school. C U in a few days.

He pressed the send icon. He figured this would keep
Hannah and her parents from calling the cops for a
while longer. Without the police involved, he could hold
on to Eden's phone. No one would be trying to track
down its whereabouts yet. He liked getting those distressed, angry texts and voice mails from Hannah. There
was something titillating about it—almost as pleasura-
ble as watching Hannah on the nanny-cam, alone in her
room at night. He'd seen her naked a few times now, and
he often reran that footage again and again. Like most
surveillance videos, it was murky and grainy. But it was
still a turn-on just seeing her undressed and so unaware
of his spying eyes.

He stood at the end of his driveway by the large rural
mailbox. The illuminated screen of Eden's phone lit up
his smiling face.

Stars filled the night sky, and everything was so still.
This close to autumn, even the crickets were quiet. He

couldn't hear anything—no city sounds, no traffic noise, no dogs barking.

No one screaming for help.

He ambled down the driveway, toward the house. From the outside, the dilapidated, two-story farmhouse looked unoccupied. Even with the lights on, as they were now, it appeared as if someone had left them on in the long-deserted house to discourage squatters and break-ins—not that there were many homeless people out here in the middle of nowhere.

Though it was a clear night, he kept the phone light on to navigate around the potholes in the driveway. He had found the phone in Eden's purse, which her abductors had stashed in the back of the SUV—along with two shovels and a saw. Obviously, once they'd gotten whatever they wanted from Eden, her two captors had planned to make sure no one would ever find her.

He'd been following Hannah's half-sister most of Friday night before realizing he had company. He'd been hoping Eden would stay out past midnight because it was imperative he take her on the twelfth. That was the fiftieth anniversary of Crystal Juneau's disappearance. He'd already loaded up the minivan with a policeman's nightstick, pepper spray, duct tape, and a blanket to cover her up in the back of the van.

But all his plans had seemed spoiled by the ominous presence of the gray SUV. It was almost as if they had the same plan he did. He'd been watching Eden for several nights now. She'd used that shortcut through the woods to town and back. It had seemed like the ideal spot to abduct her—close to where the trail ended, so he'd have the minivan parked nearby. The guys in the SUV were waiting for her in that same location. He had to hand it to them for their theatricality. They were dressed as nuns. He'd watched them load Eden into the SUV, and then he followed them to the self-storage lot in North Waukegan. He'd been worried they might catch on that someone was on their tail. But apparently, the SOBs were pretty cocky about how clever they were.

He was pretty clever himself. On Saturday morning, he'd rented a locker in the same lot so he'd have a code to come and go as he pleased. He never went far. He watched them for most of the day, sometimes from his minivan with a pair of binoculars and sometimes from a better angle in the woods on the other side of the tall barbed-wire fence. Late Saturday night, he made his move.

He'd figured it might be tough going, since the guys were pros. But he'd caught them by surprise. The biggest challenge had been making sure he killed them out of range of the cameras stationed around the self-storage lot.

After loading Eden into their SUV, he'd gone back and taken their wallets. Then he locked up the storage unit. Unless they had a third partner, it could be weeks before anyone found their bodies in there.

He'd left his minivan parked two blocks away from the lot on a residential street with dumpy-looking houses. The van was a piece of shit, and it was a safe bet no one would want it.

At just past midnight, almost twenty-four hours ago, he'd driven Eden in the SUV back here—to her new lodgings in his backyard.

He planned on getting rid of the SUV tomorrow, maybe park it somewhere with the keys inside. He'd take it to some sketchy neighborhood in North Chicago. The SUV would probably get stolen or stripped before he even finished Ubering back to where he'd left his minivan near the storage lot.

On Google, he didn't find anything about the dead guys. Obviously the IDs were fake, and the names aliases. No surprise there. The guys were criminals. The funny thing was, if they were kidnappers, they'd picked the wrong girl from bungalow twenty to abduct. The Bonners were the ones with all the money.

He had a theory about why Eden O'Rourke had been taken—and what they wanted from her. He'd have to ask her what had happened during those twenty-six hours she'd been held prisoner inside that storage unit. They might have talked freely in front of her, since they'd planned on killing her and burying the body.

But he really wasn't in a position to chat with Eden right now. Sonny Boy had strict orders not to fraternize with the prisoner.

He walked around the side of the house through the overgrown weeds. In the backyard, he stopped to pick a few burrs off his socks. The old tire swing was perfectly still as it hung from the big tree limb.

He didn't hear a sound from the shed.

As he moved closer to the shed, he put away Eden's phone and took out his own. He turned on Elton John's "The Bitch Is Back." He cranked it up. He found a small stone on the ground and hurled it at the shed. It ricocheted off the wood siding.

He switched off the music.

That was when he finally heard her.

But even as he stood a mere ten feet away from the shed, the screams inside were still muffled. She banged on the door. "Is anyone there?" she cried. "Can you hear me? Please, help me!"

On his phone, he switched over to what was being monitored inside the shed. With the camera bracketed so close to the ceiling, he felt as if he were God looking down at her. The lighting was bad, and the image was fuzzy, but it was thrilling just the same. He couldn't help feeling powerful. She was so vulnerable, totally at his mercy. She kept pounding on the door and kicking it.

She didn't have a lot of room to move around in there—less room than the dog had had last week. This time, his captive bitch had a cot, a desk and chair, and a deep pan with a lid that doubled as a chamber pot in the corner. He'd stocked the place with plenty of bottled water, juice boxes, granola bars, and other snacks. He even got her a toothbrush, toothpaste, and some moist toilet packs. And as Lyle had done for Crystal fifty years before, he'd provided her with a Bible, too.

Eden continued to scream out in agony. The microphone inside the shed was picking it up—making for a slight delay as the screams came over his phone. She kept beating at the door. But she looked like she was getting tired.

"Nobody can hear you, Eden," he finally called to her.

"Who's there?" she cried. "Goddamn it, where am I?"

"Far away from ears other than my own," he said, proud of how poetic he sounded. "So you can make all the noise you want. I don't mind. It's easy to tune you out."

On the phone screen, he watched her back away from the door. She plopped down in the chair. He could hear her muffled sobbing on his phone.

"Eden?" he called. "Wish me luck tomorrow, okay?"

On the screen, she looked up at the camera. She was a smart one. She seemed to know he was watching her. "Wish you luck?" she said to the camera. "What the hell for?"

"I'm killing the first one tomorrow night," he said.

Then he switched off the phone and started toward the house.

CHAPTER TWENTY-FOUR

Monday, September 14, 2:00 P.M.

Hannah hurried into the classroom with the last wave of students. She stopped by Ellie's desk. "Could I talk with you after class?" she whispered, a fretful look on her face.

"Sure," Ellie murmured, nodding briskly.

Ellie thought about the chewing out she'd gotten yesterday from Father O'Hurley. He'd warned her to stop seeing Hannah outside of class. *Okay, so we'll talk in the classroom*, Ellie figured.

Hannah probably wanted to talk to her about Rachel again. Or maybe it had something to do with the fact that Hannah's other half-sister, Eden, hadn't shown up to class today.

All during the session, Ellie kept glancing over at Eden's empty chair. From what she could tell, Eden seemed like the type who wouldn't give a second thought to skipping a class.

Now and then, Ellie glanced at Nick Jensen in the back row. Sometimes, their eyes met, and it made her nervous. He really was handsome, as a few of his massage clients had pointed out in their reviews. Was that why she couldn't trust him, because on some level, she was attracted to him?

At the end of class, Ellie noticed Nick joining the bottleneck of students headed for the classroom door.

Hannah came up to the front of the room, where Ellie sat on the edge of her desk. Ellie felt a strange knee-jerk reaction to this little conference—a barrier automatically going up because the two of them weren't supposed to be socializing. She managed to smile at Hannah. "How was your weekend?"

"Okay, I guess," Hannah said. "Listen, I just wanted to double-check that you won't tell anyone what we talked about on Friday." Her voice dropped to a whisper. "Y'know, about Rachel and me being half-sisters?"

Ellie glanced over toward the classroom door and spotted Nick Jensen lingering in the hallway. Hopping off the edge of the desk, she marched to the door. "Did you need anything, Nick?" she asked pointedly. "Are you waiting to see me or Hannah about something?"

Smiling, he backed away. "I—I just wanted to ask you if I need to use footnotes for that article due on Wednesday."

She frowned. "Get yourself a copy of the *Tribune* and see how often reporters use footnotes in their articles. Then you figure out if you should use them in your article. Does that help you? Does that answer your question?"

"Yes, thanks," he said with a dazed laugh, obviously at her officious tone. He backed away a few more steps. Then he turned and continued down the corridor.

Ellie stepped back into the classroom and closed the door behind her.

Hannah looked amused. "You really don't like him, do you?"

Ellie shook her head. "I don't trust him. Haven't you noticed? Every time you and I talk, he's hovering nearby." She sighed. "Anyway, regarding your situation with Rachel, my lips are sealed. I don't intend to tell anyone about it. Did you mention to Rachel that I know?"

Hannah nodded. "She wasn't too happy about it."

"Neither were her parents. I gather Rachel said something to them, because they called the vice president of the university, and he called me in yesterday for a little chat."

Hannah grimaced. "Oh my God, did I get you in trouble?"

Ellie stole a look toward the window in the classroom door. She didn't see anyone in the hallway. She turned to Hannah again. "Don't worry about it. I'm a big girl."

She wanted to say something to Hannah about making other friends or finding someone else she could make her confidant. As out of line as Father O'Hurley had been yesterday regarding their *disconcerting* teacher-student relationship, he had a point. She was Hannah's teacher, not her BFF.

She took a deep breath. "Listen, Hannah, maybe you should talk to Eden more about this, and get her perspective . . ."

"She's gone." Hannah heaved a sigh. "Didn't you notice?"

"Yes, I noticed. I just figured she'd skipped class. What do you mean *gone*?"

"She went out Friday night and never came back." Hannah shrugged, but still had a distressed look on her face. "She's done this before—disappeared for days at a time. She switches off her phone and won't answer any calls or texts. It drives my parents crazy. Anyway, I figured she'd show up last night—in time to get some sleep before classes today. Then around midnight I got this weird text."

"*Weird* in what way?" Ellie asked.

"She told me she'd taken the train to Chicago. She said she'd already made some friends there, and she was staying with them. She also said, *screw school*, and told me not to worry about her."

"Well, I guess that explains it," Ellie said.

"I know it sounds crazy, but it didn't seem like Eden."

"Hannah, I don't know your sister very well, but it—it sounds like her to me."

"I keep thinking she didn't send that text. I mean, she's texted me a lot, and I know her style. She never uses 'D' for the word 'the.' That was just one thing that was off. She also told me not to worry about her. Eden doesn't think that way. The woman who raised her, I don't think she gave a shit if Eden disappeared for hours or days at a time. So it always seemed to surprise Eden that my parents worried about her when she went off on her little adventures. My point is, it would never dawn on Eden that I'd be worried about her. So why would she say that in her text?"

"Have you talked to your parents about this?" Ellie asked.

"I talked to my brother on Saturday morning. He wasn't really concerned. Like I say, it's happened before with Eden. It's just this text last night . . ."

"You think something might have happened to Eden, and someone else sent this text?" Ellie asked.

Hannah nodded. "You'll think this is crazy, too. But

after we talked on Friday, I went online and read about those murders here on campus fifty years ago. That fire in the laundry room the other night, it happened exactly fifty years after the girl killed her baby and set it on fire, right? Well, this other girl—her name was Crystal Juneau—she was abducted just three days after the baby-killing incident, September twelfth. I keep thinking, Eden might have been out on her own Friday night—past midnight. Saturday was the twelfth. Maybe someone abducted her on Saturday, maybe the same person who started that fire Wednesday night . . ."

With a hand over her heart, Ellie stared at Hannah. "You think someone is copying the timetable of the Immaculate Conception Killer?" she whispered.

Hannah sighed. "Like I said, I know it sounds crazy."

Not really, Ellie thought. As a reporter, she'd encountered crazier things. But she didn't want to encourage Hannah to think along those lines. The poor girl already seemed worried enough.

Ellie reached over to stroke her arm, but then she thought of O'Hurley again and his assessment of their relationship. She touched Hannah's arm for just a second before pulling away. "Listen, Hannah, I'm sure it's nothing. But why don't you text Eden back or call her? Tell her that you need to hear from her. Tell her that if you don't hear from her, you'll have to call the police. In the meantime, it wouldn't hurt to talk to your parents about this."

She nodded. "You're right. Thanks."

"And Hannah, by the way, could you do me a favor?" Ellie couldn't believe she was going to ask this of her. But she went ahead: "Could you not say anything to Rachel about our talk here? She—well, her parents have the wrong idea about me. Because I'm a reporter, they'd just as soon you weren't confiding in me about anything—especially delicate family matters."

"I understand," Hannah said.

"Thanks," Ellie said. "Keep me posted about your sister, okay?"

Hannah nodded. Then she suddenly hugged her.

Ellie felt her body become rigid. Her arms stayed at her sides. She hated that the talk with O'Hurley had made her so cautious and self-conscious—over nothing.

But Hannah didn't seem to notice. "Thanks, Ellie," she said. Then she hurried out of the classroom.

CHAPTER TWENTY-FIVE

Monday, 9:33 P.M.

"**W**ell, I know the text might not sound like her, honey," Hannah's mother said over the phone. "But with Eden, you think you know her, you expect her to behave a certain way, and then she pulls the rug out from under you and does something else entirely."

"There's no predicting her," Hannah's father chimed in.

Her parents had been washing the dinner dishes when Hannah had called. She'd started talking to her mother, but once Hannah had mentioned Eden was missing, they'd turned it into a conference call on the other end. She pictured her mom and dad sitting together at the breakfast table with the phone between them. They were deeply concerned. The only other time Eden had been AWOL this long had been her spontaneous trip to Oregon last year, when, for three days, nobody had known where she'd gone. Her parents seemed to take the text as a positive sign. Eden was finally showing a little consideration.

Hannah sat at the mid-century modern bar that separated the kitchen area from the living room. Rachel was upstairs in her room, listening to Frank Sinatra and studying. Hannah had decided not to tell her parents her theory that Eden might have been abducted by someone copying the Immaculate Conception Killer's actions fifty years ago. It suddenly seemed like a pretty far-fetched notion. She figured, if her mom and dad didn't totally freak out about it, they'd think she was completely nuts. Neither reaction would be helpful right now.

"Did anything happen prior to Eden going out on Friday night?" her mother asked.

"I wasn't here when she left. I was at a sorority thing. Rachel was out with her friend. So Eden was here by herself."

"Had you two been fighting or anything?" her dad asked. "I mean, any more than usual?"

"Honey, no one's blaming you," her mother chimed in. "But this whole thing about you asking Eden to move out, do you think it might have had anything to do with her going off on her own? I know she's never needed an excuse to disappear before, but maybe this time, there's a reason."

Since arriving at Our Lady of the Cove, Hannah had talked to her parents twice and texted them several times. They'd also been following her on social media. She'd been dying to post something on Instagram about the fire on Wednesday night, but Eden had talked her out of it. Eden had pointed out that if their parents knew about the fire, they'd only end up panicking that a pyromaniac was loose on the campus. She was probably right, as much as Hannah hated to admit it. She and Eden had also agreed to keep mum about Rachel's role in getting them their scholarships. Hannah figured if she said anything to her parents about it, she'd have to explain how they were all related to Rachel. And no one was ready for that.

"Hannah?" her mother said. "Are you there?"

"Yeah, I was just thinking. I know I talked to Eden about moving out. But I'm pretty sure that isn't why she took off. In fact, just the other day, I told Eden that I wanted her to stay."

"Well, that's good news," her mother said, sounding surprised.

"It's one for *Ripley's*," her father added. "So you two are getting along better? That's great, honey. How about this Rachel? I know you like her. How are she and Eden getting along?"

"They get along okay." *Like sisters*, Hannah thought.

"So, it's been three days," her mother sighed. "It's concerning. If it were anyone else but Eden, I'd be really alarmed—"

"She's over eighteen," Hannah's father said. "That's the first thing the police will tell us if we try to report this. And then there's the text. If she said she wanted to explore Chicago for the weekend, well, that sounds like Eden to me. I don't like her missing a whole day of classes. But then, I guess that's pretty damn typical . . ."

"It certainly won't be the first time," her mother remarked. "But three days and nights? And who are these strangers who took her in? I swear, that girl's going to give me an ulcer."

"Han, you said you texted her earlier tonight?" her father asked.

"Yes. I told her that, for all I know, someone could've stolen her phone. I mean, the password couldn't be any easier. It's her birthday—oh-seven-oh-one. I caught her punching in the numbers about a month ago. Seriously, all anyone has to do is look at her driver's license and give it a try. Anyway, I told her that I needed to hear from her in person or I'd call the police."

"Well, we'll try calling her, too," her father said. "Let us know if you hear from her. And we'll keep in touch. If we haven't heard back from her by tomorrow night, I'll contact the police there in Delmar—or maybe Chicago. We'll take the next step—whatever that may be. In the meantime, honey, don't worry about it. This is classic Eden behavior. She'll probably show up on your doorstep tomorrow morning, wondering what all the fuss was about."

"You're right," Hannah murmured, frowning.

"So, what else is going on there, honey?" her mother asked.

"Besides Eden driving me crazy? Nothing much."

"No, something else is bothering you, I can tell," her mother said. "Is everything okay with you and Rachel? She was all you could talk about for the first few days. But since the middle of last week, you haven't so much as mentioned her in any of your texts or your posts. Did you two have a falling out? Did something happen?"

Her mouth open, Hannah gaped at the phone in her grasp. Was her mother psychic or something? She straightened up on the barstool and cleared her throat. "No, everything's fine."

"Are you sure?"

Hannah hesitated. Her mom must have read something into her silence.

"Oh God, it's something bad, isn't it?" her mother said finally. "It's even worse than Eden disappearing, because you're afraid to tell us."

Hannah said nothing. In high school, she used to think her parents were utterly clueless. And here they were, thousands of miles away, picking up vibes from the sound of her voice in a phone conversation.

"Is it the reason Eden took off?" her mom asked. "Why she ran away?"

"You just said, like, five minutes ago that Eden never needed a reason to disappear," Hannah pointed out. "I'm practically positive this thing has nothing to do with her taking off like she did."

"Wait a minute," her father cut in. "What are you talking about, honey? What exactly is *this thing*? What happened?"

"I knew it," her mother was saying—while her dad was talking.

Hannah suddenly felt sick to her stomach.

"What don't you want to tell us?" her dad asked. "Listen, it's bad enough your sister has vanished and we don't know where she is. Don't leave us hanging about this other thing."

"I can't talk about it," Hannah said, wincing.

"Does it have anything to do with drugs?" her father pressed.

"No."

"Thank God," he said.

"Well, are you or Eden in some kind of trouble?" her mother asked. "Did something happen with a guy?"

"No, Mom—"

"Are you going to make us keep guessing?" her father asked impatiently. "For God's sake, Hannah, what is it? Does it have anything to do with school? Are they taking away your scholarship or something?"

"The scholarship," Hannah repeated and then gave a sad, little laugh. "Do you know who got us the scholarship? Rachel did. The Slate-Gannon Group is her father's company. Rachel set up the whole thing so she could meet Eden and me."

"Because we were in the news?" her father asked.

"No, not because we were in the news. It's because of you, Dad."

"What are you talking about?" Hannah's mother asked.

"Mr. and Mrs. Bonner adopted Rachel. They got her when she was an infant. Her real mother was a college student in Eugene. Rachel just found out about it last year. We're all related. The college student was Aunt Molly. Rachel showed me the original birth certificate. Her mother was Aunt Molly, and it showed the father was you, Dad."

"Oh Jesus," her father whispered.

Hannah didn't wait to hear her mother's reaction. She decided to get it all out there. "Rachel told us on Wednesday. The three of us are half-sisters. And Rachel's your niece, Mom. Anyway, I don't think that's why Eden took off the way she did. In fact, she's been handling this whole thing better than me. She said the woman who raised her, Cassandra, had hired some detective to investigate you, Dad. He found out there was another illegitimate child out there. Eden didn't have any of the details, but she's known about this other kid. She didn't find out who it was until Rachel told us last week."

There was silence on the other end.

"I shouldn't be surprised," Hannah's mother finally muttered.

"Listen, I'm sorry," her dad said. "But in the last two years, ever since we were in the news, how many fake *illegitimate children* have I had? How many forged birth certificates have we seen?"

"Dad, Rachel's parents are filthy rich and very influential. They'd like to keep a lid on the whole thing. They'd have absolutely nothing to gain—"

"Yes, but someone else might. I'm not trying to weasel out of anything here. Everyone knows what happened with Molly and me. Hell, some of the news stories even got their digs in, implying there was an affair. But I'm pretty certain Molly would have told me if she'd had my baby. She couldn't have kept that to herself for nine months."

"Goddamn it!" Hannah heard her mother cry. There was a bang, like she'd slammed a door or knocked something over. Hannah flinched.

"Is Mom okay?" she asked shakily.

"No, I'm afraid not," her dad answered. "She's gone upstairs. Listen, when was Rachel born? What's her birthday?"

"From what I remember reading, she's twenty, and I think her birthday is around—"

"December third."

Hannah turned and saw Rachel standing at the foot of the stairs. She was wearing a T-shirt and sweatpants.

Hannah took a hard swallow. "December third," she said into the phone.

"I'm sorry," her dad said. "I know it sounds callous. But I'm going to insist she take a paternity test. I'm sure the Bonners are honest people. But for all we know, someone could be providing them with bad information, fake documents. I'll get my doctor to FedEx Rachel a DNA kit. Once we get the test results back, we'll figure out what to do from there."

"Okay," Hannah whispered. Tears in her eyes, she glanced back at Rachel. She looked as if she were about to start crying, too.

"I better go talk to your mom," he said soberly. "Honey, I'm so sorry you've had to go through this. And

I'm sorry this kind of crap keeps coming up because of the way I was. I—I've changed. I hope you know that."

"I know," she murmured.

"We'll talk with you tomorrow. And call us the minute you hear from Eden, okay?"

"Okay. G'night, Dad."

"G'night, sweetie," he said. Then he hung up.

Hannah clicked off the line. She turned toward Rachel again. She figured Rachel would be angry that she'd told her parents the big secret. "I'm really sorry," Hannah said. "I didn't want to tell them. They just knew something was wrong . . ."

"I could hear him—our father—on the other end of the line," Rachel said, coming to lean on the bar. She took a cocktail napkin from the end of the counter and wiped her eyes. "If one more O'Rourke says they're sorry, I'll scream. It's not your fault, Hannah. Shit, it's nobody's fault. But he's my birth father. He knew I was here. And he didn't even want to talk to me. Neither did my aunt."

"I'm—" Hannah stifled the apology. "Ever since we became infamous, my parents have had all these phony claims from people saying they're my dad's long-lost illegitimate kids. I have no idea why. It's not like we have any money. I guess people are just crazy. Did you hear what he said about a paternity test?"

Rachel nodded. "I guess I can't blame him. Ever since I told my parents that you guys know, they've been acting totally psycho. I shouldn't have jumped on your case the other night for talking to Ellie Goodwin. You had to confide in someone."

Walking around to the other side of the bar, she bent down and pulled out a Seagram's bottle. She set it on the bar counter. "I feel like getting drunk, sis. Do you feel like getting drunk?"

Wiping her eyes, Hannah took a deep breath. "Hell, yes," she said.

Rachel set two crystal Old-fashioned glasses on the bar and started pouring. "When he calls tomorrow," she said, "tell our father that I'll take his stupid paternity test."

CHAPTER TWENTY-SIX

Monday, 10:16 P.M.

Diana Mackie shoved her books and her laptop into her Art Institute of Chicago tote bag with Georges Seurat's *A Sunday Afternoon on the Island of La Grande Jatte* depicted on it. The college's library was practically empty tonight, but then it was only the beginning of the school year. By mid-terms, the joint would be jumping. Diana was there because her roommate, Tara, had the TV on all the time, even when she was studying or falling asleep. So, for Diana, it was either study at the library or flunk all her classes.

She noticed a few crumbs in the Nestlé Crunch wrapper on the desk in her cubicle. Though she desperately wanted to lose weight, Diana also felt the need to reward herself for getting her homework done, and Nestlé Crunch was her guilty pleasure of choice. She licked her index finger, picked up the chocolate crumbs with her moist fingertip, and then savored the last remnants of her "study snack."

Stashing the candy wrapper in the tote, Diana grabbed her cardigan and left the cubicle. As she headed down the stairs to the first floor, she thought about J.T., who hadn't called or texted since their date on Saturday.

Was he waiting another day so he could do that three-day-waiting thing some guys did before calling again after the first date? Or was it supposed to be a three-day-wait before asking a girl out once meeting her? Whatever, she hadn't heard a peep from him. Maybe she should have gone swimming naked with him—though she wasn't ready to show him her body. Maybe she should have let him put his hand under her sweater. *Shoulda, woulda, coulda.*

Ellie had texted earlier today, apologizing for cutting short yesterday's coffee date. They planned to meet again on Wednesday—for dinner and another post-date analysis. It would be more like a post-date postmortem by then. What did it say about her that she cared more about the date analysis with Ellie than a second date with J.T.? What did it say about J.T.?

Diana had become good friends with several girls at Our Lady of the Cove last year. But she still felt Ellie Goodwin knew her better than anybody else. Ellie was a great listener. It really was a lost art. No wonder she'd won so many awards as a journalist. She was smart, pretty, and funny. But she didn't seem to have any friends her own age—and absolutely no potential boyfriends, not even a crush. Diana had gotten her to admit that. Ellie hadn't had a single date since breaking up with her husband eighteen months ago. Diana considered Ellie her lifeline, but she sometimes wondered if it was the other way around.

Stepping outside, Diana felt a chill in the night air. The library was the hub of the campus, where the old and new sections met. Just across the quad was the student union, the Campus Grounds, and the Grub Hub.

The mini-market was the only one still open. She caught a glimpse of some kids heading in there.

By the library entrance, Diana stopped to put on her sweater. She thought about going to the store for another snack, but decided against it. No, she'd just take the bridge across the ravine to the girls' dorm, O'Donnell Hall. She'd make it back in time to catch *The Tonight Show*. By the commercial before the last guest, she'd be washed up and ready for bed—and Tara would be asleep. Then Diana would switch off the TV, curl up in bed, and get back to *Rebecca*.

She slung the strap to her tote bag over her shoulder and started for the bridge.

"Diana?" someone called.

She stopped.

For a second, Diana thought it was J.T. But she didn't recognize the man who stepped up from the stairs by the bridge. He had shaggy, sand-colored hair, a handlebar mustache, and thick glasses. "Ellie said you'd be at the library," he said, approaching her.

She might have backed away from this stranger, but he had mentioned Ellie. With a bewildered smile, Diana stared at him.

He took a quick glance around them. "I've got some bad news," he whispered.

Diana glanced around, too. There was no one else nearby. Her eyes narrowed at the man. "Who are you?"

"I'm a friend of Ellie's. She's been asking for you. She's been shot."

"What?" Diana automatically dug into her tote and pulled out her phone.

"No, you don't want to do that, Diana," he said, taking the phone from her.

She noticed he was wearing thin rubber gloves—the kind a surgeon would use. This close to him, she noticed something else: his shaggy hair looked like a wig; the glasses and mustache seemed to be part of a disguise.

He slipped her phone into the pocket of his corduroy jacket.

"Wait a minute," Diana started to say. "What—"

She fell silent as he furtively took out a revolver and jabbed it in her side. Diana froze.

He slid his other arm around her while the gun barrel dug into the fold of flesh just above her waist. "Come with me, keep your head down, and do what I say," he whispered.

He started leading her back past the library—toward the stately former mansion that housed the administration offices. Beyond Logan Hall, Diana could see all the windows were dark in the older buildings that housed classrooms. This part of the campus became deserted after night classes got out at nine o'clock.

Diana stole one last look at the Grub Hub. Through the window, inside, she could see a foursome of students laughing and clowning around as they headed toward the checkout counter with their drinks and snacks. They were too far away. If she tried to trip this guy or run, he could shoot her and flee before anyone in the store even noticed.

Her legs felt weak, and she was shaking. But Diana kept walking—with her head down, just as he'd instructed. "Where are you taking me?" she whispered, her voice quavering. "Did you mean that about Ellie? Did someone really shoot her?"

"They will if you don't cooperate with me, Diana."

They passed the rose garden with a tall statue of

St. Mary on a pedestal in the center. Diana looked up at it for a moment. She felt the gun barrel poking into her rib cage. She was so scared she couldn't quite get a breath. They headed toward the church at the edge of the campus. She spotted two nuns, walking toward them on the other side of the street.

"So far, you've been a real good girl," he said in a hushed voice. His hand on her shoulder took on a vise-like grip. It almost hurt. "You don't want to spoil it now. Things have gone very smoothly. In fact, it's perfect that you went to the library. I couldn't have asked for it to be more ideal. Fifty years ago tonight, the library was the last place Greta Mae Louden was seen alive. Do you know about her? Have you ever seen her picture, Diana? She was found the next morning in the ravine, her schoolbooks scattered near her corpse. You know about the Immaculate Conception murders, don't you? Greta was the first one he killed, the first holy slut . . ."

Diana wanted to scream, push him away, and make a run for it. But she was too terrified. She never thought she'd be so passive in this kind of situation. But Diana kept thinking, *Do what he says, and you'll be okay.* Yet, all the while, she knew it was a lie.

They kept moving—past the old church, toward a small, fenced-off arboretum area. He led her up to the tall, wrought iron gate. He finally released her shoulder and then reached into his pocket. He handed her a key. "Unlock it for me, Greta."

Why did he call me by the dead girl's name? Diana thought. *Had he done it on purpose?*

Her hand shook so much that she could hardly fit the key in the lock. She'd been in this garden a few times, but only during the daytime, never at night. It was pretty—with trees, plants, shrubs, and a winding path that led to a stairway that went down to the beach. There was also a grotto, a cave-like shrine that housed a nine-foot statue of Christ. The last time Diana had been there, she'd noticed the paint on the statue of Jesus was faded and peeling. His red robe had turned pale pink. In front of the sacred effigy were racks of votive candles and a long kneeler. She remembered there were a couple of pews as well. Diana wondered if he was taking her there—or to the beach. This area was closed after dark. Only certain members of the college's administration or the custodial staff had the keys to it.

She finally got the key in the lock and gave it a turn.

The heavy gate squeaked as he pushed it open. Diana handed the key to him. "What are you going to do to me?" she asked. She tried to hold back her tears. "Is Ellie here?"

"You'll see," he said. He nodded for her to lead the way.

Diana reluctantly headed into the garden. He kept nudging her in the back with his gun. The treetops blocked out the moonlight, and in the darkness, Diana could barely make out the gravel trail in front of her. She heard the waves lapping on the shore below. From a distance, and in the shadows, the grotto looked like a large, dark recess between two huge trees. But as Diana came closer, she recognized the man-made stone cave with its rounded roof. A slightly battered-looking crucifix hung over the arched entrance.

Diana felt the gun prodding her toward the entryway. "You might feel like praying," he said. "Go on in . . ."

She passed under the archway but then hesitated. The cave was dank and pitch-black inside. It felt cold—like death. His hand pressed against her back, gently pushing her to the left. Then a light went on. Diana glanced over her shoulder to see he had one hand on a light switch on the wall. His other hand still held the revolver.

Turning forward again, she realized they were standing in front of the shrine. Ornately covered lights hung from beams that ran across the ceiling of the cave. They weren't very bright. Without the votives illuminating Jesus' face, the statue looked almost menacing.

Diana spotted a tall ladder behind the statue. At first, she thought some renovation work was being done on the shrine. But then, just above the top of the ladder, she saw a rope tied to one of the ceiling beams. At the bottom of the rope was a noose.

"I want you to climb up on that ladder," he said.

She turned to him, searching for a human being behind that clumsy disguise. "Why are you doing this to me?" she whimpered.

"Because you look like the first one," he said in a quiet, cold voice. "Get up on the ladder, Greta. Jesus can't help you now."

CHAPTER TWENTY-SEVEN

Monday, 10:34 P.M.

In terrible trouble. Am at d grotto by d church. Please come meet me. Need 2 C U now. Counting on U. Please hurry.

Ellie was grading papers at the kitchen table when she got the text. She had on her "comfy clothes"— a long-sleeve T-shirt and drawstring pants. Joni Mitchell serenaded her from the sound system in the living room. She'd been thinking about going to bed early when her phone had buzzed.

The cryptic text didn't seem like something Diana would send. She wasn't the overly dramatic type. And if it was a true emergency, she would have telephoned.

Ellie phoned her and got Diana's voice mail. She impatiently waited for the beep. "Hey, Di, what's going on? I just got this weird text. What are you doing at the grotto? Isn't it closed this time of night? Anyway, call me when you get this. I was just about to go to bed, but I—I'll head over there. Call me if you can, let me know what this is about, okay?"

She clicked off. "Shit."

Ellie threw on a sweater and a pair of jeans and was out the door within five minutes. She'd hoped Diana would call back in time to spare her this trip, but no such luck. She had the phone in her lap while driving toward the campus. She kept thinking that Diana must have run into J.T. and he'd taken her to the wooded park, where things got out of hand. Maybe he'd tried to rape her. Maybe he'd succeeded.

It usually took Ellie about twenty minutes to get to work, but she made it to the campus in less than fifteen. As she drove up Maple Hill Road, which ran parallel to the lake, Ellie saw the church ahead—and beyond that, the swirling lights.

An ambulance, three patrol vehicles, another one marked CAMPUS SECURITY, and a few other cars were parked by the entrance to the small arboretum.

"Oh God, no," Ellie murmured. She'd already felt anxious. But now a wave of dread rushed over her. Had Diana called the police after sending her that text?

Ellie pulled over and parked on the other side of the street. Jumping out of the car, she ran to the garden gate. Several bystanders—one of them a priest—were milling around, craning their necks to look into the wooded area. Two cops blocked the entrance.

Ellie approached them. "My name's Ellie Goodwin," she said to the tall, lanky policewoman. "I teach here at the school. I got a text twenty minutes ago from Diana Mackie, asking me to meet her here."

The policewoman glanced over at her colleague, a ruddy-faced, thirty-something man with dark hair. He took a step back and muttered something into his shoulder mic. "What's your name again, ma'am?" he asked, looking at Ellie.

"Ellie Goodwin," she said, trying to get her breath. On her tiptoes, she glanced past the policewoman's shoulder. The lights were on in the little park, and she could see the winding gravel trail. "What's happened? Is Diana in there?"

Although Ellie hadn't so much as taken one step forward, the policewoman put a hand up as if to stop her. "Hold on just a minute, ma'am."

Ellie shrugged at her. "What?"

The other cop finished murmuring into his shoulder mic. "Castino says to let her through," he told the policewoman. "One of us better take her. I can handle things here if you want."

The policewoman nodded at Ellie and opened the gate. "All right, let's go."

Her stomach clenched, Ellie followed the woman down the gravel path bordered by trees, plants, and shrubs. "Is Diana hurt?" she asked. "Can't you tell me what happened?"

"Detective Castino's in charge of the investigation," the cop said with her back to Ellie. "Detective Anton Castino—"

"*Investigation?*" Ellie repeated.

"Yes, I'm sure Detective Castino would like a few words with you," she said.

As they approached the grotto, Ellie passed another uniformed cop and two paramedics with a collapsible gurney—still folded up. One of the EMS guys was talking into his phone. Ellie hesitated before stepping under the grotto's archway. She'd been to the shrine a few times. It always struck her as a serene place. Not tonight. Though no one was yelling, there was a buzz of activity and several people talking at once.

Following the policewoman through a tiny foyer, Ellie turned to her left. She entered the shrine—only to be blinded by a flash. It took her a moment to see again. A police photographer was at the edge of the altar, taking pictures. The flash kept going off. Behind him, another cop talked into his shoulder mic. And behind the cop, standing between two pews that faced the altar, stood a short, stout man in a cheap-looking suit. He looked like a plainclothes detective and reminded her of Danny DeVito. He was dictating into a little recorder.

On the altar, beside the bigger-than-life statue of Jesus, a ladder had fallen and smashed into a rack of votives. Among the mess and the shards of glass on the floor, Ellie recognized Diana's tote bag—the one from the Art Institute. The aftereffects of the flash were still playing tricks with her eyes. She made herself focus on the books that had fallen out of Diana's bag. *Look Homeward, Angel* was among them—open and face-down at the edge of the step to the altar. There was a school library sticker on the back cover.

Ellie still didn't see Diana. She took another step toward the shrine and noticed a priest on the altar, standing behind the statue. Looking up, he murmured a prayer. Ellie couldn't hear his words amid all the other talking. And from where she stood, she couldn't see what he was looking at.

She took one more step and glimpsed her young friend, Diana, hanging from the end of a rope. The other end was tied around one of the ceiling beams.

Horrified, Ellie let out a cry. Covering her mouth, she backed away and bumped into the wall.

"Who is this?" the little plainclothes man hissed. His voice echoed inside the cave.

"It's Ellie Goodwin," the policewoman whispered. "You said to bring her in here."

"I said to bring her here, not *in here*," he growled. "Take her outside, damn it. I'll be out to talk with her in a couple of minutes. And for God's sake, get that priest out of here, too. He's trampling all over my crime scene. He can pray over her after we take her down from there. She won't be any less dead than she is now."

In shock, Ellie was barely aware of the policewoman taking her by the arm. She was still gazing up at her friend. She couldn't comprehend how this could have happened. It didn't seem real.

The policewoman started to lead her toward the exit. With tears in her eyes, Ellie glanced over her shoulder. But she couldn't see Diana anymore. The statue was in the way. The washed-out face of Jesus looked calm— almost indifferent to what was going on around him.

Ellie let the policewoman guide her outside. Once she felt the cool night air, she broke down and wept.

Tuesday, 1:34 A.M.

Ellie turned the key in her front door and realized it was unlocked.

She was tired and emotional—and now she was scared.

She always locked the door whenever she left her townhouse. It was an automatic thing. Ellie stood on the front stoop for a few moments. She'd left the light on in the living room, and she could see from the doorway that nothing looked different. The place hadn't been ransacked. Nothing appeared to be missing.

Biting her lip, she finally stepped inside. She left the door open behind her for a quick escape. Then she peeked into the kitchen and the powder room. She glanced up the stairs. The hallway light was on. She was pretty sure she'd left it that way.

She closed the front door and double-locked it. Then she headed into the kitchen and opened the utensils drawer. The rattle of the utensils broke the silence in the townhouse. Ellie took out a steak knife. She returned to the foot of the stairs and then stopped to listen for a minute. Not a sound. Ellie forced herself to go up the steps. She checked the guest room and the closet, the bathroom, and then her bedroom. The bedroom closet was open and the light was on. That was a trademark of break-ins. Bedroom closets were where people often hid guns or stashed valuables. It was one of the spots in a house where a burglar would really dig in and look for things. But from what Ellie could see, nothing was out of place. She'd been in such a hurry to change her clothes that she'd probably just left the light on and the door open.

Taking the knife back downstairs to the kitchen, she poured a glass of red wine for herself. Then, in a daze, she wandered into her living room and sank down on the sofa. Grabbing the remote, she switched on the TV. A *Frasier* rerun was on. She turned down the volume. She didn't really want to watch anything. But it was nice to look at familiar faces—and hear them talking in the background. She took a big gulp of wine.

She'd just spent the last hour and a half at the Delmar Police Station, talking at a café table in the break room with the Danny DeVito lookalike, Detective Castino. He was actually very nice. He'd gotten her a 7UP from one of the vending machines—and a Dr Pepper and a Little Debbie for himself.

They'd already spoken outside of the grotto, but he wanted to go over everything again. Ellie showed him her cell phone and the text from Diana. She told him how the text didn't seem like something Diana would send.

She couldn't accept the idea that her friend might have taken her own life. Diana hadn't been depressed. None of it made any sense.

Castino said the timing of Diana's text made perfect sense. It had been sent at 10:34 P.M. Then, at approximately 10:45, one of the college's philosophy teachers, Father Gillespie, on his nightly constitutional, had heard a loud crash—coming from somewhere in the arboretum park. He'd hurried back to the rectory and called campus security.

"You shouldn't blame yourself. She gave you only ten minutes to get there before she gave up. It's obvious the crash Father Gillespie heard was when Diana kicked the ladder out from under herself. She must have been alone, because Father Gillespie said he didn't see anyone in the woods after he heard the racket. And she still had the key the custodian—what's-his-name—Lance—reported stolen. It was in her purse."

"Someone could have planted that key in her purse and run away in the other direction—down to the beach," Ellie pointed out.

Castino seemed to dismiss the idea. He asked if Diana had a boyfriend or anyone special in her life.

Ellie told him about Diana's unspectacular date with J.T. "I really don't think she would have killed herself over him," she said. "It was just a mild crush. She was really ambivalent about him." She told Castino that J.T. had a reputation for having had sex with about half the girls on campus. She figured that every detail might be helpful, so she also mentioned how J.T. had surreptitiously taken a photo of her and Hannah at the pool on Friday.

This little tidbit seemed to interest the detective. But

apparently, it didn't change his mind that Diana's death was a suicide.

"But it doesn't make sense," Ellie argued. "Why would she kill herself there? She had to go to all that trouble stealing the keys, dragging the ladder from *wherever*, and getting the rope. O'Donnell Hall is eight stories high. She could have easily jumped out of one of the top-floor windows of her dorm and killed herself that way. It's no secret that, over the decades, other girls have done it. Diana never even mentioned the grotto to me until the text tonight. I keep thinking it was set up to look like a suicide. The whole thing is crazy."

"I've seen a lot crazier," Castino said. "I'm sure, as a reporter, you have, too."

Those had been his closing words. He'd given her his card and thanked her for her cooperation.

Ellie had wept most of the way home from the police station.

Her wineglass was now empty. On TV, *Frasier* had been succeeded by *The Golden Girls*.

Ellie kept thinking about something else that didn't make sense. It was a small matter, but one that gnawed at her. She hadn't shared it with Detective Castino because it seemed so trivial. But why were Diana's books scattered on the floor like that? Had she taken her tote bag up on the ladder with her? Why would she do that? And the way the books were strewn looked sort of arranged. She kept thinking about *Look Homeward, Angel*. Diana and she used to discuss the books they were reading. Diana had been in the middle of reading *Rebecca*. She hadn't mentioned Thomas Wolfe or *Look Homeward, Angel*. The book had been left open on the altar floor—with the cover and spine facing up. Ellie

couldn't help wondering if Diana—or maybe her killer—
had positioned the book that way on purpose. Was there
a crucial quote on that particular page, one that might
hint at why Diana was dead?

"Okay, now you're grabbing at straws," she muttered
to herself.

Ellie got to her feet, went into the kitchen, and
poured another glass of wine. Before taking another sip,
while she still had a clear head, she went around and
checked all the first-floor windows to make sure they
were closed and locked. She also double-checked the
back door. Then she grabbed her purse and returned to
the sofa. Taking out her phone, she looked at Diana's
text again:

> In terrible trouble. Am at d grotto by d church. Please come
> meet me. Need 2 C U now. Counting on U. Please hurry.

She scrolled back to the last text Diana had sent
before that:

> OK, we're on for dinner Wed night at 6:30. This time U
> will hear all the gory details about the date w/JT. He still
> hasn't called by the way. To hell with him. Looking forward
> to seeing U!

The two texts weren't written by the same person,
Ellie was sure of it. Diana spelled out "see" and "to."
She didn't substitute "C" and "2" for them. She also
spelled out "the."

Ellie remembered Hannah telling her the same thing
about the text she'd gotten from her missing sister: *I
mean, she's texted me a lot, and I know her style. She*

never uses "D" for the word "the." That was just one thing that was off . . .

"It's the same person," Ellie whispered.

She imagined Detective Castino pointing out that a hell of a lot of people use "D" instead of "the" when texting. Still, Ellie couldn't help thinking that Diana's "suicide text" and the text from Hannah's missing sister had been written by the same person.

On her phone, Ellie looked up Hannah's email address from her class list. Then she composed an email to her with the subject heading *Have You Heard from Eden Yet?*

Dear Hannah,

I was wondering if you've heard from Eden again. If she won't meet with you in person, I'd make sure she talks to you on the phone. I think you're right not to believe any texts or emails from her. It's very possible someone might have gotten a hold of her phone. Please, let me know if you hear from her.

Thanks,

Ellie Goodwin

Ellie sent the email and took another gulp of wine. She hoped to numb herself. Otherwise, she'd start crying again and never stop.

CHAPTER TWENTY-EIGHT

Tuesday, September 15, 7:55 P.M.

Hannah noticed the sign when she stepped into the Sunnyside Up Café: PLEASE SEAT YOURSELF. This was her first time here, and the place wasn't as bad as her instant assessment of it from the train station nearly two weeks ago. She realized she'd been in a haggard, snotty mood at the time. Actually, it was a nice little dive with kitschy old ads on the walls, some *Do-Do-Ron-Ron* oldie on the jukebox, and the smell of bacon coming from the kitchen behind the counter. The place was nearly full, and a lot of the diners looked like students from the college.

She took a seat at the counter. The skinny, older waitress was taking orders at a table at the other side of the restaurant. Hannah figured it might be a while before the woman made her way over, which was fine. Hannah wasn't very hungry. She'd already eaten dinner at the cafeteria in O'Donnell Hall.

Hannah had come here tonight because Eden liked the place. She figured maybe Eden had swung by on Friday night—before she'd disappeared. Maybe someone had seen her. Maybe Eden had said something to somebody here about catching the Metra to Chicago later. Hannah just wanted someone to tell her that, and then she'd stop worrying.

Her mom and dad had texted her today—separately. Apparently, they'd also each left Eden voice mails that hadn't been answered yet. The two of them seemed more annoyed with her half-sister than worried. Hannah kept having to remind herself that they'd been through this disappearance routine with Eden on numerous occasions in the past—and Hannah herself hadn't given it much thought at the time. Her mom and dad seemed to believe the weird "screw school" text had been from Eden and no one else. In her communiqué today, Hannah's mother had said maybe they should wait one more day before calling the police to report Eden missing.

Obviously, as far as her mom and dad were concerned, the more pressing crisis had to do with Rachel's real parentage. Hannah's mom didn't say anything about it in her text. But her dad wanted to know if Rachel had agreed to take the DNA test. His doctor had sent the kit by FedEx this morning. Hannah texted back that Rachel was fine with it.

Hannah had briefly talked with her brother Steve this afternoon, catching him during his lunch period at school. She'd wanted the lowdown on how her parents were handling the bombshell about Rachel. "Well, Mom went out for a long walk last night. Then later, around bedtime, I heard her crying alone in their bedroom. Dad slept in Eden's room. So things are kind of tense. Aren't you glad you asked? Hey, y'know, I looked up Rachel Bonner on Google, and it's weird because she sure looks like the photos of Aunt Molly."

Her parents had said they'd call tonight. Because of the time difference, Hannah realized she probably wouldn't hear from them until after nine-thirty. She wondered if either one of them would want to talk to Rachel.

Her new big sister was being very sweet and supportive lately. Rachel kept saying she felt responsible for this whole mess. She even apologized for getting so upset at Ellie Goodwin. "I know she's your friend and that you like her. You had to talk to somebody about all this, and our sister isn't around, so it's understandable you'd turn to Ellie. I get it. It's just that my parents are freaking out and all up my ass about it."

Right now, Ellie and Rachel were the only ones around here in whom she could confide. They were also the only ones who seemed to share her concern over Eden's disappearance. Hannah had woken up this morning to an email from Ellie, urging her to get in touch with Eden again and insist on talking with her—if not in person, then at least on the phone.

So Hannah had done just that—in what must have been her twentieth text to Eden since Friday night. She'd sent the text this morning.

And of course, no response.

Hannah was so deep in thought she didn't even realize the waitress was now behind the counter. The woman set a glass of water in front of her. "You get a chance to look at the menu yet, hon?" she asked.

"That's okay," Hannah said, pulling out her phone. "I'll just have a Diet Coke, please."

While the waitress got her soda, Hannah found a photo of Eden, one of the scant few she had of her half-sister. Her dad had taken a picture of them together at Sea-Tac Airport the morning they'd left for college. Neither one of them had been in the mood for a photo-op, but it had actually turned out to be a pretty cute picture. It was the most recent shot Hannah had of Eden, and she couldn't help thinking that it might be the last one ever.

"Here you go," said the waitress, setting a tall plastic tumbler of Diet Coke and a paper straw in front of her.

"Thanks," Hannah said. "Listen, I know you're busy, but I was wondering if you recognize the girl here in this picture with me." She held up the phone for her to see.

The waitress squinted at the phone screen and then adjusted her glasses. "Oh, yeah, sure, that's Eden."

"Were you working on Friday night? Do you know if Eden was in here?"

The waitress seemed to think about the question for a moment, and then she nodded. "She was sitting just about where you are now."

"Do you remember what time it was on Friday night?"

"Hmm, around nine o'clock."

Hannah was surprised at how late Eden had been there. It would have been pretty stupid of her half-sister to catch a train some time after nine-thirty at night so she could go explore Chicago. It would have made a lot more sense to start out on a Saturday morning. Then again, Hannah often had no clue as to how Eden's brain worked.

The waitress started to move away as she wiped down the counter.

"Excuse me again," Hannah said. "Did Eden say anything to you about where she was going later?"

"Not to me. But she was chatting with some guy here at the counter. In fact, he bought dinner for her. Maybe she told him where she was heading. Why? Is she missing?"

"Kind of," Hannah said. "You haven't seen her since Friday night, have you?"

The waitress shook her head. "I'm sorry, hon."

"What about this guy she was talking with, do you know him? Is he a regular customer?"

The woman shook her head again. "Nope, at least I'd never seen him before."

"Could you describe him?"

"Well, he was quite easy on the eyes, I'll say that much. And he was a good tipper."

"You mean, he was nice-looking?"

She nodded. "Very."

"Did they leave together?" Hannah asked.

She pondered it for a moment. "No, Eden left first. In fact, now I remember. He stuck around for about five minutes after that. He barely touched his food. As soon as I gave him the check, he was—*phffft*—out of here."

"Was this guy another student, do you think? Was he around my age?"

"No, he was an older fella, maybe thirty or so."

"Besides him being handsome, do you remember anything else about him?"

The waitress cracked a smile. "You mean, like hair color, distinguishing marks, that kind of thing?"

Hannah nodded eagerly.

"He had dark blond hair, and—oh yeah, he had some scars on his arm. Does that help? Does that sound like someone you know?"

Hannah stared at her and nodded. "Yes, it does. Thank you."

Tuesday, 8:40 P.M.

A slightly chubby student aide with a goatee and an ugly plum-colored sweater stood behind the information desk on the first floor in the college library. "*Look Homeward, Angel* by Thomas Wolfe?" he asked.

Ellie nodded. "I know it's checked out. I'm wondering when it was checked out."

He turned to his computer monitor and started typing on the keyboard.

Ellie couldn't stop thinking about the books that had fallen out of Diana's tote bag at the scene of her "suicide." She knew she'd become obsessed over what seemed to be an insignificant detail. Still, she'd gotten in touch with Diana's two liberal arts teachers to find out if *Look Homeward, Angel* was part of their curriculum. It wasn't. So Diana wasn't reading the book for school.

Ellie remembered the book had been an edition from the college library. How long had Diana had the book checked out?

"Um, we have two copies of *Look Homeward, Angel*," the librarian told her. "Both are in, so you're in luck. In fact, one of them is brand new. You'll be the first one to check it out."

Ellie shook her head. "That can't be right. One copy is definitely checked out. Are you sure you don't have three copies?"

"No, just two copies—"

"Well, was one of them returned today?" She couldn't imagine that someone from the Delmar Police Department had decided to return Diana's library book for her.

"Nope," he sighed, obviously getting a bit tired of her questions. He looked at the computer monitor again. "The last time this title got checked out was in May—last semester. Before that, back in April, the other copy was reported missing. It must have been stolen or something.

We replaced it two weeks ago. So, would you like to check out the book?"

Bewildered, Ellie shook her head. "No . . . thanks," she murmured. "Thank you for your help."

Four minutes later, she was in the library's vestibule, which was practically floor-to-ceiling windows. From one vantage point, the windows looked down at the ravine; and from another, there was a view of the student union across the quad. Ellie leaned against a beam separating the windows on the ravine side. "Don't you see?" she whispered into her phone. "The book was stolen from the library six months ago. I knew Diana pretty damn well, and she wasn't the type of person who stole. But someone else took that book, and they left it there by Diana's body for a reason." Her voice cracked a little. "I think they left it there after they killed her."

There was silence on the other end of the line. Ellie waited for Detective Castino to say something. "All right, that's an interesting theory," he said, at last. "But I can think of a hell of a lot of other explanations for why your friend ended up with a stolen library book. She could have bought it at a secondhand store or at a flea market. A lot of stolen stuff inadvertently ends up in the hands of honest people . . ."

Ellie could tell the detective wasn't exactly thrilled about her call. When he'd given her his business card with his home number scribbled on it, he probably hadn't expected her to use it—certainly not at a quarter to nine at night. "I know you'd like to give some significance to this book—and the way it landed on the floor," he said. "Maybe Diana wanted us to see a quote or a passage from the book that would tell us something. You're looking for a reason or a motive, something to explain why she took her own life. But in most cases I've come across, suicides aren't so conveniently explained away. For the survivors, it's often easier to think what happened was an accident—or even a homicide. That way, they don't have to blame themselves—or the deceased."

This time, Ellie was the one who was silent for a moment. *Spare me the pop psychology*, she wanted to say. But she held her tongue.

"Are you still there, Ms. Goodwin?"

"Yes," she sighed. "Did you talk to J.T.?"

"Yes, he told us that he had a date with Diana on Saturday—dinner at the student union, followed by a movie, and then he took her to the recreation center where they had a make-out session by the pool. In true *kiss and tell* fashion, he said he got only as far as second base. Then he walked Diana back to O'Donnell Hall. Does that sound right to you?"

"Yes," she said. "It jibes with what Diana told me on Sunday." She'd almost wished she'd caught J.T. in a lie. Maybe Castino was right with his Psych 101 speech; she was looking for someone to blame.

"This lifeguard fella claims he didn't see her or talk to her again after that," Castino said. "By the way, you know that business with the photos? He has about five hundred of them on his phone—all candids of pretty girls by the pool. I don't think we can charge him with anything. But if you want to raise a stink about it with the school or his boss at the recreation center, I'll be happy to back you up."

"Did you see the photos?" Ellie asked quietly. "Was Diana one of his unaware *models*?"

"No. I'm afraid he wasn't very serious about her.

Apparently, he was just looking for a good time on Saturday night. He admitted that he didn't plan to go out of his way to impress her. He made it pretty clear that he thought Diana would be a—well, I'm not sure how to put it . . ."

"An easy lay?"

"Yes, I'm sorry. Do you suppose Diana might have sensed that?"

"It's possible. But I know that Diana wasn't all that crazy for him. She really didn't know how she felt about him."

"Still, it must be hard for a young woman to know she's regarded that way—even if it's by some guy she's not even crazy about. We spoke with her family. Diana's parents and her older sister said that Diana suffered bouts of depression. Her roommate, Tara Bernhardt, described her as 'gloomy' and 'moody.'"

"That's because Tara had the TV on all the time, and it drove Diana crazy," Ellie pointed out. "Diana had to go to the library to do her homework."

"Well, that's where she told her roommate she was going last night at eight o'clock."

"Listen, I know you think I'm in denial about this whole thing," Ellie said. "But I keep coming back to the text Diana supposedly sent. It just didn't seem like her. It had all these abbreviations that Diana never used—like the number two for 'to' and the letter 'D' for 'the.' I can't help thinking that someone else wrote that text on Diana's phone. In fact, a friend of mine—another student—her sister disappeared sometime around Friday night or early Saturday morning. And on Sunday, she got a text—supposedly from her sister—saying she was fine and in Chicago. But it was the same thing. The text had a bunch of abbreviations her sister didn't ordinarily use—like 'D' for 'the' and so on . . ."

"What, are you saying the same person who sent Diana's text also sent this other girl's text?" He sounded incredulous. "Do you know how many millions of people use 'D' for 'the' when they text? And how do you consider your friend's sister *missing* when she sent a text telling her where she is and that she's fine? I'd say she's pretty much accounted for."

Then you're not a very good detective, Ellie wanted to reply. But she didn't wish to agitate him any more than she already had. Besides, everything he said made sense. Her theories sounded pretty wild and far-fetched when she said them out loud.

"Listen," he said. "I know you're trying to help, and I appreciate it. But you should think about helping yourself, Ms. Goodwin. You're grieving over the loss of your friend. It might help you to talk to someone about it—a counselor or maybe a priest. You'd certainly have your pick of them there at the college."

Ellie closed her eyes and sighed. "I'll take that under advisement. Thank you, Detective Castino."

After she hung up the phone, Ellie just stared out at the dark ravine for a few moments. Once again, she remembered the memorial wreath someone had set there around this time last year to commemorate the anniversary of the first victim of the Immaculate Conception murders. Like Diana, the girl had been at the library the night she'd been killed.

Ellie brought up Google on her phone. She typed in *Immaculate Conception Killings, Blessed Heart of Mary*.

The first result was a lengthy Wikipedia article about the murders. She wanted to find the date of the first murder. And there it was in a sidebar listing of Lyle Duncan Wheeler's victims: *Greta Mae Louden, 19 (strangled) 9/14/70.*

That was fifty years ago last night.

Diana died on the fiftieth anniversary of the first murder.

Ellie returned to Google, selected *Images* and typed in *Greta Mae Louden.*

A slightly blurry black-and-white high school senior portrait of the girl came up: fair-haired, slightly chubby, a cute smile. She looked a lot like Diana—almost a dead ringer.

Ellie always thought the teachers' parking lot behind the old science building, Martinsen Hall, could have used some more lights. It was slightly sinister at night. It didn't help that the lot was practically empty now. As she approached her Toyota, Ellie could see the front gate to the grotto arboretum across the street.

With her key already out, she pressed the device on the fob to unlock the car door. She picked up her pace as she got closer to the car.

Ellie remembered what Hannah had said about the fiftieth anniversary of the Immaculate Conception murders: The laundry room fire last week had occurred on the same date as a student had murdered her new-born baby and set him on fire in one of the bungalows in 1970; and Eden O'Rourke had vanished Friday evening or, more likely, early on Saturday—the same date Lyle Duncan Wheeler had abducted Crystal Juneau. Then yesterday, exactly fifty years after Greta Mae

Louden had been strangled, her lookalike, Diana, died in an apparent suicide.

Ellie was tempted to phone Detective Castino again and point out how all these recent incidents matched up with the Immaculate Conception Killer's timeline. But the detective would probably just dismiss it as another of her wild theories.

Ellie finally reached her car, opened the door, and ducked inside. Shutting the door, she immediately locked it.

Her phone buzzed, startling her. The caller ID said: *O'Rourke, Hannah*. It wasn't a text. She was calling to talk.

"Hello, Hannah?" Ellie said into the phone.

"Hi. I'm sorry to call you this late—"

"It's only nine o'clock. What's going on? You sound a little stressed."

"I just came back from the Sunnyside Up Café. Actually, I *ran* back. I talked to a waitress there. She said Eden had dinner at the café on Friday night—and she was talking with somebody. He even paid for her dinner. This is right before she disappeared . . ."

"Did the waitress there have any idea who the guy was?" Ellie asked anxiously.

"She described him to me. It was the guy from our class, the same one who was talking to me at the pool on Friday . . ."

"Nick Jensen?"

"Yeah, Nick Jensen, the guy you warned me about . . ."

Tuesday, 9:50 P.M.

It didn't look like Nick Jensen was home.

Ellie had his address in her notebook inside her

purse: 812 Sunset Ridge Road, number 17 in Highland Park. It was a working-class neighborhood. The apartment building looked as if it had been built in the sixties: an L-shaped two-story structure with a beige brick facade. All of the apartments had outside entries. On the second story, flower boxes hung from the railing along the walkway, but most of the plants in the boxes looked dead.

Ellie slowly drove around the building and noted that each apartment had a back door that opened onto a fire escape walkway. She parked across the street, climbed out of the car, and hurried to where the mailboxes were. She found *N. Jensen* printed with a label-maker on mailbox number seventeen.

She found his apartment on the upper level. The drapes were shut, but it looked like a light was on. She couldn't imagine he'd be able to keep Eden captive in the apartment—unless she was drugged, gagged, and tied to his bed.

Ellie wanted to bang on the door and confront him right now. But how stupid and reckless would that be?

Retreating to her car, she tried to think about the best strategy. If she could break into his apartment while he was gone, maybe she could find some evidence linking him to Eden's disappearance and Diana's murder—something she could show Detective Castino.

She wondered if Nick Jensen was the one who had stolen *Look Homeward, Angel* from the library. The earliest record she had of him was a customer review of his massage work in April, the same month the book had been listed as missing.

Ellie took out her phone and checked Nick's customer reviews again. Every few moments, she looked up to make sure the curtain in his apartment hadn't moved. With her phone light on, she would be easily spotted.

She looked at the customer names and dates: *J. Reynolds, Highwood, IL (4/15/20); B. Riddle, Lake Bluff, IL (5/30/20); M. Freeman, Sheboygan, WI (6/5/20)* . . .

Why did Sheboygan ring a bell?

Then Ellie remembered. She typed in another name for a Google search and clicked on the first search result. It was the *Milwaukee Journal Sentinel* article dated June 7. The headline read:

SHEBOYGAN GIRL DIES
IN BICYCLE ACCIDENT

*Kayla Kennedy Was Known
for Heroic Rescue of
Drowning Mother and Child*

Sheboygan was about two hours away. Had Nick been spending the night there on June 5? Maybe he was making some money with massage work while in town on other "business." Kayla had been killed early the following morning.

Nick seemed to have a keen interest in Hannah and Eden. Had he been interested in Rachel's previous roommate as well? Or was it all just a coincidence?

Ellie set the phone facedown on the passenger seat to diminish the light. Then she glanced up at Nick's window again. The curtain hadn't moved.

She kept thinking about the fire escape in back. Maybe she could watch the place tomorrow night, wait until he left, and then break in somehow. Maybe she'd find a window left unlocked. But she was no master at housebreaking. It wouldn't be easy.

She spotted someone jogging toward the building and realized it was Nick.

Ellie quickly slumped down in the driver's seat. She watched him across the street as he slowed down and staggered to the apartment building's stairway. His gray T-shirt was stained with sweat. He grabbed the railing and caught his breath for a moment. Then he glanced at his watch or his pace-tracker; in the distance, Ellie couldn't tell which. He started up the stairs and continued down the walkway. When he reached his door, he glanced around and then furtively took a pot out of the flower box, grabbed something, and then turned and unlocked his door. Before he stepped inside, he returned the key to the flower box and set the plant pot on top of it.

Ellie couldn't help smiling. "Thank you, Nick," she whispered.

Maybe it would be easy after all.

CHAPTER TWENTY-NINE

Wednesday, September 16, 2:49 P.M.

From her desk, Hannah glanced up at the classroom clock. She was anxious for class to end. She'd had difficulty paying much attention to Ellie during the session. She kept thinking about how she had to get together with her—and someone else—after class.

Several times, she'd sneaked a glance over her shoulder at Nick Jensen in the back row, only to find him staring back at her with that same dopey, innocent smile on his face. She wondered exactly what part he'd played in Eden's disappearance.

As promised, her parents had phoned last night— separately. She figured her mom was giving her dad the silent treatment. They both sounded tired and on edge. They wanted to wait one more night—and if no one heard from Eden by morning, they'd call the school or the Delmar Police. Hannah didn't tell them anything about Nick Jensen buying Eden dinner on Friday night.

Class finally ended. Gathering her things, Hannah got to her feet. She surreptitiously nodded at Ellie and then joined the students heading for the door. She felt someone brush against her arm. Flinching, Hannah turned.

Nick gave her that innocent smile again. "Hey, how's it going?"

"Fine," Hannah answered. She inched away from him.

"Is your sister okay? She isn't here today, and I noticed she missed class on Monday, too."

They headed into the crowded corridor together. Hannah realized she'd have to delay her clandestine rendezvous with Ellie and company and keep walking with him for a while. "I wasn't aware that you knew Eden," she said coolly.

"Not very well," he said. "But I ran into her the other night—Friday. In fact, we sort of had dinner together at the Sunnyside Up. It wasn't a *date* or anything. She was finishing up and I was just starting . . ."

Hannah was surprised he admitted it. But maybe that was where he was being clever—pretending he had nothing to hide. "What did you two talk about?" she asked.

He shrugged. "Nothing much really."

"She didn't tell you about her plans for the weekend?"

"No. Why? What did she do over the weekend?"

"You have no idea?" Hannah asked as they stepped outside.

"I don't remember her saying anything."

Hannah didn't break her stride. She headed for the quad. "Well, Eden decided to have herself an adventure in Chicago. She's still there—as far as I know."

"You mean, she just decided to ditch her classes the last three days?"

"You didn't see her in journalism class Monday or today, so you figure it out."

"And she's been in Chicago all this time? On her own? Aren't you worried?"

Staring straight ahead, she nodded. "Yeah. We haven't heard from her since Sunday night, and even then, it was just a quick text. My parents are calling the police soon. Since you were one of the last ones to see her before she went off on this toot Friday night, the cops will probably want to talk with you."

He stopped in his tracks—but for only a second. Still, it was enough for Hannah to read his apprehension. "Um, okay, sure," he replied. "But like I say, she really didn't say anything to me about her plans."

"Just the same, could I get your number?" She stopped and took out her phone. "I'm sure they'll want to talk with you."

He nodded a few more times than necessary and gave her his phone number.

"Thanks," Hannah said. She noted the ten digits and then shoved the phone in her purse and started walking again.

"I hope she calls you or shows up soon," he said.

"Well, if she doesn't, you'll probably hear from the police."

"Anything I can do to help," he said feebly.

"Where are you off to now?" she asked. "The pool again?"

He shrugged. "Um, no . . ."

"Well, unless you'd planned on following me to the library, I'll say goodbye now."

Stopping again, he gave a bewildered laugh. "Oh, all right then. Well, nice talking to you. Keep me posted about your sister, okay?"

"Will do!" she called—with her back to him.

Hannah kept walking. She was so proud of herself for coming up with that business about the police contacting him. That really threw him for a loop. She couldn't wait to tell Ellie about it.

Five minutes later, she was standing at the top of the stairs by the bridge over the ravine, not far from the library entrance. Hannah was in the pedestrian lane, which hardly anyone ever used. From there, she had an ideal view of the quad. "You should have seen how nervous he got all of a sudden—once I mentioned the police," she said into the phone. "I thought he was going to shit a brick."

"I hope you didn't push him too far," Ellie said on the other end of the line. "We don't want him thinking you suspect anything. Where is he now?"

"Like I said, the last I saw of him, he turned and headed in the other direction, back toward Lombard Hall. It looks like he hasn't come back. Can I come join you?"

"Better wait a few more minutes—just to make sure the coast is clear," Ellie said. "And, by the way, good job throwing him off our trail. When I saw him latch on to you after class, I was afraid you wouldn't be able to shake him. See you in a few minutes."

When she walked into the student union seven minutes later, Hannah was certain Nick Jensen hadn't been following her. She had kept checking behind her, and hadn't seen him.

The union wasn't crowded. She easily spotted Ellie and Alden sitting at a four-top table. A framed vintage Our Lady of the Cove T-shirt hung on the wall above the table, with a little spotlight on it. Ellie and Alden each had a cup of coffee in front of them. They both glanced at her as she approached their table.

Hannah couldn't help focusing on Alden, who looked cute in his new glasses. He was wearing a black T-shirt and jeans, a nice edgy contrast to the Clark Kent spectacles.

"So did Ellie brief you?" she asked him as she sat down.

"You mean about the misdemeanor we're pulling off?" he replied.

"I'm the only one committing a crime in this scheme," Ellie said in a hushed tone. "Even then, I don't think it's quite breaking and entering if I'm using a key. All you're doing, Alden, is scheduling a massage with him so I know he'll be out of his apartment. By the time he gets to your dorm, realizes you aren't there, and heads home again, I'll have had about forty-five minutes to check his place."

"So—are you in?" Hannah asked him.

Alden nodded. "I've already texted him and requested a sixty-minute session—any time after four tomorrow or Friday."

Ellie glanced at her wristwatch. "Speaking of appointments, I need to meet a student at a quarter to four. I should get going." She reached over and squeezed Alden's arm. "You are a sweetheart to do this for us. Thank you. And please, let me know the minute you hear back from our suspect." Getting to her feet, she grabbed her purse and glanced at Hannah. "Can I have one quick word with you before I go?"

Hannah got up and followed her a few steps away

from the table. Ellie finally stopped and whispered to her. "Oh, Hannah, he's a peach—and so sweet."

Hannah just nodded. She didn't want to tell Ellie that Alden might be gay. She still hoped she had a chance with him. Heading back to the table, she realized this would actually be her first time alone with him for more than a few minutes.

"What was the private powwow about?" Alden asked.

"Ellie just wants me to call her later," she lied. She started to sit down.

"I'm done here," he said, nodding at his coffee. "Want to head back to the bungalow and hang out?"

"I'm pretty sure Rachel's got something after class today," Hannah said. "She might not be back until five or six."

"So? Can't just the two of us hang out together?" He stood up.

She nodded. "Sure. That's cool."

He walked alongside her, and they started for the exit. "Y'know, I'm kind of flattered you picked me for this assignment," he said.

"Well, you're the only guy I know around here—and I trust you. Anyway, thanks for agreeing to do it." She shrugged. "You might even want to consider having the massage. You might like him. He's a real hottie . . ."

As they stepped outside, Alden paused and gave her an incredulous grin. "Why would you say that?"

Hannah stopped. "Uh . . . I don't know . . ."

He laughed. "Hannah, I'm not gay. Did Rachel tell you that?" They started walking again. Alden shook his head. "Ever since she caught Jason McIntire and me *experimenting* behind the tennis courts at her parents' summer home, Rachel's been convinced I'm gay. Jason and I were eleven at the time—and it was his idea to mess around, not mine."

"So, how come you're not dating Rachel?"

"Because I grew up with her," he said. "It would be like dating my big sister—borderline incest. Plus I'm related to the help, and no daughter of Richard and Candace Bonner can let herself get involved with the son of a servant girl."

Hannah didn't say anything for a moment. She never fully realized the class chasm between Rachel and Alden. "If something like that did happen, it would be really romantic," she said as they headed toward the bridge. "It's right out of *Wuthering Heights*."

"Well, it's not going to happen," he replied. "Besides, like I say, I'm just not interested in Rachel that way. Huh, maybe that's why she's so convinced I'm into guys. Anyway, nothing's ever going to happen for me until I graduate from here."

"What do you mean?"

"I'm stuck in neutral for the duration—no girlfriends, no big life changes, nothing. I'm here on a scholarship, thanks to the Bonners—"

"So am I," Hannah said. "We're in the same boat."

"Not exactly." He frowned. "My scholarship comes with all sorts of strings attached. I work for the Bonners. I'm like the all-purpose errand boy. I do everything from helping the yard crew to running to the drugstore for Mrs. Bonner's valium prescription. I get paid just enough to cover the incidentals around here—and nothing else. If it weren't for Rachel footing the bill, I'd never go out at all. But sometimes, I feel like I'm her charity case. I'm not knocking it. I mean, she's great." He shrugged. "Anyway, I can't afford to spend money on dates or weekend trips to Chicago. What girl in her right mind would want to go out with me?"

"I'd go out with you," Hannah heard herself say. They were at the entry to St. Agnes Village. She imagined cheap dates with Alden—long walks on the beach along the lake, studying together at the library, and sharing a plate of fries at the Sunnyside Up Café. It all seemed very romantic.

"You're being nice," he said with a sad smile. "Hell, you don't have to say anything. Just because I'm throwing myself a pity party here, it doesn't mean you have to RSVP—"

"I'm not just being nice, Alden," she admitted. "From the moment I met you, I thought you were cute."

"Rachel said you were hung up on some guy named Riley at Northwestern."

She let out a jaded laugh. "That was a smartphone summer romance. I never even got to meet him. We were supposed to go out last Saturday, and he didn't follow up. He didn't even bother calling to cancel."

"God, what a douchebag. I hope you weren't too upset. I mean, hell, it's his loss."

Hannah smiled. "I was thinking the exact same thing."

They walked past the chrysanthemum garden next door to the bungalow. It was a bit neglected, wild and full of weeds. The statue of St. Ursula looked a little sad.

It dawned on Hannah that they were both getting misinformation from Rachel about their respective love lives. Was Rachel intentionally trying to keep them apart?

As they turned up the walkway to the bungalow's front door, Alden brushed his shoulder against hers. "So, you aren't seeing anybody or anything like that?"

Hannah felt a lovely breathlessness. "No. And I—I really meant what I said earlier."

At the front door, her hand trembled slightly as she took her keys out of her purse. She kept waiting for him to ask her out. Or maybe this was already their first date. The two of them would have the bungalow to themselves for the next hour.

She unlocked the door, opened it, and saw someone lumbering down the stairs—toward them. Hannah gasped and shrank back. She'd expected to walk into an empty house. Then she realized it was Rachel's cleaning woman, Alma, dragging a big laundry bag behind her down the steps.

Alden laughed at the way Hannah had jumped. The two of them stepped inside. Hannah still had a hand over her heart.

"Do you need any help with that, Alma?" Alden asked.

"I'm perfectly capable," she grumbled, plopping down the laundry bag at the bottom of the stairs. Alma was wearing her usual kitten sweatshirt and the clunky crucifix necklace. She always had an angry, wild look in her pale blue eyes. "The package is for Rachel," she said, nodding toward the small FedEx box on the coffee table. "They left it on the front stoop, and I brought it in."

"Thanks," Hannah said. "We'll see that she gets it."

Alma headed into the kitchen, where she'd left some cleaning supplies on the counter. She put them away in the broom closet in the corner. "I'm going to have a talk with Rachel," Alma said. "I'm cleaning up after three girls in that bathroom upstairs. It's three times the work. I need to be paid extra."

Standing in the middle of the living room, Hannah

turned to Alden and gave him a secret *I'm-in-trouble* grimace.

He started to crack up. With a hand over his mouth, he turned away.

Alma quickly wiped off the counter and then headed for the front door. She stopped and grabbed the laundry bag. "Tell Rachel I'll have all this cleaned and pressed by Saturday. Lance might bring it by. I'm not sure yet."

Alden still had his head turned away. His shoulders were shaking.

"I'll tell her," Hannah said, stifling a giggle. She followed Alma to the door. "Thank you!" she called. Then she shut the door after her, bent over, and started laughing.

"God, she scares the shit out of me!" Alden declared.

Catching her breath, Hannah staggered into the living room and plopped down on the sofa. "I think her son, Lance, is even scarier. Or maybe it's a draw."

Alden sat down next to her. He picked up the FedEx box. "I wonder what little bauble Rachel ordered for herself. Or maybe it's something from Daddy—a diamond tennis bracelet or pearl earrings . . ." He looked at the address label. "Seattle, Washington."

"Oh God," Hannah murmured. Suddenly, everything got serious. "That must be the DNA kit from my dad's doctor's office—for the paternity test."

Neither of them said anything. Alden set the package back on the coffee table. "Well, that's a real buzz-kill."

Hannah got to her feet. "Be right back," she said, heading toward her bedroom.

She needed to check herself in the mirror—and maybe grab a breath mint from the tin on top of her dresser while she was at it. If she was going to be alone here with Alden, she wanted to look and smell her best.

She reached the doorway and abruptly stopped. Two dresser drawers were open—the drawers where Eden kept her clothes. For a moment, Hannah thought Alma might have been in their bedroom. Then she spotted the note on Eden's bed. The piece of paper had been torn out of a spiral notebook, and the handwriting was unmistakably Eden's:

> *Dear Sis,*
>
> *Looks like I missed you. I swung by to pick up some things. Don't worry about me. I'm fine. I just needed to get away & I'm not ready to come back yet. Tell the folks not to worry. I'll be in touch. OK? Take Care.*
>
> *XXX – Me*

With the note in her hand, Hannah stood between the two beds. She wondered if Eden had shown up while Alma was here. But, no, Alma would have said something. Eden must have come by sometime earlier—in the morning.

Hannah went to the closet and saw some empty hangers on Eden's side. She glanced over at Eden's desk and noticed that the top drawer wasn't closed all the way.

There was absolutely no reason to doubt the authenticity of the note. And yet Hannah wasn't completely satisfied.

Still holding on to the note, Hannah wandered back into the living room.

Alden was on the sofa, studying his phone. He glanced up at her. "Guess who just texted me. Your mystery man masseur has confirmed my appointment for six-thirty tomorrow."

Hannah sat down and handed him the note. "And guess who came by today."

He read it and then turned to her. "So, your sister's okay. Does this mean we're calling off the massage and the misdemeanor thing?"

Hannah shrugged. "I'm not sure. To be honest, I don't think I'll stop worrying completely until I talk face-to-face with Eden and she tells me that she's fine." She took the note from him. "I guess this means everything's okay, but I still feel a little weird about it. I don't know why."

"So are we still on with this scheme tomorrow or not?"

"Let's call Ellie and find out what she thinks," Hannah said.

She frowned at Eden's note and then folded it up.

CHAPTER THIRTY

Thursday, September 17, 1:04 P.M.
Chicago

The girl was lying with her eyes open and the right side of her face pressed against a pool of blood on the wood floor. Dressed in panties that appeared too big for her and a bra, she was curled up almost in a fetal position. It looked as if she'd been crammed into the tiny, claustrophobic shack that had been her prison for the previous two weeks.

A red ink stamp was in the bottom corner of the eight-by-ten black-and-white photo:

DO NOT DUPLICATE
Property of the Chicago Tribune

Ellie turned over the picture and read the caption, typed on a yellowing label and stuck on the back:

9/27/70—The body of CRYSTAL JUNEAU, 18, in a backyard shed at the residence of BERNICE WHEELER and LYLE DUNCAN WHEELER at 756 Corliss Road, Rural Route 11, Waukegan, IL

Ellie knew that Lyle had slashed Crystal's throat. An uncontrollable morbid curiosity made her eyes instinctively go to the dead girl's neck, but Crystal's shoulder was hunched up, covering Lyle's handiwork. For that, Ellie was grateful.

She studied the crude, inhumane accommodations in Crystal's little prison: a rumpled sleeping bag stained with blood, a Bible, and some open tins of cat food. Ellie couldn't help wondering if Eden O'Rourke was currently surviving under similar conditions.

Hannah had phoned last night to say that Eden must have been by the bungalow yesterday while no one was home. She'd collected some clothes. Hannah knew her half-sister kept a journal, and it was missing from Eden's desk. On the bed was a note, in Eden's handwriting, saying she was fine but not yet ready to come back to school.

Hannah had already told her parents about the note. Though they'd expressed some lingering concern, they'd seemed relieved, too. All of it was quite typical of Eden.

Considering this new development, Hannah had wondered if Ellie still wanted to investigate Nick Jensen's apartment tonight.

Ellie had no intention of canceling their plans—as long as Alden was all right keeping the pretense of his six-thirty appointment tonight. There was so much more Ellie wanted to tell Hannah, but she didn't want to worry her even more.

It was Hannah who had first noticed the similarities between recent events and the Immaculate Conception Killer's timeline. But perhaps she didn't know or she'd forgotten that Lyle Duncan Wheeler had forced Crystal Juneau to write her sister a note, saying she was fine and just needed to get away for a while. Everyone had believed the note—until the murders started. Ellie knew only because she'd been reading so much about the murders. But she had kept mum about it.

Until she got a look inside Nick Jensen's apartment, Ellie didn't want to say anything that would cause Hannah or her parents any undue panic.

Hannah didn't even know about Ellie's friendship with Diana Mackie. So much of tonight's prospective investigation was propelled by Diana's mysterious suicide. No one except the police had any idea about Ellie's connection to the case. Her name didn't come up in any of the news releases about Diana's death. In fact, there was very little written about her death at all. The university must have seen to that. It would have looked bad for the school.

The social media buzz among the students regarding Diana was vague and unspectacular. There were tweets about a "suicide by hanging," but people weren't sure exactly where it had happened or why. One tweet had Diana hanging herself in the church, and another had her swinging from a tree in the arboretum. No one seemed to know that she'd been found in the grotto. And only a few people seemed to really care.

Diana's family was having a very private funeral for her in Eau Claire. No local memorial was being planned.

Ellie felt like she was the only one who gave a damn. That was why after her Thursday class had gotten out at eleven, she'd driven to her old digs, the *Chicago Tribune* offices in the Tribune Tower. Now, she was at a desk in the staff room of the newspaper's library and archives. She was a longtime acquaintance of the head librarian, Jim Mitchell, who had always reminded her of Morgan Freeman. He knew everything that went on at the newspaper and had an encyclopedic knowledge of Chicago history. Jim had given her free rein to pore over the newspaper's files on the 1970 Immaculate Conception murders.

Ellie had tried online to find crime scene photos of Greta Mae Louden's murder. She'd wanted to compare them with what she'd seen in the grotto on Monday night. All she'd uncovered online was one blurry black-and-white shot of Greta's body at a distance—a vague, faceless shape in the wooded ravine by the campus library. It could have been a mannequin.

Ellie knew the newspaper would have plenty of photographs in their archives, including photos too grisly for newspaper publication. And here was the proof in this shot of Crystal Juneau's corpse. Next in the thick pile of photos was a shot of the dilapidated shed in the Wheelers' yard. The little shed sat beside a thorny-looking shrub in the mostly dirt yard. A dead tree and a ramshackle house stood in the background.

Then there was a picture of Crystal on the slab in the morgue. It was a close-up of her droopy, splotchy face—with her mouth slightly open. Someone had closed her eyes. The mortal wound on her throat looked like a black smile.

Wincing, Ellie forced herself to keep going through the collection of documents and photos. She found one of a chubby blond girl lying on a blood-strewn, tiled bathroom floor. Her head was near the toilet, which had one of those rug-like covers on the lid. The summer nightgown she wore was hiked up over her matching panties to reveal slash marks on her torso. The photo was too graphic for Ellie, and she quickly turned it over. The typed label on the back read:

9/27/70—The body of APRIL HUNNICUTT, 19, in the upstairs bathroom of her dorm residence: Bungalow 18, St. Agnes Village, Blessed Heart of Mary College, Delmar, IL

The very next photo was of a partially dressed body amid a pile of leaves under a bridge. It was taken at a distance, but Ellie could see the girl's blouse was open, and from the waist down, she had on only a pair of pantyhose and one shoe. Her face was discolored and dark compared to her pale body. Ellie flipped over the photograph:

9/20/70—20-year-old JANE MARIE EGGERT, strangled, body discovered under Sycamore Way Bridge, Delmar, IL

"I think some of these photos might be out of order," Ellie called to Jim. He was on the other side of the room, at his desk, eating a Milky Way and typing on his computer keyboard.

He barely glanced up from his work. "Don't look at me," he said. "You can blame Mike McGoldrick. He was the last one to go through that file."

"What for?" Ellie asked. "Did he give you a reason?"

Jim sat back and finally looked at her. "He wanted to do a feature story on the fiftieth anniversary of the murders. He even scheduled interviews with the families of some of the victims. Then he tried to get in to see a nun at a rest home run by the archdiocese. She was close to two of the girls who died. The archdiocese got wind of what Mike was doing, and they put the kibosh on the whole project. Suddenly none of the victims' families would talk to Mike. Apparently, the university didn't want to see that old nasty business dredged up again. I mean, they changed their name from Blessed Heart of Mary to Our Lady of the Cove hoping to distance themselves from what happened there, hoping people would forget. Anyway, Mike wasn't a happy camper for a few days after that. Want part of my Milky Way?"

Staring wide-eyed at him, Ellie shook her head. "No, thanks."

"So I hope you were on the level with me earlier when you said you were just curious," Jim said, "because if you plan to write anything about those killings, you're going to run into a lot of interference, Ellie."

With a sigh, she nodded at him. "Thanks, Jim."

She went back to the pile of photos in front of her. Each one was gruesome or disturbing or just plain heartbreaking. Some she couldn't look at for more than a second. In others she studied every detail for clues— even though she wasn't sure what she was looking for.

Among the collection, she found a police composite sketch of the Immaculate Conception Killer before he'd been identified as Lyle Duncan Wheeler. The drawing was based on a witness's description of a "non-student" in his mid-twenties seen outside the library walking with Greta Mae Louden on the night she was killed. It showed a cold, cruel-looking stranger with shaggy, light brown hair, glasses, and a thick mustache. The sketch didn't look much like the photo of Wheeler, taken when he was being escorted to a police car in handcuffs—

with his short, dark hair, a wide smile, and demonic, staring eyes that reminded Ellie of Charles Manson.

She also came across a clear photo of the note Crystal Juneau had been forced to write to her sister, assuring her that she was fine. The penmanship was perfect. Ellie imagined Crystal's grade school nuns must have taught her cursive very well. Ellie furtively took a photo of the note with her phone, in case she needed to show it to Hannah later. Jim didn't seem to notice.

A few photos farther down in the stack, Ellie found what she was looking for.

It was a shot of Greta Mae Louden's corpse sprawled among the leaves and dirt in the ravine by the campus library. Her face was slightly turned away, but the wavy, pale-colored hair looked so much like Diana's. She wore a cardigan, a shirt with a Peter Pan collar, a kilt skirt, and knee socks. A purse and some books were scattered on the ground beside the body.

Ellie had brought a magnifying glass with her. She'd known she might need it.

The same way she already knew the title of one of the books by Greta Mae's corpse.

Ellie held the magnifying glass over the photograph and focused on the cover to *Look Homeward, Angel* by Thomas Wolfe.

Ellie glanced at the dashboard clock: 5:17 P.M.

She was passing Bahai Temple, the majestic shrine on the lake in Wilmette. She'd always thought it looked like an old-fashioned citrus juicer. No matter how many times she'd driven by, she had to admire it. Ellie also considered the temple as a milepost whenever she drove back from Chicago on Lake Shore Drive to Sheridan Road. It usually meant she had about an hour until she was home—if traffic was decent.

That didn't give her much time to get ready for to-night's break-in operation. She'd have to drive directly to Nick Jensen's apartment in Highland Park. She could brief Alden and Hannah over the phone. They didn't really have to do anything except watch Alden's dorm for Nick's arrival, and then call to let her know once Nick headed back to his car.

Ellie told herself this undertaking tonight wouldn't be too risky or challenging—not if the key was where Nick had left it Tuesday night. Still, she had an awful feeling in the pit of her stomach. She felt a bit woozy, too. Of course, looking at all those horrific photos at the newspaper's library hadn't helped.

Ellie kept her window open, and the cool breeze off the lake seemed to help.

She hadn't intended to take so long looking through the files. In addition to the photographs, she'd also studied several articles on the Immaculate Conception killings and taken notes.

At one point, she'd waited until Jim left the room for a few minutes. Then she used her phone's camera to take a picture of the crime scene photo of Greta Mae Louden's body in the ravine. Ellie tried for a second shot while holding the magnifying glass over the image of the book. It took her a few tries before she got it so that the title, *Look Homeward, Angel*, was at least par-tially readable.

After that, from the lobby of the Tribune Tower, she texted the two photos to Detective Castino—along with a message:

Det. Castino: This is a photo of the first victim of the
Immaculate Conception Killer. She was murdered on 9/14/70,
exactly 50 yrs before Diana Mackie's death. She too was last
seen leaving the college library. Note the books scattered
around the scene. Note the title of one book, magnified in the
other photo: Look Homeward, Angel. Do you still think the
book is insignificant? The girl's name was Greta Mae Louden,
and she looked like Diana. I think we have a copycat killer.
Please call me and we'll discuss. Thank you.

It had occurred to Ellie while she'd been examining
the more gruesome photos in the newspaper's files:
How had this copycat killer picked up such a minute
detail from an old crime scene? She'd needed a magnifying glass to discern that one of the books around
Greta's corpse was *Look Homeward, Angel*. That photo
hadn't been published in the newspaper or online. Had
it been written up in some obscure article exactly what
books had fallen out of Greta's bag the night she'd been
strangled?

Ellie had walked over to Jim's desk and showed
him the photo. "How could someone get a hold of an
unpublished picture like this one? Somebody I know
described to me in detail this photo—right down to the
title of one of the books here in the foreground."

He'd grinned at her. "Well, I'd say that's one morbid
son of a bitch."

Ellie had given a weak laugh. But no sooner had she
asked the question than she thought of a possible
answer. Maybe the copycat killer was a reporter or a
policeman—or, more likely, the son of a reporter or a cop
who had covered the case fifty years ago.

"Still, I'm wondering how this guy could know about everything in this photo," Ellie had pressed.

Jim had shrugged. "Some of these murders and serial killings have fans. They can be very resourceful. They go online and swap unpublished photos with other fans. Some will even pay good money for an uncensored crime scene photo—especially if it's a murder that really fascinates them. A picture like that one could easily go for a couple of hundred—maybe even a grand for the negative. Hell, if I weren't such an honest, scrupulous guy, I'd be rich . . ."

As Ellie drove past the tall brick pylon at Winnetka's Tower Road beach, she wondered if tonight, in Nick Jensen's apartment, she'd find photos like the ones she'd seen in the *Trib*'s archives.

Her smartphone rang. She had it bracketed to the dashboard. She glanced at the screen for a second: *Det. Castino, Anton*. Ellie reached past the steering wheel and touched the phone screen to put him on speaker mode. "Detective Castino?"

"Hello, Ms. Goodwin," he said cheerlessly. "I got your text. And you're right. It's a very interesting coincidence—and something we'll be sure to investigate further. But I don't want you jumping to any quick conclusions that Diana's death was the result of some copycat killer. Talk like that can cause a panic."

"I understand," she said, tightening her grip on the steering wheel. "But look at what's happened: first, the fire in the laundry bungalow exactly fifty years after the baby-killing incident. Then, on the fiftieth anniversary of Crystal Juneau's disappearance, Eden O'Rourke disappears—"

"Is this the girl who sent a text to her sister saying

she was fine and coming back soon?" Castino asked, his tone dripping with irony.

"Crystal's sister got a note just like it—and all the while, Crystal was being held prisoner in a shack in Lyle Duncan Wheeler's backyard. And look at the similarities between Greta Mae Louden's murder and Diana's death on Monday night. Did you even bother to look up Greta online and check her picture? Did you see how much she looks like Diana?"

"Yes, I *bothered*," he replied. "And, yes, I see a similarity between the girls—"

"They were both in the library before they were killed. The same book was found by their bodies. Diana was killed on the fiftieth anniversary of Greta Mae's murder."

"The problem here is that you're looking at all the tiny similarities, Ms. Goodwin, and not the big, big differences. You say there's a copycat killer on the loose. But if that's true, he's not really copying the murders, is he? Another consideration—serial killers, especially copycats, most of them are publicity hounds. They want their work to be noticed. So why would this 'copycat' go to such lengths to make Diana's death look like a suicide? For a copycat, he's sure working under the radar, and he's very, very subtle."

"So he doesn't fit the normal profile," Ellie argued, glancing at her phone for a second. "That doesn't mean he isn't out there."

"Ms. Goodwin," he said with a heavy sigh. She could picture the Danny DeVito lookalike at his messy desk with his Dr Pepper and Little Debbie. "You've had quite a shock. And you may even feel responsible for what happened to Diana, because she turned to you for help and you weren't able to get to her on time. But no one's blaming you. I think you're grasping at straws. Someone pulled a sick prank and set a small fire on the fiftieth anniversary of something. So you want to take it seriously because it will help explain away what happened to your friend. I know you have the best of intentions. Have you thought about what we discussed last time? Have you spoken with a grief counselor or one of the priests there at the university?"

"Not yet," Ellie growled, squirming in the driver's seat.

"Well, I'm sure if you consulted with one of the fathers there, he'd agree with me. This talk about a possible copycat killer, it could really hurt the school. I'm sure you don't want that. Diana's parents strike me as very private people who want to keep their grief private, too. You don't want to cause them any more pain, do you?"

"Of course not," she sighed.

"Listen, I have another call right now," he said. Ellie figured that was a lie. "Anyway, I appreciate that you're trying to help . . ."

Another lie.

"I'll give you a call in a couple of days and let you know if any of this information you gave us pans out. Okay?"

And still another lie.

"Thank you, Detective," she said, frowning. She reached up and pressed the hang-up icon on her phone screen.

Ellie thought about Jane Marie Eggert, found strangled under a bridge along Sycamore Way on September 20, 1970.

Three days from now.

How was Detective Castino going to feel if another girl died on Saturday?

More important, Ellie thought, *how am I going to feel?*

If she had any reservations about breaking into Nick Jensen's apartment tonight, they were gone now.

The bogus appointment Alden had made with him was in less than an hour.

Ellie shifted in the driver's seat and pressed harder on the gas pedal.

CHAPTER THIRTY-ONE

Thursday, 6:09 P.M.

Sitting in the front seat of her parked Toyota, Ellie watched Nick Jensen's apartment building across the street. For the last ten minutes, she'd been keeping her eyes on the front window of his second-floor unit. The curtains were open. It was just starting to get dark. The streetlights were on. She could see a light was on in his apartment, too. But from where she sat, she couldn't tell if anyone was home.

She'd called Hannah to check in with her. According to Hannah, she and Alden had gotten an outside table at Campus Grounds with an unobstructed view of everyone coming and going from O'Leary Hall. Alden had his phone with him—in case Jensen called to cancel or anything. They would phone her once they spotted him heading into the dorm—and then again, when they saw him leaving.

It occurred to Ellie while she waited that Jensen might not even be home right now. He could have just left the light on. Maybe he was out on another appointment and planned to leave from there for O'Leary Hall. Instead of wasting valuable time sitting here in the car, waiting for him to appear, she could be in his apartment, searching the place.

She glanced at her wristwatch. He should have left for O'Leary Hall by now. It took about twenty minutes to get to the campus from here.

Ellie decided to give it five more minutes, and then she'd go up there and try to peek through the window. Her stomach rumbled, and she could feel herself perspiring. *What if the stupid key wasn't in the flower box?* she thought, *then this whole thing would be for nothing.*

She saw his window curtains shut. A moment later, the door opened.

Ellie slouched down behind the wheel and watched as Jensen carried his folded-up massage table out of the apartment. He was dressed in black shorts, a gray T-shirt, and a gray sweatshirt, unzipped in front. He shut the door behind him, gave it a twist to check it, and then carried the table down the walkway to the stairs.

She watched him lug the contraption across the parking lot. He glanced around a couple of times— almost as if he thought someone was watching him. Ellie slumped even lower in the seat. Could it be he knew he was being set up?

He loaded the table in the trunk of his car, an old red Ford Fiesta. Then he looked around again and climbed into the car. After a couple of minutes, the car lights went on and he pulled out of the lot.

Ellie told herself to sit still for another sixty seconds—just in case he realized he'd forgotten something. That minute seemed to drag by. Finally, she grabbed her purse and phone and stepped out of the car. She hurried across the street to the L-shaped building. She headed up the stairs, and as she reached the top step, Ellie heard a door open. She stopped dead.

A woman emerged from another unit. She was talking on her phone. Ellie stepped aside and smiled at the woman. Without even a glance her way, Nick's neighbor headed down the stairs. Ellie leisurely walked toward unit seventeen and knocked on the door. She knew the woman could see her from the parking lot if she bothered to look up. Ellie dug into her purse, took out her phone, and pretended to make a call. All the while, she watched the woman down in the lot. Once the woman had driven out of the lot and turned down the street, Ellie shoved the phone back in her purse. Then she glanced around and stepped over to the flower box. She lifted up the first of three small flowerpots. She didn't see a key.

"Shit!" she hissed.

She put the pot back and tried the next pot. There it was.

She snatched up the key, put the pot back, and then, with a shaky hand, she slipped the key into the lock for unit seventeen. She heard a click and opened the door. For a moment, she held her breath, waiting for an alarm to go off.

Nothing.

Ellie put the key back under the flowerpot, and then she quickly turned around and slipped inside the apartment. Her mouth was dry and her heart raced.

The place was clean, but stark—with only a few furnishings. Everything looked like it was from Ikea. There was a sofa, and above it, the only thing on the otherwise bare beige walls—a large, unframed print of Edward Hopper's *Nighthawks*. Ellie had always thought everyone in that painting looked so lonely and sad. A small TV sat on a folding table and beside that, another folding table with a computer on it and a chair. A solitary barstool was at the counter bar that divided the tiny kitchen from the living area.

Everything looked so temporary—like he hadn't been there long and didn't intend to stay long either.

Ellie checked the computer to see if he was still logged in. But as soon as the monitor came on, a password request appeared. She tried *Nick*. That didn't work.

Then she got an idea that made her shudder. She typed in *Lyle*.

That didn't work either. She decided not to push her luck and risk a third incorrect guess that would lock up the computer. She didn't want him to know anyone had been in the apartment.

She noticed a spiral notebook by the computer, but when she opened it, there were only a couple of pages of notes he'd taken in her class—and some doodling. The rest of the notebook was blank.

On the floor, to the side of the sofa, she noticed two books—both from the university's library: *East of Eden* by John Steinbeck and *The Cider House Rules* by John Irving. Ellie made a mental note to check later with the library to find out if the books had been checked out or stolen.

She detected a pleasant, subtle spicy-musky scent from one of the two rooms off the small hallway. She switched on the light in the bathroom. It was tidy, but the light fixture and the cheap, pressed-wood cabinet looked outdated. She opened up the medicine chest, but didn't see any prescription bottles amid the toothpaste and other toiletries. She'd been hoping to find out if he went by another name.

The pleasing aroma came from the room next door. It was also the homiest room in the place. There were two comfortable-looking chairs and a handsome dresser with a phone port and speakers and a couple of sleek glass candleholders on top of it. A standing oscillating fan stood in the corner. A dark curtain covered the window. Two framed Jackson Pollock prints hung on the walls. Ellie realized that this was where he gave massages. There was a big gap in the middle of the room where he must have had the massage table set up when not on house calls. She wondered where he slept.

She opened the dresser drawers and found neatly folded sheets and towels—along with an array of lotions and bottles of essential oils. Peeking behind the dresser and underneath, she didn't discover anything he was hiding. She didn't have much luck in the closet either. His limited wardrobe was nice and conservative, except for the one Hawaiian shirt she didn't like. The shelf along the top held a couple of sweaters and nothing else. There were no mysterious boxes or storage bins—just a laundry bag with some sheets and clothing in it.

Heading back into the living room, Ellie lifted the seat cushions on the sofa. Nothing was hidden there—except the sofa bed. Now, at least she knew where he slept.

She was checking under the couch when her phone rang. It was too soon for Jensen to have made it to the campus already. Ellie grabbed the phone out of her purse and checked the caller's name on the screen: *O'Hurley, Robert.*

It took her only a moment to realize why Father O'Hurley was calling. Obviously, Detective Castino had contacted him because she was being a pain in the ass. "Well, that didn't take long," she muttered to herself, shoving the phone back in her bag.

Finding nothing hidden in the living room, she looped around the counter bar and checked the kitchen cupboards. Jensen certainly had a healthy diet—not a bag of chips or candy in sight. On the top shelf, she saw a big box of Honey Nut Cheerios and a large container of Quaker Oats. The Quaker Oats container seemed like the ideal hiding place for a gun, a computer file, or even some rolled-up documents. On her tiptoes, she reached up and grabbed the Quaker Oats. She opened the container. It was about half-full—with Quaker Oats. She even shook the oats around, but nothing was hidden at the bottom of the container.

Frowning, she put the Quaker Oats back on the shelf and reached for the Honey Nut Cheerios. The box was too heavy for cereal. The top flaps on the box were worn and slightly frayed—as if they'd been opened and closed repeatedly and for a long time. She opened the flaps and found the cereal box stuffed with papers. Ellie carefully pulled them out. There were three manila folders full of documents. Ellie thought she might find a collection of grisly photos like the ones she'd just seen in that file at the *Tribune*'s library.

In the first folder, on top of a stack of papers, was a printout of Hannah's Instagram page—with a selfie of her and Rachel Bonner eating pizza:

My new favorite pizza place is Bellini's in Delmar! Best. Pizza. Ever. #gobellinis #carbfeast #cantgetenoughpizza

The rest of the folder was full of printouts of other social media posts from Hannah, along with newspaper clippings and stories about her and Eden.

It looked like Jensen was obsessed with the two of them.

Ellie flipped through the next folder. It was the thickest of the three, crammed with printouts and clippings about Rachel Bonner and her parents.

The third folder was the thinnest—just a few pieces of paper. Ellie stared at what was on top of the papers: a newspaper clipping with the headline

SHEBOYGAN GIRL DIES IN BICYCLE ACCIDENT

*Kayla Kennedy Was Known
for Heroic Rescue of
Drowning Mother and Child*

"Shit," he said, pulling over to the side of the road.

He was about half way between his apartment and the campus.

He didn't have a good feeling about the massage appointment with this Patrick Murphy kid. First, most of his clients were adults. This was a student at the university, and the kid wanted the massage to take place in his dorm room at O'Leary Hall. A noisy dormitory for boys hardly seemed like the ideal setting for a massage session. And how many students could afford to drop a hundred dollars for a massage? It seemed like a setup. Somebody was punking somebody else—and at his expense, too.

On his phone, he found a number for O'Leary Hall.

Though he figured he'd get a recording, he gave it a try anyway.

A man answered: "O'Leary Hall, front desk."

"Hi, yeah, I have a pizza delivery for Patrick Murphy in room four-oh-three. I just want to make sure he's in."

"Let me check for you. Hold on a sec."

While he waited, a few cars passed him on the road.

"Hello?" The desk clerk came back on the line. "Jim Munchel and Anthony Wingarter are in room four-oh-three, and neither one of them ordered a pizza."

"Thanks," he said, frowning.

He clicked off the line, glanced in his rearview mirror, and started to turn the car around.

"Would you relax?" Alden said. "He couldn't possibly trace this to you."

At their outside table at Campus Grounds, Hannah sat facing the quad and the front entrance to O'Leary Hall across the way. The men's dorm was one of the more modern buildings on campus—a cold-looking, five-story, concrete-and-glass structure. But the entryway was well lit, and she could see people coming and going.

Night had fallen, and Hannah felt a slight chill creeping through the air. She sipped her decaf latte and nervously rubbed her arms. "Ellie and I didn't think everything through when we asked you to do this," she said. "This Jensen guy knows me. I've posted pictures of Rachel and me on Instagram. And through Rachel, he could easily link you to me."

Alden put his hand on top of hers. Hannah felt a pleasant little rush.

"Don't sweat it, okay?" He smiled. "Have you seen me in any of Rachel's social media posts? Like I told you yesterday, Richard and Candace Bonner's girl does not associate with the help. My name isn't linked with Rachel's anywhere. So we're safe. Plus I have my phone under my middle name—Patrick. It helps me screen the unsolicited calls. I also gave the guy a bad room number. There are three other Murphys in that piece-of-shit dorm, and by the time he goes through the three of them and gets to Alden Murphy, I'll just deny, deny, deny. Easy breezy. And you don't have to look for him yet. Our appointment isn't until six-thirty. We have another ten minutes . . ."

Alden's words were reassuring. And he still had his hand on hers, which was even more comforting. Just the same, Hannah kept looking over at the quad and O'Leary Hall.

"We're not going to miss him," Alden said. "He'll be easy to spot. He said he was bringing his massage table."

"Well, don't you two look cozy?"

Hannah glanced up at Rachel, standing by their table. With a straw, she sipped some iced coffee concoction in a clear, tall, plastic glass.

Alden pulled his hand away.

She sat down with them. "Don't mind me. Has Mr. Rub-a-Dub-Dub shown up yet?"

"Not yet," Hannah said nervously.

Alden smiled at her again. "Relax," he whispered. Then he looked at Rachel. "Where were you?"

"Talking with the parental units," she sighed. She turned to Hannah. "I finally opened up the FedEx package. As promised, your father—*our* father—had his doctor send me a DNA kit. It came with very easy, very impersonal instructions. I'm to spit in a vial and stick the vial inside a special envelope and take it to the FedEx office, all pre-paid. Wasn't that thoughtful of our dear dad?"

Hannah felt so ashamed. "I'm sorry, Rachel. Like I tried to explain the other night, they've had so many false alarms—"

"Yeah, well, I'm not some stranger pulling a hoax. I'm your roommate. I'm the one who . . ." She trailed off.

"You're the one who paid for my scholarship," Hannah finished for her. "Eden's scholarship, too."

"Not that she's getting much use out of it this week," Rachel muttered. She patted Hannah's shoulder. "Listen, forget it. I didn't really mean to go there with the scholarship thing. That's my parents talking."

"And how are Dick and Candy?" Alden asked.

"Peachy," she answered, frowning. She sipped her iced coffee drink. "They were all up my ass about this paternity test. They don't want me to take it. They said it's beneath me. My dad says that . . ." She turned to Hannah, "He says that *our* dad will only arrange things with his doctor to fudge the test so it'll look like I'm not really his daughter . . ."

"I don't think he'd do that," Hannah said. She took a quick glance over toward the quad and the dorm again. "He just needs to make certain . . ."

Rachel didn't seem to be listening. "My mom was all, 'Why do you even want anything to do with him? He's given you absolutely nothing.' And blah, blah, blah. They asked me not to take the test until they've talked to me in person. They want me to come home and spend the night on Saturday. I told them, fine." She nudged Hannah under the table. "Listen, would you like to come with?"

Hannah hesitated. "Are you kidding? I'm from the enemy camp."

"My parents have nothing against *you*."

"Well, are you sure they wouldn't mind?"

Rachel rolled her eyes. "Oh, please, they won't even know you're there. It'll be fun . . ."

"Believe me," Alden interjected. "When you see how big the house is, you'll know she isn't kidding."

"It's settled, you're sleeping over Saturday night," Rachel said. "Besides, if Eden doesn't come back before the weekend, I'd hate to leave you alone here. I mean, what with all this weirdness going on right now. Plus that place is creepy when you're alone there at night . . ."

"Wait a minute," Alden said, looking toward the quad. "I think I see our guy . . ."

Hannah followed his gaze. "That's not Nick Jensen. And the man's carrying a painting and an easel."

"Put your glasses on, stupid," Rachel said.

Alden's phone rang. Sitting up, he pulled the phone out of his pocket and gaped at the screen. "It's him," he whispered.

"Put it on speaker," Rachel said.

He took a deep breath and touched the screen. "Hello?"

With a hand over her mouth, Hannah stared at him.

"You gave me the wrong room number, Patrick," Nick Jensen said evenly.

Alden seemed stumped. "Um, really? Gosh, I'm sorry. Where are you?"

"More important, where are you right now? We have an appointment."

"Yeah, I know." Alden gave Hannah a helpless look. "Listen, I'm sorry, but something came up, and I can't make it. I meant to call you—"

"I know what you're up to," Jensen said. "I'm watching you right now."

"What?" Alden asked.

Hannah heard a click.

"Oh, fuck me," Alden whispered. Wide-eyed, he stared at the phone.

"God, do you think he really means it?" Rachel asked.

Panic-stricken, Hannah glanced around. But there were just too many people, all the buildings with windows, all those bushes and trees, too many places where he could be hiding.

"Call Ellie," she said. "We need to call her right now. Tell her what just happened . . ."

"He obviously knows he's been set up," Hannah urgently whispered on the other end of the line. "He said he's watching us now, but—well, I think we'll be okay. We're headed over to the bungalow. Rachel has a bodyguard, and she just called him. He's on his way. He'll be here in, like, five minutes. He'll stay with the three of us. Rachel says he'll stay with us all night if he has to."

"Good," Ellie said. She stood over Nick Jensen's kitchen counter with his files spread out in front of her. "Listen, tell Alden and Rachel I'm sorry I got them into this—"

"It's okay!" she heard Alden yell in the background. "Just get out of there!"

"He's right," Hannah said. "Finish up and get out of there."

"Will do," Ellie answered. "By the way, I found some stuff. It's very interesting. I'll tell you about it later."

"Call us as soon as you're safe and in your car, okay?"

"Okay. Bye." Ellie hung up. Her hands were shaking as she tried to put all the paperwork from Nick Jensen's files back in order.

Amid the clippings, printouts, and scribbled notes, she hadn't found anything about the Immaculate Conception murders from fifty years ago. There was nothing about Diana either. But he was clearly obsessed with Rachel Bonner, her family, and her roommates. She'd found detailed notes from discussions he'd had with Hannah and Eden. But Ellie couldn't quite decipher them because of his penmanship and all the abbreviations.

She wished she had more time to go over everything, maybe even take some photos of his notes, but she couldn't risk hanging around there any longer.

She heard a car in the parking lot outside. Her heart racing, Ellie hurried to the window and moved the curtain a tiny bit—just enough to peek down at the lot. It was one of Jensen's neighbors. She watched a station wagon pull out of the lot and onto the street.

Ellie told herself that it was too soon for Jensen to have already returned from the campus—unless he was lying to Alden on the phone. Was he really watching Hannah, Alden, and Rachel—or was he just trying to intimidate them? Ellie hated the idea that she may have put Hannah and her friends in danger.

She was about to move away from the window when she spotted the red Ford Fiesta already parked in the lot—the same spot Jensen had been in before.

It looked like the car was empty.

Ellie heard someone coming up the outside stairs.

Backing away from the window, she helplessly looked around for some place to hide—or something she could use as a weapon.

She froze at the sound of the key in the door.

There was a click, and then the door opened. From the threshold, Nick Jensen glared at her.

Ellie couldn't move or talk. Standing in the middle of his living room, she gaped back at him. He was blocking the exit.

"What are you doing?" he asked finally. "Is someone else here with you?"

She shook her head.

"So what the hell are you doing in my apartment?" He stepped inside and shut the door behind him.

Ellie swallowed hard. "Why do you have files on Rachel Bonner and the O'Rourke sisters—and that girl who died?"

He didn't answer. He looked over toward the papers spread across his kitchen counter.

"What have you done with Eden O'Rourke?" Ellie dared to ask.

"Nothing," he replied, still standing by the closed door. He shoved his hands into the pockets of his sweatshirt. "I ran into her at the Sunnyside Up Café last Friday night and haven't seen her since."

"*No one* has seen her since," Ellie said.

He let out a sigh. "I had a bad feeling that was the case. Her sister told me yesterday afternoon that Eden went off by herself to Chicago for a while. But the way Hannah acted when she talked to me, I wasn't sure what to think . . ."

Ellie warily studied his face. Was his concern real—

or just part of the innocent routine she'd seen him do before?

She was still scared, but impatient, too. She frowned at him. "I'll ask you again. Why do you have files on those girls? Why do Eden O'Rourke's whereabouts matter to you?"

"Because Eden is Rachel Bonner's roommate," he said. "And that's not a good thing to be. Last year, Rachel's roommate, a girl named Kayla, was going to help me when she suddenly met up with a fatal *accident* . . ."

Ellie kept staring at him. In his track shorts, T-shirt, and open sweatshirt, it didn't look like he was carrying any concealed weapons. He hadn't attacked her or even threatened her yet, and he easily could have. "Who are you?" she asked. "Is Nick Jensen even your real name?"

He didn't answer. Wincing, he rubbed his forehead. Then he walked past her to his refrigerator and opened it up. "Would you like a beer? I could sure use one. I also have bottled water in here, a Sprite, and a couple of Cokes."

"Never mind that," Ellie said. Her heart was still racing. "Why did you enroll in my journalism class?"

"Because Hannah O'Rourke tweeted about it over the summer," he replied, taking out a beer and a bottle of water. Then he shut the refrigerator door with his elbow. He handed her the water. "Here. Let me know if you'd like something livelier. In her tweet, Hannah said she was looking forward to taking your class, and they were making a movie about you. She mentioned that Eden was taking the same class. I figured, if I took your course, I'd have a good chance of getting to know at least one of them."

"Why is it so important to know the O'Rourke girls?" Ellie asked.

"Because in an earlier tweet, Hannah said she and Eden were going to be roommates with Rachel Bonner. And that interested me very much." He walked over to his sofa and sat down.

Ellie narrowed her eyes at him. "Why? I don't understand any of this . . ."

He opened his beer. "Well, first off, you're right. Nick Jensen isn't my real name." He let out a dazed little laugh. "Jesus, after two years, it sounds weird to hear myself actually saying that to somebody."

He raised his beer can as if toasting her. "My name's Nate Bergquist. I'm from Portland, Oregon, Ms. Goodwin. And I'm supposed to be dead . . ."

CHAPTER THIRTY-TWO

Thursday, 6:53 P.M.

"After the explosion, I don't remember anything until I woke up a few days later," he said, sitting on one end of the sofa with the beer in his hand.

Ellie was at the other end of the couch. She'd switched from bottled water to beer. As a reporter, she was used to listening to people's stories. She could usually tell when someone was lying, and so far, she believed what Nate Bergquist was telling her about the assault on him, his detective brother, and their girlfriends in a remote cabin in Oregon two years ago.

"I found myself in a strange bed and in the care of this middle-aged woman," he continued. "It was a scene right out of *Misery*. I kept thinking that's how I would have described it to my brother, Gil. We always compared real life to the movies. I was just like James Caan in the film, really banged up. I had a broken leg, a broken arm, fractures, bruises, all these horrible cuts and burns. The burns were the worst . . ." He pointed to the scar on his forehead and then rolled up the sleeve of his sweatshirt to show her his arm. "You noticed this the other day. I didn't get it in a motorcycle accident when I was a teenager. I got it two years ago—in the explosion."

Ellie grimaced. She suddenly felt stupid, thinking he was with that group of arsonists.

"Anyway, the woman was a nurse. And she wasn't Annie Wilkes or Kathy Bates. Her name was Ruth, and she put me back together again. She was a godsend. It helped that I was a physical therapist and knew what to do to heal faster. Just the same, I was laid up in Ruth's house in Beaverton for months. I was hiding, too. Ruth was friends with a guy who worked for my brother. His name was Frank Pomeroy. He was Gil's 'invisible partner.' Nobody knew about him. Remember I mentioned that, after those two creeps showed up at the cabin, I thought Gil might have secretly phoned somebody? Well, he did. He called Frank."

Nate Bergquist shrugged and then sipped his beer. "I guess Gil knew we were in trouble. He knew some terrible people were out to get him. According to Frank, after he got the call from my brother, he drove like a bat out of hell to the cabin. He was off the highway and on the private road to the cabin when he saw the explosion. He managed to save me. It was too late for the others. He loaded me into his car and drove me to Ruth's. The fire from the blast did a lot of damage to the woods around there. There was nothing left of the cabin. There was nothing left of my girlfriend, Rene, either, nothing to identify her . . ."

He started to tear up and quickly wiped his eyes. "Sorry, I've never really discussed this with anybody. I'm not used to it." He let out a shaky sigh. "Anyway, there were enough remains to identify the others. But both Rene and I were assumed dead."

He cleared his throat and took a swallow of beer. "Whoever employed those two thugs, they must have had some influence with the local police or bribed somebody, because it came out that my brother was running a crystal meth lab in the cabin, and that's why the place exploded. There were even stories about me stealing and selling drugs from the veterans hospital where I worked. I found out about it days later, when I was recovering at Ruth's house. Eventually, the investigators put it together that the crystal meth story was bogus. But they knew something was up because of the criminal records and various aliases for the two creeps who had showed up at the cabin that night."

"Did they ever figure it out?" Ellie asked.

Nate shook his head.

"Why didn't you go to the police?"

"Frank convinced me I'd be a lot better off if everyone thought I was dead. He was worried people were watching him. He persuaded me to stay in hiding at Ruth's place. He'd saved my life. I didn't want to put him in any more danger than he already was."

"Did you ever find out what Rachel Bonner had to do with all this?" Ellie asked.

He frowned. "Well, we figured Gil must have discovered something about Rachel or her family during one of his private investigations. Gil was my brother, and I loved him. But he definitely had a sleazy side. I think he was trying to extort money from the Bonners or an associate of the Bonners. That's how he got himself in trouble—and how he got himself killed. While I was convalescing, Frank dug up what he could about Gil's various jobs in the months leading up to his death. He'd been doing some work on and off for a woman named Cassandra Farrell in Portland. She'd first hired him about fifteen years before, and again, every few years after that . . ."

"Cassandra Farrell," Ellie repeated. "You mean the woman who raised Eden O'Rourke?"

"Exactly," Nate said, nodding. "Gil had been investigating Dylan and Sheila O'Rourke for her."

"He must have found out about Sheila's sister and the affair with Dylan—and the baby the Bonners adopted. There's the Rachel connection."

"Yeah, but at the time, Frank had no idea what Gil discovered. My brother did a good job covering his tracks—and his findings. I'm sure that's why no one ever connected him to the O'Rourkes when they were in the headlines a couple of years ago. So, back when I was convalescing at Ruth's, we didn't see a link between the O'Rourkes and Rachel Bonner. We still had no idea what Gil had found out. I became pretty obsessed about it. I wanted to know why my girlfriend, my brother, and his girlfriend were all killed. I wanted to know why my life had been destroyed. Frank told me that I'd live a lot longer if I just let it go. He even pulled back on his own investigation into it."

Nate took another drag of his beer. "So, I focused on getting better. Good old Frank, like Gil, he had a few shady business associates. And through one of them, they got me a new identity—and all the fake documents to go with it. They even gave me a name close to my own—*Nick, Nate*. Anyway, after four months living off the kindness of Frank Pomeroy and Ruth, *Nick Jensen* moved to Taos, New Mexico. I laid low for a year, got a massage license, and saved my money."

Wincing, he shifted around a bit on the sofa. "I was there only a couple of months when Ruth got word to me that Frank was shot and killed in what looked like a random mugging. I didn't buy that it was *random*. I still think it had something to do with whatever Gil started. Fortunately, Ruth's okay. We still check in with each other every few weeks."

"Then you moved here in April," Ellie said.

Nodding, he let out a surprised little laugh. "How did you figure that out?"

"A lucky guess," Ellie explained. "Your massage reviews online, the earliest one is in April."

"By then, I figured things had blown over, and maybe I was safe enough to move closer to where the Bonners live," he said. "I couldn't let go of what happened. I made it my mission to find out all I could about Rachel Bonner, her family, and her father's business associates. I hung around here at the school and got to know Rachel's roommate, Kayla Kennedy. The two of them had started out as friends, but it soured after a couple of months. Still, while they were chums, Rachel confided in Kayla quite a lot. And Kayla confided in me. I found out that Rachel has a bodyguard-chauffeur named Perry, living close by in town. Rachel's parents have her on a short leash. They're worried about her getting kidnapped. But they're also worried about her getting into trouble. According to Kayla, this Perry is also a babysitter-watchdog of sorts. I guess the Bonners had good reason to be concerned. Rachel admitted to Kayla that, when she was sixteen, she had a two-month affair with a married business associate of her father's."

"My God," Ellie murmured. Still, she told herself she shouldn't be too surprised. From everything she knew about Rachel Bonner, the girl had always seemed too sophisticated for her own good. Or maybe she was just terribly naive.

"I wondered if this was the piece of information Gil had picked up," Nate explained, "the tidbit he'd used to try to extort money from someone. Kayla didn't have the name of Rachel's onetime lover. Kayla was trying to get back in Rachel's good graces so she could find out for me. She did some digging. We were supposed to get together near her home in Sheboygan when she was killed in a *bike accident*."

"Yes, I read about that," Ellie murmured.

"I think she was murdered because she knew something—or because she was poking around asking too many questions, the same reason Frank was killed. I'm sure someone intentionally ran her off that road. I can't help feeling responsible. I mean, if she hadn't agreed to help me, she'd probably be alive today."

"You didn't kill her," Ellie whispered. "It wasn't your fault."

"Just the same," he muttered. He didn't seem to be listening to her. "I'm pretty sure Rachel had nothing to do with it. She was in Paris when it happened. She flew home in time to attend the funeral. I figured the guilty party was someone hired by Richard Bonner's business associate: a professional hit man, someone like that. But with Kayla dead, I was kind of at a dead end. I mean, Richard Bonner has a hell of a lot of businesses—and business associates. The guy responsible for all of these murders could be one among hundreds . . ."

Ellie heard footsteps on the walkway outside. It sounded like someone approaching his door. She could feel the floor vibrate. Alarmed, she looked at Nate and started to stand up.

But he smiled and shook his head. "Relax, it's just my neighbor. Bigfoot, I call him. There's a lot of coming and going around here this time of night."

Ellie settled back down on the sofa. She couldn't help feeling anxious and on edge. She felt overwhelmed, too. She didn't doubt Nate Bergquist's story. But it didn't have anything to do with the Immaculate Conception murders or what had happened to Diana or Eden—at least, on the surface, it didn't.

"So where was I?" he asked.

"At a dead end."

"Yeah, well, I'd been following Rachel on social media, and about two months ago, her name came up on that tweet from Hannah O'Rourke. They were going to be roommates . . ."

"And suddenly, you had a link between Rachel and your brother's investigation of the O'Rourkes for this Cassandra woman."

"Exactly." He nodded. "Then, like I told you, when I read a tweet from Hannah saying she and Eden had enrolled in your journalism class, I signed up, too." He cracked a smile. "I also signed up because I heard you were a brilliant teacher."

Ellie let out a little laugh. "Yeah, right, thanks."

He glanced down. "Actually, I shouldn't make light of it. I've botched things up something fierce. I don't have my brother's detective skills. In fact, I suck at it. I mean, you had my number the first day in class. You could tell right away that I had an ulterior motive for being there."

"I had a theory about who you were and what you were up to," Ellie admitted. "I'll share it with you later. Anyhow, I was way off base."

"You also caught me eavesdropping on you and Hannah at the pool . . ."

"And she mentioned a private investigator who had been working for the woman who had raised Eden. So of course you were listening . . ."

Nate nodded. "She was talking about Gil. That night, I followed Eden to the Sunnyside Up Café. I was hoping she could tell me more. But I truly must lack my brother's charm or his knack for getting information out of people. As soon as I started asking her questions, Eden clammed up. Shortly after that, she left."

With a look of regret on his handsome face, he leaned back. "And no one has seen her since. The thing of it is—I told myself I'd take a different tack with Hannah and Eden. After Kayla, I wanted to make sure nothing happened to either one of them. Jesus, I hope I didn't screw things up for Eden. I hope she's okay."

"I may as well tell you now," Ellie said. She took her last swig of beer and set the empty can down on the floor. "You were such a mystery man that we thought you might have abducted her. That's why we set this whole thing up tonight—"

"Wait, who's *we*?"

"Hannah, Rachel, and her friend, Alden. He's the one who scheduled the massage appointment with you tonight. It was all so I could break in here and search the place while you were gone."

"Alden *Murphy*," he murmured. "Shit, I'm so stupid, I didn't make the connection. Kayla told me about him. She said he was like Rachel's pet puppy dog. She didn't like him much, but I'm afraid a lot of that had to do with the fact that he's gay and Kayla was a pretty rigid, conservative small-town girl—not exactly open-minded.

Between Rachel's affair with a married man and Alden's sexuality, Kayla was convinced the two of them were going to hell."

Ellie gave him a wary sidelong glance. "How reliable a source do you think she was?"

He shrugged. "I'm not sure. But she was the only source I had." He got to his feet and started to pace in front of her. "So, Rachel, Alden, and Hannah all suspect I'm up to no good . . ."

"Thanks mostly to me, I'm afraid," Ellie admitted.

"So much for me keeping a low profile," he muttered. "And I had plenty to do with blowing my own cover. I thought Alden was some kid pulling a prank. So I told him I was *watching* him."

Ellie nodded. "Yeah, and it worked. You had them all pretty concerned."

"We have to figure out something you can tell them that will put their minds to rest about me. Otherwise, I better buy myself a one-way ticket back to Taos, New Mexico. Listen, you can't tell Hannah or anyone else who I really am." He quickly shook his head. "Actually, I didn't put that right. I'm *asking* you to please not say anything to anyone about my real identity."

Ellie's phone rang. Jumping up from the sofa, she hurried to the kitchen counter, where she'd left her purse. "Oh God, I'm sure that's Hannah. I was supposed to call her."

She dug the phone out of her purse and glanced at the screen: *O'Rourke, Hannah*.

"Wait a minute," Nate whispered urgently. "What are you going to tell her?"

"I don't know yet," she said. Then she touched the

phone screen. "Hannah, I'm so sorry, I completely lost track of the time . . ."

"Are you okay?" Hannah asked anxiously. "We were convinced he'd walked in on you and killed you or something."

"No, he—he returned only a couple of minutes after I got out of the apartment, not long after you and I talked. I saw him from my car. So—I don't think he was watching you guys after all. I think he was just trying to scare Alden."

"Where are you? Why didn't you call me? It's been like a half hour . . ."

"I—I saw a neighbor of his in the parking lot," Ellie lied. "She was taking her dog out for a walk. I caught up with her and got the lowdown on him. I think we were totally wrong about Nick Jensen. This neighbor knows him pretty well. She says he's a real nice guy. He's divorced and dating a widow from Highwood with two kids."

Nate gave her an incredulous look. Ellie just shrugged.

"Well, earlier, you said you found something in his apartment," Hannah pointed out.

"Yeah, he had a—a gun hidden in his closet. I think I made it out to be a lot more *menacing* than it really is. Where are you right now?"

"Rachel, Alden, and I are at the bungalow—with her bodyguard, Perry."

"Well, you can call off the bodyguard," Ellie said. "Nick has been in his apartment for the last half hour. And we really don't have to worry about him. I don't think he had anything to do with Eden's disappearance."

"So, you no longer think he was following me around or anything like that?"

"Nope, no hidden agenda," Ellie replied. "He seems to be just who he says he is. Anyway, I'm sorry to put you guys through all this for nothing. Listen, I'm starving. I'm going to head home and get something to eat. You can call me later tonight if you want. Otherwise, I'll see you in class tomorrow."

"Well, okay," Hannah said, still sounding a bit uncertain. "I'm glad you're safe."

"Be sure to thank everyone there for me, okay?" Ellie said. "Take care."

"Bye," Hannah said.

Ellie touched the phone screen and hung up. She looked at Nate and sighed.

"So you don't think I'm this major creep anymore?" he asked. "You believe me about everything?"

Ellie gave him a dazed smile. "I guess I do. Because I've just lied for you."

CHAPTER THIRTY-THREE

All the other entries in this stupid journal have the date and time at the beginning. That's the way I always do it. But I haven't a fucking clue about the time or what day it is.

So there.

He gave me my journal yesterday—along with some of my clothes, & a copy of Rebecca that he must have ripped off from someone named Diana Mackie (her name's written at the top of the inside cover). He also gave me some more bottles of water, juice boxes (yeah, real delicious lukewarm), granola & power bars, & some fruit. And he dumped out my portable toilet (a tall stew pot with a lid), which is quickly stinking up the place again.

Or maybe it's me that stinks. I think I've been here for about a week. I haven't had a shower or a bath this whole time. He gave me a supply of moist towelettes (sp?) & I've been using them every once in a while to keep from feeling totally disgusting.

Though I got the journal yesterday, I didn't start writing in here until now. I'm sure he'll

*want to read this after he's killed me & I don't
want to give him the satisfaction. In fact, I was
tempted to use the pen he gave me to scratch out
all my other entries in here up until now. But
damn, I liked reading everything I wrote in here
over the summer. The big joke is that all I did
was bitch & moan while I wrote in the comfort
of my bedroom at home back in Seattle & then
I compare it to where I am right now. Anyway, I
figured it'd be a waste using up this Bic just to
scratch out a bunch of shit the guy has probably
already read.*

*Besides, it feels good writing in here now—
like I'm actually doing something, like I'm
talking with somebody, even if it's just myself.
I don't feel so damn bored & lonely & scared.
Plus it sure beats staring at these four
windowless walls (so, so, SO SICK OF THEM!).*

*I'm also glad he left me a good book. All I
had to read before Rebecca was THE good book.
Yeah, the asshole stuck a Bible in here. I guess
that was supposed to keep me enthralled. If I
never have to read the word BEGAT again, I'll
be happy. So—if I'm dead & you're reading this
now, asshole, thanks a lot.*

*I'm still not completely sure what the hell this
is all about. I kept thinking the guy who jumped
me in the woods was that Nick guy from class &
the café. But now, I'm pretty sure it wasn't him. I
have no idea who those two guys at the storage
unit were. But obviously, they were working for
somebody & they thought I knew something
about the detective Cassandra hired. The whole*

episode is cloudy. I was drugged up half the time.

Then I thought someone had come to save me. I have to admit, it scared the shit out of me when he got all Rambo on them & cut that one guy's throat. But I was excited too & grateful as hell. Because I thought I was being rescued—right up until the son of a bitch knocked me out.

Then I woke up on the cot in this little shack. At first, I thought it was a big closet, but then I heard the outside sounds too clearly—the rain or the birds chirping or the insects buzzing. It's happening just on the other side of all four walls. I feel it get colder, and I know night is falling. I feel it on the fake wood floor (some sort of cheap laminate) especially. I think I'm in a tool shed in someone's backyard. The walls— these awful walls—they look like they've been reinforced & maybe even soundproofed. The door & the lock are strong as hell, too. I've kicked & pounded on it & it doesn't seem to do any good.

The light is on here 24/7, but he's got it on some kind of timer so it gets pretty dim for several hours. This is when I'm supposed to sleep, I guess. But fuck him. I stay up. Not that there's anything to do here in the dark. But I refuse to be his lab rat & sleep when he wants me to. So I exercise or eat or go to the bathroom or sing in the dark—just to defy him.

I'm guessing it's never so dark in here that the camera can't see me. I've come to hate it, knowing his prying eyes are watching me all the

*time. But in a weird way, it's company, too. I
don't feel so completely alone. Still, I also have
no privacy at all.*

*So far, he's come in here 3 times—to restock
my supplies & empty the toilet. I know the drill
now. He announces over the speaker (up near
the ceiling) that he's coming. I have to place all
the garbage & the pot by the door. I must lay (or
is it lie?) face-down on the cot with my hands
behind me & a black pillowcase over my head.
Inside of a minute, he collects the trash, dumps
the pot, drops off a new bag of supplies & food
& then he gives the place a spray of Lysol or
something that smells like fresh laundry—
correction, FAKE fresh laundry.*

*Those few moments when he has the door
open are the only time I can feel & smell the
outdoors. I yearn to see what it's like out there,
just a glimpse. I wouldn't mind a mirror either.
I must look like shit. I'd also like to see myself
to know I haven't really disappeared—because I
know that's what everyone thinks has happened.
I haven't really vanished. I'm here . . .
someplace.*

*I think about the black pillowcase & I tell
myself that he makes me put it over my head so I
can't identify him after he lets me out of here.
Maybe that's wishful thinking. Because I'm 90%
sure he's doing this to be like the Immaculate
Conception Killer 50 years ago. It all matches
up with Rosie's description of what the killer did
to that one girl. She told me about it my first
night at the Sunnyside Up. The psycho abducted*

a girl & kept her locked in a shed in his backyard for 2 weeks while he went on his killing spree. He also tortured her.

This guy hasn't hurt me (so far). He hasn't even touched me except for when he knocked me out that first day.

It's more psychological harassment than physical. He'll talk to me over the speaker system, most of the time, praying or throwing Bible quotes at me. I want to tell him to shove it up his ass. But I don't say anything, because I figure that's why he's doing it—just to get a reaction from me. He calls me a "holy slut." I remember Rosie saying that was what the Immaculate Conception Killer called his victims. I also remember Rosie saying that—after he strangled & stabbed all those girls—he came back home & killed the girl in the backyard shed. He cut her throat—just like St. Agnes.

The other day, he told me he was going to kill his first victim. I think he meant it, too. I'm pretty sure he's already murdered her by now.

And he's going to murder me if I don't figure out how to escape from here.

A part of me thinks his heart isn't completely in this whole thing. I feel like someone else has forced him to do this. The first Immaculate Conception Killer had his mother telling him what to do. Is this the same thing? Maybe that means I have a chance of surviving this if I can just talk to him & get him to like me, if I can get him to see me as something other than some "holy slut" he has to kill. Or maybe he feels like

*he has something to prove & no matter what I
do, he'll cut my throat.*

   *Last night, I couldn't stop crying. I'm better
today. I realize that crying isn't going to get me
out of here. I keep thinking that he might've
made a real mistake giving me this pen. I could
use it to poke a hole in the black pillowcase.
Then I could hide the pen on the cot & lay on
top of it when he comes to collect the trash. I'll
be able to see him & I can use the pen to stab the
son of a bitch in the throat . . .*

Eden stopped writing.

Then, with the pen she contemplated using to kill her
captor, she thoroughly scratched out the last paragraph.
There was always the chance he'd take the journal away
and read it.

Eden told herself that just because she'd obliterated
the words on paper, it didn't mean the idea was gone.

CHAPTER THIRTY-FOUR

Friday, September 18, 12:40 P.M.

"Those murders were tragic—and a stain on this university's otherwise excellent reputation," Father O'Hurley said. He sat in the big, leather chair behind his desk under the sanctimonious gaze of his mother as St. Anne in the portrait. "People don't need to be reminded about something that happened fifty years ago. We'd all just as soon forget . . ."

Sitting across from him once again in the astonishingly uncomfortable straight-back antique chair, Ellie just nodded. She'd already pointed out that she hadn't shared her theory about a copycat killer with anyone except Detective Castino. "And that was in an effort to help him with his investigation into a student's death," she'd added.

But now, she just remained silent. She didn't mention *Look Homeward, Angel* again or how much Diana looked like the first victim of the Immaculate Conception murders, Greta Mae Louden. She'd already told him. But he continued to chew her out over her call to Detective Castino.

Ellie guessed that a part of him was aggravated because she'd waited until this morning to return his call.

It also must have unnerved him a bit that she didn't act contrite, throw herself at his mercy, and ask to do a dozen Hail Marys and a dozen Our Fathers as penance.

The ironic thing was that, since talking with Nate Bergquist last night, she wasn't quite as fixated on the Immaculate Conception murders as before. A part of her was almost willing to accept that Eden O'Rourke might have indeed gone off of her own volition and was perfectly fine right now. And perhaps Diana had, sadly, taken her own life. The theories she had about those events were just that—theories, speculation.

She'd been distracted and sidetracked by everything Nate had told her last night. She'd stayed at his place, talking with him until close to nine o'clock. He'd even ordered them a pizza. While they'd eaten, he'd shown her a second file, which he'd hidden—along with a revolver Frank had given him—under the floorboard of the kitchen cabinet. In the file were articles and photos from Portland newspapers about the explosion at his family cabin. Then she'd come home and read even more about the incident online, including an article debunking the story about the cabin being a crystal meth lab. The piece had several testimonials from Nate's former patients and colleagues at the veterans hospital. Ellie came to the conclusion that Nate Bergquist was a damn nice guy. And he needed her help.

So, for at least one night, she'd lost focus on the Immaculate Conception murders and the possibility that a copycat killer was now on the loose.

She was almost grateful to Father O'Hurley for reminding her just how important that was.

"That was a terrible time in the history of this university," he said. In the big picture window behind him, the sky was darkening over the lake. "I won't let you dredge it up again and cause a panic at the school with all this loose, irresponsible talk about a copycat killer. Do you understand, Ms. Goodwin?"

"Completely, Father." She got to her feet. "And I'm sorry to have taken up your time with all this. I know you're busy."

He seemed a bit flummoxed that she'd gotten up before he was ready to dismiss her. "Yes, well, I hope I won't have to talk to you again about this," he grumbled, rising from his chair.

Ellie stopped in front of his office door and turned to him. "I hope not," she said. "But then, we'll know for sure by Sunday, won't we?"

His eyes narrowed. "What do you mean?"

"Jane Marie Eggert," Ellie said. "She was last seen at a bar in Highwood on the night of September nineteenth, 1970. Her body was found under a bridge on Sycamore Way the following morning. She'd been strangled. This Sunday is the fiftieth anniversary of when they found Jane's body."

He glared at her.

"Have a nice weekend, Father," Ellie said. "I truly hope it's uneventful."

Then she walked out of his office.

CHAPTER THIRTY-FIVE

Saturday, September 19, 11:52 A.M.
Chicago

At first, Hannah thought the immaculate four-story art deco edifice was a condominium for a select few rich residents. Tucked between two tall apartment buildings along Lake Shore Drive, it had a gated driveway, perfectly trimmed hedges, and a flagpole in front.

She stared at the building from the backseat of the Lincoln Town Car. Rachel was at her side. Rachel's driver, Perry, stopped at the end of the short driveway, and the gate opened.

"Here we are," Rachel announced, "home sweet home."

"For some reason, I thought you lived in a *house*," Hannah said as the car pulled up to the front door.

"Yeah, I do. This is my house. C'mon. Perry will get our stuff . . ."

As they climbed out of the car, Hannah couldn't stop gaping at the house. The front door opened, and a stout, fifty-something brunette waited for them in the doorway. She had a pretty smile, and wore a plain black short-sleeve dress and a pearl necklace. "Welcome home.

Rachel!" she said cheerfully. "And you brought a friend. How lovely . . ."

Rachel gave her a hug. "Alida, this is Hannah."

The woman shook Hannah's hand. "It's so nice to meet you," she said. She had a very pleasant demeanor that seemed sincere, yet restrained.

"Alida is the glue that holds this place together," Rachel explained, stepping into the house. "We're all helpless without her."

Hannah followed Rachel into the grand foyer—with a polished wood parquet floor, a dramatic, curved staircase, and a beautiful chandelier overhead. A huge, framed painting hung on the wall above a mirrored table. The early 1900s portrait of a woman in white looked like it belonged in a museum. Hannah was in awe of the place, which seemed stately, but not stuffy. She'd only seen houses like this in the movies—and in *Architectural Digest*.

With their overnight bags in tow, Perry quietly moved past them and then up the stairs.

"Your mom and dad should be home any minute," Alida said to Rachel. "They left the club a little while ago. They're looking forward to having lunch with you, Rachel. Your mom wants to eat out on the terrace. Hildie's fixing your favorite, BLTs."

"Cool." Rachel turned to Hannah. "Our cook, Hildie, makes the best BLTs. Is that okay with you?"

"Sure," Hannah answered, shrugging.

"We'll be up in my room," Rachel told the housekeeper. "Give us a shout when lunch is ready."

"I'll let Hildie know there'll be one more," Alida said.

Hannah followed Rachel up the stairs. "Your parents

are expecting me, aren't they?" she whispered. "I mean, you told them I'm spending the night, didn't you?"

"Hey, it's not a problem," Rachel said, heading down the spacious hallway decorated with more museum-quality art. "This is my house, too. I can have my friends over any time I want."

Rachel's bedroom had a queen-size, four-poster bed with a pale pink silk coverlet. Everything was white, pale pink, or mint-colored, and all those hues were incorporated in the plush, rose-patterned carpet. The windows provided a view of the Chicago cityscape. There was a TV on one of the dressers and, above the desk, a pretty portrait of Rachel that must have been painted a couple of years ago. And there was a fireplace, too, of course.

Hannah's concern about her unanticipated presence in the house was set aside as she got a look at Rachel's exquisite bathroom—with a vanity, walk-in shower, huge tub, and separate stall for the toilet. Her walk-in closet was as big as Hannah's bedroom at home, and it featured a remote-controlled revolving shoe rack with what seemed like a hundred pairs of shoes.

They both unpacked their overnight bags.

When Alida came to the bedroom door and announced that Rachel's parents were home and ready for lunch, Hannah got all nervous again.

Last night, in preparation for this visit, Hannah had googled *Richard and Candace Bonner*. She watched a YouTube video of their appearance on a local evening show, *Chicago PM,* over the summer. Mr. Bonner was interviewed outside on the lakefront about some charity yacht race. He was a handsome, slightly jowly older businessman. But he also looked sporty in his baseball cap and Izod shirt. What with all the sailing terms he used, Hannah hadn't had a clue what he was talking about, but he spoke with authority. Mrs. Bonner was on the same show, but in the studio with the host. She was so elegant and stylish in her Chanel suit. She had that older Princess Grace thing going for her. Yet she seemed down to earth as she traded quips with the *Chicago PM* hosts. She was promoting a charity event tied to the yacht race, with a who's who of guests: "Our good friend Harry Connick Junior has agreed to sing a few songs for us, and of course, the mayor will be there . . ."

Hannah couldn't help feeling anxious about meeting them. These were the same two people who had been on TV a few weeks ago. Sure, she'd been on TV, too, but only because of a horribly humiliating national news story about her screwed-up family. Rachel's parents were local celebrities. Plus they were paying for Hannah's schooling and her room and board. All of that was intimidating enough, but as a bonus, Rachel hadn't told them that Hannah was here—and spending the night, no less. And the Bonners had a pretty low opinion of her father, so the whole thing promised to be awkward as hell.

She and Rachel headed downstairs. On their way to the terrace, they passed by the formal dining room with a huge fireplace, a table that must have sat thirty people, and above it, three chandeliers. Then they moved through the paneled study with yet another fireplace and a wet bar. The terrace was just outside a pair of open French doors.

"I heard we had a guest for lunch, but Alida didn't say anything about how pretty she was," Mr. Bonner announced, getting up from the beautifully set glass-top table on their terrace. It was in the shade of a green awning. "Or is that chauvinistic of me to say?"

"Very, Dad," Rachel said, planting a kiss on his cheek.

He gave her a fierce hug and then shook Hannah's hand. "Great to meet you," he said.

He was the same middle-aged, husky business-tycoon Hannah had seen on TV—only friendlier than she'd expected. He barely resembled the young stud in the framed photograph in Rachel's bedroom at the bungalow.

Hannah's mother was even more beautiful in person—with flawless skin and soft, delicate features that the TV cameras hadn't quite captured. She looked closer to forty than to fifty-something. She wore a tennis outfit, but didn't appear as if she'd broken a sweat any time recently. Sitting at the table with a tall glass of iced tea in her hand, she seemed so composed and regal. She and Rachel merely brushed cheeks for a greeting. "Oh, I still can't get used to what you've done with your hair," she murmured.

"It's great to see you, too, Mom," Rachel muttered, sinking into her chair.

Rachel's mother turned to Hannah. "She looks just like Mia Farrow in *Rosemary's Baby*, doesn't she?"

Hannah shrugged. "I'm afraid I've never seen that movie. I—I absolutely love your house. It's gorgeous. And I can't get over your garden . . ."

She was thinking of her mother, who was always toiling away in her backyard garden at home—her far-from-glamorous mother, and their modest four-bedroom house. The Bonners' terrace had a beautiful old stone fountain, potted flowers and plants, and overlooked a courtyard with a koi pond and lush gardens.

Rachel's mother smiled at her. "Well, thank you, dear

What can we get you to drink? Iced tea, Perrier, a soft drink?"

A skinny, gray-haired, uniformed maid set a glass of iced tea in front of Rachel.

"Thanks, Sylvia," Rachel sighed. "How's your arthritis?"

"Manageable, thanks for asking, Miss Rachel," she answered quietly. Then she turned toward Hannah. "To drink, miss?"

She saw that everyone else had iced tea. "I'd love an iced tea, thank you very much," Hannah said just to be agreeable, even though she craved a Diet Coke.

"Well, a polite one," Mr. Bonner said. "You can come over for lunch any time, young lady."

"So what are you two planning to do with your afternoon?" Rachel's mother asked.

"Well, since Hannah hasn't ever been to Chicago, I figured I'd take her to the Art Institute and Millennium Park," Rachel said.

"How nice," Mrs. Bonner said with a pleasant smile. "Where are you from, Anna?"

"It's *Hannah*, Mom," Rachel said. "*Hannah O'Rourke*, you know, my *sister*? And she's from Seattle. But I think you already knew that."

Mrs. Bonner turned to gaze at Hannah. She kept the same pleasant smile plastered on her face. But from the rest of her expression, she may as well have had a mouthful of broken glass.

"When we invited you to come home this weekend, we didn't say you could bring a friend along," Mrs. Bonner declared in a shrill voice, "and especially this girl—of all people. If you'd bothered to tell us in advance—or even ask—we would've told you no. I suppose that's why you didn't ask. Did you enjoy putting your father and me on the spot like that? How could you? You know how we feel about her father. Do you have any idea what an imposition this is for your father and me? Are you listening to me, young lady?"

"Yeah, it's like *absolutely no* imposition on you guys!" Rachel shot back. "You'd think we didn't have a household staff! You won't even know she's here. You don't have to lift a goddamn finger for her—"

"That's not the point, and you know it!" Mrs. Bonner barked.

Mr. Bonner said something in a low voice. Hannah could only make out the tone of his voice. It sounded like he was whispering and trying to calm down Rachel and her mother.

Hannah sat on the edge of the tub in Rachel's bathroom. The vent in there made it all too easy for her to hear the Bonners' discussion downstairs in the study.

She'd managed to get through the awkward lunch. Once they'd found out who she was, Mr. and Mrs. Bonner seemed to have difficulty even so much as looking at her. Mr. Bonner kept clearing his throat—like something was stuck in the back of it. He addressed Hannah only twice: first, to ask how she liked Our Lady of the Cove, and second, to ask if it was true that it rained a lot in Seattle. He also talked about his golf game. At least, he tried. Mrs. Bonner barely spoke. She ate one half of her sandwich, excused herself, and said she had to make some calls. Then she left the table.

That was when Rachel turned to her father and told

him: "You might as well know, Daddy. I took that paternity test and mailed it in this morning."

He cleared his throat again, wiped his mouth with his napkin, and said: "We'll discuss this later. I've lost my appetite." Then he left, too.

Hannah couldn't eat anything after that. The BLTs weren't really all that sensational—too much mayonnaise. But Rachel finished up her sandwich and fries. Then the two of them went up to Rachel's bedroom.

Rachel was apologizing for her parents, when there was a knock on the bedroom door. It was Alida, telling Rachel that her parents wanted to talk with her alone downstairs in the study.

That had been fifteen minutes ago, and for a while, all Hannah had heard was a hushed, angry murmuring. Then, the voices had gotten louder, and she'd figured out the sound was coming from the bathroom vent.

"How dare you!" Rachel's mother bellowed.

After trying to decipher more muffled conversation for the last minute or two, Hannah was startled to hear Mrs. Bonner's voice now at full volume: "Where do you get off, young lady, calling me rude? You're the rude one, parading that girl in front of us, giving us absolutely no warning about who she is. And you were rude to her, too! You put that poor girl in a terrible position. Have you even thought about tonight? What are you going to tell her now? Talk about awkward. We've already told your grandmother that you're coming to dinner . . ."

"Well, why can't Hannah come, too?" Rachel asked.

"You're not bringing her to the club," her mother said. "This is family only!"

"Well, Hannah's family! She's *my* family!"

"Nana wouldn't understand! I swear to God if you say anything to your grandmother about this non-sense . . ."

Hannah heard Mr. Bonner shush them. Then there was more murmuring.

She'd had enough. Slump-shouldered, Hannah wandered back into Rachel's bedroom and started to pack her overnight bag. She figured she could Uber to the train station and catch the commuter train back to Delmar. So she'd have to sleep in the bungalow by herself tonight. It beat staying someplace where she wasn't wanted. She never should have let Rachel talk her into this.

Yet, twenty-five minutes later, Rachel talked her into staying: "My parents aren't mad at you. They're mad at me. If you leave now, believe me, it'll just make everything worse. I'm going to this stupid dinner with my parents for only, like, two hours. The rest of the time, we can hang out and have fun. You don't want to go back and spend the night alone . . ."

Perry drove them to the Art Institute. It was kind of difficult for Hannah to appreciate all the wonderful, famous art while Rachel went on and on about what a bitch her mother was. Hannah agreed with her, but was careful not to say anything. After all, her scholarship was riding on the generosity of Rachel's parents. Hannah kept thinking about how poised and chic Mrs. Bonner had seemed on TV, but when things didn't go her way, she really was pretty horrible.

"I'm so glad she isn't my real mother," Rachel said in front of the masterpieces of Monet. "I wish you knew more about your aunt Molly. I'll bet she was really sweet. I can't wait to meet your mom and ask her . . ."

They checked out Millennium Park, and Hannah took some selfies of them in front of "The Bean" sculpture for Instagram.

With so many people in the park, Hannah kept thinking they might run into Eden. It was silly, considering how huge Chicago was. But she figured her chances of seeing Eden there were better than bumping into her on campus any time soon. But of course, they didn't see her.

Perry drove them back to the house on North Lake Shore Drive at five-thirty.

While Rachel showered and dressed to go out with her parents, she told Hannah to feel free to check out any of the house's thirty-eight rooms—including a game room and a gym with a sauna in the basement, and a home movie theater on the third floor. Alida had gone home, but the cook, Hildie, was on duty tonight especially for her. So whatever Hannah wanted for dinner, Hildie would cook. Perry was spending the night in the servants' quarters, so she didn't have to worry about getting spooked in the big house. If she needed anything, all she had to do was pick up the house phone, and Perry or Hildie would take care of it for her.

Hannah remained in Rachel's bedroom—and avoided Rachel's parents—until they'd gone off to their family dinner. Then she started exploring. She felt funny checking out the rooms on the second and first floors. She didn't even want to turn on the lights. She was afraid she'd break something. Though two other people were in the house, Hannah still felt like she was all alone. It was a creepy sensation. In some of the bigger rooms, her footsteps echoed.

The basement somehow seemed more accessible

and welcoming than the rest of the house—like it was made for guests. And what could she break in the game room or the gym? The game room had a wet bar and a mini-kitchen with a fridge stocked with sodas, beer, and bottled waters. There was a ping-pong table, two pinball machines, an old player piano, and one of those flashy jukeboxes from the 1950s. Hannah poked her head into the mini-gym and checked out the dry sauna next door. It was cold right now, but she noticed a switch and a timer on the wall. Next door was a full bathroom with a Jacuzzi. Down the corridor she discovered an extra bedroom. It seemed like a guest room for not-so-special guests. The room was furnished with a pair of twin beds, a dresser, a desk and chair, and on the walls, framed vintage Illinois Central Railroad posters. But it was a room that could have been in anyone else's basement. Hannah wondered if the furniture had belonged to Mr. Bonner before he'd married Mrs. Bonner and become rich. It dawned on her that it might even be Alden's bedroom. But it looked too generic. Plus when she opened the desk and dresser drawers, they were empty.

Heading back upstairs, Hannah found the large, up-to-date kitchen—and the cook, Hildie, sitting at a built-in breakfast table. She was watching *Wheel of Fortune* on a TV bracketed to the wall and had a half-full tumbler of red wine in front of her. Hildie was a scrawny, wry-faced, beige-haired woman of about seventy. In a British accent that made Hannah feel like she'd walked into an episode of *Downton Abbey*, Hildie asked her what she wanted to eat for dinner.

Hannah figured a hamburger and fries wouldn't be too much trouble. And she remembered to tell her to hold the mayo. By the time Hildie served up the dinner, she'd already polished off her wine and refilled the tumbler. Hannah could tell Hildie wasn't exactly thrilled she had to work tonight, and maybe that was why she was a little tipsy. It was easy to get her talking, and Hannah found out that Alden's room was in the servants' quarters on the fourth floor. He shared a bathroom with Mr. and Mrs. Bonner's chauffeur. Hannah was dying to check it out, but she didn't dare ask.

She sat with Hildie at the breakfast table, and they muted the TV. She could tell she'd won her over because Hildie asked in a confidential whisper if she wanted some wine. Hannah took a Diet Coke instead. The hamburger was actually first-class restaurant quality. Hannah kept offering Hildie some of her fries while asking more about Alden.

She remembered what Rachel had told her about Alden's mother coming over from Ireland, single with a baby, and taking a job as a maid in the Bonners' house.

"Oh, she was a quiet, dreary little thing," Hildie said in her crisp British accent, "and with this beautiful little boy. I had to wonder what the father must have looked like—the handsome scoundrel who'd left her in a family way without so much as a fare-thee-well . . ."

Hildie finally tried one of Hannah's fries, and then she had a few more. "Anyway, the poor thing started getting sick about the time Alden was seven or eight— headaches and dizzy spells. He was so devoted to her, always helping her around the house with her chores. It was heartbreaking to see him realize she was slipping away. God bless the Bonners. Say what you will about them, they're still very generous people. They paid her hospital and funeral bills—and made sure that boy had a home here. Of course, they knew there'd be hell to pay from little Miss Rachel if anything happened to her baby boy. We all adored him, but Rachel most of all. As kids, they were inseparable. In fact, the old housekeeper, Vivien Houghton—she was here before Alida—she thought it was an 'unhealthy relationship.'"

"What did she mean by that?" Hannah asked.

Hildie helped herself to another French fry and then got to her feet. "I think Ms. Houghton caught them naked in Rachel's bathroom on a couple of occasions, normal kid stuff." She took a jug of Gallo wine out of the cupboard and refilled her tumbler. "The children were just playing doctor or some such thing. But Ms. Houghton was such a prude, her and her nightly novenas. Maybe she saw something else. I don't know . . ."

Hannah left only a couple of bites of her hamburger before she pushed her plate away. "I wonder what she could have seen," she murmured almost to herself.

"Well, if you want the whole story, you'd have to call on Vivien Houghton at Mary of the Rosary Rest Home." Hildie raised her glass as if toasting her. "Ms. Houghton was working for Mrs. Bonner's family even before Mr. Bonner came along. She knows about all the family skeletons . . ."

CHAPTER THIRTY-SIX

Sunday, September 20, 2:17 A.M.

Ellie studied the blurry photo on her phone: the body of Jane Marie Eggert, discarded in a leafy ravine under a bridge on Sycamore Way. It was a poor copy she'd bootlegged from the crime scene photo she'd found in the *Tribune* archives. But it made her recall details from the original picture: how from the waist down, Jane wore only pantyhose and one shoe, and the discoloration in her face after having been strangled.

From the front seat of Nate's Ford Fiesta, she and Nate had an unobstructed view of the bridge. They'd parked a quarter of a block away—across from a small, deserted playground at the tip of some woods. The old, weathered stone bridge cut through the trees and led to a well-to-do residential neighborhood on Sycamore Way. The crossing was only three or four car-lengths long and about twenty feet above the creek running through the ravine.

Except for a few more trees, the site hadn't changed much since 1970.

Ellie was convinced the copycat killer couldn't resist returning to the "scene of the crime" tonight. If they were lucky, they'd catch him before he killed the "holy slut" he planned to dispose of in this spot.

Nate had brought along the revolver his brother's partner, Frank, had given him. He'd admitted to Ellie that he'd never fired it. Right now, the gun was wedged between the car door and the driver's seat.

Ellie switched off her phone. She didn't want the illuminated screen to give them away. Nate had purposely parked as far as he could from the streetlights for their stakeout. Ellie had brought along a pair of binoculars.

Every time they spotted a pair of headlights from a car coming down Sycamore Way—in either direction—they both ducked down in the front seat and peered over the dashboard. But there was hardly any traffic this time of night. In three hours, only a dozen cars had passed by, the last one about forty-five minutes ago.

It occurred to Ellie that, just a couple of days ago, she couldn't have imagined sitting alone in a car at two o'clock in the morning with this man—and not another soul in sight. Her assessment of "Nick Jensen" had turned around ninety-eight percent since finding out his real name was Nate Bergquist. Ellie believed his story—enough so she worried that Hannah's and Eden's relationship with Rachel Bonner might have endangered them; enough so that she wanted to help Nate; and enough so that she felt attracted to him. But there was that lingering two percent of uncertainty about Nate that made her cautious.

She glanced over her shoulder for any approaching vehicles and then turned to look at the bridge again. "Do you really think Hannah's okay at the Bonners' home tonight?" she asked.

"I doubt anything will happen to her while she's there

at the house," he said. "Hell, it might even be the safest place for her right now."

Ellie nodded. If the copycat killer was looking for a new victim tonight, Hannah was better off nowhere near the campus.

Her half-sister's fate was still a mystery. Ellie was pretty certain that Eden had been abducted by the copycat, who, right now, could have her locked up in a shed somewhere. And there was always a chance that Eden was fine, exploring downtown Chicago nightlife this very minute. But after what Nate had told her about Kayla Kennedy, Ellie couldn't help wondering if Eden had "disappeared" because she knew something about Rachel or her family—which meant she was probably dead.

"Speaking of Hannah," Nate said. "I keep thinking about how useful she could be in getting us information about the Bonners—and Rachel."

"The same way Kayla Kennedy was useful to you?" Ellie asked.

He nodded glumly. "I know. I'm worried about that, too. Hannah could already be in danger, and I don't want to make it worse. But my brother, Gil, investigated Dylan O'Rourke and the Bonners shortly after they adopted Rachel. I'm pretty sure, much later on, Gil found out about Rachel's affair with her dad's business associate. I think what Gil knew—about the adoption or the affair or both—I think that got him killed. Hannah and Rachel are close right now. With a little coaxing, Hannah might get Rachel to open up to her, confide in her."

"So you want Hannah to go undercover for you."

"I guess so, only she can't know she's doing it for me.

That would put her in more danger—along with the two of us."

"Let me get this straight," Ellie said. "You'd like me to manipulate Hannah into spying on Rachel for us without her really knowing why. And she can't know about the risks involved either."

He tipped his head back on the headrest and sighed. "Shit. When I thought of it earlier today, the whole scheme didn't seem quite so horribly callous. But hearing you put it that way, hearing the reality of it . . . well, I'm sorry. Please, forget I said anything."

Ellie saw a shadow sweep across the landscape in front of them. She looked over her shoulder and spotted the headlights of a car coming up Sycamore Way. "Duck!" she whispered.

They both slid down in their seats just moments before the approaching car's headlights illuminated the inside of Nate's Ford. Ellie heard the tires humming and the occasional pebble ricocheting against the underside of the car as it came closer. She listened to the car slow down. Then it passed. She and Nate peeked over the dashboard.

It was a black BMW. The headlights went off as the vehicle came to a stop in front of the bridge.

"Jesus, I think this is it," Nate murmured.

The BMW sat there for a few moments. With the binoculars, Ellie tried to get a look inside the car, but it was too dark. All she could think was that the copycat killer could be in there, strangling his latest victim right now. "We can't just sit here," she whispered. "We have to do something."

"Stay here," Nate said. He grabbed the gun, opened the driver's door, and crept out of the car. He quietly closed the door again, and the interior light went off. Ellie prayed the driver of the other car hadn't noticed.

Gun in hand, Nate darted toward the idling BMW. Then he ducked behind a tree.

The BMW's front door opened, and the inside light went on. Ellie gazed through the binoculars. The driver stepped out of the car. He was a gangly-looking teenager. He wore white high-top sneakers and had a mop of unruly brown hair. Ellie didn't see anyone in the passenger seat or in the back.

The teenager glanced around nervously and then hurried around the front of the BMW to the passenger door. He opened it.

Nate skulked toward the kid, who was taking a black plastic bag from the passenger side of the car. From what Ellie could see, the boy didn't look like a murderer. But then, some of the arsonists she'd helped put in prison hadn't been much older than him. And anything could have been inside that plastic bag—from a dead girl's clothes to a human head. He moved toward the side of the bridge with it.

Brandishing the revolver, Nate closed in on the unaware teen. "Hold it!" he yelled.

Ellie grabbed her phone and jumped out of the car.

Both Nate and the teenager were in some kind of wordless standoff. The kid looked absolutely petrified.

As Ellie got closer, she could see the boy was trembling. He gawked at her, and she knew from his fawn-in-the-headlights expressions that she and Nate had made a mistake.

"What have you got there?" Nate asked warily.

"Porn," the kid answered—with a crack in his voice.

"What do you mean?"

"*Playboy, Penthouse*, a couple of copies of *Hustler*. It was my friend Steve's father's stash. He threw them out. So Stevie dug them out of the trash and had them for a while. He didn't want them anymore, and since my folks were out of town, he gave them to me . . ." With a shaky hand, the teen reached into the bag and pulled out a *Penthouse* magazine.

Ellie shone her phone flashlight on the Vaseline-on-the-lens cover photo of a half-naked woman. The date along the top of the photo was July 1999. From how heavy the bag looked, the kid must have had about a dozen magazines.

Nate stashed the revolver in the pocket of his jacket. But the poor teenager seemed to crack under pressure. He wouldn't stop talking.

"Anyway, my folks are coming home tomorrow, and I have no place to hide these. So I was going to dump them here. My parents would kill me if they find I have porn—especially my mom. They're already monitoring my computer and my phone—"

"Okay, okay," Nate gently interrupted. "I get the picture. Why didn't you just toss them in a Dumpster?"

"I was afraid somebody might see me."

"Yeah, well, throwing them away this close to a playground, where a bunch of little kids hang out, that's not such a great idea either," Nate remarked.

"I never thought about that," the kid mumbled. "What are you guys going to do to me? Was that gun real?"

"No, don't worry about it," Nate replied.

"It's okay," Ellie said. "Relax. We thought you were someone else."

"Do you want us to take the magazines?" Nate offered. "We can throw them out for you. No one will ever trace them back to you."

"You'd do that?"

"Sure, don't sweat it," Nate said.

The teenager handed the bulky black plastic bag to him. "Well, thanks," he stammered. "Thanks a lot, man." Then he hurried back toward his parents' BMW, hopped inside, gunned the engine, and peeled away.

Nate stood there for a moment with the lumpy-looking bag in his grasp. "Poor kid, I think we scared the shit out of him." He chuckled. "You want to hear the funny part? I remember that issue of *Penthouse*. My brother had it. I'll bet I've seen at least half the magazines in here."

They turned and started walking back to Nate's car. "So, are you really going to get rid of those magazines, or are you keeping them?" Ellie asked.

"Well, as tempted as I am to take a trip down *mammary lane*, after hearing the list of previous owners, there's not enough hand sanitizer in the world." When they reached the Fiesta, Nate opened the trunk and set the bag inside. "Don't forget to remind me we have these back here. First Dumpster we see . . ." He shut the trunk and glanced at his wristwatch. "It's a quarter to three. Do you want to call it a night?"

Ellie hesitated. The smile faded from her face. She thought about how Jane Marie Eggert was last seen in a local tavern fifty years ago tonight. The bars in the vicinity usually closed at two in the morning. "Could we give it another half hour—just to be sure?" she asked.

He opened her door for her. "It's fine with me. I like the company."

She climbed into the car. "Thanks, me too," she murmured.

Nate shut the door for her, and then went around to

the driver's side. He got behind the wheel. They both sat there in the dark for a moment.

Ellie finally sighed. "Give me some time. I'll try to figure out how to get Hannah to help us without putting her in too much danger."

CHAPTER THIRTY-SEVEN

Sunday, 2:46 A.M.

Seventeen blocks from the bridge on Sycamore Way, a junior named Justine Everly was leaving a party at one of the upperclassmen resident houses. The redbrick estate was home to thirty-two young men—and the only one of them to show any interest in her was a nerdy business major named Darrell. He was nice enough, but boring. Plus he just seemed so utterly desperate. All the hot guys there were taken. It was one of the pitfalls of attending a school where the girls outnumbered the guys four to one.

Justine realized as soon as she stepped outside that she'd had too much to drink. But the large consumption of alcohol had failed to make Darrell seem any more attractive. So at the door, when he offered to walk her home, she insisted that she was fine.

But she wasn't. She walked away frustrated and disappointed.

So far, after only two weeks, her junior year at Our Lady of the Cove was a major bust. She hated all her classes. Also, due to a housing shortage, they'd stuck her in Campbell Hall with a bunch of freshmen and

sophomores. And just to rub it in, her pretty blond sophomore roommate, Stephanie, had a cute steady boyfriend at Illinois State, and Stephanie had plastered
pictures of them on the wall all over her side of the dorm
room. At least she'd be spending most of her week-
ends with him in Normal, which was sort of a break
for Justine.

Campbell Hall was one of the newer dorms, about
five blocks away. But Justine would have to walk
through the old section of campus, which was often deserted and a bit scary late at night. There were too many
trees, gardens, and saintly statues lurking along the way.
As she crossed Maple Hill Road, Justine kind of re-
gretted not letting Darrell walk her to the dorm. All the
windows were dark in back of the old mansion that was
now the administration building, Emery Hall. The place
always reminded her of a haunted house.

A slight chill blew in from the lake, and Justine
rubbed her bare arms. She'd worn a sleeveless top, fool-
ishly thinking more visible skin might bring her more
luck with the guys.

As she hurried past Emery Hall, Justine glanced
around and didn't see anyone else in the area. She'd
thought more students would be out partying on a Saturday night. Now she wished she hadn't stayed so long
at the party and drunk so much. She felt her stomach
rumble—a bad combination of nerves and Pabst Blue
Ribbon. She peeked over her shoulder. The party
house was at least a block away now. She didn't notice
anyone on the street or the sidewalk in back of her.
But then, she blinked and she could have sworn someone had just darted behind a tree. It was far enough

away that Justine wondered if what she saw was real. Or maybe it was merely her beer-fueled imagination running wild.

She picked up her pace and hurried past another dark, empty, spooky building.

"Hey, pretty lady . . ." someone called in a low, teasing singsong voice. "Where are you going?"

The voice came from behind her. Her heart racing, Justine didn't dare look back. After a brief hesitation, she walked faster—toward the lights and wide open space of the quad. Maybe she'd see a few students milling around there.

But the place was deserted. Grub Hub closed at two. All the lights were out in the student union building.

"Are you all alone, pretty lady?" the singsong voice called in sort of a stage whisper.

"FUCK OFF!" Justine finally screamed. Then she started running.

Her dorm was still about two blocks away. They locked the lobby door at two. She'd need her key to get in.

Justine kept moving and didn't look back. In only a block, she'd pass the boys' dorm, O'Leary Hall, and if she screamed, at least someone there would hear it. Someone would help her.

She raced through the quad toward the dorms. Behind her, more and more distant, she heard his laughter—an awful, menacing cackle.

"Justine!" he called.

He knew her name. How long had he been stalking her?

Justine tried to keep running, but she had to slow down to find her keys in her purse. Where were they?

Frantic, she hurried past O'Leary Hall. She didn't think she had the breath to scream.

Just a little farther and she'd reach her dorm. She kept rifling through her purse.

Glancing over her shoulder, she didn't see anyone. There were fewer trees in this newer section of the campus, fewer places for her pursuer to hide. Had he given up?

At last, she found her keys.

Staggering up to the glass door to Campbell Hall's lobby, Justine tried to get the key into the lock. But her hand was shaking too much. "Calm down," she managed to tell herself between gasps for air.

She finally inserted the key into the lock, opened the door, and ducked inside.

Still trying to get her breath, she shut the door behind her. She looked out the glass door for her tormentor. But she didn't see anyone.

Justine felt dizzy and nauseous as she tottered through the lobby and reached the elevator. She pressed the up button. The doors opened immediately. Stepping aboard, she pressed the button for the third floor. As soon as the doors shut, her phone rang.

She reached into her purse and grabbed the phone. She thought she might be sick. Her hands were still shaking. She saw the caller ID: *Johnston, Darrell.*

"Good God," Justine murmured. "Give up already. I'm not interested." She let it go to voice mail.

She decided to wait until her hands stopped shaking before she called the police. Or maybe it was something she needed to take up with campus security. Either way, once they heard her explain what had happened, they'd probably put it together that she was drunk.

Still, she needed to call them. It was pretty damn creepy that the guy knew her name.

The elevator doors opened. Her legs wobbly, Justine headed down the quiet, empty third-floor corridor to her room. Her phone beeped, signifying that Darrell had finally finished leaving his stupid message.

Her hand shook a bit less as she unlocked her door. She pressed the icon on her phone screen to play back Darrell's voice mail. Then she opened her door and stepped inside the darkened room. She was about to switch on the overhead light when she noticed that Stephanie's bed was occupied. Her roommate had planned to spend the weekend with her boyfriend. But she must have had a change in plans.

Justine left the light off. She closed and locked the door behind her.

Hi, Justine! Darrell said in his voice mail. It was too loud. Justine realized she must have put her phone in speaker mode. Darrell laughed. *That was me following you. I was just clowning around. I'm sorry. I didn't mean to frighten you . . .*

"Idiot," Justine muttered under her breath. The speaker mode was still on, but she managed to turn down the volume a bit. She glanced over to see if Darrell's babbling had woken up Stephanie.

The covers shifted, and someone sat up in the bed. But it wasn't her roommate.

It was a man.

In the darkness, Justine couldn't make out his face—only his outline as he climbed out of Stephanie's bed.

He had a gun in his hand. That much Justine saw.

She let out a little shriek and dropped the phone.

. . . But I have to admit, it was kind of funny to watch you take off like that . . .

Justine froze.

"Don't scream," the man whispered. "Sit down at your desk. Then everything will be fine."

I just wanted to make sure you made it back to your dorm safely. Looks like you did . . .

Terrified, Justine felt her stomach lurch. She did what he said and slowly sank down into her desk chair. She felt him creeping up behind her. "Is—is this another joke?" she asked in a shaky voice. She tried to laugh, but it just came out as a whimper. "Do I know you?"

"I know you," he whispered. "Justine Michelle Everly. Someone else had those same initials, and she died fifty years ago tonight . . ."

Hey, I'm still here in the quad if you want to come back. I'll apologize in person. I didn't mean to freak you out. I hope you'll forgive me. I'd really like to get together with you sometime. Are you free next weekend? I think you're really nice . . .

Trembling, Justine felt the man's hands covering her ears—until she could hardly hear Darrell talking anymore.

"Here's the important question," the man said, hovering behind her. He seemed to ease off the pressure against her left ear so she could hear him. "Will you come with me, Justine? Will you let me take you under the little bridge over by the library? It's not too far. Would you like to die there?"

She started to cry. "No . . ."

"Then I'll have to kill you here," he said.

Suddenly he jerked her head to one side.

The last thing Justine heard was Darrell's muffled voice—and the horrible sound of her neck snapping.

CHAPTER THIRTY-EIGHT

I think something has happened to him & it's the worst feeling in the world.

Judging from the lights dimming, I'm pretty sure it's been 3 days since he's talked to me over the speaker, 4 days since he's restocked supplies & emptied out the toilet. It smells awful in here, and the air is so stagnant. I'm surprised I haven't suffocated yet. There must be a vent hidden somewhere up near the ceiling. Otherwise, I'd be dead.

I'm down to 1 & ½ bottles of water & a granola bar. I'm thirsty & hungry, but I'm trying to pace myself in case this is it for the next few days. I hate that he's made me rely on him so much. The thought that he's gone & might not be coming back (maybe dead or in an accident) scares the shit out of me. I keep thinking I'll die in this place before anyone finds me. It makes me feel so hopeless . . .

Eden realized a while back that she couldn't break out of the shed on her own. She couldn't knock down the door, manipulate the lock, or tunnel her way out. In all the time she'd been a prisoner, she hadn't heard a single voice outside except his. There were no traffic sounds. She hadn't even heard a dog barking. So it wasn't likely anyone would come to her aid. Her only chance for escape was overpowering him when he collected her trash and restocked her supplies.

Time seemed to go by faster as she planned her surprise attack. Poking a hole in the black pillowcase only took a few minutes one night. She'd hunched over the work, and kept her back to the camera. She would watch him through the hole in the pillowcase. She'd come to realize the point to her putting the black pillowcase over her head was not so that she couldn't identify him later, but so that she remained blind and helpless while the shed door was open. She'd already tested the pillowcase to make sure the hole was at eye level—and it worked. She would have the pen on the cot where she could quickly reach it. She'd wait until he was emptying the toilet. Of all the chores during his brief visits, that one probably took the longest. She imagined he might even wince and close his eyes as he poured out the shit and urine. That was when she'd tear off the pillowcase and lunge at him with the pen.

Eden's need for food and supplies wasn't what made this long wait for his "restocking" visit so excruciating. No, it was her champing at the bit for the opportunity to carry out her plan and escape.

In the meantime, she thanked God for Daphne du Maurier. For a couple of days, *Rebecca* gave her something to do, something to take her mind off of this place. She'd already started reading it again.

She'd also written at least thirty pages in her journal. She worried about the pen running out of ink. She read

the journal over and over, too. It was like a lifeline—
someone to communicate with, even if it was just
herself. She hadn't realized how much she'd written
in her journal over the summer. Reading it now took
her back to the sights, sounds, and smells of Seattle. It
took her back to all the adventures on her own and to
all the little dramas at home during the last two years
with her adopted family. Reliving these episodes through
her journal entries made her so terribly homesick. She
just ached inside and sobbed. But strangely, the entries
filled her with hope, too. Her journal felt like a connection to the outside world—*her* world, before it was
reduced to this tiny space and these four awful walls.

"I see you're writing in your journal, Eden," his voice
said over the speaker.

Startled, Eden sat up in the chair at her tiny desk. She
quickly shut the diary.

"It's very therapeutic, isn't it?" he said. "Well, no
more therapy for you, Eden. You lost that privilege when
you poked a hole in your pillowcase. You thought I
didn't see that? I see everything, Eden. I'm like God.
I'm going to restock in about five minutes. I want you
to leave the journal and the pen there by the door with
your chamber pot and all the other garbage . . ."

"No!" she cried, glaring up at the camera and hugging the diary to her chest. "You can't do that . . . please,
don't take it away . . ."

"You can leave *Rebecca* there with the trash, too," he
said, talking over her protests. "But you may keep the
Bible. It might do you some good to read those passages
about obedience. Now, you know the drill. I want you
on the cot, with the pillowcase over your head. Just
make sure the hole is in back. Hands behind you . . ."

Getting to her feet, Eden stared up at the camera. She shook her head over and over. "Please, let me keep it," she begged. Tears filled her eyes. "It's the only thing I have in here that I care about. Please? I'm sorry. I promise I won't do anything to make you mad again . . ."

She heard a little click, which must have been him turning off the speaker or whatever he used to listen to her. She'd just heard something else, too: her pleading with him, promising to be a good little prisoner—until he was ready to slit her throat.

Eden hated herself for whining, begging, and sucking up to him like that.

She started shaking as she set the trash bag by the door—along with the shit-pot and *Rebecca*. A rage built up inside her. It wasn't just the horribly disappointing failure of her escape plan. It was giving up her journal that infuriated her.

And she'd be damned if she'd let that asshole read it.

She set the pen down by the door. Then she stared at the diary in her trembling hand. Before she knew it, Eden started ripping the pages from her journal and tearing them up into small pieces. Something about this wild act of defiance gave her a little jolt of pleasure. She couldn't stop herself. She kept tearing apart the diary and throwing the shredded pages up in the air. The page edges sliced into her fingers and gave her paper cuts. Some scraps of her writing rained down with blood on them. She finally threw the empty binder at the door.

Eden stopped just short of picking up the shit-pot and hurling it across the tiny room. She came to her senses before letting that happen.

Exhausted and gasping for air, she plopped down on

the cot. The floor was littered with bits and pieces of paper that bore her handwriting. She was hot and sweaty and miserable. But she felt she'd won a tiny victory. Too bad the cost was so dear.

She finally got her breath and stood up. She felt a bit dizzy. Wiping the tears from her eyes, she wandered over to the corner of the shed. Her hands were still shaky and bleeding as she reached over to the near-empty supply shelf and grabbed the black pillowcase. She sat down on the cot and put the pillowcase over her head like a good little prisoner.

As she started to lie down, she heard him talking to someone, his voice, faint and muffled outside the sound-proofed walls.

I'm tired, Mama . . . You're asking too much of me . . .

That was all Eden heard as she lay facedown on the cot and put her hands behind her.

She realized she'd been right earlier: Someone else was making him do all of this. It was just like the Immaculate Conception Killer. He was doing it for his mother.

But Eden didn't hear another voice.

Was he on the phone? Or was he talking to himself?

It was so quiet out there now.

Eden kept waiting to hear the key in the door lock.

She knew he was able to watch her every move on his phone—thanks to the camera overhead. That was how he knew when she was in position for him to come in. She wondered why he was taking so long. Was he still on the phone with his mother? Or was he simply lording his power over her and making her wait in this submissive, uncomfortable position with the black pillowcase over her head? Eden wondered how much longer she would have to lie there. She counted to one hundred.

"I'm ready!" she finally called in a shaky voice.

No response. She waited a little longer.

"Are you out there?" she called.

"You're not getting anything until you clean up the mess you've made," he finally answered over the speaker. "Maybe I'll be back tomorrow. I have a lot on my plate—including a very dangerous mission . . ."

Eden sat up and pulled the pillowcase off her head. She looked up at the camera.

"If I were you," he said, "I'd pray nothing happens to me. Pray hard, Eden."

CHAPTER THIRTY-NINE

Monday, September 21, 9:34 A.M.

"It was an accident," Detective Castino said.

"Oh, come on, give me a break!" Ellie said into her phone. She was headed across the quad toward Campus Grounds for some coffee-to-go before her ten o'clock class. "I warned you this was going to happen— and damn it, in this case, I really hate being right. Did my two texts and the photos I sent yesterday make any impression on you at all?"

Ellie had gotten only a few hours of sleep after Nate dropped her off at the townhouse early Sunday morning. She'd woken up at eight-fifteen and immediately checked online for news of any local deaths. She'd tried different combinations of keywords: *Our Lady of the Cove, Death, Delmar, Bridge*, and *Student*. But she hadn't come up with anything. She'd called a friend at the *Tribune* for breaking news about the death of a student from Our Lady of the Cove. All they'd had was the brief report about Diana's "suicide" last week.

Ellie had started to think she'd been wrong and maybe all her worrying had been for nothing. But late Sunday afternoon, she'd found something on Instagram. A senior at the university, Laurie Tanner, had been jogging at 5:30 in the morning when she saw a girl sprawled at the bottom of the stairs that wound under the bridge near the campus library. By the time the local police and paramedics arrived, several students from nearby dorms had taken photos of the scene and posted them on social media.

Ellie examined the photos before they were pulled off Instagram because of their disturbing content. The dead girl's sleeveless top was bunched up, exposing most of her stomach, and one of her shoes had fallen off. It was just like Jane Marie Eggert fifty years ago.

After more digging around, Ellie managed to find out the identity of the victim. The girl was a junior named Justine Michelle Everly—J.M.E., the same initials as Jane Marie.

Ellie had fired off two texts to Castino last night, pointing out all the similarities between both deaths— exactly fifty years apart. She'd included photos of the two dead girls. She figured he could no longer debunk her copycat killer theory.

Castino hadn't called or texted her back last night.

But he'd picked up when she'd called him ten minutes ago.

As she neared Campus Grounds, Ellie slowed down. She stared at the stone bridge just beyond the quad. Strips of yellow police tape blocked the stairway access. She couldn't help thinking—for the umpteenth time—that she and Nate had chosen the wrong bridge for their stakeout on Saturday night.

With the phone to her ear, she veered past the coffee shop and continued toward the bridge. "How can you tell me it was just an accident?" she said.

Castino let out a loud sigh. "The girl left a party on

the other side of campus around three in the morning. She was drunk. We talked to several kids from the party who confirmed this. One guy followed her back to Campbell Hall. I guess he meant to tease her and gave her a little scare. He called her and left a message, apologizing. He asked her out—and asked her to come outside again so he could apologize in person. He waited around for her for ten or fifteen minutes before going back to his residence. We checked with his roommates, and his story jibes. We think Justine must have gone out again, fell down the stairs by the ravine bridge, and broke her neck. That's the fourth accident someone has had on those stairs this year—the first fatality."

"So, you're chalking it up to coincidence that it's the same date as Jane Marie's murder, the same initials, the body under a bridge, the missing shoe . . ."

"One was very clearly a murder, and the other is very clearly an accident," he replied. "Listen, Ellie, if you look for similarities between two separate events, you'll always come up with stuff. You just happen to have the Immaculate Conception killings on the mind and you're finding coincidences. Look at all the coincidences with the Lincoln and Kennedy assassinations. Just because there are similarities, it doesn't mean there's a connection—or a copycat at work. You don't think Lee Harvey Oswald figured, 'Hey, I have fifteen letters in my name, just like John Wilkes Booth. I'm going after the president who was elected one hundred years after Lincoln. I'll shoot him on a Friday—in the head, while he's with his wife and another couple, and I'll wound the other guy. And when he's dead, another Vice President Johnson will take over. But I'll shake it up a little, and instead of shooting the president in a theater and having the police catch up with me in a warehouse, I'll do it the other way around—'"

"Okay, I get the picture," Ellie cut in. She couldn't believe he was throwing the old list of Lincoln and Kennedy assassination coincidences at her. "So until someone's blatantly murdered, you won't even consider the possibility that there's a copycat killer at work. Is that right?"

"I'll answer that question with another question. How can you call these deaths the work of a copycat murderer when they don't even look like murders?"

Ellie said nothing. She slowed down as she approached the bridge. She stared at the police tape across the top of the stairs. It fluttered in the breeze.

"Is that it?" Castino asked. "Is there anything else?"

"I suppose you're going to call Father O'Hurley now and tell him I was bothering you again. So I can expect another chewing out from him."

"He chewed you out?" Castino asked. "Ellie, it's true I called him after we talked the other day. But I was trying to help. I wanted him to offer you some grief counseling . . ."

She let out a sad, little laugh. It was bad enough to think that he considered her a pain in the ass, but he actually considered her a *crazy* pain in the ass. Either way, he didn't take her seriously. "I appreciate your concern," she said finally. "But I wish you'd shift some of that concern over to Eden O'Rourke. She's been missing for nine days, and no one seems to care."

"Actually, we just got word from her parents yesterday," Castino said. "They wanted to report her as a runaway, but the girl's over eighteen. So they're hiring a private detective. In the meantime, we're working with the Chicago Police to do what we can."

"And I suppose no one is taking into account that Eden disappeared exactly fifty years after Crystal Juneau was abducted by the Immaculate Conception Killer, and Eden—like Crystal—has a sister attending the university. The killer left Crystal's sister a note—in Crystal's handwriting—saying she was fine, the same way Hannah O'Rourke got a note—"

"What we're taking into account is Eden's history," Castino interrupted. "She grew up being shuffled back and forth between two unfit mothers. Her guardians for the last two years admit that she often went missing, for days sometimes—usually, without any kind of provocation. Eden disappeared nine days ago. Then last week, she came by her dorm bungalow, took some of her clothes and things, and left a note for her sister saying that she was fine and not ready to come back to school. No one has heard from her since. To me, that seems like a runaway situation."

"I wonder if the O'Rourkes know about the Immaculate Conception Killer and all these 'coincidences,'" Ellie said, walking to the center of the bridge. "Everyone's so worried about causing a panic that they're totally ignoring the obvious. I wonder what you and Father O'Hurley are going to say when a teacher dies on Wednesday night—from something that looks like an accident or a suicide. That's two days away, Detective, the fiftieth anniversary of Valerie Toomey's murder . . ."

Ellie looked over the side of the bridge. Because of the police tape at the stairway's access, some students must have used the other stairs behind the playfield to access the ravine walkway below. Ellie gazed down at the flowers and candles they'd left near the spot where Justine's body had been found.

"I really hope we won't be having this same conversation again on Thursday morning, Detective Castino," she said.

"You and me both, Ellie," he replied, "you and me both."

Then he hung up.

Monday, 2:52 P.M.

As she approached Ellie's desk, Hannah glanced over toward the classroom door. Nick was filing out with the other students. He looked her way, and their eyes met for a fleeting second before he headed out the door.

"God, he makes my skin crawl," she whispered to Ellie. "I can't believe I used to think he was cute. But ever since that whole 'I'm watching you' thing with Alden, I can't stand him."

"I think he was just angry at Alden for wasting his time, and that's my fault," Ellie said, sitting on the edge of her desk. "I really don't think he's that bad. I misjudged him. Anyway, I wanted to talk with you because I heard your parents contacted the school and the local police about Eden."

Hannah nodded glumly. "Yeah, it's official now. Everybody thinks she's run away."

"And what do you think?"

Glancing around the empty classroom, she sighed. "I feel shitty about the whole thing," she admitted. "Let me tell you about my weekend—so you'll know what I'm talking about. After a rocky start, I ended up having a great time with Rachel at her parents' incredible place in Chicago on Saturday. And the only time I gave any thought to Eden was when Rachel and I went to Millennium Park. With all the people, I imagined maybe we'd run into Eden there." She rolled her eyes. "Yeah, dumb, I know. Anyway, Rachel had to go to some dinner thing with her parents on Saturday night. But when she came back, we made popcorn and watched *La La Land* on a gigantic screen in their home theater. After that, we stayed up until four in the morning, talking and drinking champagne. Then yesterday, we slept in, and she took me to a fancy brunch at the Drake Hotel and we got chauffeured back to the bungalow. And here's where I feel like a total shit. I was kind of glad Eden wasn't around. I was happy it was just Rachel and me at the bungalow. Then I got a call from my parents, and I guess it's official—Eden is a *missing person*. So, this policeman came over and interviewed me at the bungalow last night. He made out a police report and gave me a case number. Like I say, all very official. Talk about weird . . ."

"Was it Detective Castino by any chance?" Ellie asked. "A short, stubby guy, about fifty—in a sloppy suit?"

Hannah shook her head. "No, he was about forty and tall, wearing a police uniform. Anyway, you know what I was thinking the whole time? Actually, I was thinking *two* things. First, it felt like Eden was dead, like I'd never see her again." Hannah sort of laughed, but her eyes filled with tears. "And that was a real awful feeling, y'know? While I was having a grand time in Chicago with my new sister, my other sister was probably dead."

Ellie reached into her purse and pulled out a small travel packet of Kleenex.

Hannah took one and blew her nose. "Thanks.

Anyway, the other thing that occurred to me was that Eden lived with my family for two years, and yeah, it was rough going sometimes, and she disappeared on occasion. Still, she always came back, and we all made it work. But it took only two weeks with me before she ran away and disappeared for good. I—I could have been a better sister to her . . ."

"You can't blame yourself." Ellie offered her more Kleenex. "You told me the other day that before Eden disappeared, you felt like the two of you were getting closer."

Hannah grabbed another tissue and wiped her eyes again. "God, I'm sorry to be blubbering like this."

"Remember you mentioned how maybe Eden's disappearance was connected to the fire in the laundry room? You said that someone following the Immaculate Conception Killer's timeline could've abducted Eden."

Hannah nodded and took a deep breath to steady herself. But she kept the tissue in her hand in case she started crying again. "Yeah, kind of crazy, I know."

"No, not so crazy," Ellie said. "Did you tell your parents or the police about that?"

She nodded again. "I told them both yesterday."

"What did they say?"

"Well, the cop didn't say anything. He just wrote it down. My parents didn't seem to take it very seriously. My brother is kind of ghoulish when it comes to reading up on serial killings, and he told my folks about the Immaculate Conception murders. So they knew what I was talking about. My dad said he had a hard time taking seriously someone who would set a baby doll on fire. He said it sounded more like a prank, and he didn't think the same person would actually abduct somebody and hold them against their will for over a week."

"That makes sense, actually," Ellie sighed. She seemed disappointed. "Listen, Hannah, what you said earlier about Eden running away after only two weeks with you, the thing is, she spent those two weeks with Rachel as well. You have to admit, Rachel has been full of surprises. Maybe Eden found out something about Rachel that upset her—and that's why she ran away."

Hannah just stared and blinked at her. She'd never considered that before. She took a step back and sat on the edge of the long table in the front row of the classroom.

"Maybe Eden found out something about the adoption," Ellie continued. "Didn't you mention at the pool the other day that there was a detective looking into your father and your aunt—and their baby?"

"Yeah, but that was old news to Eden," Hannah murmured.

"Well, maybe there's more to the story than Eden knew. Maybe Rachel told her something, and it upset her enough that she ran away. Or maybe Eden discovered something about Rachel . . ."

Hannah shrugged and wiped her nose again. "I don't know what Eden could have discovered. And I doubt Rachel told her anything in confidence, at least, nothing that she wouldn't tell me. I mean, they weren't exactly close. I don't think the two of them ever had a conversation that lasted over two minutes."

"Well, you never know with Rachel," Ellie said. "She strikes me as a young lady with a lot of secrets."

Hannah said nothing. But she felt the same way. Rachel was still kind of a mystery to her, but she was also her friend and her half-sister. Plus Rachel had shown her a wonderful time this weekend. Hannah was grateful for their friendship.

"Has she ever mentioned to you anything about an older, married man—a business associate of her father's that she was close to?" Ellie asked.

Mystified, Hannah shook her head.

"I'm just trying to think of someone who could tell us more about Rachel and her family. You know, as a reporter, I always found I got more useful information on a person from their friends and associates than I did from the actual person."

"Well, there's always Alden," Hannah suggested. "He's known Rachel all his life, and he grew up in her house. There's also a housekeeper named Alida. She seems close to Rachel. On Saturday night, I spent a lot of time talking to the Bonners' cook, Hildie. And Hildie said there was another housekeeper before Alida, and she knew *everything* about the Bonners . . ."

"Do you remember this former housekeeper's name?" Ellie asked anxiously.

Hannah couldn't recall. She'd been too distracted by Hildie's story about the old housekeeper discovering Rachel and Alden when they were kids, naked and "experimenting." She shrugged. "Her name began with a 'V.' It's all that comes to mind right now. She's retired and in a rest home, Our Lady of the Something. I guess I could find out from Alden . . ."

"Well, if you can get the woman's name, I can track her down and talk to her. And, like I said, I heard something about Rachel being close to one of her father's business associates. If you could manage to find out his name, too, I'll talk to the guy . . ."

Hannah frowned at her. "So, basically, you want me to help you find these people who—who might have some dirt on Rachel or her family. Is that right?"

Ellie sighed. "I know it's a long shot, but if it can bring us any closer in determining why Eden disappeared, don't you think it's worth a try? On the plus side, maybe we won't find anything bad at all. Maybe Rachel and her family have nothing to hide. You're just getting to know her as a friend and a sister. Wouldn't you like to know as much as you can about her? Aren't you curious?"

"I suppose," Hannah admitted.

"All you have to do is ask Alden about the house-keeper—and if Rachel was close to one of Mr. Bonner's business associates. Bring it up casually. Say you heard a rumor . . ."

"Well, what do you mean when you say Rachel was *close* to this older, married guy? Did she have an affair with him or something?"

"I don't know exactly," Ellie said. "It's merely something I heard. It was very vague. I'm hoping Alden might have a better idea what it's about. Only when you talk to Alden, please, leave me out of the conversation. He—well, he knows I was a reporter. I don't want him to think I'm poking into Rachel's personal life for some kind of big scoop. I'm just worried about Eden, and I have good reason to believe her disappearance has something to do with Rachel . . ."

Hannah couldn't help feeling funny about the whole thing. But she didn't want to disappoint Ellie. And at least it was an excuse to get together with just Alden and no one else.

She nodded. "Rachel has classes until five tomorrow,

and I think Alden is free. I'll see what I can find out for you . . ."

Monday, 6:40 P.M.

"I feel terrible. I mean it. I hate myself right now."

"I know," Nate said. "I'm really sorry I put you in that position." He refilled her wineglass. "I feel lousy about it, too."

"Thanks." Ellie took the glass and sipped her Cabernet. She stood over a pot of spaghetti sauce on the stove in his kitchenette. "I looked her right in the eye and lied to that girl. And I totally manipulated her into spying for us."

"What do you mean you *lied* to her?" Nate asked. He stood beside Ellie and noticed she wouldn't look at him. It was something Rene used to do when she was ticked off at him.

"I lied when I said I thought Eden's disappearance was linked to Rachel. It was the excuse I used to recruit her into getting those names for us—and a lame, convoluted excuse at that. I'm not sure she even believed me. I didn't believe me. Why should she?"

Leaning against the counter, Nate took a sip of wine and said nothing.

He wished he could just enjoy the fact that Ellie was there cooking dinner for him. Since moving into this dump six months ago, she was the first non-client to visit his apartment, the first woman—and a nice, beautiful woman, too. After so many frozen dinners from Trader Joe's and takeout, this home-cooked dinner was another first. This afternoon, he'd been so thrilled at the prospect, he'd gone out and bought a second barstool. So what if it didn't match? The important thing was they could sit and eat together at his counter-bar. He'd also bought a good bottle of wine, some decent plates, and even a few votive candles for a little ambience. In the last year and a half of feeling so isolated, he'd finally found someone in whom he could confide. Even Kayla Kennedy hadn't known who he really was. He couldn't risk letting anyone know, not until Ellie forced it out of him. And Nate was glad she did.

In Taos, he hadn't let himself get close to anyone. He'd been too afraid of putting some unsuspecting woman in danger. He kept thinking of Rene. They'd been together for three years before that night at his family cabin. In a way, he'd died with her there.

The closest he came to making friends in Taos were his regular massage clients. And the closest he came to having sex was when he got the occasional pass from onetime clients—female and male. He'd always tactfully averted messing around with them. It had been tough keeping things professional with some of the women. Not that he was a total saint; in fact, he'd often kick himself for passing up those opportunities for some meaningless sex. But that was all it would have been.

For the last year and a half, everyone had felt like a stranger.

Nate didn't realize how lonely he'd been until he talked to Ellie on Thursday evening. It felt so good to connect with someone again. And it felt so right that it was Ellie. He couldn't help thinking of tonight as a date.

Ellie had arrived forty minutes ago with a grocery bag full of food. But she'd also arrived angry. Though Ellie said she was mad at herself, Nate knew it was his fault. She'd asked Hannah to spy on Rachel in order to help him.

And now she'd just made it clear that she didn't even believe Eden's disappearance had anything to do with Rachel Bonner. To Nate, that meant she didn't believe much in him.

He took some flatware out of the utensils drawer and washed it off at the sink. Living alone and never having company, he always used the same knife, fork, and spoon over and over again. After six months, the unused utensils had gathered dust.

"I've read up on the Immaculate Conception murders," he said. "And I think you're right about someone copying those murders. It's quite possible the same guy abducted Eden O'Rourke, and he's holding her prisoner right now. But I also think she could have disappeared because someone thought she knew something about Rachel Bonner. You didn't lie to Hannah this afternoon."

"Well, I felt like a liar," she muttered, stirring the spaghetti sauce.

He arranged a couple of place settings on the counter-bar. "Listen, two years ago, some guy held a gun to my head and asked me what I knew about Rachel Bonner. He and his partner asked my brother the same question while torturing him. I've been hiding and constantly looking over my shoulder ever since. Two of the three people who have helped me were killed under very mysterious circumstances. One of them was Rachel's roommate . . ."

He set the three votive candles on the counter-bar and lit them. "Eden O'Rourke knew about my brother working for the woman who raised her. I found out about that pretty easily—merely by eavesdropping on you and Hannah at the pool. Someone else could have found out just as easily from Hannah, Eden, or Rachel. My brother was killed because he'd discovered something abou Rachel or the Bonners. Eden might have 'disappeared for the same reason."

Nate turned to see her leaning against the counter facing him. "You didn't lie to Hannah today," he said "You have your theory about why Eden disappeared and I have mine. But I'm allowing for the possibility that you're right. Can't you do the same for me? Can' you at least acknowledge that I could be right, too?"

She let out a sigh. "Of course. I just feel shitty abou putting Hannah in this position."

"Believe me, so do I," he admitted. He was thinking of Kayla and Frank.

"And the way I manipulated her . . ."

"On the plus side, she just needs to get a couple o names for us. And that could lead to a real break through. We're talking about someone who ran the Bonners' household business for years and somebody else who very well could have ordered my brother' murder. And I think Hannah will be okay, I really do. don't think she's in any real danger."

"I hope you're right," Ellie said. She moved over to the sink and filled a pot with water. Then she set it on the stove to boil. "You know, you're a rare breed, Nate. It' not very often nowadays that I run into someone who' willing to accept another person's point of view on an issue. Shows you have an open mind. So, you don' think my copycat killer theory is full of holes?"

"No, not at all," he said. "In fact, I believe in it so much that I'm worried about you being alone on Wednesday night. Isn't that the fiftieth anniversary o when the Immaculate Conception Killer broke into that teacher's house and strangled her?"

Ellie nodded. "Valerie Toomey. She was the same age as me when she was killed."

He came over next to her and leaned against the counter. "Do I know you well enough to invite myself over to spend the night at your place on Wednesday?"

Her eyes met his, and she nodded. "I'd like that. Thank you."

For a moment, Nate thought about kissing her. But she turned away and stirred the spaghetti sauce again.

"Good," he said. "You shouldn't be alone."

CHAPTER FORTY

Tuesday, September 22, 3:20 P.M.

The fifth-floor hallway of the boys' dorm, O'Leary Hall, smelled like sweat socks—at least Hannah thought so. Someone had that old "Tubthumping" song—"I get knocked down, but I get up again"—blaring from his room. Hannah had dressed in a cute red pullover and her sexiest jeans for this seemingly impromptu visit to Alden's room. She'd texted him five minutes ago and asked if they could get together.

He'd texted back:

M at my dorm. Come on up! Room 508.

Now she knocked on his door.

Seconds later, Alden opened it. He wore a gray T-shirt and jeans, and was barefoot. He gave her a big smile. "Hey, what's going on?"

"Nothing much," she said. "It's been a while, and I just felt like seeing you . . ."

This, of course, was a lie. She was there on a mission for Ellie, and she felt a bit nervous about it. Now that she was face-to-face with Alden, alone with him, and about to enter his bedroom, her heart was racing.

"Yeah, not since Thursday night, when Perry had us in lockdown at the bungalow—after that creepy massage guy said he was watching us." Alden opened the door wider. "C'mon in. *Mi casa, su casa . . .*"

The narrow room had a big window with a view of the playfield and the woods beyond. It was easy to guess which side was Alden's. There were two Irish posters—one a collage of Irish beers, and another a beautiful photo of the Irish countryside. Hannah didn't even have to ask who had given him the large, framed poster from the original Frank Sinatra *Ocean's 11*. His side of the room was tidy—in contrast to his roommate's, whose sloppiness rivaled Eden's. It looked like the roommate's bed was all rumpled beneath the hastily arranged bedspread. Beer and hockey posters decorated the wall on that side. As Alden closed the door, Hannah noticed a dartboard on the back of it—along with at least a hundred little holes in the door and the doorway frame.

"Have a seat," Alden said, indicating his bed. He sank down in his desk chair. "I should warn you that Turner, the Flatulence King, should be back at any minute, and promised I'd go with him to this place in Highwood and help him load some shit into his brother's pickup for him. I don't know how I got suckered into that. Anyway, how are you? Have you heard anything new about Eden?"

Settling on his bed, Hannah leaned back against the wall. "No. But she's an official missing person now. The police and the school are in on the case. And yesterday, my parents hired a private investigator."

"God, I'm really sorry," he murmured. "Must be tough."

Hannah just nodded. There was an awkward silence

while she tried to think of a way to steer the conversation toward the Bonners' former housekeeper and the married guy with whom Rachel might have had an affair.

"So how was your Saturday night at Chez Bonner?" Alden asked. "Cute, rustic little shack they've got there, huh? What did you think of Dick and Candy?"

"Talk about awkward," Hannah admitted with the roll of her eyes. "We had a really strained lunch, and that was the only time I set eyes on them."

"Yeah, Rachel told me about that. I hear they ditched you to go out for dinner."

Nodding, Hannah sat up a little. This was exactly where she needed the conversation to go. "Yes, in fact, I spent a lot of time in the kitchen, talking with Hildie, the cook."

"Was she hammered? She always gets kind of shit-faced when the Bonners go out to dinner. And I'll bet the TV was on the whole time. She always has the TV on."

Hannah giggled. "Yeah, she was pretty drunk, and she had the game shows on." Hannah imagined Alden keeping the tipsy British cook company in that kitchen when the house was practically empty. "We talked about you part of the time. Hildie told me a story about the old housekeeper—what was her name again?"

He made a sour face. "Vivien?"

"Yes, *Vivien* Something . . ."

He tipped the chair back against the edge of his desk. "Vivien Houghton. The old bitch was running the house back when it belonged to Candy's parents, before she married Dick. Under her domination, everything in the household had to be just so. A tight-ass who ran tight ship, that was Vivien. Growing up, she scared the shit out of my mother and me. What story did Hildie tell about her?"

"Something about her finding you and Rachel when you were kids, naked and messing around. According to Hildie, Ms. Houghton was convinced the two of you had an 'unnatural relationship.'"

He let out an awkward laugh. "And that was just the one time we got caught."

"And you were the one who told me that any relationship between you and Rachel would be incestuous. What exactly did you guys do?"

He tipped the chair forward—so the front two legs met the floor again. "Jesus, I don't remember. I was, like, six, and Rachel was eight. She wanted us to get naked, so I got naked for her. I always did what I was told. Ms. Houghton thought we were a couple of little perverts, and she was probably right. In fact, you want to hear something weird? A few years back, I mentioned those peek-a-boo sessions to Rachel, and she claimed she didn't remember any of it, acted like it never happened. I guess she repressed it. She even got a little pissy when I tried to remind her . . ."

Alden stared down at the floor for a moment, and then his eyes met hers. "I hope you didn't mention anything about this kinky kids' stuff to Rachel."

Hannah quickly shook her head. "No, I didn't."

"Well, I wouldn't if I were you." He chuckled again. "Hildie and her big mouth, three or four glasses of wine, and she's revealing all the family secrets. What other scandalous tales did she tell you?"

"That was the juiciest. Otherwise, she had nothing but nice things to say about you." Hannah paused. She saw a potential segue there, and she decided to take it.

"Speaking of scandals, I heard these two girls talking in the cafeteria yesterday. One of them said something about Rachel being really close to some older, married guy, a business associate of her father's . . ."

Eyes narrowed at her, Alden leaned forward in his chair. "Who said this?"

"I don't know—some girl one table over from me at lunch," Hannah lied. "She was talking with her friend. I have no idea who she was. I didn't recognize either one of them."

"Can you remember what she said exactly?" Alden pressed. He stared at her intently. "Did she mention where she'd heard this?"

Hannah shrugged. Suddenly, she couldn't look him in the eye. "I don't remember her exact words. I heard her mention something about Rachel being *close* to an older married guy. Then she said, 'I think he's a business associate of her father's.' Anyway, it got me wondering. Is it true?"

Alden seemed to force a smile. He shook his head. "Don't pay attention to that shit. People are always gossiping and making up stories about Rachel because she's rich. So, when you were in the cafeteria yesterday, did you have the pizza for lunch? Wasn't it horrible?"

Hannah laughed. "It was so gross . . ."

Alden said nothing for a moment, but he was still smiling. "Hannah," he whispered finally. "They didn't serve pizza for lunch yesterday. The lunch special was their watery macaroni and cheese. C'mon, fess up. You didn't hear this rumor about Rachel from a couple of girls in the cafeteria, did you?"

Hannah just stared at him.

"I'll bet you heard it from your friend, Ellie. Am

right?" He seemed more amused than mad. "Ellie Goodwin, Our Lady of the Cove's own Lois Lane, I'm sure she's behind this. I know you like her, but I'm sorry. She's kind of a user. Look how she got me into trouble with that whack-job massage creep. I'll bet Ellie asked you if this rumor about Rachel and an older guy was true, and you decided to ask me . . ."

Hannah shook her head. "No, God . . ." She laughed nervously. "I swear, I heard these two bitches talking in the cafeteria. And I had a salad for lunch. I always eat a salad for lunch. I was just agreeing with you about the pizza, because I tried it once. And you're right. Their pizza sucks." She let out a dramatic sigh and gave him a smile. "The girl who was talking about Rachel had blond hair with black roots, and she wore it in a ponytail with a scrunchie. Oh, and she had dark blue fingernail polish . . ." Hannah figured these details might lend a little credence to her story. "I don't remember what the other girl looked like."

Slouching in his desk chair, Alden just smirked at her. Hannah couldn't tell if he believed her or not.

The bedroom door opened. A stocky, cute, but dumb-looking guy stepped into the room. He had a camouflage backpack slung over his shoulder. "Hey . . ." he mumbled.

Alden got to his feet. "Turner meet Hannah. Hannah meet Turner."

"Hey . . ." Alden's roommate grinned at her and tossed his backpack on the hastily made bed.

"How's it going?" Hannah smiled and gave a nod.

He turned to Alden. "You still helping me out this afternoon?"

Hannah quickly got up. "I was just leaving. Nice meeting you, Turner . . ."

He grunted in response.

Alden walked her out to the hallway and closed the door behind him. "That was Turner," he whispered. "Charming, isn't he?"

"Delightful." She giggled and touched his arm for a moment. "Well, thanks for having me over . . ."

"Drop in any time," he said.

Hannah was about to head for the elevator, but she hesitated. "Y'know, you never really answered my question. What the girls were talking about, is it true? Was Rachel ever involved with some older, married guy?"

"Are you kidding me?" Alden chuckled. "The way her parents keep tabs on her? Rachel couldn't get away with anything like that. Her dad would hunt the guy down and murder him—or he'd have one of his people do it for him."

Hannah nodded. It struck her that Alden was dead serious. She felt his hand on her shoulder.

"Nice seeing you," he whispered. Then he leaned in and gently kissed her on the lips.

For Hannah, the kiss was over way too quickly. He seemed very casual about it.

"See ya," she murmured.

Alden ducked back into his room and closed the door.

Mesmerized, she stood there in the noisy, smelly hallway. For a few moments, she forgot the reason for her visit.

It wasn't until Hannah wandered onto the elevator that she remembered she needed to report to Ellie.

Tuesday, 4:03 P.M.

"I think I convinced him that you had nothing to do with it, but he was definitely suspicious. I mean, he asked me flat out if you were the one who said something to me about Rachel and this married business associate of her father's."

"It's okay," Ellie said. "You did well."

Hannah sat in the only spare chair in Ellie's office. At her desk, Ellie still had a pen in her hand from the brief notes she'd taken on a yellow legal pad:

> *Vivien Houghton (or Haughton?)*
> *Affair story may be true . . .*
> *ALDEN SUSPECTS!!!*

"The weird thing is," Hannah said, "when I brought up the affair thing, Alden didn't deny it right away. He seemed more concerned about where I'd heard it . . ."

"Good observation," Ellie replied. "As a reporter, that's one of the things you learn pretty quickly. If you fire a question at someone, and they don't want to answer it, the first thing they ask is where you heard the story. It's a way to deflect—and usually a sign that your question hit a nerve." Holding the click-end of the pen against her lower lip, Ellie sat back in her chair. "So— I think you better not bring this up with Alden again, and definitely not with Rachel. If he broaches the subject, stick to your story about hearing those girls talking in the cafeteria. And act like you haven't even given it another thought. Okay?"

Hannah nodded. But she still looked a bit apprehensive.

"You did well," Ellie told her again. She put the pen down. "And I won't ask you to do anything else. Thank you, Hannah."

"I'm not sure how this will help us figure out what

happened to Eden," Hannah said, squirming in the chair. "But . . ."

"I'm not sure either," Ellie admitted. "But I can take it from here."

She hoped the information would be useful to Nate. She also hoped she wouldn't have to break her promise to Hannah. She didn't want the poor girl sticking her neck out for them again.

Ellie noticed someone hovering outside her office door. He ducked back, so she couldn't see his face; but he still lingered out in the corridor.

"Excuse me?" Ellie called.

Hannah glanced over her shoulder.

"Excuse me! Are you waiting to see me?" Ellie called again.

The custodian, Lance, backed into her doorway. He rested the handle of a push broom on his shoulder and took out his earbuds. "You talking to me?" he asked.

Ellie worked up a smile. "I'm sorry, Lance. I saw someone out there, and didn't realize it was you."

He seemed slightly annoyed—until he looked at Hannah and then he grinned. "Hey, how's it goin'?"

"Fine, thanks," she said with a pained, cordial smile. Then she turned toward Ellie again.

Lance put the earbuds back in and then moved on down the hall with his push broom.

With the way the janitor sometimes lurked around, Ellie wondered if he was spying on her—maybe even for O'Hurley. "Do you know him?" she whispered to Hannah.

Grimacing, she nodded. "His mother works for Rachel as a cleaning woman. She also comes by and picks up or drops off laundry for Rachel. Sometimes his mother sends Lance. Rachel says he's creepy but harmless. So, before she took off, Eden and I used to call him C-B-H Lance. Creepy But Harmless."

"Have you heard from your parents since yesterday?" Ellie asked. "Are there any updates on Eden?"

Hannah sighed. "They just called, like, fifteen minutes ago—when I was on my way over from O'Leary Hall. It looks like Eden got rid of her phone. The last activity they got was her deleting a bunch of our texts on Friday night. The phone went out of whack shortly after that, somewhere near downtown Chicago. I guess I might as well stop texting her now."

"Did they say where in downtown Chicago?" Ellie asked.

Hannah thought for a moment. "According to the private detective they hired, it was North Clark and West Wacker Drive. Is that right? Is there really a street downtown called Wacker?"

Ellie nodded. "That's the Clark Street Bridge—over the Chicago River."

She figured the copycat killer had tossed Eden's phone into the river.

He must have had bridges on his mind this weekend.

"I had no idea Eden was so serious about not wanting anyone to find her," Hannah murmured. "I mean, I can't imagine getting rid of my phone like that. Then again, she had hers turned off more than she ever had it turned on. Still . . ."

"Do you really believe she ran away?" Ellie asked quietly.

"I don't know. I keep thinking of those texts that

didn't sound like her—same thing with that note she left in our room. She began it, *Dear Sis.* She's never called me 'sis'—except maybe a few times when she was trying to be a wise ass."

"Wait a minute," Ellie said. She reached into her purse. "Do you still have that note someplace?"

"Yeah, in fact, I have it on my phone. I took a picture of it to text to my parents. I wanted them to see what she said . . ."

"Find it, will you?" Ellie grabbed her phone out of her purse and started hunting for the photos she'd taken from files in the *Tribune*'s archives. She briefly glanced up to see Hannah swiping and searching her phone screen as well.

Ellie finally found what she was looking for. "'Dear Sis,'" she read aloud. "'Looks like I missed you. I swung by to pick up some things. Don't worry about me. I'm fine . . .'" Ellie looked up to see that Hannah was reading along on her phone screen.

They both started reading in unison: "'. . . *I just needed to get away and I'm not ready to come back yet. Tell the folks not to worry. I'll be in touch. Okay?*'"

Hannah stopped reading aloud, but Ellie continued: "'Take care. X-X-X, Me.'"

Glancing up from the phone, Ellie found Hannah gaping at her.

"How did you get a hold of Eden's note?" Hannah asked.

Ellie shook her head. "It's not Eden's. It's the note Crystal Juneau was forced to write to her sister while the Immaculate Conception Killer kept her locked up in that shack in his backyard. It's the same thing, word for word. The copycat didn't change a syllable."

"My God," Hannah whispered.

"I'm going to text you this photo of the original note—from 1970." Ellie worked her fingers over the phone. "And I'm texting you some other pictures—along with some texts I've sent to our local law enforcement. You know that girl who supposedly killed herself last week—and the girl who fell down those stairs and broke her neck over the weekend?"

Wide-eyed, Hannah nodded at her.

"I'm pretty certain those girls were murdered by someone copying the Immaculate Conception killings. It's an idea you first put in my head."

"The one nobody took seriously," Hannah said.

"Yes, no one took it seriously. But the similarities between these recent . . . 'fatalities' and the murders that occurred exactly fifty years before are irrefutable. I've been trying to convince Detective Castino of the Delmar Police, but he's chalking it all up to a bunch of bizarre coincidences. He won't listen to me. But maybe he'll listen to your parents. He's sure to pay attention to them after they show him the two letters."

Ellie glanced up from her phone for a moment. 'Now, before you forward this material to your folks and call them, maybe I should tell you what I'm talking about and what these texts mean . . ."

Hannah was studying her phone and working her thumbs over the screen. Ellie could only see the top of her head. "Hannah, are you listening to me?"

"Yes, my mom and dad aren't getting back from work until about seven-thirty our time." Hannah was still looking at her phone. "So I'll send the texts as soon as we finish up here, and then I'll talk to them around a quarter to eight."

Hannah finally looked up at her. She seemed dazed. "God, I can't believe these two letters. They're exactly the same. How can anybody call this just a coincidence?"

"They can't, Hannah," she replied. "They can't."

CHAPTER FORTY-ONE

"It didn't go over so well," Hannah said on the other end of the line, "at least, not how we expected."

Sitting at her kitchen table, Ellie held the phone to her ear. This was a crushing blow.

She'd had such hope. The two handwritten notes between the two sets of sisters, fifty years apart, had felt like a breakthrough. With those two letters, how could the police keep denying the existence of a copycat killer? Ellie had figured that, at last, local law enforcement would get busy looking for Eden O'Rourke. And they'd start the search for the man holding her prisoner, the same man who had already killed two young women.

Ellie rubbed her forehead. "Didn't the two notes make any kind of impression?"

"My dad got my brother to Google Crystal's letter, and it took him less than two minutes to find the entire contents of it. Everyone seemed to agree, copying that note was the kind of thing that Eden might do—just to be perverse."

"No, you can't be serious!" Ellie moaned. "C'mon, who would do that?"

"Eden would," Hannah said glumly. "They're right. She knew a lot about those murders. She read up on them after the fire in the laundry room. It would be just like Eden to write the exact same note as the abducted girl—to screw around with me. Even if I never made the connection, she'd do something like that for the mere fun of it."

"I can't believe this," Ellie said. With the phone to her ear, she got up from the table, opened the kitchen cabinet, and took out a bottle of Cabernet. "Didn't any of the photos or the other evidence sway them at all?"

"Yeah—at first," Hannah replied. "They called this Detective Castino with the Delmar Police, and they called the school, too. I guess my dad was on the phone with them for at least a half hour. The Castino guy said he knew all about your copycat theories. He said you were *grieving* because the girl who hung herself was your friend. The priest in charge here at the school said you've been trying to write a news story about Rachel, Eden, and me—"

"That's not true," Ellie said, setting the wine bottle on the counter.

"He thought you were a bad influence on me. He said you were using me. It's funny, because Alden said the same thing this afternoon—about you using me."

"Hannah . . ."

"I told them they were wrong. I told them you were my friend. Anyway, this priest said he'd warned you over a week ago to stop seeing me outside of class. He was really upset that you went ahead and kept getting together with me. I—I hope I didn't get you into trouble with him . . ."

"Hannah, this priest, this Father O'Hurley, he has the

wrong idea about me. He's made all these assumptions. And I'm sorry, I know he's a priest, but he's a total jerk. He and Castino are so worried about causing a panic at the school that they want to bury this whole thing. I warned them in advance about the girl dying on September 20, but they wouldn't listen . . ."

"Ellie?"

She took a deep breath and then sank down on the kitchen chair. She'd left the open wine bottle and a clean, empty glass on the kitchen counter. "Yes, Hannah?"

"You weren't really using me for some big story, were you?"

"No, I wasn't. I'm your friend, Hannah. I care about you. And I want them to find your sister before it's too late."

"You know how you said maybe Eden found out something and it upset her so much that she ran away?"

Ellie hesitated. "Yes?"

"You said maybe she knew something about Rachel's adoption that she didn't tell us." Hannah's tone was listless and dejected. "Maybe she knew we might not get to keep our scholarships."

"What do you mean?"

"My dad got the paternity test results back from his doctor tonight. It turns out Rachel isn't his daughter. She's not our half-sister. Maybe Eden already knew that, and she figured Rachel would cancel our scholarships. My dad thinks maybe that's why she ran away and decided to stay in Chicago for a while."

"Oh, Hannah," Ellie murmured. "Are you okay? How do you feel about that?"

"I don't know," she whimpered. "It's all so weird. If the birth certificate is right about my aunt Molly being her mother—which is a lot harder to fake—then, well, I guess Rachel and I are still cousins. Eden wouldn't be related to her at all. The important question is how Rachel will feel when I tell her about all this. She doesn't know yet. Her parents already predicted that the test would come back negative. They figured my dad would make his doctor fudge the results so he wouldn't be held accountable for another illegitimate kid—which is bullshit. He wouldn't do that even if he could get away with it. Anyway, I need to talk to Rachel sometime soon and face the music. Am I the shallowest person alive to be worried she'll cancel my scholarship?"

Ellie closed her eyes. "I don't think it's shallow of you to be worried about your education—and how all of this will affect you."

"Well, I still feel terrible," Hannah said. "I feel like I've let you down, too. But at the same time, I can't help hoping that you're wrong about what happened to Eden."

"I hope I'm wrong, too," Ellie said. She heard a call-waiting click on the phone and glanced at the screen: *O'Hurley, Robert.*

"Well, that didn't take long," she muttered. Then she cleared her throat. "Listen, Hannah, I need to take this call. Can we talk tomorrow?"

"Yeah, sure, no problem," she murmured. "Listen, take care, okay?"

"You too—and thanks for calling." Ellie switched off and picked up the incoming call. She got to her feet. "Hello, Father O'Hurley. I've been expecting to hear from you. I understand you had a long talk with the O'Rourkes tonight . . ."

She moved to the counter and poured herself that glass of wine.

"Ms. Goodwin, I don't usually call teachers this late in the evening," he said. "And I've never dismissed a teacher over the phone before. But in your case, I'm making an exception. If you report to Lombard Hall tomorrow morning at eight-thirty, someone from campus security will escort you to your office so you can clean out your desk and hand over your keys."

CHAPTER FORTY-TWO

Wednesday, September 23, 6:18 P.M.

Hannah sat in the backseat of the Uber car with a bouquet of flowers she'd bought for Ellie at the Jewel-Osco. It was her pathetic apology/condolence token for helping get Ellie fired.

She'd shown up to journalism class at Lombard Hall this afternoon, only to find a note on the door saying classes were canceled for the remainder of the week. Practically all the other students from the class were there in the hallway—with the strange exception of Nick Jensen. Hannah overheard someone say that Ellie had been "shit-canned," and they would have a new instructor on Monday. Apparently, the announcement was on an automatic reply on Ellie's school email.

Hannah checked, sending a quick email to Ellie: *Have you been fired?*

Sure enough, she received an automatic reply:

Ellie Goodwin is no longer at Our Lady of the Cove and cannot be reached at this email address. Emails cannot be forwarded. Written correspondences addressed to Ms. Goodwin at the university will be forwarded for a limited time only. All written correspondences should be sent to:

Ellie Goodwin
9203 Larkdale Road #3
Lake Forest, IL 60022

From everything her parents had said about their conversation with Father O'Hurley, Hannah had thought that Ellie might get reprimanded. But she hadn't expected Ellie to get the ax. And it seemed so careless of the university to give out Ellie's home address on their email server. Didn't they know about all the threats and hate mail she had received because of her reporting on those arsonists? Ellie had mentioned it in class.

Hannah sent her a text, asking what had happened, and if she was okay.

Ellie's text back was brief:

I'm fine, just overwhelmed right now. Hope UR OK. We'll talk tonight.

Hannah called her mother and told her that Ellie had been fired—probably because of them. Wasn't there anything they could do to persuade Father O'Hurley to give Ellie back her job?

"Oh, honey, I really don't think we're to blame," her mother said. "And I don't know what we can do or say on her behalf. We're the parents of a couple of charity scholarship students at that school. We don't have much clout there at all. The Bonners are the ones with all the influence. And from what you've told me, they're not exactly fans of Ellie Goodwin."

With journalism class canceled, Hannah went back to the bungalow. Rachel was home. Hannah told her the news about Ellie.

"Well, that's too bad," Rachel remarked, slouched on their living room sofa with a laptop at her side. "I know you like her, but to be perfectly honest, I always thought it was weird—a thirty-something woman getting all palsy-walsy with her eighteen-year-old student. I couldn't help thinking she was trying to get a news story out of you because you were such a big deal a couple of years ago. And I still hate the idea that she knows we're sisters . . ."

"Yeah, well, about that," Hannah said, her stomach in knots. She sat down in the chair across from her. "I've been meaning to tell you. My dad got the paternity test results—"

"Forget it," Rachel cut her off.

"What do you mean?" Hannah asked, wide-eyed.

"You just said, 'my father,' not '*our* father,' and you didn't even stop to correct yourself." Rachel gave an off-hand shrug, like it didn't matter. "Obviously, the test came back negative."

Hannah reluctantly nodded.

"My parents said that would happen. I've already scouted out some clinics, and there's a place in Lake Bluff. The two of us can go in there, get tested, and have the results in twenty-four to forty-eight hours. It'll prove we're sisters. I don't have anything going on this afternoon. And now that your journalism class is canceled, you're free, too, right? What do you say we go get tested right now?"

So Perry drove them to a rather posh clinic in Lake Bluff. A nurse took a swab sample from the inside of Hannah's and Rachel's cheeks. They said they'd have the results by Friday at the latest.

On the way back, Hannah had asked Perry to drop

her off at the Jewel-Osco. She'd decided to buy Ellie some flowers and go check in on her.

Hannah hated siding with everyone else who thought Ellie's copycat killer theory was irresponsible, panic-inducing nonsense. But she didn't want to think of Eden locked up in some lunatic's backyard tool shed. She didn't want to think the same psycho had been in her bedroom, collecting Eden's things and leaving that note. She hated the idea that this same guy still had Eden's keys and could break into the bungalow any time he wanted.

Though she'd made up her mind to discount Ellie's copycat killer hypothesis, Hannah refused to discount Ellie—no matter what everyone else said about her. Hannah wanted to show her teacher and friend that she cared and supported her.

Hannah noticed the street sign as the Uber car was turning down Larkdale. She smelled the bouquet she'd bought for Ellie and started to check the address numbers of the houses.

The driver slowed down as they approached a row of two-story, brick townhouses. A system of water sprinklers showered the well-manicured front lawn. Hannah could see the address in front, and it was Ellie's complex. She could also see someone ambling up a walkway to the doorway marked *3*.

"Could you stop here, please?" Hannah asked the driver.

He stopped in front of Ellie's neighbor's townhouse.

It was just starting to get dark, and Hannah couldn't quite see the face of the tall man approaching Ellie's door. He had an overnight bag in one hand, and in the other, a plastic bag that looked like it held carry-out food. He set down the overnight bag and rang the bell.

The front light went on. That was when Hannah recognized Nick Jensen.

She watched the front door open. Ellie greeted him with a hug. Then Nick Jensen picked up his overnight bag and she led him inside. The door closed.

Hannah didn't understand. Nick Jensen was the guy Ellie didn't like or trust. At the pool last week, Ellie had warned her about him. This was the same creep who had told Alden, "I'm watching you." The sound of his voice had made Hannah's skin crawl. And here was Ellie, acting like they were old friends or lovers. Were the two of them in on something together, some sort of scheme? Was everyone right about her?

And she thought Ellie was so open and honest with her.

"Ah, listen, I—I've changed my mind," Hannah said. "Could you turn around and take me back to Delmar? I need to go to the Our Lady of the Cove campus, Saint Agnes Village . . ."

CHAPTER FORTY-THREE

Wednesday, 7:11 P.M.

Sitting across from Nate at the café table in her kitchen, Ellie wondered once again about his intentions for tonight.

He'd brought over the Chinese dinner they'd just eaten. Seven mostly full carryout containers were lined up on her counter. She'd be eating Chinese for the next few days.

Tonight was the fiftieth anniversary of Valerie Toomey's murder. Toomey was the thirty-three-year-old teacher at Blessed Heart of Mary strangled by Lyle Duncan Wheeler—the third victim in the Immaculate Conception killings. Ellie remembered the picture of Valerie's corpse from the crime scene photos in the *Tribune* archives: a black-and-white shot of a slim brunette, in a terrycloth bathrobe, lying on her side on her kitchen floor. Wheeler had used the bathrobe sash to strangle her.

Thinking of that photograph now, Ellie was glad she didn't own a terrycloth bathrobe. She was also grateful Nate had volunteered to sleep over. She didn't want to risk being alone tonight.

So it seemed Nate was there to offer his protection—and nothing more. At least, that was how she'd interpreted things so far this evening. In his overnight bag, he'd brought along the revolver his brother's partner, Frank, had given him.

If Ellie was correct, the copycat killer was going to murder a teacher tonight.

Of course, she'd been fired yesterday evening, so technically, she was no longer an instructor at Our Lady of the Cove. But the copycat killer might not know that.

Cleaning out her office this morning, Ellie had managed not to break down crying in front of the campus security guard—a short, pale, forty-something mustached guy who barked instructions at her. He chewed his gum loudly and walked with a macho swagger. She'd felt his beady eyes staring at her as she'd removed all her writing awards and framed citations from the wall.

Adding to her hurt and humiliation, someone in campus administration had posted her home address on her now-defunct university email account. Ellie imagined Father O'Hurley dictating the officious message to Grandma Walton as she typed up the notice. They'd also blocked Ellie from contacting anyone through the university email system. So she couldn't send out a warning to her fellow teachers about tonight.

At least she'd managed to get her home address deleted from the email message they'd posted, but it had been up there for several hours for anyone to see—including her "fans" with the American Family Preservationists. That was another reason she appreciated Nate's company right now.

But she also felt vulnerable, sad, lonely—and suddenly

without purpose. Would it be crossing a line if she wanted more than just a bodyguard tonight?

She couldn't help feeling as if this was strictly another vigil, like their stakeout in the wee hours of Sunday morning. Once again, they were merely waiting out the night together while a killer was out there. And they had to brace themselves for the possibility of seeing him face-to-face some time in the next few hours.

The circumstances were hardly conducive to an evening of wild, hot passion. She wasn't expecting that. Still, she would have given anything for Nate to take her in his arms and comfort her.

But right now, as they sat at her kitchen table together—like buddies or business partners—that kind of intimacy seemed out of place. He hadn't even put his hand on hers. The hug she'd given him at her front door had been the only time they'd touched.

There had been at least a couple of moments during Monday night's dinner date—if it was even a date—that she'd been certain he was about to kiss her. Maybe she'd been projecting. Yet she had good reason to believe they felt the same way about each other. And he seemed as extra-cautious as she was.

So they'd kept things merely cordial over dinner. Nate told her how he'd spent his day trying to track down Vivien Houghton. After checking with dozens of local nursing homes, he'd finally located the Bonners' former housekeeper at Mary of the Rosary Nursing and Rehabilitation Center in Wilmette. He would visit her tomorrow. There hadn't been much about Vivien Houghton online, not even her age. Nate said he hoped she was still sharp enough to answer some questions about Rachel and her family.

He felt they'd gotten as much information as they could from Alden in regard to Rachel's older, married lover. Alden's reaction when Hannah had questioned him about it seemed to give credence to Kayla's story. Nate wondered out loud if Ms. Houghton might know something about it.

"I'm still not sure how I'll get this old woman to open up to me, but I guess I'll figure something out," Nate said. He crumpled up his napkin and set it on his plate. "I'm trying not to invest too much hope in this. For all I know, this Houghton woman could totally clam up on me. Or she could talk my ear off and still not tell me a thing that would give us any insight as to why Gil, Cheryl, and Rene were killed—or why Eden O'Rourke disappeared."

Ellie got up from the table and gathered their plates and flatware. "I still say this copycat killer has her locked up in a shed somewhere."

"I'd like to think you're right. At least, with your theory, Eden is still alive."

Ellie grimaced at the thought of the poor girl already dead—like Kayla Kennedy. She set the dishes in the sink and turned on the hot water. "Well, you're the only one who even *almost* agrees with me," Ellie sighed. "It looks like Hannah now concurs with her parents that Eden ran away because she was afraid of losing her scholarship or some such nonsense." With another sigh, she started washing the dishes. "Though I guess it's logical on some level. Hannah's father made a good point about the laundry room fire and Eden's disappearance . . ."

"You mean that the person who set fire to the doll can't be taken seriously?" Nate came up beside her and handed her the ladling spoons and serving forks. "And how that same guy couldn't have done something as grave as abducting a girl and holding her against her will for over a week? I've been thinking about that, and I have a nice rebuttal for Mr. O'Rourke. The Immaculate Conception Killer didn't murder a baby fifty years ago. The infant's poor delusional young mother did. Why would this copycat murder a child if he didn't have to? The original guy didn't do it. And if this new guy used a real baby, he'd have had the police and the press swarming all over the campus in record time. So he set fire to a doll as a reminder of what had happened fifty years before. Everyone called it a prank, right? That was probably just what he wanted. If people took it seriously, he couldn't keep operating under the radar the way he has."

Ellie turned off the water and turned toward him. "You've thought about this a lot, haven't you?"

Nodding, Nate moved over to the carryout containers and started closing all the lids. "If I'm wrong and you're right about why Eden O'Rourke disappeared, then this copycat certainly picked the perfect girl for it."

Ellie dried off her hands with a dishtowel. "Yes, just like Crystal, Eden has a sister also attending the school . . ."

"Not just that," Nate said. "He chose a girl who has a history of running away and disappearing for days at a time. I told you how I started following Hannah on social media over the summer. Well, she mentioned in at least a couple of tweets about Eden disappearing— much to her parents' annoyance. If I found out so easily about Eden's penchant for vanishing, chances are this guy found out about it, too."

"So the copycat knew he could abduct Eden on the anniversary of Crystal Juneau's disappearance without anybody seeing a connection. It would be Eden O'Rourke, going off on her own again. It allowed him days to keep working before anyone started to worry or suspect anything."

"Like I said, he's working under the radar." Nate glanced at the containers on the counter. "I hope you have room in your refrigerator for all this . . ."

"Just leave it—leave it," Ellie said distractedly. She grabbed his arm and led him back to the table. They sat down again. "'Under the radar,'" she repeated. "Detective Castino used that same expression. He said there couldn't be a copycat killer, because, if there was, the guy was '*sure working under the radar*.' Castino kept saying that's not how a copycat killer would operate."

"He's right," Nate replied. "This guy isn't a copycat. If it had looked like Justine or your friend Diana had been murdered, the whole campus would be on alert. He couldn't get anywhere near his next victim."

"So, instead, we have an apparent suicide and an apparent accident," Ellie said. Then she shuddered. "The original victims were strangled. So this new guy did something to the new girls' necks. He must have forced Diana to go up that ladder and put the noose over her head . . ."

Nate nodded. "And he probably broke Justine Everly's neck before he threw her down those stairs."

"The way he's chosen the victims," Ellie said. "Diana looked like Greta Mae, and Justine had the same initials as Jane Marie Eggert. Plus he left some little calling card behind to link their deaths to the original murders—the book *Look Homeward, Angel* with Diana, and the shoe that fell off of Justine's foot."

"But that doesn't make him a copycat," Nate said.

"No," Ellie whispered. She clutched at a napkin still on the table. "No, that's where I was wrong. These murders are *tributes*."

Nate nodded. He put his hand over hers.

Neither of them said anything for a few moments.

"Are you going to call Detective Castino or the school and tell them any of this?" Nate finally asked.

Ellie slowly shook her head. "They wouldn't listen. I've already tried and tried with them. Besides, I wouldn't be offering them any real proof. I'd just be expounding on my theory."

"I suppose you're right," he said.

Ellie looked down at his hand on top of hers.

She found some comfort from his touch. Still, she couldn't help feeling that, right now, some teacher at Our Lady of the Cove was going about her business—and had no idea she'd be dead by morning.

Wednesday, 10:13 P.M.

"Aren't you going to invite me in?"

"I'd love to," Pamela said. "But I have an eight-thirty class in the morning—and papers to grade tonight."

She had the door unlocked and open. She inched toward the threshold. Ron still lingered on her front stoop.

It was the end of their first date—and the end of their brief association as far as Pamela Rothschild was concerned.

She was a forty-six-year-old divorcée and a psychology professor at Our Lady of the Cove. Pamela had two kids in college and still lived in the same split-level home they'd grown up in on Greenwood Avenue in Delmar. Over the summer, her well-meaning daughter had signed her up on Cupid.com.

Ron was pretty typical of the guys she'd met through the dating site so far. He looked about ten years older than the photo he'd posted on his profile. She'd been willing to overlook that—along with a few chauvinistic remarks he'd made during dinner at Bellini's. And she'd been fine about splitting the bill. But as they'd walked out of Bellini's, Ron had made a joke about bulimia. Pamela had forced a laugh but then started to share with him a few facts about the disorder. She didn't mention that she'd suffered from bulimia for a short spell after her divorce—or that she'd published an article about her experiences in a psychology journal two years ago. She just wanted to educate him a little. It wasn't as if she was giving him a thirty-minute lecture. She'd been talking for only a minute or two when he interrupted with some story about a woman cutting him off in traffic. It didn't have anything to do with bulimia.

By the time he finished his story, Pamela had decided they were finished, too. She wasn't really attracted to him anyway.

But Ron seemed to think he'd swept her off her feet.

"C'mon, just one drink," he said, still hovering by her front door. He looked like he was leaning in to kiss her. "The night's still young . . ."

"Not for us, Ron," she said. "But seriously, thank you for dinner—or at least, for driving us to dinner. Good night and good luck."

Pamela slipped inside and closed the door on him. She turned both locks and applied the chain. Then she prayed he didn't knock or ring the bell. She just wanted him to go.

She stood in the dark front hallway, listening to his retreating footsteps. Then she moved over toward the shadowy living room and looked out the front window. Because of the streetlight in front of her house, she had a clear view of Ron as he climbed into his car. Once the headlights went on and the car pulled away from the curb, Pamela began to breathe easily again.

But that feeling of relief lasted only a few moments.

As she started to peel off her coat, Pamela realized that, if not for the streetlamp outside, the house would be completely dark. The outside light came through the living room windows, making the furniture cast long shadows across the carpet.

This wasn't right.

Whenever she went out at night, Pamela always left a light on in the front hall and in the kitchen, above the breakfast table. It had become an established routine now that she was an empty-nester. Had she been so pre-occupied about her date that she'd forgotten her routine earlier tonight?

She switched on the overhead in the front hall and then hung up her coat in the closet.

With a bit of trepidation, Pamela poked her head into the kitchen and then reached in and flicked on the over-head light.

A place was set at her kitchen table—with a whole small cooked chicken, a cluster of grapes, and a bowl of cherries. A white terrycloth robe that wasn't hers had been draped over the back of one of the chairs.

From the dining room doorway, a man stepped out of the dark—into the lighted kitchen.

Pamela gasped. He was strange-looking, with shaggy dark blond hair, a mustache, and thick glasses. All of it seemed like a disguise. With his mustard-colored turtleneck, brown vest, and oatmeal-colored bell-bottom corduroys, he looked like he was on his way to a 1970s theme party. Everything about him seemed fake—except for the gun in his hand.

Pamela's heart stopped. She opened her mouth to speak but couldn't get any words out.

He pointed the gun toward the place setting on the table—and then at her. "I made you a late-night snack, Pam."

She glanced at the food he'd set out for her. She noticed there wasn't a glass of water to help wash any of it down. It took a moment before she could speak. "You—you expect me to eat all of that?" she asked timidly.

"No," he whispered. "I expect you to choke on it."

CHAPTER FORTY-FOUR

Wednesday evening

All the food had been put away and the dishes washed. After dinner, they sat on opposite ends of the sofa and watched *Sweet Smell of Success* on TV. They'd both taken off their shoes. Nate's overnight bag—with the gun in it—was beside the couch, on the floor.

Nate said the movie was one of his favorites. He'd seen it with his brother about ten times. But Ellie had a tough time concentrating on the film. About halfway through, Nate asked if she wanted to watch something else. She said no, she was fine, just a little tense. Then he asked if she wanted a foot rub. She said yes.

It was heaven. He knew all the pressure points. At times, Ellie couldn't help moaning or shuddering gratefully. It was strange to feel so relaxed and stimulated at the same time. She now knew why he'd received so many five-star reviews on the massage sites.

But even with her feet resting on his thigh, Nate remained very professional about everything. He kept watching the movie while his hands worked their magic on her heels, ankles, arches, and toes. His face looked so handsome in the flickering light from the TV screen.

Once in a while, he'd look at her and smile. "Is this okay?" he'd ask.

"Wonderful," she murmured each time.

Ellie didn't remember when he'd stopped—or when she'd fallen asleep.

She'd thought she'd merely closed her eyes for a few minutes. But opening them again, Ellie saw some obscure movie from the early thirties on TV. She didn't recognize any of the stars, and everyone seemed to talk in muffled, squeaky voices over the crackling soundtrack. The clock on the cable box read 12:13. Ellie's bare feet were wedged between the cushion and Nate's left thigh. He still had one hand on her ankle. But he was slouched over in the other direction, asleep with his head on the armrest pillow.

My, what a sexy couple we are, Ellie thought drolly.

But then the refrigerator kicked in with a noise that gave her a start, and Ellie remembered why Nate was with her tonight. Suddenly, she was on edge again. She'd been lucky just to get comfortable enough to fall asleep for a couple of hours. And for all she knew, the tribute killer may have already struck. According to one article she'd read online, Valerie Toomey's approximate time of death had been eleven at night.

Ellie listened to the refrigerator humming. She muted the TV so she could clearly hear any other noises—from inside and outside the townhouse. A part of her wanted to wake Nate, but she didn't have the heart. From the hall closet, she pulled out an afghan with reindeer on it her parents had given her several Christmases ago. She covered Nate from the chest down with it. He barely stirred.

Creeping to the window, she moved aside the curtain and peered outside. Everything seemed quiet. Nate's Ford Fiesta was parked across the street, a couple of houses down. She didn't see any other strange cars, nothing new at least.

In the kitchen, she checked the back door and glanced out the window again. She'd left the back light on—and it would remain on until morning. She had a view of her garden and the small backyard, bordered by hedges. There was only one tree, a big elm. Its branches were still. Standing by the window, Ellie remembered the police composite sketch of Lyle Duncan Wheeler in the disguise he used—the shaggy-haired, mustached man with glasses. She wondered if his self-appointed disciple was out there someplace. She shuddered.

"Nobody's there," Ellie told herself, backing away from the window. She took a couple of deep breaths and tried to relax.

She cracked open a fortune cookie from the take-out dessert bag they'd left on the kitchen counter. She read the fortune:

The year ahead will bring much travel.

Munching on the cookie bits, Ellie figured the fortune wasn't too far off. If she survived the evening, she'd soon be looking for another job, possibly in another city.

She set her laptop on the kitchen table and turned it on. It was probably way too soon for the police to discover anything, but Ellie went to Google News and tried searches with keywords like *Our Lady of the Cove*, *death*, and *teacher*. Nothing came up. She found a site with live audio feed of local police and fire dispatches.

She listened for twenty-five minutes, but didn't hear anything that sounded too serious.

Ellie wished she'd tried harder to warn all the other teachers at the school. She didn't know any of them very well. They probably would have thought she was crazy.

She wondered what kind of fatal "accident" would befall the woman he'd selected for tonight. It would have to be something involving the neck or throat again because Valerie Toomey had been strangled. Would it look like the victim had slipped in the shower and broken her neck—or possibly fallen against the shower door and severed her throat on the broken glass? Maybe he'd set it up to look like an automobile accident. He could break her neck ahead of time, place her in the driver's seat, and push her car off a bluff. Or maybe he'd somehow even set it up to look like Isadora Duncan's fatal car ride—her long, flowing scarf choking her to death as it snagged in the wheel of a speeding sports car. What kind of creative, sick scenario had this killer dreamed up for tonight's "tribute"?

And how quickly would Detective Castino and Father O'Hurley accept it as another unfortunate accident?

Ellie left the laptop on and returned to the living room. With the remote, she switched off the muted TV. Then she opened the drapes. She usually kept them open anyway. For the last few hours, it had felt slightly claustrophobic in there.

In the darkened living room, she sat down on the couch and stared out the window. The night was still. Nothing was moving out there. The wet grass of the recently watered front lawn glistened in the moonlight. An old beat-up station wagon was parked across the street. It hadn't been there when she'd last checked half hour ago. All the lights were off in the house across the way. So, who was this new arrival?

She glanced at Nate again. In the dim light, the faint burn scar on one side of his forehead was barely noticeable. But Nate's souvenir from the cabin explosion reminded Ellie that he was a hunted man. This tribute killer wasn't their only concern. Someone else was out there, someone who may have murdered Kayla Kennedy and been involved in the "murder" of Nate, as well as the murders of his brother and their two girlfriends.

She heard a clanking sound—like bottles banging together in a bag. It came from the front yard. Straightening up, Ellie stared out the window. She saw a man dart behind a tree on the front lawn.

"Nate!" she whispered, reaching over and shaking him. "Someone's outside!"

He quickly sat up. He started putting on his shoes.

Beside the same tree, Ellie glimpsed a small flame—from a match or a lighter the man was holding. The flame suddenly swelled into a flare. She realized he'd just ignited a Molotov.

"Go out the back!" Nate urged her. He reached into his bag. "Call the police!"

Ellie jumped up from the sofa, but froze for a second as she saw the man hurl the Molotov toward the front window. It smashed against the outer ledge and burst into flames.

She suddenly realized two men were out there. She didn't recognize the second guy. But the one who had thrown the bottle was Larry Deacon, whom she'd helped put in prison two years ago. He'd served eighteen months for arson. She was almost positive it was him.

But she didn't have much time to study his face before the fire and smoke outside her window obscured her view.

Nate finally found his gun and stood up.

All at once, another Molotov smashed through the front window.

Ellie screamed at the explosion of fire and glass. With a roar, flames shot up from the carpeted floor, igniting the curtains.

"Die, you bitch!" she heard one of them shout.

Nate pushed her toward the kitchen. "Go! Get out the back way . . ."

Ellie heard glass smashing again, but it was too far off to be the front window. It must have been a Molotov that missed the house.

With the gun in his hand, Nate turned and ran to the front door. He struggled with the locks but finally got the door open and ducked outside.

Ellie heard car doors slamming and then the squeal of tires.

She hurried to the hallway closet and grabbed the fire extinguisher. She'd prepared for an attack like this. There was another extinguisher in the kitchen and another upstairs in her bedroom closet. With the extinguisher in her hands, she turned toward the living room rapidly filling with smoke. She could feel the heat on her face. The fire seemed centered around the front window. Flames started to snake out along the carpeted floor; from the curtains, they licked the ceiling. Ellie could hear crackling. The smell was pungent.

Ellie held her breath as she pulled the pin to unlock the extinguisher's discharge lever. Bracing herself, she stepped forward and aimed the hose nozzle at the floor.

where the flames were the worst. She squeezed the lever, and the CO_2 shot out with a loud hiss. Trying to keep her hands steady, she swept the vapor stream back and forth over the fire. Between the smoke and the plumes from the carbon dioxide, she couldn't see much. But to her relief, she could no longer see any flames or sparks either. Still, Ellie kept squeezing the lever just to make certain the fire was out. Finally, she let the canister slip out of her hands and fall to the floor. It made a muffled, hollow thud.

Nate staggered back inside. He plopped the gun down on the hallway table, took her by the arms, and led her toward the kitchen, almost carrying her. She was surprised at his strength. He stood her by the kitchen counter and then looked her over—apparently to make sure she was all right. He started coughing and turned away to make a beeline to the back door. He unlocked and opened it.

Dazed, Ellie braced a hand on the counter. She watched him move over to the kitchen windows and open them.

"Front lawn's wet," he gasped. "The fire didn't last out there. Are you okay?"

He didn't wait for her to answer. Brushing past her, he hurried back into the front hallway and checked the living room. "You've put it out. You're good . . ."

Ellie's heart was still pounding. "Thanks," she started to say, but then she choked on the word and went into a coughing fit.

"You okay?" Nate asked again.

She nodded, but covered her mouth as her coughing subsided.

He hovered by her for another moment. Then he

turned and started searching around. He seemed to find what he was looking for—a pen and a pad of paper at the end of the counter. "I saw them," he said, scribbling on the pad. "They were two white guys, late twenties . . ."

"I know one of them, Larry Deacon," Ellie said, getting her breath back. She cleared her throat. "I helped put him in jail."

"The two of them took off in a station wagon, a Chrysler, early two-thousand-something, I think, license plate N-F-B, nine-something . . ." Nate was still hunched over the counter, writing. "You need to call the police now. I'm sorry, but I can't be here when they arrive . . ."

He handed her the piece of paper with his scribbling on it. "I can't risk any contact with the cops. I've managed to avoid them for the last two years, and I'd like to keep it that way. Plus it won't be good for you if anyone knew I was here. Your neighbor across the street came outside, but I don't think he saw me. I'm pretty sure he's called nine-one-one by now. You need to call them, too. I'm sorry. I wish I could stick around, but I can't . . ."

Ellie nodded. "It's okay. Go . . ."

He quickly kissed her on the cheek. Pulling away, he rushed into the hallway again and, moments later, came back with his revolver and overnight bag. He handed the gun to her. "Here, you should hold on to this until the police arrive . . ."

Then he bolted out the back door.

Ellie realized he was probably right about her neighbor calling the police.

In the distance, she heard the sirens.

At least they would be there for one teacher tonight.

Thursday, September 24, 2:36 A.M.

Ellie applied a few more pieces of duct tape to secure the flattened cardboard box and the Hefty bag that covered her broken window. One of the cops—a stocky, baby-faced young guy with red hair—had stuck around to help her tape everything in place. He must have felt sorry for her. Or maybe he'd been flirting with her. She really couldn't tell anymore, it had been so long. But he'd helped her clean up the place a little. He'd left about five minutes ago.

Nate was right about a neighbor phoning the police. In fact, two neighbors had already called 911 before Ellie finally contacted them. The police and the fire department showed up two minutes after Nate had slipped out the back door.

While the police were there, Ellie offered each of them Cokes, coffee, and water. She'd also asked the young cop if they'd had any reports of a fellow teacher at Our Lady of the Cove who had been involved in an accident. He had no idea what she was talking about. She made up some explanation about having a weird premonition and left it at that.

The damage to her living room wasn't as bad as Ellie had first thought. Right now, it was a mess. She needed a new window—including a sill and frame, new curtains, and a new living room carpet. The entire room would need to be repainted. And there was irreparable smoke and water damage to an occasional chair she'd never liked that much. She'd gotten off easy.

Still, she felt vulnerable and shaky—like it might happen again at any minute. She was also exhausted.

When her phone rang, Ellie almost jumped out of her skin.

Setting down the roll of duct tape, she hurried into the kitchen and grabbed the phone off the café table. The caller ID read *Jensen, Nick*.

She touched the phone screen. "Where are you?" she asked.

She hadn't seen Nate's car parked down the street when she'd walked the Good Samaritan cop to her front door. She'd figured Nate must have quietly driven away during all the police activity.

"I'm still in the neighborhood," he said. "I kept coming back to check if the police were still there. Do you know if they got the guys yet?"

"Yes, thank God," she sighed.

The Highwood police had caught Larry Deacon and his accomplice speeding down Waukegan Avenue. They'd found all the ingredients for making Molotov cocktails in the backseat of their 2005 Chrysler station wagon. Larry, like many of the guys she'd helped put away, was no criminal mastermind—not even very adept at pitching, it turned out. Ellie was scheduled to come into the station and identify the dim duo in a lineup at ten in the morning.

"It looks like the last patrol car pulled away a few minutes ago," Nate said.

"You can see that from where you are now?"

"Yeah, and I don't think you should be alone. Would you like me to come over?"

Ellie paused. "No, that's okay. I've got your gun."

There was silence on the other end.

She laughed. "I'm kidding. Yes, Nate. Yes, please, come over."

"Be there in a minute," he said.

CHAPTER FORTY-FIVE

Thursday, September 24, 11:40 A.M.

Ellie felt as if she were trespassing as she cut through the campus. She hadn't dared to use her parking space in the teachers' lot, and parked on Maple Hill Road instead. She kept thinking someone would spot her and call campus security to escort her off the premises—probably by that same short, swaggering, gun-chewing security guard who had watched her clean out her office yesterday.

She'd slept with Nate last night, just slept—she in a T-shirt and sweatpants, he in his underwear. They'd both been so exhausted, but it had felt right falling asleep in his arms.

When Ellie had awoken, he was already dressed and down in the kitchen making coffee. In the harsh light of morning, the charred, ravaged living room was a depressing sight. At least the coffee smell sort of covered up the odor of burnt, damp carpeting.

They ate breakfast together and listened to a live audio feed of local police dispatches on her laptop. There was nothing about a teacher from Our Lady of the Cove dying from a suicide or some bizarre accident.

In the middle of breakfast, the police called to remind

her that she was needed at the station at ten. Then Ellie was on the phone with her insurance company for twenty minutes.

Nate wanted to go home and put on a tie and blazer to look respectable for Vivien Houghton this morning. He decided to leave by the back door—in case any of the neighbors were watching the house. He still had to keep a low profile, and her burnt-out front window seemed to be the neighborhood curiosity. At the kitchen door, he gave her a kiss on the lips—their first.

It was a surprise that left Ellie a little breathless. His lips were soft, and he was gentle about it. Then he was out the door.

There was no time for Ellie to think about the kiss or what it meant. She had to leave for the Lake Forest Police Station.

She positively identified Larry Deacon as the man who threw an incendiary device through her window. His accomplice was identified as Brent Mayhew of Oak Park. An American Family Preservationist member, he had a prior arrest for assault and two DUIs. His ex-wife had also recently sworn out a complaint on him for failure to pay child support.

Ellie spent at least an hour at the police station, answering questions and signing forms. While there, she confided in a forty-something, kind-faced cop: "I know it sounds crazy, but before all this happened last night I was kind of nervous anyway because it was the fiftieth anniversary of when the Immaculate Conception Killer murdered a teacher from Blessed Heart of Mary College. You haven't gotten any reports in this morning about a murder or fatal accident or anything like that involving a teacher from the university in Delmar, have you?"

The policeman did an expert job of pretending her inquiry wasn't completely ludicrous. He even checked with the front desk before telling her no, she was the only teacher from Our Lady of the Cove who had had an "incident" last night.

That was when she'd decided to head to the campus to find out for sure whether or not the tribute killer had struck again.

Ellie kept her head down as she ducked into Emery Hall. She headed up to the bursar's office and waved at her friend, Jeanne, sitting at her desk behind the counter. Jeanne looked surprised to see her. She quickly glanced over at her two coworkers in the office. As far as Ellie could tell, they hadn't spotted her yet.

Jeanne hurried up to the counter. "Well, nice to see you," she whispered. "But what the hell are you doing here?"

Ellie smiled, but winced a bit, too. "Asking you for a favor, Jeanne."

"That's aiding and abetting the enemy. You're persona non grata around here, honey." Jeanne peeked over her shoulder for a moment and then faced Ellie again. "If it's any consolation, the general consensus around here is that you got a raw deal. What can I do for you, Ellie?"

"Thanks, Jeanne," she said in a hushed voice. With the counter between them, Ellie leaned in closer to her. "Is there a way to find out if any teachers—besides me—didn't show up for work today?"

Our Lady of the Rosary Nursing and Rehabilitation Center was a sprawling two-story, redbrick building with white shutters. The double-door front entrance looked impressive with its four-columned portico.

But the inside was depressing. The kitchen staff must have been frying some cut-rate frozen fish for lunch. The greasy, acrid smell hit Nate the moment he stepped inside the facility. At the front desk, by a statue of Mary, a sour-faced receptionist told him that Vivien Houghton was probably in the dayroom—down the hall. She made Nate print and sign his name on a visitor's check-in sheet on a clipboard. She didn't ask to see his ID, so he signed in as Sidney Falco, Tony Curtis's character in *Sweet Smell of Success*. The receptionist wrote the name on a label that said VISITOR across the top. Nate stuck the label to his blazer.

The long hallway had handrails on both sides—and a color scheme that was popular in 1990: beige, hunter green, and mauve. Nate didn't peek inside any of the rooms as he passed the open doors. Parked outside several of them were patients slouched in wheelchairs, many of them asleep. They all looked like they'd been waiting for someone who had forgotten to take them somewhere. A few of the patients were in pajamas and robes, and others had been dressed hastily in a combination of street clothes and nightwear—so one old woman wore a pretty cardigan with her nightgown, and an eighty-something gentleman with a walker had on a food-stained V-neck T-shirt and a loud pair of checkered golf pants he must have bought in the pro shop back in 1979.

Nate found the dayroom at the end of the hallway. It was a large space with big windows looking out at the parking lot. One entire wall had bookshelves crammed with books. There was also a gas fireplace with a mantel made of cheap fake wood. The tables and chairs all looked like they were made of that same laminate material. And again, the color scheme was beige, hunter green, and mauve—only it looked more faded, like everything had been dusted with a fine coat of baby powder. All the framed prints on the walls were of Jesus, Mary, or some saint. The tabletop decorations were crucifixes or vases with plastic flowers. The syrupy music piped over the sound system must have been Nurse Ratched's playlist from *One Flew over the Cuckoo's Nest*.

About a dozen people were using the room—including two old ladies, each with a set of visitors. A few wheelchairs had been temporarily abandoned by their occupants, who were seated nearby in comfy-looking chairs, reading, working crossword puzzles, or dozing. Two elderly women played cards at a table in the corner. And at another table—over by the window, an emaciated blond woman sat alone in front of a jigsaw puzzle. She was very neatly dressed in a navy blue skirt and lavender blouse. A four-prong cane stood beside her chair. She didn't seem to fit in with this crowd at all. She looked like she belonged in some posh country-club type of rest home instead.

Nate had a feeling he'd found the Bonners' former housekeeper.

She didn't look up as he approached her. She seemed focused on her puzzle. The box for the jigsaw puzzle was on the spare chair: one thousand pieces of Van Gogh's *Café Terrace at Night*. She'd already put together all the outside pieces.

"Excuse me," Nate said. "Are you Vivien Houghton?"

She finally looked up. "Yes, I'm Ms. Houghton. Who are you?"

He hesitated and then glanced down at his visitor ID: "I'm Sidney. You don't know me, Ms. Houghton. I was friends with a girl named Molly Driscoll from Portland, Oregon. Actually, she was my babysitter when I was a kid. Does that name sound familiar to you? Molly Driscoll?"

She gave a tiny smile—almost like she saw right through him and was amused by his pathetic charade. "How are you at jigsaw puzzles, Mr. Falco?" she asked.

Nate shrugged. "Okay, I guess."

"Well, why don't you sit down and help me out? You can set aside the blue and black pieces in separate piles, and I'll take the orange, yellow, and all the other colors." She grabbed the box off the chair and set it on the floor.

Nate sat down. "Does that name, Molly Driscoll, ring a bell?" he asked.

Staring down at the puzzle, she nodded while she sorted her pieces in stacks.

Nate wasn't sure she completely understood. But he went on with his excuse for why Molly Driscoll was so important to him. "Molly saved my life when I was seven. I'd gotten a hold of a lighter and set my bed on fire. She rescued me. I still have some scars from where I got burned . . ." He pointed to his forehead. "I'm sure I would have died if it weren't for her . . ."

She frowned at him. "I thought you agreed to help me. Why aren't you picking out the black or blue pieces?" With her bony finger she pointed out several of them.

Nate got to work collecting the puzzle pieces and separating them by color. He wasn't sure if she followed anything he said. "Anyway, I know Molly died. I was also able to find out that she had a baby when she was nineteen, and she gave it up for adoption. I tracked the child to Richard and Candace Bonner."

"And how did you do that?" Ms. Houghton asked, her old eyes studying the puzzle.

"I hired a private detective, and he got a lot of the information for me. But he was killed in a—an accident before he got everything I wanted to find out."

"Yes, accidents happen, don't they?" she said, not looking up. "Just what were you hoping to find out?"

"Well, I understand you worked for the Bonners for many years."

"Most of my life," she said. "I was the head housekeeper for the Pierces at their Lake Shore Drive house for seventeen years before Mr. Bonner came upon the scene." She suddenly slapped him on the hand. "That piece has yellow in it! Put the two-color ones in a separate stack. For pity's sake . . ."

"Sorry," Nate muttered. "So you've known Candace Pierce Bonner since she was a young girl . . ."

Ms. Houghton nodded. "I had a hand in her upbringing—along with her mother, of course, and a series of nannies. Candace grew into a very lovely young woman. Then twenty-six years ago, she married Mr. Bonner. And when Mr. Pierce became ill, Mr. Bonner took over his father-in-law's business. After Mr. Pierce died, Candace and her husband moved back into the house. Mrs. Pierce, the poor thing, she outlived her husband by only a couple of years. She never got to become a grandmother—and she really wanted that, too. We used to say a novena every night together, praying for a granddaughter. Candace was trying everything to conceive for the longest time. They finally arranged a private adoption. But I suppose you know this already, don't you?"

Nate nodded. "Some of it."

"Then you must already know that the infant girl they adopted from your former babysitter is their daughter, Rachel."

Nate stopped collecting the puzzle pieces. "Yes, but it wasn't quite that simple, was it? I have a feeling there were complications, other things involved that no one knows about."

Hunched over the puzzle, she smiled cryptically. "The Bonners pay certain people a lot of money to control what the public knows and doesn't know about them."

"Yes, I tried to find out who handles public relations and security for them—you know, keeping secrets secret and all that. But they're doing such a good job I couldn't even get the name of their public relations firm or security specialists."

"My niece gave me this jigsaw puzzle," Ms. Houghton said, fitting together some orange pieces. "She lives in Columbus, Ohio. Would you believe I have a niece who is seventy-eight years old? Well, I'm ninety-four, so I guess it figures." She looked up and scowled at him. "But what I can't figure, Mr. Falco, is just what you're after."

His eyes wrestled with hers, and then he took a deep breath. "I have a feeling something happened with this adoption that the Bonners need to keep secret," he admitted. "In fact, I think they'd stop at nothing to keep it under wraps."

"You might even say it's dangerous for people to go

poking around asking questions about it." Ms. Houghton looked at something past Nate's left shoulder.

He glanced back and noticed a camera up near the ceiling in the corner of the room. He figured it was there for the staff to keep an eye on the patients. It didn't seem likely the camera had a direct feed to some nefarious security company working for the Bonners.

Nate turned forward again and caught a tiny smirk on Ms. Houghton's wrinkled face. The smart old lady was messing around with him.

"You had me going for a minute there," Nate said.

"I wouldn't be so quick to dismiss it," she said, her smile fading. She studied her jigsaw puzzle again. "Donald Sloane and his people have eyes and ears in many, many places."

"Donald Sloane?"

"He's the keeper of secrets. His company handles security for the Bonners. And you're right, he's very good, though I suppose 'good' isn't how I'd describe the work he does. Maybe 'thorough' is a better word." She added another piece to an orange section she'd fit together. "In your research into what happened to your former babysitter, did you ever come across the name Marcia Lindahl?"

Nate shook his head. "No." He wondered about the spelling, and tried to commit the name to memory—along with Donald Sloane.

"Marcia was a very nice lady who died in a rather mysterious car accident. Mr. Sloane and his associates did a *thorough* job keeping the story out of the newspapers. Marcia Lindahl worked as Mrs. Bonner's personal assistant for twelve years. They kept that out of the

newspapers, too. Marcia was fiercely loyal to Candace—
up to a point."

"Was she involved in the adoption process?"

"No. Mr. Bonner handled most of it through his attorneys and Sloane. He tracked down your babysitter
friend. Molly Driscoll was a college student in Eugene
at the time. The story was that she was pregnant with
her brother-in-law's baby, but he knew nothing about it.
Molly was paid a good deal of money to give up her
infant baby to the Bonners. But some time later, Molly
demanded more money. Of course, by that time, the
Bonners had come to regard Rachel as their own child.
The Driscoll girl raised such a fuss that Candace and
Marcia flew to Portland to meet with her. It was summer,
and the girl was living with her sickly mother in a high-
rise. They hoped to reason or negotiate with her. It was
all very secret. Sloane had someone in Portland working
with them, acting as a chauffeur and bodyguard of sorts.
I hear he was in on the negotiations, too."

"And this was—what—twenty years ago?" Nate
asked.

"Yes, just about. Rachel was eighteen months old at
the time," Ms. Houghton said. She'd been holding the
same puzzle piece in her hand for the last couple of
minutes. "As head housekeeper, I was aware of practically everything that happened with the Bonners. But
regarding that Portland trip, all I heard were rumors.
While these 'negotiations' went on, something happened. Molly Driscoll fell—or jumped—off the roof of
her mother's seventeen-story apartment building."

"Or she might have been thrown off," Nate suggested.

"Or pushed," Ms. Houghton said, finally fixing the
puzzle piece to a corner section of the picture. "Whatever

happened there, Sloane kept a tight lid on it for years and years afterward. Still, Marcia was never the same after that trip, and neither was Mrs. Bonner. Marcia kept working for her—right up until about eight years ago, shortly after I retired. At eighty-five, I was getting too old to run a household that size. The Bonners set me up in my own apartment for a while, but then that got to be too much for me. I had a couple of falls. So the Bonners moved me here two years ago. One of my first visitors was Marcia. In fact, we were sitting right here . . ."

Ms. Houghton nodded at him. "Yes, I recall she was right where you are now. And I was working on another jigsaw puzzle. I think it was a Klimt. Or maybe it was a Matisse. It was one of the masterpieces. They're a little more expensive than the others, but those are the jigsaw puzzles I like best . . ."

"So Marcia was sitting right here," Nate said, trying to get her back on track.

Ms. Houghton sighed. "And she was scared. She told me about that night Molly Driscoll was killed. Marcia went with Mrs. Bonner and Sloane's man to meet Molly at a restaurant in downtown Portland. They'd hoped to reason with her. They'd paid her a lot of money up front to sign over her baby to them. But apparently, Molly had gone through the money like grease through a tin horn. And she was demanding more . . ."

"Well, if she'd signed a contract, how could she make all these new demands? Why didn't the Bonners put their attorneys to work on it?"

"Molly Driscoll had something on them that she was using as—a bargaining tool. It gave her some leverage to negotiate."

"What was it?" Nate asked. "Did it have something to do with the baby's father?"

Ms. Houghton raised her eyebrows and nodded.

"Was it because Dylan O'Rourke didn't know about the baby? Was that what Molly lorded over them?"

Ms. Houghton didn't answer. But she frowned a bit— as if his speculation was a bit off. "The negotiations didn't go well for Candace and company," she continued, letting Nate's question go unanswered. "Sloane's man followed Molly back to her mother's apartment building, and the girl was dead two hours later. The police weren't sure if it was an accident or suicide. Marcia told me when she was visiting here that she always knew the girl didn't jump or fall. It was Sloane's man. It might have even been Candace—along with Sloane's man, up there on the roof with that girl. Marcia said she couldn't really account for Mrs. Bonner's whereabouts after they took a taxi back to their Portland hotel. Marcia never asked her about it. She never said anything to me either, and Marcia and I were close. For the longest time, certainly for the duration of her employment with the Bonners, Marcia diligently kept mum on the subject. Then she met a man about two years ago. He was a very charming salesman named Gil. At least, he said he was a salesman . . ."

Nate tried not to flinch or give away that the name meant something to him.

"This Gil character swept Marcia off her feet," Ms. Houghton continued. "She was a very smart woman, but not *worldly*—if you know what I mean. She was also rather plain looking, mousy. This smooth-talking man—about ten years younger—came into her life, and she simply lost her head. She was so foolish. She thought it was love. He asked her about the Bonners and kept digging and digging until she told him everything. Shortly after that, he dumped her. He just disappeared. As I mentioned, Marcia was a smart woman, and eventually, she did some digging of her own and put it together that this Gil fellow was a private investigator. That was when Marcia came to me. She was terrified it would get back to the Bonners that she'd talked."

Ms. Houghton let out a long sigh and looked down at the jigsaw puzzle again. "A few days after her visit here, Marcia died in that car wreck. Like I said, accidents will happen. But this one was very strange. She hit a utility pole on an open, lonely road in the middle of the night. No one else was around, and there was no reason she would be out driving at such an hour . . ."

Nate thought about Kayla Kennedy's bizarre "accident." He wondered how long Marcia Lindahl had been dead. "Do you remember when she visited you here—and when this accident happened?"

She nodded. "Marcia was killed early in the morning of October third, two years ago."

Nate felt a little stab to his heart. That was just three days before Gil, Rene, and Gil's girlfriend died in the explosion at the cabin—and his entire world was blown apart.

CHAPTER FORTY-SIX

Thursday, 12:14 P.M.

Ellie pulled over and parked her car in front of Pamela Rothschild's modest mid-century modern split-level house. A red Hyundai was parked in the driveway. Everything looked quiet. But Ellie noticed the outside light above the front door was still on—in the middle of the day.

Climbing out of her car, she started up the driveway. She saw the Our Lady of the Cove parking sticker on the Hyundai's windshield. So it must have been Pamela's car—and an indication that she was home right now.

Pamela Rothschild, a professor in the Department of Psychology, was the only absent teacher who hadn't called in today. Jeanne had given Ellie her address and phone number. "Good luck getting a hold of her," Jeanne had said. "We tried to call and email, but didn't get an answer. We had to cancel her morning class."

Ellie remembered meeting Pamela at the New Teachers' Open House last year. She was in her mid-forties, which made her at least a decade older than Valerie Toomey at the time of her death in 1970. But they were both brunettes. Ellie remembered Pamela telling her at the open house: "Well, it's nice to meet another divorcée. You'll find the rest of the faculty here aren't exactly all warm, fuzzy, and friendly toward us *fallen women*. The few single ones view us as competition, and the married ones don't want us anywhere near their husbands. So—welcome to the very exclusive sorority . . ."

At the time, Ellie had thought she and Pamela might end up as friends, but that wasn't the case. Being in different departments, they simply hadn't run into each other much after that. But Pamela had been right about how ostracizing it could be for a divorcée teaching at Our Lady of the Cove.

As Ellie approached the front door—and frowned at the light glowing above it—she had a feeling she'd missed her chance of ever making friends with Pamela Rothschild.

She rang the doorbell and waited.

She didn't hear any activity inside the house. She rang the bell again and then knocked.

Nothing.

Biting her lip, Ellie tried the door handle. Locked.

She was almost relieved. Then again, if the tribute killer wanted this latest murder to look like an accident, he wouldn't leave doors unlocked.

The curtains in the front windows were open, and Ellie could see into the living room. She didn't spot anyone in there. But then she realized, if the killer had struck last night, Pamela wouldn't be in the living room.

Ellie headed down a narrow walkway beside the garage to the back of the house. A tall fence separated Pamela's yard from her neighbors. By the back door and right up to the kitchen windows was a leaf-littered patio with some slightly beat-up plastic furniture.

The light was on in the kitchen, and it didn't need to be at this hour.

Ellie stopped and stood in the middle of the patio—about five feet from the window. She didn't want to look.

All she could see now were the cupboards, the top half of the refrigerator, and a Tiffany-style light fixture, which hung over a kitchen table or breakfast nook.

"Please, God," she whispered.

She didn't want to be right about a teacher getting killed last night.

Forcing herself to step closer to the window, Ellie moved aside a plastic patio chair and peered through the glass.

The white Formica breakfast table had been set for one. The place mat was askew. A plate held the remnants of a small chicken and a cluster of grapes. A bowl of cherries had been tipped over. Several grapes and cherries were scattered over the table.

There were three chairs; but the fourth—for the place setting—was missing.

Ellie took one more step closer to the window—until her face was almost against the glass. She could see the black-and-white-tiled floor. The fourth chair had tipped over. Pamela Rothschild was spread out beside it. She wore a white terrycloth robe. Her face was turned toward the window. Her hand was on her throat, and her mouth was open.

Her sad, dead eyes stared back at Ellie.

A bell chimed, but Ms. Houghton didn't look up from her jigsaw puzzle.

"What was that?" Nate asked.

"Lunch is being served in the dining room." She frowned. "I already saw the menu. The fish here is terrible. They serve it with canned string beans and som sort of potatoes swimming in artery-hardening death sauce. I swear, they're trying to kill us. I'd just as soon starve."

"May I take you out someplace for lunch?" Nate offered.

Ms. Houghton had a puzzle piece in her hand. She dropped it on the table. "Let me freshen up and get my coat."

With her four-prong cane, she slowly shuffled away. Nate realized he'd have plenty of time to take out his phone and Google *Donald Sloane*. Among the results, he didn't see anyone who seemed even remotely connected to the Bonners or any security specialist firm. He tried the spelling, *Slone*, and even added *security* to the keywords. But his luck wasn't any better. Either Ms. Houghton had given him the wrong name, or Donald Sloane was so "*thorough*" about managing the flow of information that he and his firm didn't even exist on the Internet.

Nate tried looking up *Marcia Lindahl*, and got her obituary from the *Chicago Tribune*. It was dated October 6, 2018, the same date the cabin had exploded. She was forty-nine. There was no mention of a car crash. She'd simply "*died suddenly.*" There was a list of survivors, a brother and sister, and their families; her parents were both deceased. But there was nothing about her employment history. The Bonners weren't mentioned.

He found another obituary for Marcia on the Donnellan Funeral Home website, but it was the same as the one in the *Tribune*.

Nate tried linking her name to *Bonner* and got no results.

He figured Donald Sloane's company had already taken care of that.

Ms. Houghton returned, wearing a black velvet

sweater-jacket. She said she'd already signed them out at the front desk. She'd also written a note on Our Lady of the Rosary letterhead stationery:

Do Not Touch! 9/24

She set it on top of the unfinished jigsaw puzzle. Then she took a small crucifix on a stand from a nearby table and placed it on top of the note—so it wouldn't blow away.

It took her a while to get to his car—and into the passenger seat. Patiently walking alongside her, Nate was reminded of driving his mother to and from her doctors' appointments when she'd been so ill. He also thought of all the disabled vets he used to work with.

Ms. Houghton said she wanted to have lunch at Convito Café, which was only a couple of blocks away in the Plaza del Lago on Sheridan Road. She knew the way and barked directions at him until he pulled into the shopping mall across the street from the lakefront.

"I can't believe we're really here," she murmured once he pulled into a parking spot near the restaurant. She laughed. "Did you decide I deserved one last meal or something?"

Turning off the engine, Nate gave her a mystified grin. "I beg your pardon?"

"You don't work for Sloane?" she asked. "I thought for sure you were one of Sloane's goons, checking up on me—trying to figure out whether or not I was a liability."

"No." He laughed. "I don't understand . . ."

"Do you know what else I'm fond of besides jigsaw puzzles?" she said.

Nate shook his head. She wasn't making any sense.

"I like old movies, Mr. Falco," she said. "*Sweet Smell of Success*, 1957, Burt Lancaster as J. J. Hunsecker and Tony Curtis as Sidney Falco—they showed it on TV last night. The minute I saw that nametag on your lapel, I knew you were a phony."

"You thought I worked for Sloane?"

"His men have come by and tested me before, pretending to be someone else as they asked me about the Bonners. It's always been kind of scary, but less so with each random visit. I found that I just have to act a little daffy, and they leave me alone."

"I still don't understand," Nate said. "If you thought I was one of Sloane's goons, why did you tell me so much?"

"I'm ninety-four years old. Everything aches. I hate where I live. Every day, I see people getting sicker and crazier. It's just downhill from here. I'd like to go quickly. So—when you walked into the dayroom, and I saw the name on your guest pass, I figured, *Here's your chance, Vivien. He has good taste in movies, and he's handsome, polite, and charming. If he's one of Sloane's crew sent to test you, then make sure he's the one who kills you. He'll be a gentleman about it . . .*"

Gaping at her, Nate shrugged. "Well, I'm sorry, Ms. Loughton, I have no intention of doing away with you."

"So I told you all of that for nothing," she said, frowning.

"Not for nothing," Nate replied. "You've been very helpful."

"Well, who are you then?"

Hesitating, he tapped his fingers on the steering wheel.

"Never mind," she said, waving away the question. "I might forget myself and say something about you to the next henchman Sloane sends to question me. Better I just don't know. But now that I think about it, I wonder if your private detective who died in an accident is the same one who swept Marcia off her feet . . ." She quickly shook her head. "No, don't tell me. I don't want to know that either. If anyone ever asks, you were Sidney Falco, a handsome charmer who took me to lunch so he could dig up some dirt on the Bonners—just like in the movie. Now, help me out of this car so we can go eat . . ."

Now that Ms. Houghton's candor was no longer part of her secret death wish, Nate had expected her to clam up during lunch.

Instead, over her chicken Caesar salad, she vented about having to suffer in silence for over two decades while working for a man she utterly despised.

"Richard Bonner is a good businessman, but a terrible human being," she said. "Candace was a kind, lovely woman when they first got married. But she changed after that. He changed her. He was psychologically abusive. He berated her and was forever critical of her parents. He blamed her for not being able to have children. He cheated on her all the time, everyone knew. He publicly humiliated her . . ."

Ms. Houghton wasn't a fan of "daddy's little girl" either. The Bonners considered their adopted baby a blessing, but according to Ms. Houghton, little Rachel turned out to be a curse. "He spoiled that girl rotten," she said, fishing a crouton out of her salad. Her hand shook as she set it on the edge of her plate with the other croutons. "That's the word for her, all right, *rotten*. Rachel had a habit of loving every new toy she received—loving it to death. As soon as she got bored with it, she'd break it. That included a pony she go when she was eight. She adored it for a few weeks. Then one day, the stable hand made the mistake of leaving her alone with the pony for a few minutes. And in that time, little Rachel beat the poor thing with a rake. Fortunately, they didn't have to put the animal down. But after that, Candace wouldn't allow her to have any pets. Little Rachel was always begging for a dog or a cat. Mr. Bonner didn't see the harm in it, of course, because his little girl could do no wrong. But Candace stuck to her guns, thank God."

Ms. Houghton glanced out the window. From their table, they had a view of the parking lot and, across the street, Lake Michigan. "Rachel had a little girlfriend for a while," she said, frowning. "Karen was a neighbor's child from the apartment building next door. They were thick as thieves for about a month. Then Karen came over to spend the night. Rachel got into some kerosene we had in the storeroom. They used to have gas lights out in front of the house. Rachel and Karen had gone to the basement to play. I still remember hearing the shrieks from that poor child. And the whole time, Rachel didn't utter a peep . . ." Ms. Houghton slowly shook her head. "Rachel wasn't hurt at all, of course. The other girl had third-degree burns up her arm, on part of her torso, and along the side of her neck. I suppose you know what that's like—if your story about setting your bed on fire is true. That sweet little girl, she was a pretty thing, too. The Bonners paid for the best surgeons to perform the skin grafts. But the girl ended up scarred for life. Her parents were paid off to keep quiet about it. Donald D. Sloane saw to that."

"What about Alden?" Nate asked. "I hear he and Rachel have been friends since they were kids. How did he manage to survive?"

"I think all his scars are on the inside," Ms. Houghton said, staring pensively out at the lake. "He's two years younger than her. He spent his whole childhood trying to please her, putting up with her mixture of warped love and abuse. At a very young age, she was making him do sexual things with her and for her. I did my best to protect him from her, but they were always together, and I had a household to run. That poor child—and such a handsome boy, too—he never had a chance. She made certain he never had any friends except her. Rachel held it over him that all she had to do was say the word, and he'd be out on the street with no place to live. I remember hearing her say that to him once, when she was eleven and he was nine. 'I just have to snap my fingers,' she said, 'and you'll end up in some foster home.' Poor Alden, he lost his mother so young. He got passed around from servant to servant. He wandered around that big house without anyone ever really noticing him. He didn't have anyone else, just Rachel . . ."

"By all reports, he seems to be doing okay now," Nate said. "He's in college with Rachel at Our Lady of the Cove."

"Where she can keep him all to herself," Ms. Houghton murmured. She sipped her iced tea and straightened in her chair. "The last time I laid eyes on Rachel Bonner, she was twelve years old. I'd like to think maybe she's changed. But I still hear from a few of the people who stayed on at the house after I left, and they told me she hasn't changed much. She has some people fooled because she's pretty and she knows how to wear the right clothes. She's involved in a lot of charities, but she doesn't do a damn thing but attend their parties, sit a the VIP table, and get her picture in the newspaper. At least, that's what I hear."

Nate nodded. This confirmed what Kayla Kennedy had told him about Rachel. It made sense now that her parents had a bodyguard/chauffeur keeping tabs on her while she was at school. The guy was probably hired by Sloane's firm.

"Did you ever hear anything about Rachel getting involved with a married business associate of her father's?" Nate asked.

Ms. Houghton sighed. She suddenly looked fatigued. "No, but I'm not surprised."

"Do you want to get back to the ranch—and your jigsaw puzzle?"

"After dessert." She smiled tiredly. "They have good ice cream here. I'm not in any hurry to go back. No one will touch my puzzle. Everyone's scared of me there. Now that I think about it, back when I worked for the Pierces and the Bonners, the rest of the staff there was pretty scared of me, too. But I had a big household to run. I had to be tough. You know the only one who wasn't scared of me?"

"Rachel?"

She nodded. "That little bitch wasn't scared of anything."

CHAPTER FORTY-SEVEN

Thursday, 3:48 P.M.

She had to hand it to Lance, the creepy custodian He'd done a pretty good job cleaning up the laundry room since the fire in there two weeks ago. He'd ever repainted the ceiling and one wall. Hannah had two loads going in the washers. She was alone, sitting in a folding chair and trying to get through a chapter in he philosophy book that had to be read by tomorrow.

She'd decided to get out of the bungalow because Lance's crazy mother, Alma, was cleaning the place and even though the woman stayed out of Hannah' bedroom, she made a lot of noise and was always talk ing to herself or humming. Hannah didn't want to con tend with that—or Alma's constant dirty looks.

She needed to wash her favorite pajamas for tomor row night anyway.

Rachel's parents were headed to their summer hom in Lake Geneva for the weekend, and all the staff at th Lake Shore Drive house would be taking off. So Rache was hosting a "secret slumber party" there. She alread had two other friends coming—Kim Langford an Madison "Maddie" Coughlin, both juniors, and bot slightly stuck-up. Alden was trying to recruit a posse of guys to come "crash" the slumber party. "We don't wa your roommate, Turner, the Fart Machine, coming and polluting the place," Rachel had insisted—in front of Hannah. "The guys need to be cute—and nice. Three guys besides you, one for each girl . . ."

Hannah imagined pairing up with Alden tomorrow night. Rachel had already figured out that the boys could sleep in the extra bedroom in the basement—or on the sofas in the game room. The girls would all be together in her room. "But I won't keep track of where everyone ends up," she'd told Hannah with a wink and a giggle. "So who knows what the night will bring?"

The whole evening was being planned on the sly. Mr. and Mrs. Bonner had no idea their home was being invaded. Maddie had a car, so she'd be driving them. ("That's mostly the reason I invited her," Rachel had confided to Hannah.) Rachel planned on giving Perry the slip. She didn't want any of this to get back to her parents. Alden and the guys would probably take the train downtown and Uber it from there.

So it was crucial that Hannah's cutest pair of pajamas was clean.

As she listened to the washer machine churning, it occurred to her that the timing of this slumber party was perfect. Tomorrow night would mark the fiftieth anniversary of the Immaculate Conception Killer's "doubleheader" in the bungalow that used to be next door to her and Rachel's place. Hannah was glad to be spending the night miles and miles away—with seven other kids.

Her phone rang, and she glanced at the screen. It was Ellie again. She'd texted about two hours ago:

Give me a call as soon U can, will U? Need 2 talk.

But Hannah had purposely blown her off. It had been so disturbing to see Ellie hug that slimy massage

guy and invite him into her house last night. Okay, so
recently, Ellie had claimed he wasn't such a creep. But
they'd looked so chummy-chummy, it was positively
gross. If Ellie was involved with him, why hadn't she
said something? And how long had they been *friendly*?
What was the big secret?

Staring at the phone, Hannah debated whether or not
to answer. With a labored sigh, she finally touched the
phone screen to take the call. "Yes, hello," she said flatly.

"Hi, Hannah, did I catch you at an okay time?"

"I guess so. I'm just sitting here doing laundry."

"Sorry if I sound weird. I'm in my car on the express
way, talking to you on the speaker phone."

Hannah didn't think the connection was bad. But
Ellie sounded kind of rushed. "It's okay," Hannah said
listlessly.

"Listen, you know the whole Immaculate Conception
copycat theory, the one that no one was taking seriously.
Well, there's been a new development—a disturbing
sad, new development. I can't remember if you're taking
Psych one-oh-one or not . . ."

"No, I'm waiting until next year."

"Then you didn't know Professor Rothschild, who
teaches that class . . ."

"I've heard of her. Why? What's this about?" Hannah
was getting impatient.

"Professor Rothschild was killed last night—on the
anniversary of the day the Immaculate Conception
Killer strangled a teacher from the school. Pamela
Rothschild died in her kitchen, wearing a terrycloth
bathrobe—just like the teacher murdered in 1970."

Bewildered, Hannah didn't say anything. This upsetting
"new development" suddenly gave credence to Ellie

copycat theory. But Hannah was still so disillusioned about her teacher-friend that she didn't know what to think.

She'd told Rachel about seeing Ellie with Nick Jensen last night. "That's fucked-up," Rachel had concluded. "What kind of game is she playing? I've always thought she was a user. I wouldn't trust her . . ."

Even if everything Ellie said right now was true, Hannah couldn't help wondering if she was working some kind of angle.

"You know how Diana's death looked like a suicide, and Justine's death looked like an accident?" Ellie asked. "Well, I guess, last night was supposed to look like another accident—like Professor Rothschild had choked to death. In my research on her this afternoon, I found she published a piece about her one-time struggle with bulimia. I'm pretty sure this copycat killer read the same article. Actually, we decided he's not really a copycat, these murders are more like *tributes* . . ."

"Who's *we*?" Hannah asked pointedly. She wondered if Ellie was working on this case with Nick Jensen. Though, from what she saw, they looked like work partners with benefits.

"Just—just a general *we*," Ellie replied haltingly. "I think it was supposed to look like Professor Rothschild choked to death while gorging herself. But things must not have gone according to plan, because the police found ligature marks on her wrists. The police think someone must have tied her hands behind her and then force-fed her until she choked. You see what the killer was trying to do? He couldn't strangle her, so he did something to her neck or throat—just like the others. I was at the scene. In fact, I discovered the body and called the police."

"What were you doing there?" Hannah asked.

"It's a long story. Anyway, all the food on the table in front of Pamela was a choking hazard of sorts. Detective Castino showed up after the first round of nine-one-one responders, and even he admitted the whole thing looked suspicious. There were signs of a struggle and food stains on the robe. The police think it's even possible there were two killers. They figured someone had to be holding Professor Rothschild at knifepoint or gunpoint while the other tied her wrists behind her. Anyway, this changes everything. Now the copycat or tribute killer hypothesis is something they're taking very seriously. They're going back to reexamine the deaths of Justine Everly and Diana. This is where you come in, Hannah. I'm talking about Eden—and the very real possibility that she didn't run away. If someone's out there pulling off these tribute killings, it seems more and more likely that Eden was abducted, and right now, that same someone is holding her prisoner . . ."

Hannah didn't know what to say. It was all coming to her so fast—and from somebody she no longer completely trusted. She imagined Eden trapped in a shed in some lunatic's backyard, subject to all sorts of horrors.

The humming mechanics of the washer seemed to get louder and louder.

"Hannah, are you there?" Ellie asked. "Did we get cut off?"

She cleared her throat. "I'm here. I'm listening."

"The thing is," Ellie said, "as you know, I got fired. So, I don't have to tiptoe around Father O'Hurley anymore. I'm getting together with a reporter friend o mine from the *Tribune*, Garth Trotter, and we're going to write about these tribute-murders. That's where I'm headed right now—the Tribune Tower. We have five hours to put this story together for tomorrow's edition. Eden is an important part of this piece—and so are you. She's missing—like Crystal Juneau went missing fifty years ago. And that makes her a major player. But also, both you and Eden already have some notoriety. People remember you from everything that happened in Seattle two years ago."

"In other words, our names in this story are going to help you sell newspapers," Hannah said. She realized Rachel was right about Ellie. She was a user. Maybe Ellie had been using her from the start.

"That's not it at all," Ellie said. "Hannah, you sound upset. Are you angry at me?"

"Well, I'm sorry. But I feel like you're exploiting Eden and me for some big news story," she admitted.

"Hannah, I'm trying to help you guys," she said. "This story could save Eden's life. More people will be looking for her after the newspaper comes out tomorrow. Don't you see? The police will start working on the case in earnest. Even if I'm wrong and Eden has run away—well, if she reads this article, she'll probably call you or your parents. Either way, this article might help reunite you with Eden . . ."

Hannah remained silent.

"Hannah, what's wrong?" Ellie asked. "Why are you acting like this? I have a feeling Rachel has been bad-mouthing me to you again. Honey, you need to be careful with her. I've heard some things about Rachel Bonner . . ."

"So now you're going to pick on Rachel?" Hannah asked indignantly.

"I'm just saying you should proceed with caution there and not believe everything Rachel tells you. I won't go into it now with you, because I don't have time. But please, listen to me. We've always been honest with each other—"

"Really? Were you being honest when you warned me not to trust Nick Jensen?"

"I've told you, I was wrong about him."

"Well, you sure changed your mind about him in an awful hurry."

"What are you talking about?"

"I came by your place around six last night, and I saw him knocking at your door. He had an overnight bag with him. You kissed him and took him inside—like he was your boyfriend or something. This is the same creep who threatened Alden just last week."

"Like I said, I was wrong about him," Ellie explained, sounding a bit impatient. "And he didn't mean what he said to Alden. He was just upset that we'd wasted his time with the bogus massage appointment. That's my fault, I admit it. I've already explained all this—"

"How come he was following me—after class and at the pool? He was following Eden around, too. Do you really think he just 'ran into' her at the Sunnyside Up? Has he been working with you? Did he spend the night with you last night?"

"No!" Ellie cried. "God, this is all just a big misunderstanding. He hasn't been working with me. He's not my boyfriend. And he didn't spend the night. That was a gym bag he had with him. I invited him over for dinner because I felt bad about misjudging him. I'd been prett rude to him. I wanted to apologize. He—he's actually a very nice person . . ."

Hannah heard her sigh on the other end. "You'll just have to trust me about this, Hannah. Now, I'm getting close to downtown, and the traffic is pretty nuts. I can't hang on the line. For the newspaper story, I really need that statement from you or your parents about Eden's disappearance. If you can't think of anything to say right now, can you call me back in an hour or have your parents call me?"

"Sure, one of us will call you back, I guess," Hannah mumbled. The washer finished the spin cycle, and she got to her feet.

"Thank you," Ellie said. "Like I said, this article is going to help people. It'll be out tomorrow morning—in time to alert everyone on campus. You know, tomorrow's the anniversary of the double homicide."

"I know," Hannah said, standing beside the washer. "I live right next door to where it happened, remember?"

"My God, that's right. Are you going to be okay? Maybe you shouldn't stay there tomorrow night . . ."

Ellie actually sounded concerned. Maybe she really cared.

"I'll be okay," Hannah sighed. "Listen, you have traffic, and I have a couple of loads to take out of the wash. I don't have anything to say for your newspaper story right now. But maybe I'll text you in an hour or so if my parents don't. Bye."

Hannah hung up before Ellie got another word out.

Thursday, 7:51 P.M.

"Anyway, I tried my best at damage control," Ellie whispered on the other end of the line. "But after what she saw last night, Hannah is convinced the two of us are up to something. And of course, I couldn't tell her who you really are, so naturally, she's suspicious . . ."

"It sounds like you handled it the best anyone could," Nate said, sitting at his kitchen counter-bar.

They'd talked and texted several times since his noon meeting with Ms. Houghton today. They'd both had major breakthroughs.

But Nate felt frustrated. After learning so much from the Bonners' longtime housekeeper, he wasn't sure what to do with the information. Sloane and company had made it impossible to track down any of the leads online.

Nate had already read everything he could about Dylan O'Rourke and the mysterious death of his sister-in-law, Molly Driscoll. He wondered how much Marcia Lindahl had told his brother. If Gil had known that Molly Driscoll was murdered trying to extort money from the Bonners, how in the world could he be foolish enough to turn around and attempt the same thing? Of course, sometimes Gil thought he was invincible. But he should have known the Bonners wouldn't hesitate to have him murdered, too.

Nate had all this information. But it was just hearsay. For him, nothing had really changed. He still felt like a fugitive. He was still hiding. It was as if his hands were tied.

And he still had no idea about Rachel's older, married lover. Had Gil known?

Meanwhile, Ellie was taking action. She was running all over the city, making calls, interviewing people, digging up facts—and getting ready to go public with her story. Nate was happy for her. But he couldn't help feeling a bit envious.

As busy as she was, Ellie had still offered to discreetly ask some of her reporter friends what they knew about Donald Sloane or Marcia Lindahl. For that, Nate was grateful.

He figured she wouldn't want to spend tonight alone at her place. So in an earlier text, he'd invited her to stay at his place tonight. Ellie had texted back, saying it sounded like a wonderful idea.

He'd gone out and bought some of the same snacks he'd noticed in her cupboard—along with two nice bottles of wine, and food for breakfast in the morning. For dinner tonight, he figured they'd stay in and order out.

Nate hadn't expected her before eight o'clock, because she had a seven-thirty deadline for her story. He wasn't really surprised when she'd phoned five minutes ago and said she was still at the Tribune Tower. He'd just finished straightening up his place—and had even lit some candles set out on the counter-bar in front of him.

"Anyway, Hannah seems to think I'm exploiting her," Ellie said. "I'm almost positive Rachel has been getting her digs in about me. I tried to warn Hannah about her. There wasn't enough time to tell her any of the things Vivien shared with you about Richard Bonner's precious little girl . . ."

"Well, you need to sit down and talk with her about it, Ellie," Nate said. "Tell her about the pony—and the little girlfriend. That ought to scare the shit out of her."

"I will, I promise. Meanwhile, I'd asked her for a quote to use in the story. And all I got was a text from her father, 'speaking for the family': '*We're doing all we can to find Eden, and we continue to hope and pray for her safe return and blah, blah, blah.*' They didn't say squat about why they waited nearly two weeks before finally putting a private detective on the case. I don't know. Maybe they don't care how bad that looks. They don't seem to realize I'm trying to help them. But I did get better quotes from Diana's and Justine's parents, heartbreaking stuff. I swear, Nate, I was crying when I took down what they said. These poor families. And Pamela Rothschild's son said something that was practically poetic about his mother. It really makes you feel the loss and the pain—the tragedy behind the whole thing. Such a waste . . ."

She let out a long sigh. "Oh, and speaking of quotes, Father O'Hurley of Our Lady of the Cove isn't available for comment. Big surprise there. He suddenly had to rush to the bedside of a conveniently sick relative. So it was left up to a vice principal of the school to give some generic remark about *the university doing everything it can to ensure the safety of its students.* It's hardly worth the cost of the ink to print it. And of course, he had nothing to say about my firing."

"Well, you were more than fair," Nate said. "You gave them a chance to explain, and they blew it. Anyway, you're all finished? You made your deadline?"

"Whew, yes, I still can't believe we got it done in time."

"And you feel good about it?"

"Yeah, in fact, I feel great. I didn't realize how much I'd missed this, and everything about it—the excitement and the intensity. Of course, I had a big, personal stake in this story. A part of me feels conflicted, because I'm so keyed up about this. But people are dead, and Eden is still missing. I keep thinking maybe Hannah's right. Maybe I am exploiting her."

"Well, if you are, you're also helping all these

people," Nate reminded her. "Anyway, when can I expect you?"

"Oh God," she groaned. "Yeah, about that, Garth and I have a mountain of stuff here for a follow-up story for Saturday's edition. So we decided to just break for a quick dinner and get back to work. I'm probably going to crash on Garth and his wife's couch tonight. They have an apartment here in the city. I'm sorry. I hope you didn't go to any trouble for me."

"No, not at all," Nate said. "Don't worry about it. You're busy. Sounds like you're going to be busy all day tomorrow, too."

"Pretty much," Ellie said. "But I haven't forgotten about Donald Sloane or Marcia Lindahl. I doubt I'll get a chance to see you, but let's talk, okay?"

"Definitely. And congratulations on getting the job done."

"Thanks, Nate. Thanks for everything."

"Good night," he said.

Nate hung up and set the phone on the counter. Getting up from the barstool, he glanced around his dingy, barely furnished apartment. He blew out the candles on the counter.

Then he went to the refrigerator and took a small Trader Joe's pizza out of the freezer.

CHAPTER FORTY-EIGHT

Friday, September 25, 2:40 P.M.

"Eden has been missing for two weeks," the reporter said into her handheld mic. She had a stiff-looking helmet of blond hair and wore a red suit. "Yet the police and the school weren't contacted until only a few days ago. Can you explain why that is, Hannah?"

She told herself to stay composed and keep the polite half-smile on her face. Hannah remembered two years ago, someone online criticizing her because she'd smiled too much during a TV interview after *the thing that happened* to her family. In yet another interview, some classmate had twittered that she looked tired and pissed off. So Hannah had found a polite, halfhearted smile was best in crisis situations like this. A few reporters had tried to get her to cry during some of the impromptu mini-interviews today, asking if she missed her sister, and if she thought she'd ever see Eden again. But Hannah managed to keep it together. She figured Eden wouldn't stop throwing up or mocking her if she cried over her in a TV interview.

They were shooting in front of the library, the most impressive building on the campus. Hannah had refused to be interviewed in front of her bungalow, because she didn't want people figuring out where she lived. She wouldn't be filmed in front of St. Ursula's chrysanthemum garden either, because that was too close to her bungalow—and just plain morbid.

The copycat-murders story had broken in this morning's *Chicago Tribune*, as Ellie had told her it would. Hannah had awoken at eight o'clock to her phone ringing and a clamor outside her bedroom window. TV news vans were parked in front of the chrysanthemum garden next door. From the living room window, she and Rachel could see the bouquets, candles, pinwheels, and even a couple of anchored helium balloons that people had placed on the sidewalk in front of the garden. Someone had also left cheaply framed photos of the double-homicide victims, April Hunnicutt and Debbie Metzger, as part of the makeshift shrine. All this—and classes hadn't even started yet.

It was surreal to switch on the TV and see the garden next door on the morning news. Still in their pajamas, she and Rachel sat on the sofa and watched Ellie being interviewed about the copycat killings—on at least three stations. Rachel kept switching channels with the remote and groaning whenever Ellie came on.

In one interview, Ellie talked about Connie Woolrich, the pretty brunette who had escaped from bungalow eighteen that night fifty years ago, and then went on to identify Lyle Duncan Wheeler as the killer of her two roommates. Now sixty-nine, Connie Woolrich was living somewhere in Minnesota under her married name, enjoying her anonymity and not granting interviews.

The *Today Show* coverage included a montage of candid family photos of the five students and the teacher murdered back in 1970, black-and-white shots and washed-out color pictures that made the victims seem all too human. There were also photos of the two girls and the teacher recently killed. Then Hannah's heart stopped for a moment when they showed a picture of Eden on TV. It was disturbing to see her sister lumped in there with the rest of the dead. They talked about her going missing on the fiftieth anniversary of Crystal Juneau's disappearance.

Hannah suddenly found it hard to agree with her parents' assertion that Eden had merely run away.

Apparently, the news reporters and their camera crews were all over the campus by eight o'clock in the morning. The local TV news caught girls on their way to classes and asked if they felt safe on the school grounds tonight. "I think I'm okay in the dorm, but I'm definitely double-locking my door," one student said.

"My dad doesn't want me anywhere near the campus tonight," another girl said. "So I'm catching the train home to Milwaukee this afternoon."

The whole campus seemed to be on alert. One reporter, standing in front of the garden, even predicted that St. Agnes Village would be deserted by sundown. "And those who are staying will certainly have a long night ahead," she ominously concluded.

Hannah couldn't even get through all the phone messages from reporters requesting interviews. Among the missed calls was a voice mail from her dad, who wanted to make sure she wouldn't be alone tonight. Did she have a school friend whose parents lived nearby? Could she go stay with them? He was flying into Chicago early tomorrow evening to see her and confer with local police about Eden. Hannah texted back that she was staying with Rachel at her parents' house downtown tonight and couldn't wait to see him tomorrow.

Ellie had left a similar voice mail: "Hey, Hannah. You're probably still asleep. We really need to talk. I want to make sure you're okay. I hope you're not staying at the bungalow tonight, and I hope you're not staying with Rachel either. We have to talk about her. I know some things, and Rachel's not a good friend to have. That's understating it, honey. Call me as soon as you can. We'll figure out where you can stay tonight. I can get you deluxe accommodations at some swanky downtown hotel through the *Tribune*. But that's just an option. Anyway, please, call me."

She didn't respond. She didn't feel like talking to Ellie—or even texting her. She wondered why Ellie was trying to turn her against Rachel. Maybe she knew that Rachel didn't like her much either. Hannah felt caught in the middle.

She kept thinking how Ellie had gotten exactly what she wanted—a reporter's dream: a big national news story, and with herself as the star attraction.

Sitting on the sofa in front of the TV with her, Rachel seemed to think Hannah was the real star attraction. She was the one with the missing sister, the one who had been in another hot national news story two years ago. People still remembered her.

"They're all waiting outside, just dying to talk to you," Rachel had said. "Why don't you do something with your hair and face, get dressed, and go out there. I can give you something of mine to wear if you want to look nice. Don't you want to be on TV?"

Hannah couldn't get excited about it. She'd already done the media circus thing.

And what the hell did Rachel mean about giving her something of *hers* to wear if she wanted to look nice?

Hannah had dressed—in her own clothes—for her morning philosophy class and snuck out the back door.

Someone must have given her class schedule to a reporter, because a whole bunch of them had been waiting for her when class had gotten out at noon. She'd reluctantly agreed to talk to a few of them.

That had been almost three hours ago. Hannah had managed to break away for a half hour and grab a salad at O'Donnell Hall. Rachel had texted that it was "complete madness" outside the bungalow. Despite cancellation from Kim, tonight's slumber party at the Lake Shore Drive house was still on. Rachel would pack a bag for her. They'd meet at three o'clock in the lobby of Maddie's dorm, Campbell Hall. Maddie was driving them.

That was in twenty minutes.

Hannah told herself that this WGN-TV interview with the pushy helmet hair lady would be her last before she snuck away.

By now, a crowd had gathered in front of the library. Behind Ms. Helmet Hair, several other reporters were filming Hannah, holding out their mics. She noticed some students in the crowd, their phones raised in the air.

She blanked out for a moment and then remembered what the reporter had asked about the delay in contacting the school and the police after Eden's disappearance.

"Eden's always been very independent," Hannah said into the mic, the neutral half smile on her face. "So it's not unusual for her to take off on her own for a few hours—or even for a day or two. It's always driven my parents crazy. But that's how she was with the woman who raised her. Anyway, the day after she disappeared, I got a text from her saying that she was exploring Chicago, and she was okay. Then a week later, I got the note."

"The note that's a word-for-word copy of the letter the Immaculate Conception Killer forced his final victim, Crystal Juneau, to write, isn't that correct?"

Hannah nodded. "Yes, we figured that out later."

"You and Ellie Goodwin figured it out together. You two have been close friends through all of this, haven't you?"

Hannah hesitated. "Well, actually, she's my teacher . . ."

"But you turned to her when your sister disappeared. How do you feel about the college firing Ellie Goodwin?"

"Well, she's a good journalism teacher. I hope they reconsider and take her back." Hannah hated answering these questions about Ellie—especially when she still wasn't sure how she felt about her.

"Will you be staying on campus tonight, Hannah?" the reporter asked gravely.

Hannah knew Rachel would kill her if she even hinted about the slumber party. So she just shook her head. "No, I have plans to be somewhere else tonight," she said cryptically.

Ten minutes later, she managed to give the reporters the slip and took a roundabout way to Campbell Hall. She found Rachel and Alden with the suitcases, waiting in the lobby by the glass doors.

They were looking at Rachel's phone, watching one of Hannah's interviews. Rachel rolled her eyes at her. "I could have told you that blouse would look absolutely hideous on camera," she sighed. "And God, a little makeup might have helped, too. HD isn't very forgiving."

"God, catty enough?" Alden made a meowing sound. He smiled at Hannah. "I think you look pretty, and pay no attention to Rachel. She's just jealous, because she's used to being the center of attention. And now you're the one on TV, with your phone ringing off the hook—"

"Shut up!" Rachel snapped.

He chuckled. "See? I hit a nerve—"

"No, seriously, shut up," she said, punching each word.

For a second, he looked totally wounded. Glancing down, he grabbed their overnight bags and carried them out the door.

Hannah remained in the lobby with Rachel.

"I didn't mean to sound bitchy," Rachel muttered, turning off the web news and shoving the phone in her coat pocket. "I'm just in a crappy mood, that's all. The clinic where we got tested emailed me the results an hour ago. Your dad's doctor was right. We're not sisters. The results showed you and I are first cousins."

"Oh, wow," was all Hannah could say.

"I guess my mother—your aunt Molly—must have lied on the birth certificate about who my father was."

"Well, at least we're cousins," Hannah said, shrugging. "We're still family."

"Yeah, I guess that's something," Rachel said, staring out the glass doors. "Anyway, I promise I won't let ruin our slumber party tonight."

Hannah followed her gaze. Alden was outside with their bags. The curbside was crowded with several of the dorm's residents, each one with a small suitcase or overnight bag, waiting to be picked up. There seemed to be a mass exodus of students who wanted to avoid the campus tonight.

"That's Maddie's car," Rachel said, nudging Hannah.

They stepped outside as Alden loaded the overnight bags into the backseat of Maddie's Jetta.

"Don't bruise my Louis Vuitton, young man!" Rachel called in a mock regal tone.

Hannah noticed Alden barely cracked a smile. He wouldn't look at either of them. "So, I'll see you guys later tonight. And I'll be sure to bring a couple of guys worthy of your company. So far, I have two firm maybes."

"Thanks, Alden," Hannah said, touching his shoulder.

"Hannah O'Rourke!" someone called.

She turned and saw another woman reporter, this one brunette, trailed by a man with a camcorder. They weaved through the girls on the curb to descend on them.

Before Hannah realized what was happening, Rachel pushed her into the backseat of the Jetta. "Get in, get in . . ."

"Hannah, can we have a statement?" the reporter called.

Rachel shut the back door and swiveled around toward them. "Why don't you just fuck off?" she screamed.

The reporter and her cameraman stopped in their tracks.

Rachel opened the front door and jumped into the passenger seat. "C'mon, Maddie, let's get out of here," she hissed, slamming her door.

Maddie, a pretty redhead with freckles, gaped at her and laughed. "My God, Rachel . . ."

"Would you step on it?" she yelled.

"Well, yes, ma'am!" Maddie let out another laugh and then pulled away from the curb.

"I'm sick of all these stupid reporters!" Rachel declared. "And I didn't feel like being on TV."

"Well, not much danger of that happening," Hanna
said. "'*Why don't you just fuck off?*'"

Maddie started laughing again as she steered dow
a campus side street. Rachel began to giggle, too.

Hannah's phone rang, and she dug it out of her purse

But Rachel turned in her seat and swiped the phon
from Hannah's grasp. "No phones until we get settle
in tonight. I don't want anyone knowing about our secr
slumber party. And you just may let it slip . . ."

"Are you serious?" Hannah asked over the sound (
her phone ringing. Dumbfounded, she watched Rachδ
stash the phone in her purse. Then Rachel plucke
Maddie's phone from the dashboard holder, and droppϵ
that in her purse, too.

"Hey, I need that for navigation!" Maddie said.

"I know the way by heart—and the best route to tal
Friday afternoons," Rachel said.

Hannah felt helpless without her phone—and tod̮
of all days. With her hand out, she leaned forwar
"Listen, Rachel, I'm sorry, but I really need my phon
My dad's calling later. He's flying in tomorrow nigʰ
and I need to get his flight information . . ."

"You can talk to him later, after we get settleϲ
Rachel decreed. "No phones until after dinner. Tho
are the slumber party hostess's rules."

She turned around and faced forward.

Hannah stared at the back of her head. She listenϵ
to the muffled ringing inside Rachel's purse. Then, finaˡ
it stopped.

She sat back and wondered what she was gettiₙ
herself into tonight.

CHAPTER FORTY-NINE

Friday, 3:22 P.M.

"Could you wait for me?" Nate asked the taxi driver, a middle-aged East Indian man with a gray mustache and a blue turban.

"I can do that," the driver answered with a trace of an accent.

"Thanks." Nate handed him the fare along with an extra twenty-dollar bill and a piece of notebook paper. "Keep the meter running. If I'm not out in ten minutes, honk and then call the number there . . ."

The driver glanced at the piece of paper. "I know this name . . ." He took a folded copy of the *Chicago Tribune* from the front passenger seat and waved it. "Is this the same Ellie Goodwin, the newspaper reporter on TV this morning?"

"Sure is." Nate nodded. "And my name's Nate. If I don't come out of there, call her and tell her where I am . . ."

"Got it," said the cabbie. "Whatever it is you're up to, good luck."

"Thanks, I need it," Nate said. Taking a deep breath, he stepped out of the taxi. He had on the same tie and blazer he'd worn yesterday for his meeting with

Ms. Houghton. He carried a large FedEx envelope he'd
stuffed with two newspapers and then sealed. He'd filled
out a label he'd also picked up from FedEx and stuck it
on the front of the envelope:

Richard J. Bonner
c/o Donald Sloane
Chicago, IL 60606

He'd purposely made the middle line with the street
address totally illegible.

Nate stopped to look at the Bonners' art deco four
story mansion, squeezed between two tall apartment
buildings on Lake Shore Drive. He'd gotten the Bonners' address from Frank ages ago. When he'd first
moved to the Chicago area, Nate had made a habit of
walking by the house and studying it whenever he
could. Now he hoped to get inside.

He realized there was still time to turn around, jump
into the cab, and have the driver take him back two
miles to the U-Park lot where he'd left his car. He'd
hailed the cab from there so, if he had to make a quick
getaway, no one working for the Bonners could take
down his license plate number.

He'd been so frustrated, getting all that valuable information from Vivien Houghton, but not being able to
act on it. Meanwhile, in comparison, Ellie had made
such a tremendous breakthrough today. She was a genuine mover and shaker.

Nate couldn't just sit still and remain in hiding. He'd
already had two years of that, and where had it gotten
him? He had to do *something*—even if it was a little
reckless and impulsive. He was going in with gun

blazing. He'd gain entry into the Bonners' mansion and confront Richard or Candace Bonner. And if they called the police, that was fine by him. The last thing they probably wanted was for him to talk to the police.

This morning, he'd bought a small Sony audio recorder, which fit nicely inside the pocket of his blue blazer. He'd accuse Richard or Candace of having Molly Driscoll murdered—and then having Marcia Lindahl killed as part of a cover-up. Those names alone would get their attention. And he would record their response. Even if they denied it and threw him out, at the very least, he might catch one of them in a lie that could spark an official investigation.

Nate knew it was a brash, hurried strategy, and for all his efforts, he'd probably meet the same fate as Gil. But he had to shake things up, stir up a shit-storm. He wanted to expose these people—the way Ellie had exposed this killer. Even if he was killed or he suddenly "disappeared," Ellie wouldn't let it go. She knew everything, and she'd see to it that the Bonners were brought to justice.

Nate took another deep breath and buzzed the intercom box on the post by the front gate. Glancing up, he noticed the security camera on top of the post, pointed down at him. He brought the envelope up to his chest—so the camera was sure to capture it. He turned his head away and then glanced down at the sidewalk. He didn't want to give the camera a long, uninterrupted view of his face. He didn't want them knowing who he was—at least not until he'd confronted them.

He waited another half-minute and buzzed again. His heart was pounding.

He glanced back at the taxi, waiting for him.

There was a click on the intercom. "Yes? Who is it?" a man asked.

"Um, I have an envelope here for Mr. Bonner," Nate said, his throat going dry. "Mr. Sloane sent me over with it."

"Just a minute." There was another click from the intercom.

Nate waited for a buzzer to sound that would open the gate, but nothing happened. Instead, the front door opened, and out stepped a slim, forty-something man with thinning hair. He wore a blue suit. He looked slightly annoyed—and in a hurry. He came to the gate. "I'll take it in," he said, reaching his hand between two bars of the wrought iron gate.

Nate shook his head. "Sorry. I have strict instructions from Sloane to place this in Mr. Bonner's hands—or Mrs. Bonner's if he's not around." He briefly showed the front of the envelope to the man so he caught only a fleeting glimpse of the label.

"Well, neither one of them is around. They took off this morning for their house in Lake Geneva. They'll be back Sunday afternoon."

Nate anxiously looked over the man's shoulder at the mansion.

"The place is empty. I'm just here locking up."

"Well, I need to get this to one of the Bonners by tonight. Listen, I ought to know, but maybe you can save me some time and give me the address of the Lake Geneva House."

The man flatly stared at him for a moment. "Let's just see some ID, bub."

Nate let out an exasperated sigh. "Screw it. I'll just call the office—if you want to get all official on me.

don't have time for this shit . . ." He swiveled around and hurried back into the cab. He opened the door and jumped in.

"Get me out of here, please," he said under his breath. Then he shut the door.

As the taxi peeled away, Nate glanced out the rear window.

He saw the man must have opened the gate. He now stood in the street, at the outer edge of the parking lane. He was talking into his phone.

And he was staring up the street at him.

"Nate, are you crazy?" she whispered into her phone. "That's an awful plan! You're going to get yourself killed!"

Ellie had just recorded an interview for WGN News at their downtown studios. She was still wearing the TV makeup from the segment. She'd really needed it, too. She hadn't gotten much sleep last night and was dead tired from running around like a madwoman today. She was in the building lobby when Nate called.

"So, you won't help me?" he asked. "I tried looking it up on Google, and nothing. I figured somebody at the Tribune must know the Bonners' Lake Geneva address. You guys must have some record of it from when the place was built or when they moved there. That's all I'm asking."

"You're asking me to help you get killed," Ellie said. "Listen, there are better ways of handling this than barging into the Bonners' vacation home and accusing them of murder. You'll end up in some godforsaken woods—with one of Sloane's men holding a gun to your head while you dig your own grave. Between you and me, we have enough on them to start a detailed investigation. There's no reason to rush into this. Now, why don't you go home? I'll meet you at your place in a couple of hours—"

"It's too late," he said, cutting her off. "I have to act on this tonight. The guy who was locking up the Lake Shore Drive house for the weekend, I'm pretty sure he's one of Sloane's guys. I know I put him on alert. They have footage of me from the security cameras at the front gate. It won't take them long to ID me as Gil Bergquist's *assumed-dead* brother. I need to do this tonight, Ellie. I'm headed up to Lake Geneva right now. I just stopped to fill up at a gas station on Touhy. If you can't think of anyone at the *Tribune* who knows the Bonners' vacation home address, that's okay. I'm sure if I ask around at enough places in Lake Geneva, someone will know."

"Just—just hold on, okay?" Ellie said. "Give me a little time, and I'll get the address for you. Let me find out about the setup there. You might not be able to get past the front gate—especially if they're expecting you. And it sounds like they might be. For all we know, the Bonners could be out at some gala fundraiser or something. I'll ask the woman who runs the society page if they're attending something tonight. She might even know their favorite haunts there in Lake Geneva. In fact, now that I think of it, you'd almost be safer confronting them in front of a roomful of people. If you disappear the next day, there'll be questions. So maybe you can catch them out and about tonight." Ellie sighed. "God, I can't believe I'm helping you with this harebrained scheme . . ."

"I can't believe it either," he said, sounding awestruck.

"You're amazing, Ellie. And you were wonderful on TV today."

Ellie felt herself blushing. "Well, thanks. Listen, don't do anything until you hear back from me." She glanced at her wristwatch. "Drive safely," she said. "It's Friday, rush hour, and the last weekend in September. Lots of people are leaving town. Traffic is bound to be nuts."

"Thanks, Ellie," he said.

"Take care," she said. Then she hung up.

She quickly checked for the calls she'd missed while doing her TV spot. There were a few, but nothing from Hannah. Ellie had left her several voice mails and texts. She knew Hannah had been safe about an hour ago. At the TV studio, she'd heard they were editing a piece with an interview Hannah had given at the school from around three o'clock.

Ellie didn't want her spending the night there at the bungalow. She imagined Hannah and Rachel there alone—right next door to bungalow eighteen, where it had all happened fifty years ago tonight. Two pretty girls alone, two potential victims—the tribute killer couldn't resist.

Ellie figured, on her way up to Lake Geneva to chase down Nate, she'd swing by St. Agnes Village and make sure Hannah was safe.

She dialed her reporter friend at the *Tribune*.

"Hey, Ellie," he answered on the second ring.

"Hey, Garth, I know you want to go home, but I have something else brewing."

"I don't want to ask. But go ahead. What is it?"

"Remember yesterday, I mentioned Donald Sloane and the Bonners, and you said you might know some stuff, and we agreed to put it on the back burner for a day or two?"

"Yeah?"

"Well, it needs to go on the front burner—now. And I need to talk to someone there who knows the Bonners' Lake Geneva home address and their favorite haunts up there . . ."

"Where are you right now? Are you still over at WGN?"

"Yeah, I just finished the TV interview."

"Well, haul your ass over here, and we'll get to work."

Hannah glanced at her wristwatch. It was 5:45. She'd been without her phone for nearly three hours, and it was killing her. Her kid brother, Steve, used to kid about her being unable to breathe correctly if she didn't have her cell phone with her, and damn it, he was right.

But that wasn't the only reason she felt on edge.

It had just gotten dark out, and already Hannah was scared. She knew once Alden showed up with his friends, she'd feel safer. But right now, the house seemed too big and empty for just the three of them.

She was sitting on the end of Rachel's bed while Rachel showed Maddie her closet and the fancy shoe storage unit. Maddie was impressed. Hannah realized that Maddie didn't know Rachel very well. She seemed nice enough—especially in comparison to the way Rachel was acting. Hannah knew she was upset over the DNA test results and tried to be sympathetic. But really, did Rachel have to be so sarcastic and bitchy during the entire car ride? And Miss I-Know-the-Best-Way-to-My-House had been totally wrong about getting there

The traffic had been awful, and the trip had taken nearly two hours.

Hannah was watching the news on the TV in Rachel's bedroom. They were reporting on the Immaculate Conception killings again—the ones back in 1970 and the recent "tribute" murders. They showed the campus at dusk. St. Agnes Village looked deserted. The camera zoomed in on St. Ursula's chrysanthemum garden, where the number of flowers, balloons, and flickering candles had more than doubled since this morning.

Over the shot of the garden, they superimposed a black-and-white photo of what must have been bungalow eighteen. It looked just like the one in which Hannah lived. Then they showed photos of the victims—and the girl who had survived. *Three young women,* the reporter said in a somber voice-over, *all of them good students showing so much promise, bright futures ahead. They went to sleep in their beds fifty years ago tonight. But only one of them was still alive in the morning . . .*

Rachel sat down beside Hannah. "God, they're laying it on a little thick, don't you think?" With the remote, she turned up the volume and then started switching channels. "Let's see if you're on ABC . . ."

Hannah glanced over her shoulder at Maddie checking out the clothes and shoes in Rachel's closet.

Rachel rolled her eyes. "God, I can't stand her," she said under her breath. She kept channel surfing—until Hannah came up on the screen.

Hannah didn't like seeing and hearing herself on TV. All her insecurities went into overdrive. It seemed almost sadistic of Rachel to turn up the volume:

"*Yes, of course, I miss my sister,*" Hannah told a reporter. "*We—we fight a lot, but we also keep each other in check. I feel kind of lost without Eden. I hope*

*she's okay. I don't want to think of her as anyone's
prisoner . . ."* Hannah remembered it was the closest
she'd come to crying during any of the interviews today.
The camera zoomed in for a close-up as her eyes welled
with tears. She let out a sad laugh. *"Eden would make
a terrible prisoner because she has a mind of her own
and loves the outdoors. She loves exploring. I hope
that's what she's doing right now. I hope we're wrong
about what happened to her . . ."*

"Talk about laying it on a little thick," Rachel
groaned. "And that close-up, eek, I can see every pore
on your face. That sadistic cameraman should be shot
at sunrise. At least your hair looks good . . ."

"Thanks," Hannah said—with a pinched smile.

"Hey, I'm just being honest," she said, switching
channels again.

Hannah thought she heard a noise downstairs, like
floorboards creaking. "What was that?" she asked. "Did
you just hear something? Turn down the TV . . ."

Rachel dismissed her with the wave of a hand. "It's a
big, old house, lots of squeaking and creaking. You'll
get used to it. We're fine. The place has all the latest
home security."

Hannah couldn't help thinking someone was down
stairs. She felt so utterly helpless. "Y'know, Rachel, I'd
really like to check my messages," she sighed. "Where's
my phone?"

"In my purse, which I hid earlier while you were in
the bathroom." Rachel gave her a self-satisfied smirk.
"Relax. You'll get your stupid phone later tonight. Or if
you want, you can start looking for it. You might start
in the basement and work your way up. There are only
thirty-eight rooms . . ."

Restless, Hannah got to her feet. She walked out of the bedroom and glanced down the dim hallway—with all the expensive art on the walls, and all those doors. Some were closed, and others were open—leading into dark rooms. *Thirty-eight rooms*, total—so many places for someone to hide.

In her head, there was another number. Three.

The three of them alone here, and tonight of all nights—it was almost like they were tempting fate.

And maybe that was just the way Rachel wanted it.

CHAPTER FIFTY

Friday, 6:33 P.M.

Nate glanced in his rearview mirror. The black SUV was still behind him. He'd first noticed it on Interstate 94, forty-five minutes ago. It had stayed one or two cars back, following him across the state line into Wisconsin. Since turning onto Highway 50, Nate had noticed the damn SUV still on his tail, directly behind him. He'd given the vehicle plenty of chances to pass, but it hadn't. He couldn't get a good look in his rearview mirror at the driver, but it looked like two people in the front seat.

He told himself Lake Geneva was a popular weekend resort for Chicagoans. The odds weren't too crazy that the SUV happened to be headed there, too. Still, as he passed another exit and saw the SUV still hovering back there, it rattled him even more. "Shit," he whispered, tightening his grip on the steering wheel.

The headlights in his rearview mirror blinded him for just a moment. Nate tried to focus on the road ahead.

His phone rang. He reached over and grabbed it off the passenger seat. He saw it was Ellie calling. "Hi, how's it going?" he asked, trying not to sound too tense.

"Where are you?"

"About twenty minutes from Lake Geneva. Where are you?"

"On my way to the college," she said. "I'm going to check on Hannah. But my friends at the *Tribune* have been working for you in my absence. They just called me with some information. Can you pull over and write this down?"

"Let's see if I can remember it," he said—with his eyes on the road. "Go ahead."

"The address of the Bonners' vacation home is Three Old Timber Lane. It's where God lost His shoes, as my dad likes to say. The scuttlebutt here is that it's a big, fenced-in compound in the woods. I wouldn't go there if I were you. They could make you disappear very easily."

"Three Old Timber Lane," Nate said out loud. He figured he could pull over and look it up on Google Maps once he got to town.

"I have someone looking into where the Bonners might be tonight. I'll call you back as soon as I get any word. But one of their favorite spots is the Lake Geneva Country Club. If they're not there, they often dine at the Geneva ChopHouse or, sometimes, at Medusa Grill and Bistro. Can you remember that?"

"Yes, I've got it, thanks," Nate said, trying to commit the address and names to memory.

"Try the restaurants first," she said. "The country club will be tougher to get into, and their house will be practically impossible, I'm sure. After I check in with Hannah and make sure she's okay, I'm driving up there to meet you. If you wait, the two of us can confront them together. I have a big spotlight on me right now, and I'm with the press. So it'll be a lot harder for them to ignore us if we're together. Could you wait for me, Nate, please?"

"Okay," he lied. He didn't want to put Ellie in jeopardy. He glanced once again at the black SUV in his rearview mirror.

"I'll call you as soon as I get word about where the Bonners are tonight. Take care."

"You too," Nate said. "And thank you, Ellie."

She hung up.

Nate put the phone back on the passenger seat. He saw an exit just ahead.

He anxiously checked the rearview mirror as he passed the turnoff.

The SUV was still looming behind him.

"Shit," he said under his breath.

Driving through the campus was eerie. Things were usually hopping around dinnertime on Friday nights. But the quad was practically empty. Ellie noticed a campus security vehicle in front of the student union, and police cars parked in front of the library and O'Donnell Hall.

The windows were dark in nearly all of the bungalows in St. Agnes Village. The street was deserted except for a few people gathered in front of the garden where bungalow eighteen used to be. The makeshift shrine in front of the site had at least thirty candles flickering in the night.

Ellie parked her car two bungalows down.

The front window of bungalow twenty was dark. But Ellie noticed a glimmer of light coming from a room in the back. With her head down, she ignored the small

crowd on the other side of the front yard and started up
the paved walkway toward Hannah's bungalow. She followed the flagstone path that veered off and wound
around the side of the bungalow to the tiny backyard.
There was no lawn, just a neglected flagstone patio in
the shadow of two large trees on the other side of the
property line. Around another corner toward the other
side of the bungalow, she had a unique view of the overgrown, slightly neglected chrysanthemum garden that
had become the focus of so much attention today. Ellie
remembered Hannah saying that her bedroom window
looked out at it. That window was where the light came
from. As Ellie crept up to the barred window to peek
inside, she had a flashback to yesterday morning—
when she'd peered into Pamela Rothschild's window
and discovered her corpse on the kitchen floor.

She hesitated for a moment, then gathered up her
courage and moved closer to Hannah's window. The tiny
bedroom was empty—with both twin beds made. A box
fan was in one corner of the room. A poster of Degas's
Dancers Tying Shoes was on the wall over one of the
beds. Hannah had left the desk lamp on. It was the only
light on in the whole place.

Ellie turned away from the window and headed
through the shadowy backyard and up along the flagstone path again. As she rounded the corner of the
house, she stopped dead.

A man blocked her way.

Horrified, Ellie gasped and stepped back.

"Who are you?" he asked. The man was in his mid-
thirties, stocky, with a crew cut and a heavy five o'clock
shadow. He wore a dark suit with no tie.

Ellie stood frozen for a minute. "I—I'm a friend of

Hannah O'Rourke's," she finally answered. Her heart was pounding. "She lives here. Who are you?"

He didn't respond for a moment. Ellie could hear people murmuring next door in front of the impromptu shrine.

"I'm Perry," he said. "I take care of Rachel. I'm sort of her chauffeur-bodyguard."

Wide-eyed, Ellie nodded. Now she remembered both Hannah and Nate mentioning him.

"In fact, right now I'm looking for Rachel," he continued. "I have a feeling she and Hannah decided to sneak off on their own someplace—without telling anyone. How do you know Hannah?"

"I'm her teacher, Ellie Goodwin." She stared at him and tried not to look too intimidated.

"Do you mind if we go talk some place where it's light?"

He gave her a lopsided grin. "Sure."

He turned and lumbered along the stone pathway toward the front of the house. His back was to Ellie. "I think the girls gave me the slip about two hours ago. I've left Rachel a couple of messages and checked her regular local hangouts, but no luck . . ."

In the light of the front yard, he turned to face her. " was just about to try this place outside Waukegan, her cleaning woman's house . . ."

"Alma?" Ellie said. She remembered Hannah telling her that the cleaning woman was Lance's mother. Rachel owned the house they lived in. "Why would they go there?"

He sighed and reached for his phone. "Well, I'v driven Rachel out there before. In fact, just the other night, she brought a load of laundry there, and I ende up waiting for a couple of hours. The house is a real dump. Anyway, maybe she's there right now. The son has a car. Sometimes he drives Rachel to his house, and I'll have no idea where she is until she calls for me to come pick her up. I can't think of anywhere else she'd be—at least, none of the usual places."

Ellie wondered why in the world Rachel would be hanging around at the home of her cleaning woman and her son—unless Lance was supplying Rachel with drugs or something. That would explain all the clandestine trips there. And Lance definitely seemed like the type who might have a drug-dealing business on the side. "I can't imagine Hannah wanting to go there with her," Ellie murmured—almost to herself.

He shrugged. "Well, those two girls have been hanging around together a lot lately, I just figured, you know . . ."

Ellie pulled her phone out of her purse. "You don't have a phone number for Alma or Lance, do you?"

"No, just the address of the house," he said. "It's about twenty-five minutes away, out in the middle of nowhere . . ."

Checking his phone, Perry read the address to her. Ellie figured it was worth a shot to check out the place. What was Lance running there?

Ellie felt like a real reporter again, chasing down a lead like this. She wasn't a bit surprised that Rachel would be hanging out at such a place. But she prayed Hannah wouldn't be there. Best-case scenario: Rachel would be there and tell her that Hannah was safe and sound in one of the dorms.

She and Perry exchanged phone numbers. They

promised to call each other if one of them found out where Rachel and Hannah were.

As Ellie climbed back into her car, she realized Perry was probably employed by Donald Sloane—a "ruthless, slippery scumbag," according to Garth. But Sloane's people had no reason to be concerned about her. She'd only asked a couple of trusted reporter friends about him and the Bonners. Hannah was the only one who could link her to Nate, and no one knew his true identity. Sloane's people thought he was dead.

Ellie was entering Lance and Alma's address in her GPS when Perry tapped on her car window. She lowered it and looked up at him.

"I just put it together that you're the newspaper reporter," he said.

And I just put it together that your boss has people murdered, she thought. Ellie nodded. "Yes, that's me."

He grinned. "I'll have to get your autograph later." He tapped the hood and backed away from the car.

Rolling up her window, Ellie put the car in drive. She cruised past the small crowd in front of the shrine where the two girls were slain fifty years ago.

She didn't look back.

The black SUV was still on his tail as Nate pulled into Lake Geneva. He turned into the empty parking lot of a Chase Bank. He almost expected the SUV to follow him, but the other vehicle kept going straight down West Main Street.

Nate parked in a space marked BANK CUSTOMER ONLY. He kept his eyes glued on the taillights of th

SUV. He prayed it wouldn't turn around. Several other cars passed, and he finally lost sight of it.

Three Old Timber Lane, Lake Geneva Country Club, Geneva ChopHouse, and *Medusa Grill and Bistro*— he'd been repeating that to himself for the last half hour.

Grabbing his phone, he started searching for the addresses. Ellie was right about the Bonners' vacation home. Three Old Timber Lane was six miles away—a tiny road off some lakeside route that took him way on the other side of town. It looked like it was in the woods somewhere.

He was about to look up the location of the country club when the phone rang. It was Ellie. "Hey, how's it going?" he answered. "Did you find Hannah?"

"Not yet," she said. "I'm on my way to this place that sounds like a crack house. It's probably just a wild goose chase."

"And you're going there alone?" he asked, alarmed.

"I figure if Rachel Bonner is safe there, so am I."

"What?"

"It's a long story. Never mind. I just wish Hannah would answer her damn phone. Where are you? Are you in Lake Geneva yet?"

"Yeah, on the edge of town," Nate said.

"I found out where the Bonners are tonight."

"How did you do that?"

"A friend at the newspaper started calling up restaurants and asking if the Bonners had reservations. They're booked at the Geneva ChopHouse for eight-thirty. They're having dinner with another couple. So— just sit tight. If Hannah's actually hanging out with Rachel at this place, I'll drag her along and we can be there by nine. We can catch the Bonners before they have their dessert."

"I can't let you get involved any more than you already are," Nate said. "It's too dangerous." It suddenly occurred to him that he may have already put Ellie in harm's way. "In fact, I need to warn you. When I tried to see the Bonners at their place on Lake Shore Drive, I gave the cab driver your name and phone number. In case I didn't come out of the house, he was supposed to call you. Anyway, I'm thinking there's a chance Sloane's man got the license plate of the taxi and they tracked down the driver. So, be careful, okay? Make sure no one's following you . . ."

There was silence on the other end.

"Ellie, are you still there? Did you hear what I just said?"

"I'll keep my eyes peeled. Meanwhile, stay put. I'll give you a call after I check out this place near Waukegan. Will you wait for me?"

"I'll wait," he lied. "Be careful. And don't take any chances, okay?"

"I won't," she said.

He had a feeling she was lying, too.

After he hung up, Nate looked up the directions to the Geneva ChopHouse. It looked like it was about fifteen minutes away.

He glanced at his wristwatch. If he left in an hour, he'd catch the Bonners while they were having their cocktails.

The dilapidated farmhouse was the only residence on a dead-end road in a rural area. It was between two empty lots with barbed-wire fences and faded signs that read LOT FOR SALE. The lawn in front of the house was mostly crabgrass. A rural mailbox at the end of the long driveway had two names stenciled on it: ALMA PIERSON/LANCE PIERSON. Ellie thought it was strange that Rachel's father owned this property—and that Rachel had leased the decrepit house to her cleaning woman. Plus it wasn't exactly convenient to the school where both Alma and Lance worked.

The place looked deserted. There wasn't another car in sight. But as Ellie pulled farther into the driveway, she noticed a faint, flickering light in an upstairs window. It looked like a TV was on.

After what Nate had told her about Sloane's man possibly getting her name from the taxi driver, she had every reason to question Perry's intentions when he'd sent her here. But so far, everything jibed with what he'd said. This house was indeed a "dump," and Alma and Lance obviously lived here.

Climbing out of the car, Ellie walked up the creaky steps of the front porch and knocked on the door. The evening was so quiet. She'd almost expected to hear murmuring from the TV upstairs, but there wasn't a sound.

Ellie was about to knock again when it suddenly occurred to her. She could be standing on the tribute killer's front porch.

Lance and his crazy holy-roller mother were the perfect candidates. Was his mother spurring him on to kill the "holy sluts" as Lyle Duncan Wheeler's mother had spurred on her son? They also had a key to Rachel and Hannah's bungalow. They'd have had no problem getting into the place and leaving Hannah that note

from her "runaway" sister. And Lance probably had a
key to the grotto, too.

Ellie took a step back, and the porch floorboard
squeaked. She gazed at the slightly battered front door.
This house in the middle of nowhere was the perfect
spot to keep someone prisoner in a cellar, attic, or closet.

She noticed a front window was open a crack. It
looked like it was permanently stuck in that position.
She tried to peer through the dirty glass, but couldn't
see much. It was just a big, dark room—vacant except
for some debris on the floor. Obviously, Alma Pierson
did all her cleaning in other people's houses, and not
her own.

There still hadn't been a sound since Ellie had first
stepped up on the porch. If this was some kind of trap
with somebody lying in wait for her, they were doing a
damn good job being quiet about it.

Ellie gave the window a tug, but it didn't budge. She
glanced down at the dirt smudges on her sweater. With
a sigh, she tried the window next to it. After some re-
sistance, it started to give way, but not without a loud
scraping noise. Ellie winced at the sound. Still, she kept
pulling and jerking at the sash until the window was
about two feet open. She waited a few moments, listening again in case the noise had alerted anyone. But there
wasn't a peep.

Maybe Lance and his mother were out somewhere
closer to the school, already stalking their victims for
tonight's double homicide.

Her stomach clenched, Ellie climbed through the
window. The house had a damp, stale smell to it. She
paused and let her eyes adjust to the darkness. On
the scruffy wooden floor of the room were beer cans, a

broken chair, some dirty clothes, and a crowbar. Ellie made a beeline to the crowbar and grabbed it.

She heard a humming noise in the next room. Switching on her phone light, Ellie shone it on the arched doorway. From the banged-up, built-in hutch on one wall, she figured she was in the dining room. She shone the phone light on the floor and noticed a pathway through the layer of dust. It went from the front hall to the next room, where the mechanical hum continued.

Ellie crept through the doorway and found herself in the kitchen. The humming came from a refrigerator. It was a newer, stainless steel, smaller "apartment size" model, like the one in her townhouse—only this fridge seemed dwarfed and anachronistic in the big, old country kitchen. Biting her lip, Ellie opened the refrigerator door. It was stocked with juice, soda, fruit, yogurt, and food from the campus deli. She also noticed a bottle of champagne. What were Lance and his mother doing with an expensive-looking bottle of champagne? It seemed more Rachel's taste than theirs.

In the glow from the refrigerator light, Ellie had a better look at the kitchen. There was a grease-stained, old gas stove against the wall—with the oven door missing. But on the cracked-tile counter sat a new microwave. Ellie noticed a light switch on the wall. She gave it a flick, and a light went on—a bare bulb hanging over a card table with two folding chairs.

Something the bodyguard had said didn't make sense. He'd mentioned that Rachel brought her laundry and picked it up here. But according to Hannah, the cleaning woman always took the laundry back and forth from the bungalow. Why was Rachel making trips here with something in a laundry basket?

Ellie's theory about Rachel coming to the house for drugs suddenly didn't make sense either. If Lance was dealing drugs out of this house, security would have been a lot tighter. It wouldn't have been so easy for her to break into the place.

But it didn't seem like anyone's home either. The setup inside looked more like a safe house or some place where a mobster might bring a prisoner or hostage he needed to interrogate.

Ellie thought of Eden again.

Leaving the kitchen light on, she headed back through the dining room to the front hallway. With the crowbar in her hand, she crept up the stairs. She wanted to find that room on the second floor where someone had the TV on.

Halfway up the steps, her phone rang, and Ellie almost jumped out of her skin. If anyone else was in the house, they now knew they had an intruder.

She checked and saw it was the bodyguard, Perry calling. She touched the phone screen to pick up and stop the ringing. Then she listened for a moment. Still no footsteps. "Yes, hello?" she whispered into the phone.

"Did you find the place?" he asked. "Is anyone there?"

"Yeah, I'm here," she said, still whispering. "But the place seems to be empty. Have you actually seen Alma or Lance here?"

"No. Just Rachel coming and going. Sometimes there's a car in the driveway. I've always assumed it was Lance's. So—nothing, huh? Nobody's there?"

"Just me."

"Well, sorry to send you out there for nothing. I'm still at the bungalow. They have some priest leading prayers for the crowd next door. So are you coming back here or what?"

"I'm not sure yet," Ellie said. "I'll let you know. Talk to you later, okay?"

"Okay, so long." He clicked off.

Ellie hung up. Something else didn't make sense. She'd just been in that big kitchen with a microwave and a refrigerator—but no washer, no dryer, and no ironing board. No one was doing laundry in this house. She was convinced Lance and Alma didn't live here. Their names were on the mailbox out front, but Ellie seriously wondered if they even knew this place existed.

Tightening her grip on the crowbar, she continued up the stairs. The flickering light filled the second-floor hallway. To her surprise, it came from a room in the back—but the light bounced off a cracked mirror on the hallway wall. There were five other open doors in the corridor. But all of the rooms were dark except the one in back. Tiptoeing to the doorway, Ellie peeked inside. There was a cot pushed against one wall—with a pillow and a messy blanket. A cardboard box—for the microwave oven downstairs—was brimming with trash. But empty beer and soda cans and candy wrappers still littered the bare floor.

Ellie stepped into the room and saw a long desk against the wall. It held a computer and keyboard, speakers, some kind of sound system, and three monitors. The screen behind the keyboard was off. But the other two monitors were on. Each one had a smaller picture-within-picture at the bottom corner of the screen. The large images were the ones Ellie noticed first. One TV showed Hannah and Eden's empty bedroom. Ellie recognized the Degas poster. It looked like someone had hidden a nanny-cam in the room. The smaller image, the picture-within-picture showed a little girl curled up on a cot with a blanket bunched up around her feet. It looked like a still photo, shot from overhead.

The bigger image on the other monitor was a shot of a neglected yard. The camera must have been up in a tree, because a few bare branches almost obscured the view—though not quite. There was another tree with an old tire swing. But the camera seemed focused on a tool shed at the edge of a leafless hedgerow—a shed like the one in Lyle Duncan Wheeler's backyard.

"My God," Ellie whispered. She turned and ran to the bedroom window. She gazed down at the derelict, barren yard, the old tire swing—and the tool shed.

Breathless, she hurried back to the monitor and set the crowbar down on the desk. Her hand was shaking as she tried to manipulate the mouse on the pad in front of the monitor showing Hannah's bedroom. She clicked on the smaller image, and it suddenly filled the screen. It wasn't a still photograph, because the girl restlessly tossed and turned on the cot. Ellie found a knob that enabled her to zoom in on the image.

It was no little girl. It was Eden O'Rourke.

And she was still alive.

A movement in the small picture on the other monitor suddenly caught Ellie's eye. The bigger picture of the backyard was completely still. But a different camera picked up some activity in another location. Ellie manipulated the mouse again and clicked on the smaller picture-within-picture image. She hadn't noticed a surveillance camera earlier, but there must be one mounted somewhere above the front door. She could see the desolate front yard, her car parked in the driveway, and someone creeping past it.

She didn't need to zoom in on him. She could see that it was Perry.

He'd lied to her on the phone five minutes ago when he'd said he was waiting by the girls' bungalow. He must have been down at the end of the driveway when he'd called her. One of the first things he'd asked was if anyone else was there.

She should have listened to Nate's warning. Sloane's goons must have identified him from the security cameras at the Bonners' house. Then obviously, they'd tracked down the taxi driver and gotten her name from him.

Perry couldn't very well have nabbed her earlier at the bungalow, not with all those people gathered in front of the garden next door. So he'd persuaded her to drive out here—*in the middle of nowhere*, he'd said.

Was this a safe house for Sloane's men? Were they the ones who took Eden? Maybe Nate was right about that, too.

Or was Perry the Immaculate Conception Killer's self-appointed disciple?

Ellie grabbed the crowbar off the desk. She hurried out to the hallway and ducked into one of the front bedrooms. It was empty—except for some trash scattered on the wood floor. Ellie stood flat against the wall by the window. The tattered shade was halfway down. Past the dirty glass, she could see Sloane's man directly below, sneaking up toward the front porch.

This close, she could also see the gun in his hand.

CHAPTER FIFTY-ONE

Friday, 7:51 P.M.

Hannah heard the noise again—a distant scraping sound, like someone in another room had bumped into a chair and the legs had dragged against the floor. It seemed to come from the basement.

She sat with Rachel and Maddie in the breakfast nook, watching *The Big Bang Theory* on Hildie's TV and eating the pizza that had been delivered twenty minutes ago. Rachel had insisted they change into their pajamas before they ate. So while the pizza had gotten cold, Hannah had changed into her blue gingham pj's. At least Rachel had managed to pack the right pajamas. Rachel had on a sophisticated lacy gown with a matching robe, and Maddie wore flannel lounge pants and an old Hello Kitty T-shirt.

Hannah thought eating in their nightwear was a stupid idea—especially in this huge, drafty mansion. But the notion wasn't nearly as moronic as Rachel's quirky moratorium on phones for the evening. Hannah kept wondering when she'd be able to get hers back.

She also wondered when Alden would show up with his friends. She'd thought Rachel would have ordered a pizza for them, too. But, no, she'd gotten only one large mushroom pie—her choice. She hadn't even asked Hannah and Maddie what they'd wanted on the pizza. Why had Rachel become so selfish and snotty all of a sudden?

So far tonight, Hannah was having a miserable time, and it wasn't just because she didn't have her phone or because Rachel was acting so awful. Hannah kept thinking of Eden, alone and terrified, locked up in a shed or a closet someplace, at the mercy of some killer. Before, it had merely been a theory between her and Ellie. But now, the TV newspeople were reporting it as a very real possibility. She was hardly in a "pajama party" mood.

Hannah also thought about those two girls murdered fifty years ago tonight—two of the three students in bungalow eighteen that night.

She just wanted Alden to show up. Then she'd feel safe. Then the two of them could sneak away from the others and talk or maybe cuddle—corny as that sounded.

There was yet another noise from the basement. Hannah put down her slice of pizza. "Okay, I just heard something again . . ."

"I heard it, too," Maddie whispered.

"Turn down the TV." Hannah nudged Rachel, who, of course, had charge of the remote.

Rolling her eyes, she turned down the volume. "I told you. It's just the furnace. It does that sometimes . . ."

The three of them remained completely still at the kitchen table, waiting and listening. Hannah stared across the room at a vent by the floor.

Rachel let out a sigh and then reached for her Diet Coke and took a sip.

Hannah heard a man quietly snickering. The sound sent chills up her back. It seemed to come from the vent.

Maddie let out a little shriek and covered her mouth.

"That's Alden!" Rachel laughed. She sprung up from the table. "He must have snuck in while we were upstairs. He's screwing with us! C'mon . . ."

But Hannah didn't want to move. She could see Maddie was just as frightened as she was. "This isn't funny," Maddie said.

"I'm telling you, it's Alden," Rachel said through a giggle. "He has a key. He knows all the security codes. He's down by the vent in the basement. Who else could it be? C'mon, don't be such scaredy cats . . ."

Hesitant, Hannah finally got to her feet.

Maddie stood up as well, but she was trembling. "I don't like this," she murmured.

"Join the club," Hannah replied under her breath.

Still, she followed Rachel out of the kitchen to the basement door in the front hall. When Hannah reached the doorway, the basement light was on and Rachel was already halfway down the stairs.

She felt sick to her stomach. "Rachel!" she called down to her. "Rachel, I want my fucking phone back!"

But Rachel ignored her and continued down the steps.

"Damn it, I'm not having a fun time!" Hannah yelled. "Neither is Maddie. For God's sake . . ."

With Maddie hovering behind her, Hannah reluctantly started down the stairs. From one of the middle steps, she saw the light go on in the game room.

"Alden?" she heard Rachel call. "We know it's you. Nice try, buddy! Where are you?"

"Alden?" Hannah called in a shaky voice. "Alden, we're majorly creeped out here. The joke isn't funny anymore. If I wanted to be scared, I'd have stayed at the bungalow tonight. Now, c'mon, enough is enough—"

"I don't think this is a joke," Maddie whispered, her voice quavering.

With a hand on the banister, Hannah continued down the stairs. She glanced around the huge game room. Rachel had already moved into the back corridor—toward the mini-gym, sauna, bathroom, and the extra bedroom. The hallway light went on, and Rachel's shadow moved across the wall. "Alden, you asshole, where are you?"

Exasperated, Hannah shook her head and reluctantly started toward the back corridor.

Rachel let out a brief shriek. It was as if she was cut off mid-scream. Then suddenly, silence.

Hannah stopped dead. From the end of the hallway, she saw the light was on in the guest room. "Rachel?" she called nervously. "Rachel, what's going on?"

There was no response. From the room down at the end of the corridor, all she heard was a whimper.

Maddie clung to her arm as they headed down the hallway together. Hannah felt her heart thumping against her chest. She crept up to the doorway and saw Rachel standing in the middle of the bedroom.

With tears in her eyes, Rachel stared at something off in the corner, out of Hannah's line of vision. She seemed in shock. She kept shaking her head over and over.

The room wasn't the same as when Hannah had seen it last week. The twin beds had been shoved against opposite walls. All around the room were pots and vases with cut chrysanthemums—just like the ones in the garden where bungalow eighteen used to be.

Reaching a hand out to Rachel, Hannah stepped into the room. That was when she saw the man standing in the corner, by the closet door. He wore strange, outdated clothes. He had shaggy dark blond hair, a thick mustache, and glasses. It all looked like part of a disguise.

He pointed a gun at them.

Hannah stopped. All at once, she couldn't breathe.

Behind her, Maddie let out a little cry.

Past the bizarre disguise, the man grinned. "I want you holy sluts to get down on your knees," he whispered.

The 911 operator repeated the address.

"That's right," Ellie whispered into her phone. "It's a mile north of Waukegan, a farmhouse—on a dead-end road. The missing O'Rourke girl is in a tool shed in the backyard. She—she's alive. Someone's trying to get into the house right now, and he's got a gun . . ."

Ellie stood beside the window, clutching the crowbar in her other hand. She could hear Perry downstairs, struggling to raise the window higher. The opening must have been too small for his stocky frame.

Ellie realized if he had to climb through the window, he didn't have a key to the house. He and Sloane's men weren't using it as a hideout. Maybe he had no idea that Eden was locked in the backyard shed.

"All right, Ellie," the 911 operator said. "Stay calm, and remain on the line . . ."

Earlier, Ellie had given the woman her name, and since then, the operator had called her by name in every sentence she spoke. It was probably supposed to calm her, but it just unnerved Ellie even more.

"I can't hold on," she whispered. The crowbar almost slipped out of her hand as she hung up. She couldn't keep her hands steady. Tucking the weapon under her arm, she pressed Perry's number. She had to do something to stall him until the police arrived.

He must have had his phone on vibrate because she didn't hear it ringing.

"Shit," he grumbled. She heard that much through the open window downstairs.

There was a click. "Yeah, what's going on?" he whispered, out of breath.

"Well, I—I got inside the house," she explained in a hushed, shaky voice. "I'm in a back bedroom, and there're some TV monitors here. From one of them, it looks like somebody planted a nanny-cam or a spy-cam in Hannah's bedroom. They've been watching her . . ."

"You're kidding me," he murmured. He sounded genuinely surprised.

Ellie wondered if, when he'd sent her here, Perry had been telling the truth about never having set foot in the place. Maybe it was just like he'd said—he'd merely dropped and picked up Rachel there on a few occasions.

"Rachel didn't tell you about all the closed-circuit TV monitors here?" she asked.

"It's news to me . . ."

"Well, I'm pretty sure it's Hannah's bedroom on the TV monitor," Ellie said. "You're there by the bungalow, aren't you?" She waited for him to lie.

He hesitated. "Yeah . . ."

"Well, could you go to that window in back and check for me? You know, behind the house, where we were? I didn't get a good look at the bedroom earlier tonight. But I think it's Hannah's. On the monitor here, there's a ballet poster on the wall . . ."

There was no response.

"Perry?"

Ellie heard a beep on the line. The 911 operator was trying to get back to her. Ellie hoped the police were on their way. But it would still be at least five more minutes—maybe ten—before they arrived.

"Perry, are you still there?"

Ellie could hear the echo of her own voice—murmuring over his phone. It came from downstairs.

She heard his footsteps directly below. She swiveled toward the bedroom door as a light went on somewhere downstairs, most likely the front hallway.

Ellie quickly pressed the phone screen for the other call. "He's in the house!" she said under her breath.

"Ellie, can you find a place to hide?" the 911 operator asked. "The police are on their way . . ."

She looked across the room at the closet. She tiptoed toward it, but the floorboards creaked.

All at once, a loud shot rang out and a bullet pierced the wood floor—just inches in front of her feet.

Ellie froze. Another shot followed, and she recoiled. She saw faint beams of light and dust pour through both holes in the floor. She raced back into the hallway. She could hear him running, too. She saw his shadow below looming larger as he approached the stairs.

Terrified, she ducked into another dark, empty bedroom—across the hall.

With her back to the wall by the bedroom door, she winced at the sound of him charging up the stairs. The footsteps got louder and louder, then—nothing, just him breathing heavily. It sounded like he was just outside the bedroom.

Ellie hung up the phone and carefully tucked it in the pocket of her sweater. She prayed the 911 operator didn't call back and give her away. She tried not to make a sound. She held the crowbar with both hands, but couldn't stop shaking.

"I guess, by now, you've figured I'm not at the bungalow, Ellie," he called out with a chuckle. "The truth is you're going to get me out of some trouble. Tonight of all nights, I can't believe I let that little bitch, Rachel, give me the slip. I know she'll be okay, wherever the hell she is. She always comes out on top, that girl. I'll be doing nicely, too, thanks to you . . ." His voice kept fading in and out as he moved from room to room while he talked. "All will be forgiven, because I got you. See, they're looking for you, Ellie. Didn't you know it can be very unhealthy to associate with guys who are supposed to be dead? Didn't you know that, bitch?" His voice got louder. And the room became darker as he stepped into the doorway and blocked out the light. "Was Nate Bergquist going to be the subject of your next big news story? I don't think so. They'll be printing your obituary first. Where the fuck are you?"

A floorboard nearby squeaked.

Ellie waited until he came through the doorway. Then she swung the crowbar.

There was a loud crack as she hit him in the face.

The gun went off and flew out of his hand.

Howling in pain, Perry dropped to his knees in front of her. A red line across his forehead began seeping blood. As he leaned over, it dripped onto the dusty wood floor.

Raising the crowbar again, Ellie struck him on the back of the head.

He let out a feeble groan and finally collapsed with thud.

Suddenly, the house was so quiet again.

But then Ellie heard a muffled sound from outside.

It was someone crying for help.

CHAPTER FIFTY-TWO

Friday, 8:19 P.M.

The basement bedroom smelled of chrysanthemums and sweat.

Paralyzed with fear, Hannah remained on her knees. She kept her arms crossed in front of her. She couldn't believe this was happening. But it was no joke. Rachel wasn't laughing anymore. She looked petrified. Maddie couldn't stop crying.

When she'd read online about the Immaculate Conception murders, Hannah had seen the police composite sketch of "the suspect." The fake shaggy hair, mustache, and glasses the man in Rachel's basement wore had been copied from the disguise Lyle Duncan Wheeler had used when preying on his victims. The man now holding them at gunpoint also wore some kind of makeup that made his face look brown.

In a raspy voice, he instructed Rachel to tie up Maddie and her—just as Wheeler had made the three girls tie each other up that night fifty years ago.

On one of the beds, he'd set out measured and cut sections of rope. They were neatly arranged in three separate piles. He nodded at Maddie. "You—*Hello Kitty*—lay down on your stomach—with your hands behind you

"Please, don't hurt me," Maddie sobbed. Strands of her red hair stuck to the tears on her cheeks. Her whole body shook as she lay down on the floor.

"You there, girlie, get started," he said—with a nod at Rachel. "First, tie her wrists together—then her feet at the ankles. Those knots need to be tight, because I'm testing them."

Rachel reached for the ropes. "Listen, I can show you where my mother keeps her jewelry. I know where all the valuables are in the house—"

"No one's going to get hurt," he said. "I just need some money for a trip to Alaska."

Hannah remembered that, according to the girl who survived that night fifty years ago, Wheeler had told the girls he needed money for a trip to Mexico. Of course, it had been a lie. He hadn't stolen anything from the bungalow—except for the lives of two innocent young women.

Hannah prayed Alden and his friends would show up soon. She figured Rachel was trying to buy them some time.

"The silverware and the silver service in the dining room are worth thousands," she said in a shaky voice. "You—you can go around the world with the money from that. And it's yours for the taking . . ." She kept talking to the man, trying to bargain with him—and all the while, she hovered over Maddie, binding her wrists and ankles.

Maddie squirmed and cried out as Rachel tightened the knots.

"Your turn, sweetie," the man said, staring at Hannah. "Facedown on the floor, hands behind you . . ."

Gazing at the gun in his hand, Hannah obeyed. At

some point, he'd have to put down the gun; maybe then she could do *something*. Even if she was tied up, she might be able to trip him up or escape. She couldn't help thinking about the girl who had survived the original murders.

She felt Rachel crouched over her, tying her wrists and ankles. The man had said he would test the knots. But did Rachel really have to tie the ropes so tight? It didn't seem necessary. Hannah was losing the circulation in her hands and feet.

"The alarm system here is very sophisticated," Rachel was saying. "I don't know how or when you got in, but anything can trigger it. It's a silent alarm. The police are automatically notified. And there are security cameras everywhere—"

"Now, it's your turn," the man interrupted. "Sit down with your legs out in front of you, and tie your ankles together. And remember, I'm watching you . . ."

"Please, no, I—I don't want to be tied up—"

"Shut your hole and do it," he growled.

Rachel fell silent.

Hannah turned her head and watched Rachel tie her ankles together. Rachel started crying as she double-tied the knot.

"That's right. Good girl," the man whispered. "Now, roll over on your stomach and put your hands behind you . . ."

He tucked the gun in the waistband of his outdated bell-bottom corduroys. Then he grabbed the last section of rope and bent over Rachel, now facedown on the floor.

Hannah thought she heard a noise upstairs. It could have been someone trying to get in the front door—or

t could have just been the house settling. She wasn't
sure. But neither the man nor Rachel seemed to notice.

Rachel let out a sharp cry as he tightened the knot
around her wrists. "Ouch, God, not so tight, you stupid
shit!"

The man straightened up and backed away a step,
leaving her squirming on the floor.

Hannah wondered how Rachel had the guts to talk to
him like that.

He stood over Rachel and pulled a serrated-edge
hunting knife out of a sheath attached to the back of
his belt.

Hannah looked at his eyes. Past those fake glasses
and the rest of the masquerade, she saw the pain there.
It was the same humiliated expression she'd seen on his
face earlier today, when Rachel had told him to shut up.

"Alden?" she whispered.

She remembered what Rachel had said about him
having a key to the house and knowing all the codes.
He'd lived in the servants' quarters his entire life. He
was part of the staff. So of course Rachel could talk to
him like that.

He put the knife back in its sheath and stepped over
to Hannah.

She recoiled and started to roll away as he hovered
over her. Then his arms went around her waist and he
pulled her up onto her feet. Dragging her over to the bed,
he sat her down.

"What are you doing?" Rachel cried. "You'll ruin
everything. That's not how it's supposed to be . . ."

He turned away from Hannah. Reaching for the knife
again, he approached Maddie, who gazed up at him in
terror. "No, no, please . . ." she whimpered.

"Alden, you can't," Hannah pleaded. "This isn't you . . ."

He hesitated.

Glaring at him, Rachel squirmed on the floor. "Do it, Sonny . . . stab the holy slut. Do it, do what Mama says . . ."

With the knife in his hand, he just stared at her.

"Okay, fine, Sonny," Rachel grumbled, struggling to turn over on her side. "If you can't do it, I will—like I had to finish off that teacher the other night. What's gotten into you lately anyway? Tell you what, screw it, I'll handle everything. Just untie me. You've made the goddamn knot too tight. How am I supposed to escape when the knot's so tight? Mama's really disappointed in you, Sonny Boy."

"You're not my mother." Alden yanked off the cheap wig and glasses and let them drop to the floor. Then he peeled off the thick mustache. His brown hair was matted down, and sweat dripped into the greasy brown makeup that made him look older. "When no one else is around, I sometimes call you Mama and you call me Sonny. But it never was. I had a mother, and she was sweet to me, but she died. I was never your son, and was never your brother either." He started sobbing. "I was just a servant girl's kid—there for your amusement, running your errands and spying on people for you. Look at what you've made me do. I didn't even know those other two girls. They never did anything to me. Neither did that Riley guy. Why did all those people have to die? So you could get a thrill? So you could be on TV as the sole survivor of a serial killing spree? Yeah, maybe, but mostly so you could stick it to the school you hate and the parents you hate—"

"Untie me, goddamn it!" Rachel hissed. Now lying

on her side, hands tied behind her, she kicked her feet to loosen the rope around her ankles.

He turned toward Hannah. "She hates everyone because her real parents never wanted her. Remember, she told you that she found out about your aunt and your father sometime within the last year? Well, she lied. She's known since she was sixteen. Her dad told her while they were in Europe together. She sent texts to your brother about your aunt two years ago. She even went to Seattle and dropped off an old stuffed monkey for your father while he was in the hospital. She was going to see him and tell him who she was, but lost her nerve . . ."

"Go ahead and tell her," Rachel barked. "I don't give a shit. She's not leaving this room alive."

Alden's face was smeared with makeup and tears. He wiped his eyes with his sleeve. "I could've told you how those test results would come out." He spoke to Rachel again. "You thought your parents didn't want you, but, Rachel, your dad never stopped wanting you. You're Daddy's little girl. It's amazing how much you learn when you're just a servant's kid and nobody pays attention to you. I heard everything in that house, the gossip between the other servants, the arguments between your parents, the dirty deals your father made with his security people. Your father, Richard Bonner, is your real dad, Rachel—"

"That's a fucking lie!" she screamed, writhing on the floor.

"He was traveling back and forth to Eugene, banging college student named Molly. When he knocked her up, he insisted she keep the baby—so he could adopt the little darling. Only he made her lie on the birth certificate about who the father was. So she pretended

Dylan O'Rourke was the father, because she'd been screwing him, too."

Stunned, Hannah stopped struggling with the ropes that pinched at her wrists. The DNA tests results suddenly made sense to her.

"Molly was paid off well. She gave the Bonners their precious baby girl—along with an old stuffed monkey that used to be hers. But Molly got greedy. She demanded more money. So Candace and her assistant flew to Portland . . ." He let out a cynical laugh. "It depends on who you talked to among the household staff. Half of them thought Candace knew you were Richard's. And the other half believed the whole birth-certificate lie or thought Candace believed it . . ."

He twisted around to look at Hannah again. "Mrs. Bonner tracked down your aunt Molly at your grandmother's apartment building and confronted her up on the roof. She'd brought someone else along—a henchman for this malignant fuck who handles security for Rachel's father, a slime-ball named Sloane. Rachel's driver, Perry, works for Sloane, too. I guess the rooftop conversation between Candace and Molly didn't go on for very long. From what I overheard at the mansion, apparently Molly threatened to go public about who the real father was. They argued, and Molly lost. She landed on the pavement seventeen stories below . . ."

Hannah shook her head in wonder. She'd thought her aunt had committed suicide or accidentally fell.

"Candace's personal assistant, Marcia, knew all about it," Alden went on. "But she kept her mouth shut. She was loyal to the family—and sweet to me. But Candace ended up firing her much later. And then, a while after that, Marcia made the mistake of talking too much o some private dick. So Sloane had her killed. Then he killed the private eye and his family . . ."

He turned to Rachel again. While he was distracted, Hannah furtively resumed tugging at the rope around her wrists. She pulled and twisted at it until her skin was raw. Rachel had made the knot too tight.

"You know what's funny?" Alden said, staring down at Rachel.

"I don't care! Untie me!"

"What's funny is that you've always been so scared of becoming just like Candace. And you're *exactly* like her, Rachel. You're selfish and hateful. You're both murderers—or you've had people murder for you. Oh, and another thing, you both fucked the same guy—your father."

"Shut up!" she screamed, finally kicking the ropes loose from her ankles.

He glanced back at Hannah, and she immediately stopped squirming. "Remember the other day, you asked about a married man Rachel might have been involved with? It was her father. How's that for sickening? It started during their trip to Europe when Rachel was sixteen. That's when he showed her the birth certificate and lied to her about Dylan O'Rourke being her real father. He must have figured that would make the whole setup a little less unsavory." He swiveled around toward Rachel again. "That night you got drunk and told me about you and your father, it turned my stomach. You kept saying, 'But he's not my real father,' like that made it okay? What the hell is wrong with you? But I knew the truth the whole time—"

"You're lying!" Rachel screeched, struggling to get to her feet. "You're just a pathetic nobody, an ignorant servant girl's bastard. If it weren't for me and my family, you'd have ended up on the streets—"

"And I was grateful!" he yelled, saliva spraying from his mouth. "I was so grateful and scared and under your thumb, I even killed for you! Do you know how I managed to work up my enthusiasm to kill those girls? I imagined they were you, Rachel, that's how." He shook his head. "Jesus, the things you made me do, you bitch. Well, I can't do this anymore . . ."

"All right, fine," Rachel hissed. She stood in front of him. "Just untie me. I'll take care of this myself. I'll handle everything here. We'll talk about this later, Sonny . . ."

"I'm not your son," he whispered, reaching for his revolver. He pointed it at her.

Wide-eyed, Rachel stepped back. "You wouldn't fucking dare—"

He fired.

Horrified, Hannah recoiled at the ear-splitting bang. She watched the bullet rip through the front of Rachel's lacy nightgown.

Her mouth open, Rachel stood there in shock as a crimson stain bloomed over the satin material covering her stomach. In awe, she gazed down at it and started shaking. She remained on her feet for another few moments.

No one said anything. The only sound was Maddie's faint whimpering.

Rachel's legs finally gave out, and she crumpled to the floor.

His head down, Alden shoved the gun back into the waistband of his corduroys. Starting toward Hannah, he took out the knife.

Panic-stricken, she shrank back. She tried to resist, but he gently pushed her down on the bed, facedown. "Alden, please, no," she whispered.

She felt him tug at her wrists as he began cutting the rope. "There's an old farmhouse on Bingham Road outside Waukegan," he said. "Eden's in a tool shed in the backyard. She's alive. Rachel wanted me to torture her, rape her—like Lyle Wheeler tortured and raped the first girl. But I couldn't. I didn't hurt her—at least, not much. Tell Eden I'm sorry . . ."

Hannah felt the restraints tighten and pinch at her wrists until it was almost intolerable. But he finally sliced through the rope, and her hands were suddenly free. He set the knife down beside her.

Bewildered, Hannah started to push herself up from the bed.

He backed away from her. He accidentally knocked over a vase full of chrysanthemums, and it crashed to the floor. But Alden just kept backing away until he was in the other corner of the bedroom. "I'm sorry for everything, Hannah," he said, taking out the gun. He put it to his head.

"No!" Hannah screamed. She closed her eyes and heard the deafening shot.

When she opened her eyes again, Hannah gazed down at the knife on the bed. He'd left it there so she could cut away the ropes around her ankles—and so she could free Maddie as well. She listened to the other girl crying. "It's okay, Maddie," she said. "I'm coming . . ."

As she cut at the rope around her ankles, Hannah realized there were two survivors tonight.

With tears in her eyes, she stopped to gaze at the

blood-splattered wall across the room. From where she sat and caught her breath, Hannah couldn't see Alden's body lying on the floor.

But she knew he was there—on the other side of all the pretty flowers.

Nate felt intimidated as he climbed out of his old Ford Fiesta and headed toward the entrance of the swanky-looking Geneva ChopHouse. It was part of a big, sprawling, luxurious hotel near the lake, the Grand Geneva Resort. Nate was glad he had on his tie and blazer; otherwise he'd probably get thrown out of the posh restaurant before making it halfway to the Bonners' table.

Earlier, with over an hour to kill before the Bonners had their eight-thirty reservations, he'd thought about driving to Three Old Timber Lane and confronting the Bonners at their vacation house. But he'd realized Ellie was right. If he was going to accuse the Bonners of murder, he needed to do it in public—in front of witnesses so that his accusations might stick. If he faced them in private, they'd simply have him thrown out, or more likely, make him "disappear."

He'd been tempted to call Ellie, just to make sure she was okay. But he knew she'd try to talk him into waiting for her so they could take on the Bonners together. Nate welcomed her help behind the scenes, but for her to put herself directly in the line of fire, that was another story. He'd decided to call her when this was all over.

His stomach had been growling—a bad combination of nervousness and not having eaten in twelve hours. So he'd gone to an Arby's, used their bathroom, and

te a plain Arby's sandwich. He'd been too anxious to
onsume any more than that.

Now, his stomach was even more on edge, and he
ept burping.

He headed through the doors into the restaurant's
nnex, where he was greeted with the savory smell of
roiling steaks and chops. The chatter from diners and
lanking of silverware were accompanied by someone
laying "Cast Your Fate to the Wind" on the piano—
robably a Steinway from the looks of the place. He
oticed two men hanging out by the entrance. They
ere in their early thirties and neatly dressed—but a bit
asual for such an elegant spot. They were both looking
t their phones. But the shorter of the two, a handsome
lan with prematurely gray hair, glanced up at Nate and
eemed to smirk a bit.

Nate couldn't help thinking that the Bonners'
eople—or, more specifically, Sloane's people—might
e expecting him. Maybe he was being paranoid—as
e'd been earlier with that black SUV. But he'd probably
it the Bonners' security team on alert this afternoon.

Brushing past the two strangers, Nate headed toward
e hostess station, where a small group waited to get in.

The restaurant was huge with white tablecloths and
ndle lamps on the tables, plush booths, and a sweep-
g view of the lake. The place was crowded, and the
aitstaff looked busy, but dignified in their white
ckets and ties.

Nate figured it might take a while to find the Bon-
rs at their table. He took his phone out of his blazer
cket and glanced at the time: 8:45.

"May I help you?"

The hostess had stepped out from behind her little

podium and approached him. She was a pretty, twenty
something brunette in a black cocktail dress.

"Yes," Nate said, showing her his phone. "Could yo
point me to where Mr. and Mrs. Bonner are seated to
night? I have a call for Mrs. Bonner. I think she'll war
to take it."

The hostess looked momentarily confused. "Th
Bonners? Yes, well . . ." She turned and looked o
toward some booths against one wall—all facing out a
the restaurant and the lake. It seemed like the VIP are

In one of the booths, Nate recognized Candace an
Richard Bonner from the scores of photos and at lea
a dozen videos he'd studied. This was the first time he
ever seen them in person. Dressed in a blue blazer an
a wide red tie, Richard Bonner looked like an ex-jo
gone to seed thanks to too much of the good life. F
was balding and jowly, but still remotely handsom
Mrs. Bonner was elegant in a coral suit—almost regal-
though her blond hair appeared a bit stiff. They we
with an odd-looking couple. The man was about sixt
five, with receding slicked-back white hair and a bron
complexion that made him appear corpse-like. He w
dressed like a rich gangster with no taste: a wide, whi
tie, navy blue shirt, and a powder blue jacket. His b
jeweled thirty-something trophy wife or girlfriend look
like she'd come from a reliable escort service. The fc
of them were having cocktails.

"Actually, I think I've spotted them, thanks," N
said, starting to move away from the hostess. But he h
itated as he noticed a lean, fortyish man emerge fr
behind the group waiting to be seated. He had a shav
head and wore a black suit with no tie. With an inter
gaze, the man started to approach Nate.

Nate quickly dialed 911, and with the phone to his ear, he headed toward the Bonners' booth. He heard the operator answer: "Nine-one-one. What's your emergency?"

"Yes, a man's causing a disturbance in the Geneva ChopHouse," Nate said. "He's about forty, six feet tall, completely bald—and he just attacked this guy in the middle of the restaurant. I think the bald guy is deranged or something. The other guy wasn't doing anything . . ."

Nate hung up and put the phone away.

"Excuse me," the bald man quietly said as he closed in on him. "Hold it right there . . ."

But Nate kept walking at a faster and more determined clip—right up to the Bonners' booth. "Richard Bonner!" he said in a loud voice. His heart pounded furiously. "Do you recognize me? Do you know who I am? Or is that Donald Sloane's department?"

The man grabbed his arm, but Nate jerked away from him.

People in the restaurant started to notice. Nate heard the murmurs. A woman gasped. Nearby, a couple of waitpersons stopped in their tracks.

The Bonners and their two dinner companions looked puzzled and slightly perturbed.

"Maybe you don't even bother to learn the names and faces of the people you have killed . . ."

"What the hell is this?" Bonner asked.

Bonner's friend, the older one who looked like a bronzed corpse, glared at the bald guy. "Get him out of here," he growled.

The man grabbed Nate's left arm once more. Another man came out of nowhere and closed in on Nate's right side. Nate didn't see what he looked like because he was staring at Bonner.

"I'm Nate Bergquist!" he announced for the whole restaurant to hear. "Richard Bonner—or maybe his *security specialist*, Donald Sloane—had my brother killed! My brother, Gil, was no saint . . ."

"Shut the fuck up," the bald man whispered. He and his cohort started to lead Nate toward the exit.

But he resisted and just talked louder: "Gil might've even had it coming. I think he was trying to blackmail you, Bonner—or maybe your wife. I didn't know it at the time. I didn't have anything to do with it—and neither did my girlfriend, neither did Gil's girlfriend. But they were all killed, and I was left for dead. We were just so much collateral damage in Donald Sloane's 'cleanup' detail . . ."

Nate suddenly broke away from the bald guy, and shoved the other man aside. The second man almost stumbled into a table. The couple at the table quickly got up and stepped back. The loud happy chatter from all the restaurant patrons just a minute ago had become a hushed buzz. The woman at the piano had stopped playing. Everyone was watching him. A few people had taken out their phones to record the disturbance.

Nate saw it all in a rush before he focused on Richard Bonner and hurried toward his table again. "And what about Kayla Kennedy?" he yelled. "And your assistant, Marcia Lindahl, Mrs. Bonner? How many people were killed so your dirty little family secrets stayed secret? You murdered Molly Driscoll—the birth mother of your adopted child! What kind of dirt did she have on you?"

Glaring at him, Mrs. Bonner started to squirm in their VIP booth.

His face crimson, Bonner looked furious. He turned to his friend. "Goddamn it, Sloane, who the hell is this?" he muttered. "What am I paying you for?"

Nate realized he'd hit the jackpot. He was face-to-face with Bonner's chief henchman.

But the bald man suddenly grabbed his arm and twisted it behind his back. "Okay, that's enough—"

"Has anyone called the police?" Candace Bonner asked loudly.

"They're on their way, Mrs. Bonner!" someone answered.

As he was being dragged toward the exit, Nate noticed the man talking was the handsome, gray-haired guy he'd seen at the front door. He and his friend approached the Bonners' table. His friend had a camcorder. "Garth Trotter with the *Chicago Tribune*, Mrs. Bonner!" he announced. "Would you care to comment on these accusations from Mr. Bergquist? Did you have anything to do with the death of your adopted daughter's birth mother, Molly Driscoll, twenty years ago? Weren't you there in Portland at the time? Have people been killed as part of a cover-up? Mr. Bonner, would you care to comment? Mr. or Mrs. Sloane?"

He had to talk louder and louder over the increasing din and chaos around them. The police had arrived along with one of the resort's security guards. They immediately grabbed the bald man.

Sloane stood up, accidentally spilling his drink on himself. "Not him, goddamn it!" He pointed to Nate. The drink had stained the front of his pale checked slacks. "It's the other one who's causing all the trouble!"

"Are these charges against you true, Mr. Sloane?" the

reporter yelled. "Have you had people murdered at the behest of Mr. or Mrs. Bonner?"

It took a moment for the police to realize their mistake, and they grabbed Nate. He noticed at least four cops—and two of them were busy restraining Sloane's pissed-off henchmen.

"I'll go along quietly," Nate whispered to the policemen.

As they led him toward the exit, he glanced over his shoulder. Sloane and Bonner were yelling at the man with the camcorder. Sloane's wife covered her face. And Candace Bonner stared at Nate with hatred in her eyes.

From across the restaurant, he could clearly read her lips. "You son of a bitch," she said.

Near the doorway, the reporter caught up with Nate and the cops. "Hey, Nate!" he called. "I'm Ellie's friend, Garth. She figured you wouldn't wait for her, so she sent us here. She hoped you wouldn't mind . . ."

With a dazed smile, Nate shook his head at the man. He couldn't believe Ellie had his back like that. "Mind?" he murmured. "Are you kidding? Not at all . . ."

"Did you visit my aunt and uncle?"

The policemen escorted Nate through the doorway. Baffled, he stared at the reporter, who followed them outside. "Aunt and uncle?" Nate repeated.

"They live at Three Old Timber Lane," Garth explained. "Ellie didn't want to send you to the Bonners' house. She was afraid she'd never see you again. And she likes you—a hell of a lot! Hang in there, buddy. Someone will be at the police station to bail you out in a little bit. You got the ball rolling, Nate. You've accused them of murder. It's out there. Now, people know . . ."

One of the cops cuffed Nate by a squad car. Nate

called back to Ellie's friend. "Thanks! Thank Ellie for me, too!"

"You can thank her yourself soon," Garth called.

The cop guided Nate into the backseat of the squad car. Nate sat back and caught his breath. He thought about everything that had just happened—all the yelling, confusion, and chaos. He was sore and sweaty, and one of Sloane's men had torn the sleeve of his blazer.

But he had a triumphant smile on his face.

Ellie hurried through the kitchen—as fast as she dared to move with a gun in one hand and a crowbar in the other. She'd left Perry unconscious and facedown in the floor of the deserted bedroom upstairs. Ellie figured he might bleed to death if he didn't get some medical attention soon. When she'd left him, a small puddle of blood had already formed under his head.

At the kitchen door, she quickly set Perry's revolver on the counter and tucked the crowbar under her arm. Frazzled, she took out her phone and called 911 again. She gave the man the address of the farmhouse and explained that she'd called before. She told him they needed to send an ambulance, too. "The man who attacked me, I hit him on the head with a crowbar, and he's bleeding pretty badly . . ."

"An EMS team is on the way—along with the responders, Ellie," the 911 operator assured her. "They should be there soon. Hang on the line . . ."

It was a different 911 operator from the last call, but this guy liked to use her first name in every sentence, too.

"Thank you," Ellie said. While holding on to the phone, she unlocked the door and struggled to open it.

The crowbar slipped out from under her arm and hit the kitchen floor with a clang. She realized the door's deadbolt was still set, and unlocked it.

"Ellie, have you made contact with Eden O'Rourke yet?" the operator asked.

As she opened the door, Ellie heard an intense thumping from inside the backyard tool shed. "I—I think Eden's trying to make contact with me right now," she said.

Swiping the crowbar off the floor, she pushed open the rickety screen door and hurried outside.

"Eden!" she called out. "Eden, hang in there! I'm coming!"

The screen door slammed shut behind her.

"It's Ellie Goodwin!" she yelled, hurrying toward the tool shed at the edge of the bleak yard. "I have the police on the phone right now! They're on their way!"

Past all the pounding, she heard Eden's muffled screams: "God, get me out of here! Please . . ."

The back of the shed faced the house. Ellie ran around to the door side. Under Eden's relentless hammering, the door shook on its hinges, straining against the deadbolt and a latch with a padlock.

"Hold on," Ellie said into the phone. She shoved in the pocket of her sweater. "Eden, stop banging on the door so I can unlock it!" she called. "Can you hear me?"

The pounding on the door ceased. "I hear you! Eden's voice sounded muffled and distant. "Please hurry . . ."

Ellie pushed out the deadbolt. She tried to keep from shaking as she wedged the end of the crowbar into the padlock's U-shaped shackle. Gritting her teeth, she pushed the lock out toward her. It always looked so easy in the movies. But the lock wouldn't break. "Damn it she hissed. Putting all her weight into it, she pushed the crowbar until the shackle finally snapped. The broken padlock fell to the ground.

Stumbling, Ellie dropped the crowbar to brace herself against the shed. She regained her footing and then unfastened the latch. "Eden?" she said, pulling open the door.

The little shed smelled putrid. Ellie covered her nose and mouth.

Dressed in a soiled-looking sweatshirt, jeans, and filthy white socks, Eden stood in the center of the confined, cluttered space. The light above her was dim. But it was easy to see that she was emaciated and exhausted. Her blond hair was in greasy tangles and dark near the roots. Tears welled in her eyes as she numbly gazed at Ellie. She seemed to be in shock.

Then she took a deep breath and quietly began to cry.

Ellie heard a siren wailing in the distance. She stepped back to clear the doorway for Eden.

That was when she saw Perry standing in the kitchen doorway. He held the screen door open. He'd found where she'd left his gun. It was now in his hand. He lurched forward, and the screen door slammed behind him.

Backing away, Ellie looked at Eden and furtively shook her head.

Eden seemed to get the message. She stood perfectly still.

Ellie watched Perry stagger toward her. She could see the streaks of blood on his face—shining in the moonlight.

"What's so interesting in that shed?" he called, slurring his words. He almost sounded drunk. He raised the gun and fired.

The shot rang out, and Ellie flinched. The bullet

didn't seem to pass anywhere near her. But she realized she might not be so lucky if he fired again.

The police sirens got louder, but Perry didn't seem to notice. He kept weaving toward her. The front of his shirt was covered with blood.

Still inside the shed, Eden crouched down to the ground.

"You really are a stupid bitch!" Perry yelled at Ellie. "Leaving my gun behind like that, what were you thinking? Did you think I was dead?" He passed by the side of the tool shed. "Well, I'm not dead, bitch. You are . . ."

He stepped between her and the doorway to the shed. Blinking, he wiped the blood away from his eyes. Then he raised his gun and took careful aim this time.

He didn't see Eden behind him. The crowbar was in her hands.

She slammed it against the back of his head.

Ellie could hear the crack. It seemed even louder than the sound of the squad cars coming up the driveway, their sirens wailing.

She watched Perry crumple to the ground in front of her.

She kicked the gun away and then reached out to Eden

Dropping the crowbar, she staggered out of her little prison and took Ellie's hand. She started to cry again.

Ellie could see all the swirling, flashing lights from the police cars and the ambulance in the driveway. They illuminated a walkway along the side of the dilapidated house.

Ellie put her arm around Eden. Leaning on each other, they started up the path together.

EPILOGUE

annah's mother, Sheila O'Rourke, waited nearly
two hours in the lobby of Northwestern Memorial
ospital before she was allowed to visit her niece.

Along with her husband, Sheila had caught an early
ght from Seattle to Chicago on Saturday. They'd been
mbarded by reporters at both Sea-Tac and O'Hare. Of
urse, Dylan and she weren't strangers to this type of
dia frenzy. They'd been through it all two years ago.

They'd reserved a family suite at the Residence Inn
Lake Bluff, where they took Eden after she got an
-clear from the medical staff at Northwestern. Man-
ement at the inn did a pretty remarkable job keeping
press out of the lobby.

It was almost surreal to see Hannah and Eden getting
ng so well. Just five weeks ago, the two of them
ld barely tolerate each other. Now they seemed to
rish one another. Suddenly, they had a mutual love
respect that was startling to see.

"Let's enjoy it while we can, hon," Dylan pointed out
er.

The transformation Hannah had gone through was
nishing, too. When she'd left Seattle a month ago,

she'd been a moody, sarcastic, self-centered, phone-obsessed teen. She'd acted as if she'd been cursed to be part of their family. And of course, Sheila, in Hannah's thinking, had existed only to feed her, do her laundry and embarrass her whenever they stepped out in public together.

But then, on Saturday, when they were reunited, Hannah cried and hugged her so fiercely Sheila thought she might break. Eden, who had always been so independent and slightly aloof, was almost as clingy and affectionate as Hannah.

The girls shared a room in the hotel suite. So, by Sunday night, they were back to snapping at each other and bickering. But something had definitely changed between them. They acted more like sisters than half sisters.

Every time any of them left the hotel, they were mobbed by the press—especially the girls. Sheila and Dylan were in the spotlight, too. It seemed that people hadn't forgotten the events of two years before.

But from what Sheila saw on TV, in the newspapers and online, they had it easy compared to Richard and Candace Bonner, who were the epicenter of the media circus. Traffic along Lake Shore Drive downtown had to be rerouted to avoid the crushing media mob-scene in front of the Bonners' mansion. As accusations of murder and a cover-up mounted against them, neither one of the Bonners would comment to the press.

From all the recent news articles Sheila read, there was every indication that Candace Bonner had pushed Sheila's sister, Molly, off the roof of their mother's apartment building in Portland twenty years ago. It was that, or Candace had had a bodyguard do the pushing for her.

Sheila remembered the articles she'd read back then, in the wake of Molly's death, articles suggesting she may have pushed her own sister off that roof. Part of Sheila felt incensed that she'd been blamed for something Candace Bonner had done. But another part of her decided to reserve judgment until there was an official inquiry, which certainly seemed forthcoming.

For all Sheila knew, it may have been Candace or her husband who had finally cleared her with the hospital staff.

A policewoman escorted her up to the ICU, where two guards were on duty. The policewoman checked Sheila's purse and her bag. And after asking her permission, she even patted her down. Finally, Sheila was allowed into Rachel Bonner's private room.

From all the flowers on display in the room, no one would have ever guessed that the patient was already implicated in several murders—as were her parents.

A chubby nurse was checking something on one of the monitors hooked up to Rachel, who was propped up in the bed, unconscious.

She'd had major surgery on Saturday to repair extensive damage to her stomach, liver, and intestines. In addition to the IV in her arm, Rachel had an endotracheal tube in her mouth, attached to a respirator.

But Sheila still recognized her kid sister, Molly, in this sleeping girl, and it made her heart ache. Sheila's eyes welled with tears.

The nurse gave her a perfunctory smile. Sheila smiled back, and then she found a spot on the dresser for the vase of flowers. She took the slightly tattered stuffed monkey out of the bag and set it on Rachel's nightstand. Micky the Monkey had originally been Sheila's when she was a child, but then Molly had taken it over and made it hers—which was so like Molly. Apparently, she'd made certain the stuffed monkey accompanied her infant daughter when she'd given her up to the Bonners. Sheila was pretty amazed the Bonners had actually kept it—and she wondered if Richard Bonner had had a soft spot for Molly. Rachel had left the monkey for Dylan two years ago, when she'd thought he was her father and he'd been in the hospital.

Now Sheila was giving Micky the Monkey back to Rachel. She figured her poor, screwed-up niece could use an old friend at her side for the hard times ahead.

Sheila gently touched her cheek. She kept thinking about how Molly was nearly the same age when she'd died. Sheila stood there just a minute or two. Then she wiped away her tears, took a deep breath, and stepped away.

"She's been on and off the tube," the nurse said. "She'll probably be awake in a couple of hours. Do you want me to tell her you stopped by?"

Sheila shook her head. "That's okay. I probably won be back."

"Don't you want her to know who left the monkey?"

"She'll know," Sheila replied. She smiled at the nurse. "But thanks."

Then she quietly walked out of the hospital room.

Friday, October 9, 6:17 P.M.

Ellie stepped off the commuter train in Lake Fore and ran in the rain to her car.

After she switched on the windshield wipers and started for home, she realized she might actually eat dinner before eight o'clock—for a change. She'd finished up early at the *Tribune* tonight. She'd been working late every night for the last two weeks.

So much had happened, she could hardly keep up. The bodies of Eden's "first kidnappers" had been discovered, rotting away in a locker at a U-Store-It facility in North Chicago. They'd been identified as career criminals with links to Donald Sloane.

Rachel's bodyguard, Perry, immediately caved under police questioning, and he implicated Sloane and his cohorts in the plot to abduct Eden O'Rourke. Sloane had viewed her as a "liability." Perry also blamed Sloane for ordering the "accidental" death of Kayla Kennedy, another "liability."

Apparently, Sloane was as paranoid as he was ruthless. Perry had heard about other cover-up murders Sloane had ordered—including that of Candace Bonner's former assistant, Marcia Lindahl, and the Portland private investigator, Gil Bergquist. Perry told the police that on Friday night, he'd been instructed to "detain or dispose of" Ellie Goodwin because of her association with Nate Bergquist.

The following day, Perry recanted all his statements to the police, claiming he'd given them inaccurate information due to his "crippling head injuries" and "a form of PTSD." Then, later in the week, when it was clear that Sloane's firm planned to throw him under the bus, Perry recanted his recantation.

There was so much finger-pointing, in-fighting, and betrayal among the Bonner-Sloane allegiance, it now seemed on the verge of imploding.

Ellie kept busy at the newspaper covering "Bonner-gate," as it was now known. When she wasn't writing about the criminal charges being hurled at Candace and Richard, she wrote about the serial murders planned and hatched by their daughter, Rachel, still in the hospital after two more surgeries.

Our Lady of the Cove officially invited Ellie back to teach. Father O'Hurley was transferred to a parish outside Butte, Montana, and a layperson was hastily brought in to replace him. Ellie told the administration she'd consider returning next semester.

Her agent was fielding offers from publishing houses and film companies. The money was outrageous.

She wasn't the only one being wooed by the publishing houses and Hollywood. Nate had received offers for the rights to his story.

And someone else was after Nate: the Internal Revenue Service.

For a while, he'd been looking at a possible six years in prison and a $200,000 fine for failing to file his tax returns for two years in a row. Ellie had helped him get a pair of good attorneys, and they were working out a deal. He would get probation. And he probably wouldn't see much of his movie or book money. Most of it would go to the IRS and attorney fees.

"That's fine," Nate told her. "I never expected to make any profit on this venture. Considering that I ended up meeting you during all this, I think I came out way ahead."

Between her work and Nate's going back to school to get his physical therapist license renewed, they didn' see each other as much as she would have liked. Bu they talked practically every night.

Ellie pulled up in front of her townhouse.

The front window had been repaired, which was fortunate—especially on rainy nights like this. She climbed out of the car, opened her umbrella, and made a mad dash for the door.

Inside, the living room still had a slight new-carpet/new-paintjob smell. But it looked nice. There was no sign of any fire damage.

She put down her umbrella, peeled off her trench coat, and wandered into the kitchen. Taking her phone from her purse, she called Nate.

"Hey, you," he answered.

"If you come over here tonight and give me a foot rub, I'll cook you dinner and let you choose the movie."

"Would you like me to pick up some takeout instead? Chinese? You'll still get the foot rub . . ."

"God, I love you," she said.

"I love you, too, you know," he replied. "See you in an hour."

Then he hung up.

Monday, November 22, 1:58 P.M.

From the commuter train, Hannah took a bus and got off at the Northridge stop. She had only three blocks to walk to her destination.

In addition to her purse, Hannah carried a bulky tote bag. She'd bundled up warmly. She was learning to adapt to the Chicago weather. It was twenty degrees and windy. The weatherman had predicted six inches of snow tonight.

It would soon be too cold to make this trip.

As she forged through the chilly wind, Hannah hoped snow wouldn't screw up her travel plans. She and

Eden were due to take off for Seattle on Wednesday
afternoon for Thanksgiving break. It was kind of an expensive trip for only four days, but worth every penny.
She yearned to be home again, see her mom, dad, and
her brothers, be in her own bedroom again, and eat her
mom's cooking.

She felt so much older since the last time she'd been
home—just three months ago.

She and Eden were still at Our Lady of the Cove.
Even though the Bonners and their security specialist
had been charged with murder and about fifty other
crimes and misdemeanors, the scholarship was all paid
up. It would be the last one given out in the Bonner
name.

After a monthlong struggle and several surgeries,
Rachel had died of liver failure on Halloween. When it
had happened, Hannah and Eden had heard the jokes
circulating around campus about the ironic timing.

Neither one of them wanted to stay on at the bungalow. They ended up in different rooms on the same floor
at O'Donnell Hall, a perfect arrangement. They often
ate in the cafeteria together or hung out in the evening.
Eden liked to go into Chicago and "explore" whenever
she could. But now, she always told Hannah where she
was headed. And most of the time, she answered texts.

They'd each had guys they were interested in, but
no one special. They'd made a lot of friends in the
dorm. And both of them were wise enough to keep their
distance from the kids who just wanted to know the
notorious O'Rourke sisters for the sheer novelty of it.

Hannah could see her breath as she passed by the
wrought iron fence. She turned at the open gate. Bes-

it was a large sign: NORTHRIDGE PARK MEMORIAL CEMETERY. It was a non-denominational graveyard.

There had been a lot of fuss about burying Alden beside his mother in a Catholic cemetery, because he was a murderer. Hannah had no idea who arranged for him to be buried here. But it was where he ended up— with a very plain tombstone.

She knew how to find it. This was her fourth visit to the cemetery.

Once she was in the general area, it was hard to miss the grave. Though the tombstone was plain, it had been defaced.

The words were scrawled on the stone in Magic Marker or paint—almost obscuring his name and the years of his birth and death:

KILLER
Rot in Hell, Fucker
F.U.

Hannah got down on her knees in front of the tombstone. The cold, hard ground immediately began to chill her legs. Setting down the tote bag, she took out the rubber gloves and put them on over her cold hands. She took out the turpentine, the scrub brush, and the rags. Then she went to work.

Hannah understood why so many people were angry him.

But she cleaned off the bad words anyway.